## ALL THINGS THAT DESERVE TO

# PERISH

*A Novel of Wilhelmine Germany*

D1366252

First Edition
Printed in the United States

ISBN: 978-1-7353026-0-7 (Paperback)
ISBN: 978-1-7353026-1-4 (eBook)

ALL THINGS THAT DESERVE TO PERISH

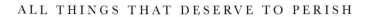

## AUTHOR'S NOTE

Many of the characters in the novel you are about to read are German aristocrats. I have at times taken the liberty of referring to these characters with their German titles and styles (styles being the formal mode of addressing a person of elevated social status—for example, "Your Royal Highness," if you happen to be addressing the Prince of Wales over a shrimp cocktail).

For ease of reading, these titles and styles are italicized only in the beginning of the book, so as to alert the reader that they are foreign words and not typos. I offer here their approximate translations:

*Graf, Gräfin*—Count, Countess
*Fürst, Fürstin*—Prince, Princess
*Durchlaucht*—Serene Highness

I also have sprinkled some German and French words and phrases throughout the novel in the hope that it helps to keep the reader rooted in a very different time and place. Where these phrases are not already familiar to the reader, I have been careful to allow them to be understood from their context.

D.M.

I once had a beautiful Fatherland.
The oak trees
grew so tall there, the violets nodding gently—
it was a dream.

My homeland kissed and spoke to me in German
(one scarcely believes,
how fair it sounded) those words, "I love you true!"—
it was a dream.

—HEINRICH HEINE *(translated by the author)*

*Part I*

# CHAPTER I

"THE FIRST THING I MUST DO TODAY—THE FIRST
thing I *really* must do," Elisabeth von Schwabacher thought, as she
coaxed herself from a state of sleep to semiconsciousness, absently
tugging at the neck of her nightgown, "is to go over that place again
exactly as Maestro Leschetizky would have insisted. I'll take it in
triplet rhythm rather than in duplets, and then in dotted rhythms,
and then all six notes together, stopping after each group of six,
then lifting my hands to root myself in the next group."

"Or else," she thought, opening her eyes just enough to see
the shape of her bedstead, "I'll never properly get it. Because the
piece goes like the wind, and yet all those notes have to be present,
and just under the surface of the melody."

These things were rather like waging war, Maestro Leschetizky
had always said. Not less worthy of meticulous preparation than
a military campaign. Every artist a soldier embarked on a sacred
quest—one doomed, of course, from the very onset; but if clev-
er and skillful and well prepared, one could delay for as long as

possible "the inevitable." And what was the inevitable? Elisabeth had once plucked up the courage to ask the Maestro, during her piano lesson. "Falling on one's sword!" he had answered. "We are all just helpless sacrifices to the gods of the muse!" And then he had guffawed. She could hear him now, hear the tone of his bass and his hearty guffaw, which as often as not tended to settle on an A-flat.

Elisabeth opened her eyes fully now, and looked around. Then she closed them again because what she saw made her ashamed. There were a host of books on her duvet. Some of them were still opened and placed on their undersides. They looked as if they had been abused in restless sleep. Papi had not failed to mention these books when he had entered her room earlier that morning. Nor had he failed to mention the filled ashtray that peeked out from under the bed skirt. ("*Lisi, mein Kind!*" he had exclaimed. "What an unappetizing sight!") Typical of Papi, there was no anger in his voice; and yet he made it clear that he was annoyed. But instead of remonstrating, he kissed her and laughed; and then he said that his daughter was surely fated to go the way of all Bluestockings. And that one day she would be a proper old maid with two pianos, three dachshunds, and a library of very peculiar first editions.

"I might end up an old maid, and will certainly have three or more pianos and a *pack* of dachshunds, Papi. But I promise to be more liberal as regards the books I collect. I mean, why collect only oddities, when one can collect everything?" Lisi stretched out her arms to him. "But you love me, despite the fact that you say my habits are disgusting. So won't you let me sleep just a little longer?"

And Papi had let her sleep in, which was good, because it was cold today. The Schwabacher home was well heated, *gemütlich* warm and fitted in all other ways too for the coming twentieth century. But Lisi could still feel the cold coming from the window.

Yes, it was a chilling cold. She stretched out her hand to catch the vicuna throw that had slipped to the foot of the bed. She drew it to her, dragging and toppling several volumes with it. The fur felt so luxuriously soft that she thought perhaps she should have given up the duvet altogether last night, and simply snuggled with the vicuna naked. But that would not have mitigated the dampness, for like so many winter days in Berlin, the dampness was penetrating. Why, she wondered, was there so little to recommend the month of March? As well as so little to recommend Berlin?

Well, never mind! That single long-lined passage, that series of gestures in groups of six would keep her from dying of boredom and loneliness today. What was Berlin in comparison to her beloved Vienna? No Maestro Leschetizky to inspire her. No male cousins to tease her out of a cross mood. No cousin Klara at home to converse with late at night. And no Aunt Anna to offer her home-baked afternoon sweets and coffee with fresh *Schlag*.

Quarters had been tight in Vienna, where she had even shared a bed with Klara. But she had gotten so many wonderful things to eat. And now she must hold hunger at bay! Well, perhaps that was why Papi had allowed her to sleep so long. It was ... let's see ... The clock read seven thirty. She knew that Papi felt bad for her that she was hungry, and that she would be kept hungry for several more weeks—that is, until the dressmaker could be confidently called in. Because as Mami so wittily put it, "I'm not saying

I would mind having two of my very dear daughter. But I'm not dressing her in double her rightful size!"

It was a shame, Lisi thought, that she had turned out such a great disappointment to Mami. She was not pretty. She lacked many of the essential social graces—the patience, elegance, and easy conversation that came so naturally to her mother. And she certainly was not slender.

Lisi loved her mother and had often resolved to make her happy by cutting down on potato, refusing cake, and cultivating the kind of small talk that amused so many women. And yet, she could never sustain these resolutions for very long. Because the only things that Lisi ever really followed through on were the things that engaged her. And those things—the very things that kept her up into the wee hours of the morning with books and piano scores and cigarettes—were unrelated to good looks and pleasantries.

Mami had said that she would soon get her own lady's maid. It was time, Mami had declared, and she wouldn't have it any other way. After all, Lisi was nearly twenty-one, and the daughter of a prominent banker—a *höhere Tochter* of marriageable age. And that, Lisi thought, as she lurched into a sitting position, was a painful status to have.

Well, never mind, Lisi thought. Let Mami bind and braid and feather her. Let a lady's maid dress her to the nines—tack her up like a prized mare! If she could fight through Beethoven and Liszt and prevail, she could certainly brave a ballroom in a tight gown.

But in the meantime, the day was to begin as every wearying day in Berlin, with the *de rigueur* family breakfast, where she would be offered a broth tea, a boiled egg, and ten almonds; and where she must watch Papi swipe his *Brotchen* with a knife he had dipped very deeply into a pot of butter, while Mami picked delicately at a small fillet of sturgeon.

*⌒———⌒*

"LOTTE FRIEDLAENDER WILL BE MARRIED. IT'S IN the paper today … A lieutenant in the First Cuirassiers, *Freiherr* von Campo."

Susannah von Schwabacher carefully folded and set down the newspaper page she had been reading. She stroked the tuft of jet black hair that rested on her brow, and gracefully tilted her head in that charming way she had of inviting others to speak. Then she placed a small piece of sturgeon on her toast, and opened her lovely mouth to receive it. "Have you met him, Maggi?" she asked, after swallowing.

Magnus von Schwabacher glanced at her from behind his newspaper. "It seems that Otto Friedlaender is more of a fool than I thought. What a sad old song, Zsuzsan!"

"We don't know that, Maggi."

"The marriage won't last a year. But *Freiherr* von Campo will manage to retain the dowry."

"You're very cynical, Papi. Perhaps they are in love," Lisi said. She had finished her broth and egg, and was slowly consuming her almonds, fingering each individually before concentratedly nibbling away at it.

Magnus put his newspaper down, removed his reading glasses, and squeezed the bridge of his bony, large nose. "Perhaps *she* is, Lisichen, if she is as naïve as I suspect. But where *he* is concerned, all I can say is, fat chance!"

"Why, Papi?"

"Have you seen Lotte Friedlaender, Lisi?"

"I have, and I think she isn't *so* horrible to look at. And remember that there is always more to a woman than physiognomy."

"Lieutenant von Campo would no doubt agree with you on that point, and will have perceived that the girl has a very rich father."

Magnus picked up the paper again, only to set it down once more when Lisi, out of a long silence, suddenly protested, "But they will *marry*, Papi, and so there must be some physiological attraction …"

"They won't have children, I can guarantee you," he said, his slender fingers closing around a soft brioche. "It's always the same story. These noblemen who marry Jewesses want only their money, and not their children."

"That's nonsense, Maggi," Susannah put in. "Just consider Prince Wittenbach, whose mother is a Jewess."

Magnus put down his knife, and looked sternly at his wife. "I don't believe that for a minute, and neither should you. That cannot be true."

"But everyone says it."

"I will believe it when Wittenbach says it. There isn't a more devoutly Catholic family in all of Germany … And besides, my dear Susannah, why is it we always have to play this game of 'Who's a Jew?'"

"It's an amusing game. Everyone plays it, and I like it a lot, Maggi." Susannah smiled a temperamental smile. "And I also wish to say that I don't like to hear you discouraging our Lisi!"

"About what, for God's sake?"

"About men, specifically about noblemen, whom you seem convinced are nothing but fortune hunters and anti-semites."

"Why do you use that word, Zsuzsan? I detest that new word. It's politically charged, and frankly sounds almost respectable!"

"Anti-Jewish, then."

"Well the vast majority are hardly friendly to Jews, my dear. And you know it."

"But *many* are open minded. And I would like my daughter to believe that she can and will be appreciated by a gentleman from a very good family."

"A Jewish gentleman, I hope you mean...."

"A gentleman, Maggi, who pleases her, of whatever religious persuasion he may be! But ... oh, dear! It's nearly eight thirty, and I have an appointment at ten, and I should go straight down to Frau Briess about Thursday supper! Maggi, did you order the burgundy?"

"It will be delivered this afternoon."

"Thank you, dear!" Susannah got up from her chair at the breakfast table, her silk dressing gown swishing as she glided to her husband's side and kissed him lightly on the cheek. "Have a good day, *mein Lieber*! And you, Lisi, my love," and here she cupped her hand and took the girl's chin in it, "will take everything your father says about young noblemen and their marriages with a very large grain of salt."

"Lisi, *Liebchen*," Magnus winked at his daughter. "I think Mami has just allowed you one large grain of salt in addition to your broth and egg and almonds!"

"If she has, Papi, I must refuse on the basis of it being at least one grain too few to make a difference."

"Well," said Madame von Schwabacher, "it seems you two rascals are determined to gang up on me. So I will go about my business."

"But Papi," continued Lisi, as her mother exited the breakfast room. "You act as if there are no pretty Jewesses at all. As if Mami weren't pretty. And what about all those Jewish actresses and artists, with their strings of gentile lovers!"

Magnus folded his paper, staring straight ahead in deliberation. "It's true there seem to be plenty of gentile lovers for famous Jewish women. But they are just that—lovers, not husbands, and certainly not fathers." Then he looked at Lisi and smiled. "When you have some experience of life, Lisi, you will understand these subtle social phenomena."

"It strikes me, Papi, that every time my elders point up so-called subtleties in social behavior that seem to elude the young, they are actually referring to preconceptions about society that are probably not verifiable—statistically, I mean.

"And therefore, you are labeling them false, out of hand."

"No, I didn't say that. I said only that they are probably unverifiable, and until they are verified, I don't think we should take the liberty of promoting them as facts."

Lisi took up the last of her almonds. "But you know what, Papi? I was also thinking the other night that the physical characteristics of my husband would be very important to me. Cousin Klara is marrying a man who possesses ears I couldn't live a day with."

"Bernhard Levin is said to be quite brilliant. Perhaps Klara doesn't care about his ears."

"Nor apparently about the fact that they may well be passed on to her children."

Magnus chuckled. "There is no accounting for taste in matters of love. But when a good man comes to tell you that he wants you to be the mother of his children, I hope that the shape of his ears won't matter."

"Unfortunately it will, Papi. And so I warn you never to bring me a suitor with large, protruding ears."

"I have no intention of bringing you any suitors. I will let the suitors bring themselves. Now, what do you say you meet me in the Behrenstrasse at noon, and I take you to Hiller's for lunch, and fill you up. Would you like that?"

"What would I tell Mami?"

"That you have an appointment with me, and that it is just between us."

"I think I shouldn't. Though I would love to …"

"You are a good girl! I shouldn't have tempted you."

"I am glad you did. It gives me confidence that you like me just as well plump as slender. And that you value my company."

"It's the best company. I missed it sorely when you were in Vienna. And I will be sorry to miss it in the next two days."

"Why? Where are you going?"

"Baron von Ehrlingen is taking me to West Pomerania to have a look at an estate."

"For purchase? Are we to have an estate? I can't imagine us in the country!"

"For a loan. I only hope the weather holds, and that I am not trapped up there in those godforsaken marshes."

"Well, how rude of Baron von Ehrlingen to force you from your family into the wilds of Pomerania. Papi, in case you don't know it, I don't much like Baron von Ehrlingen. And I even think he abuses you."

"Abuses me? Nonsense!" Magnus laughed. "I am not a man who can be abused, and you must never worry about me! But what about you? I worry you don't have enough to keep you occupied now that you're home."

"Prince Wittenbach is to come tomorrow at two o'clock to play through some Beethoven violin sonatas. And there is a lot to practice—the Brahms quintet to work on, and that Mendelssohn piece, 'Restlessness.' I don't want you worrying about me, Papi. As long as I am at the piano, I am happy."

# CHAPTER II

FROM BERLIN, THE TRIP TO THE BOENING ESTATE at Pulow, West Pomerania, in 1896, was just over seven hours. Three of these involved the main railroad line from Berlin to Greifswald. There, a regional was to carry Magnus von Schwabacher and Henning von Ehrlingen from Greifswald to Wolgast. At Wolgast, the gentlemen were to meet the estate coachman, who would take them the remaining eighteen kilometers.

Such journeys were seldom wearying for Magnus, who had the energy of a much younger man. Indeed, there was nothing Schwabacher liked more than to be in a first-class compartment with a pile of unread books and business papers. His reading glasses, Magnus liked to say, were his best companions. And yet, if one must have a traveling partner, certainly Baron Henning von Ehrlingen was not the worst choice—a reserved man of educated opinions, and a gifted musician.

Henning was as close to Magnus' physical opposite as possible—as tall and doughy as Magnus was slight and trim. Henning's short silver-gray hair, only slightly thinning, was parted neatly on the side, and straight as could be. Like many a retired military officer, he sported a smartly trimmed mustache and goatee. Of course, the clean shaven Magnus' thick strawberry-blond hair, now heavily streaked with gray, would have been a mop of unruly curls had he not kept it closely shorn. His wife, Susannah, liked to joke that he might as well go to Africa for his haircuts, at which point he would chuckle and say, "Yes, *Liebchen*, but I think the *Scheunenviertel* might be a bit closer. And there, I can get a Jewish barber who will know how to handle it."

Magnus looked up over his glasses into Henning's gray eyes. "You don't mind, Baron von Ehrlingen, that I concentrate a bit on correspondence?"

"Absolutely not, Herr von Schwabacher … I only wish I was able to read on a train. I'm afraid it makes me very motion sick."

Magnus smiled. "So there seems to be an advantage in not being a decent horseman. I can throw my head around every which way, and I never get dizzy."

Henning chuckled. "I hadn't thought of there being any connection between horsemanship and motion sickness on trains, but you may have pointed up a subject worthy of research …"

"But in case I haven't yet mentioned it," Henning added, "I am very grateful that you are making this trip."

Magnus removed his reading glasses, and leaned back. He couldn't very well ignore the Baron, who had already thanked him several times. It was obvious there was something further the man wanted to impart. So he signaled his attention with a nod of the head.

"You see, Herr von Schwabacher, I would like you to do everything you possibly can for Count Boening. I know I've mentioned that he is a great friend of mine. A good man, and a good soldier. I watched him grow up, was his commanding officer in the *Gardes du Corps*, and have known his father more than thirty-five years. And given the family friendship, which goes back several generations, I would want you too …," and here he paused for moment, "to do even a bit more than you might normally be disposed to do."

"Baron Ehrlingen," Schwabacher felt suddenly squeezed in his innards. "You are not suggesting that I lend the man money at terms that might bring me, and him, to embarrassment?"

Henning was silent for a moment, and lightly stroked his beard. Then he continued in a confidential tone. "Nobody need publicize the terms. If they are not profitable, I will pay the extra interest. *Graf* Boening is in truly difficult circumstances, and a very proud man. I think I told you that he is an *Uradel*, from one of the oldest noble families in Prussia. And he was a protégé of Prince Bismarck. But you and I know what good the latter distinction is doing him now. Since Bismarck's resignation, he is in the unhappy situation, at thirty-six years of age, of having his career at the Foreign Office play out in reverse. And at the same time, he is in danger of losing an estate that has been in his family for over seven-hundred years."

"And you wish to help him, your good friend. *Natürlich!* Well then, we will have a look, won't we, to see what we can do for the count! But it goes without saying that I would never burden you with interest on another man's debt." Magnus made for his reading glasses again, but Henning surprised him by suddenly changing the subject.

"Herr von Schwabacher, I have been thinking about your trip to America. I have been thinking I would like to join you. It wouldn't be the worst thing to combine some first-hand knowledge of my investments there with a tour out West to the Natural Wonders. I would very much like to see the Grand Canyon. To experience travel in the New World." And here Henning smiled. "Have you, by the way, read about the Harvey Girls? Imagine hiring females to cater to travelers in such remote areas!"

Magnus burst into laughter. "Who better? The world will one day belong to women, Baron Ehrlingen. I am convinced of it! And in the case of the Harvey enterprises, the girls seem to be the model of professionalism and efficiency!"

"I think," said Henning, "that we are bound to prefer them to even the most zealous waiter at Hiller's!"

And from then on, the banker and his client found a good hour and a half of easy and pleasant conversation.

⁓——⁓

IT WAS SEVEN MINUTES PAST NINE A.M., EXACT-ly, when Helmuth von Boening's steely blue eyes peered in through the study door at his son Wilhelm. "The train will have arrived at Wolgast," he said.

"Yes, *Vater*." Wilhelm pulled out his pocket watch, and lightly fingered it as he glanced down at his ledgers and bank books. "Peter will have met them just now."

"Perhaps you should have sent the sleigh."

"I think the carriage will be fine. Thank God this winter is not like the last. Only pray that Peter hasn't fallen asleep on the job."

"That man gets lazier every day."

"He's tired, Father. It's old age …"

"I'm old, and I don't fall asleep on the job. Quite the opposite. In old age, sleep is either for the sick or the lazy. And speaking of the lazy, have you told our Vietzke, and also *Mam'selle*, that this man we are hosting is a Jew?"

"I mentioned to *Mam'selle* that no pork should be served."

"What do you want to wager that *Mam'selle* puts a fat piece of bacon in the soup, and that Vietzke serves it up to this Jew without a second thought? Ha! The Jews are an unsavory people; and the most unsavory among them are the horse traders and the bankers. And yet, one always finds oneself dealing with them. Do you remember that mare I bought in '84?"

Wilhelm sighed and shook his head. "Father, I hope you are not going to warm up the tale of the lame mare for Magnus von Schwabacher. In the first place, you cannot be sure that man was a Jew."

"I know for a fact that man was a Jew. He had a Jewish face. He came from the east, and he cheated me with a lame mare."

"That may be so, *Vater*. But Ehrlingen says Schwabacher is an honorable man, and I will believe that until proven otherwise. In any case, he seems to have made Ehrlingen very rich."

"Your friend Ehrlingen was always rich. And marrying a wealthy widow didn't hurt him, either. Now she is gone, and he is left to get even richer on his own. You yourself might consider whether a nice dowry wouldn't be preferable to a loan. And may I mention also that in the particular case of the young Helge von Schwerning, it would come with a lovely looking girl!

Wilhelm did not reply.

"Do you have a mistress, Wilhelm?" Helmuth looked hard at his son.

"If I did, *Vater*, it would hardly be of relevance to this discussion."

"To the contrary. It's easy to think that a man who is as dilatory in the matter of marriage as you are would be in love with a woman he cannot marry."

Wilhelm, again, did not reply.

"In which case," his father continued, his silver-blue eyes flashing severely, "he would find himself in an unhealthy situation."

Wilhelm stood up and closed the books. He watched the lanky figure of his father as he turned into the hallway. Helmuth von Boening was a weathered man of sixty-eight, whose chin pointed permanently up, whose broad shoulders had only just begun to slack, and who still had a healthy head of hair. But under an immaculate gray mustache, his lips always seemed pursed. It was rumored that no living man or woman had ever seen him smile so that his teeth showed. His conversation, even when not insultingly blunt, was needlessly terse. And his sense of humor, on the rare occasions when he displayed one, was invariably acerbic. No wonder, then, that the ladies of the neighborhood liked to say that for a man of his age, he was unusually easy on the eye, but hard on the ear.

And yet, for all his irascibility, Helmuth von Boening was no fool; and Wilhelm knew that in pointing up his son's extended and impecunious bachelorhood, his father was only stating what was true and in need of rectification.

The problem was that the events of the past few years made Wilhelm feel like a man in retreat from an active life. Everywhere he turned, he seemed to meet a dead end—even in the direction of his distant cousin, the Countess Helge von Schwerning, whose parents hosted him often for dinner in Berlin, and who was generally thought to be his intended.

Helge was indeed pretty—fair-haired and high cheek-boned, with eyes the color of aquamarine. She was also well-mannered and demure in the impassive way of so many girls of Wilhelm's class. Thoroughly unobjectionable, if one didn't mind a young woman whose idea of conversation was to prattle about parties and mutual acquaintances. The fact was, that though Wilhelm sensed Helge liked him, he couldn't seem to get truly fond of her. Something about her, beside her conversation, made him shrink at the idea of their wedding night—as if all the charm of her face and figure would wither in the act of deflowering. He had told his father he feared she was not very intelligent, to which his father had replied that a pretty countess with a dowry of a half million gold marks could be allowed to be dull; that dullness was the very condition of virginal piety; and that if Wilhelm preferred to court a so-called intelligent woman, may the Lord protect him!

THE BOENING ESTATE HARDLY BOASTED AN IM-pressive entrance. It was true that a charming and neatly combed country road led to Pulow, but the circular driveway that fronted its manor, or *Gutshaus,* consisted of a thick mud that resisted all attempts to keep it looking well-tended. Seeing the stucco-faced brick and timber edifice on a dry summer day, when the sun shone pink on the tile roof and the back lawns could be spotted flush with wild flowers, one might have thought the ivy-blanketed edifice had some charm. But it had little architectural interest and certainly no grandeur. What it had was generous size and an awkward, settled weight. The fact was, this *Schloss* (if one was to dignify the wildly oversized cottage with such nomenclature) had been cobbled together over a period of two very disorganized centuries in the Boening family's tenure. And it seemed that the major goal of the amateur architects who directed its erection and later expansions had been to create capacious living spaces at the most modest cost possible.

One oddity of the structure was that the front door, while approached by several nicely rounded stone steps, was so small that it made the six large windows on either side of it seem disproportionate. And these generous ground floor windows, which almost dwarfed a broad, but shallow-angled second-floor gable, glaringly betrayed the fact that the balcony extending from it was an ill-advised afterthought.

Upon walking to the back, a visitor might have been better pleased with the aspect. There, two generous wings extended from the western and eastern corners of the house, their tile roofs descending gracefully, with a number of narrower and more deeply angled gables ornamented in Hanseatic style. Here also, a summer room with attending stone terrace opened out from the center of the building.

While there may have been nothing about the manor house that was particularly auspicious, there was thankfully nothing that in any way betrayed the bankruptcy now threatening the ancient

Boening family—no noticeable degeneration of the exterior, nor empty rooms. To the contrary. If the manor house was aged, it was sound and clean. And if the generous public rooms were furnished in Spartan style, if the upholstery of the chairs and couches was fraying in places, this was only typical; the East Elbian nobility had always been proudly dowdy. When Schwabacher stepped inside, he was immediately reminded of a visit he had made ten years before—in the company of his former employer, the banker Gerson von Bleichroeder—to Prince Bismarck at Friedrichsruh. Bismarck's home was far more architecturally distinctive; but one encountered the same frumpish furnishings, appointments that gave one the strange feeling of having checked into a provincial hotel.

Wilhelm, to the surprise of Magnus and Henning, had been awaiting the traveling gentlemen outside the manor house entrance upon their arrival. He was dressed in boiled wool breeches and jacket, and he sported a wool hunting cap—his tall, blond figure framed by two large gray Weimaraners. The overcast early March day was bitter cold, but Wilhelm had not donned a coat, or even gloves, and seemed unperturbed by the weather. When the carriage came to a stop, he opened the door himself, extending his hand warmly to Henning and nodding politely to Magnus. Henning jumped out, playfully greeting the dogs, whom he introduced to Magnus as "Aldo" and "Hexi."

The men had scarcely removed their respective layers of outerwear and deposited their cases in the large front hall (where a number of family portraits were on view—mainly of several generations of Boening men in full military regalia), when Wilhelm suggested a vodka to warm them. Henning immediately accepted, but Magnus demurred.

"*Graf* von Boening, I'm afraid I am reeling from the coach ride, and will need something much gentler on my stomach," Magnus said. "Are you aware your man has a dangerous tendency to nod off while driving?"

"Herr von Schwabacher, I apologize if you were distressed. And yet, Peter's very good with the horses, and we haven't lost a visitor yet. Perhaps some hot tea will do you good?"

"I would like that very much."

"Vietzke, bring Herr von Schwabacher some tea," Wilhelm said, turning to a bald, snub-nosed butler, who sported a very large belly.

Vietzke nodded and bowed as he handed off coats to a woman servant. "*So fort, Herr Graf!*" he said. "Right away!"

"Herr von Schwabacher," Wilhelm said, as they entered the drawing room, "I thought I would give you a chance to look through some records before lunch, which will be served in half an hour. And after lunch, if you wish, we can make the rounds of the estate."

"That sounds fine. How large is the property?"

"2,539 *Morgen.*"

"That would be ... let's see ... a little less than 650 hectares. And you have a resident overseer, an *Inspektor* ..."

"Naturally."

"And as for laborers?"

"We have forty-one smallholder families, and thirty cottages for the families of contracted laborers. Then there are the seasonal day-wage laborers. There seem never enough workers for the potato fields."

"And you bring mostly potatoes to market?"

Wilhelm nodded and pointed to the glass of vodka he had poured. "Our own distillery. Potatoes, yes; but wheat, barley, and rye, also."

"And livestock?"

"Well, that would be a subject of discussion. First, I would mention that we have a small fishery. Our lake, the Pulowersee, is quite deep; it yields pike, perch, and tin fish. But I am thinking we should raise more cattle and swine."

"A sound idea," Magnus replied. "Well, if you don't mind, *Graf* Boening, I think I would like to get right to it, then."

<hr>

MAGNUS WAS AN INVESTMENT BANKER AND FI-nancier who dealt with German and international industrial enterprises. If he also built portfolios for a select clientele, they were not people with mortgages. In fact, he found the mortgage business distasteful, in that it seemed so often to involve looking into the private affairs of men whose private affairs were in disarray. And here was no exception. He knew immediately upon examining the papers before him that the Boenings were to fall quite readily into a category of customers to whom he referred, in the privacy of his home, as *"unerwünscht."* There was no kinder way of saying it. Such people were undesirable clients.

It did not take a long perusal of the Boening ledgers and bank records to come to the sad conclusion that this family of ancient Prussian noble lineage had all too easy access to loans from provincial banks. And that they had used that access, like so many financially troubled families of their *Junker* class, to strip themselves, year over year, of capital—in many years paying out more in interest than their entire income. The estimated market value of Pulow, Magnus surmised, might be somewhere in the area of seven-hundred to eight-hundred thousand gold marks. It was a sum hardly to be sniffed at. But it was heavily leveraged; therefore, cashing out could not be an option for the young Count Boening.

In fact, it appeared that the young Wilhelm's circumstances were just wretched enough to encourage a tenacious nobleman to cleave to his country seat, and to make it impossible for him to pursue any more than an existence of the barest dignity in the city, where his modest salary as a government bureaucrat would hardly be much help. And this young man, thought Magnus, would certainly have his expenses in town—rooms to live in, his club, very likely a mount, and God knows what else—perhaps a mistress to support, if he didn't have a wife yet.

As Magnus fingered the ledger and papers and sipped his tea, he thought about Wilhelm von Boening. The young count was truly a strapping figure. Susannah would call him a "perfect Aryan specimen," and possibly wink as she added a sarcastic comment about the dueling scar that framed the corner of Wilhelm's right eye.

Magnus looked around him at the study. Its walls, aside from one or two paintings of interest, which he resolved to have a closer look at, were covered with hunting trophies. Its furnishings were a mass of bulky, distressed wood and worn leather. And its old ceramic tile oven radiated a settled warmth. The room seemed the picture of rooted country life. And while there was not a speck of dirt to be spotted anywhere, one could feel the earth here. This family was *bodentreu* nobility, of the land, and loyal to the land forever. That was what these *Junkers* were about, thought Magnus. So it would do no good to tell the man to sell. What was he to do with himself, especially now, with his diplomatic career in peril?

———

IT ONLY STRUCK MAGNUS WHEN SITTING DOWN to lunch that there were no women in the Boening household. When lunch was called, the old count was already standing at the far end of a very long oak trestle table in a large and dimly lit wood-paneled dining room. Wilhelm made the introductions as he took his place at the other end, but the older man scarcely acknowledged Magnus' presence, so perfunctory was his nod.

As soon as the gentlemen took their seats at the table, the elder Boening said grace *im Namen Jesu:* "Heavenly Father, bless us and these our gifts, which we receive from Your bountiful goodness through Jesus Christ, our Lord. Amen." And then he looked rather long at Magnus with his penetrating, cold blue eyes, as if trying to intuit the Jew's reaction to the invocation of Jesus.

Magnus merely nodded respectfully, smiled at the count, and broke the bread on his butter plate.

"So, Ehrlingen, what mischief are you up to in Berlin? Still playing all those instruments, and spending evenings at the Philharmonic?" Helmuth von Boening asked, as he put his napkin in his lap.

Henning nodded. *"Natürlich!* One can never have enough music, *Graf* Boening." Then he added, "The evenings I am not in the concert halls, I play quartets with Magnus von Schwabacher and your son-in-law, who introduced me to Herr von Schwabacher several years ago."

"Wittenbach?" Helmuth's piercing eyes now fixed themselves on Henning. "So the very esteemed Prince Egon is still loitering in Berlin? One wouldn't think he had children!"

Then Helmuth turned that same fixed gaze on Magnus. "You are musical, Herr Schwabacher? And did I hear a 'von' in your name earlier? How the 'von,' if I may be so bold as to ask? It seems every time one turns around these days, a 'von' is added to someone's name."

Magnus' throat tightened slightly, and he took a sip from his glass of mineral water. Could this man really believe him a fraud? "Yes, it is 'von.' And you are correct. Quite recently."

"How recent, then, *is* your patent?"

Magnus glanced across the table at Henning, whose face was a study in neutrality, and then he turned toward Wilhelm, whose eyes seemed to register only a slight impatience.

Magnus was a scrupulously polite man. But the elder count Boening was beginning to annoy him. He answered in measured tones. "*Graf* von Boening, you embarrass me. I am a guest here in the home of an *Uradel*, at the table of a man whose family drove the Slavs from this province more than seven-hundred years ago. My patent of nobility is six years young. One might, in comparison, ignore it entirely. And you may do so, if you wish. I will certainly answer to the name Schwabacher alone, which I assure you can stand with dignity on its own." He paused, then added, "Although one hardly wishes to insult the Kaiser by ignoring an honorific."

Having finished this little speech, Schwabacher noticed two things: That a steaming bowl of split pea soup had been set before him; and that the corners of Henning's mouth had turned up, and by the looks of it, against the man's will.

"We are all loyal servants of the Kaiser, Herr von Schwabacher," Helmuth responded. "And be he ever so foolish a Kaiser, we must comport ourselves with Christian humility, and accept all his honors, as well as his insults, with perfect equanimity."

Magnus didn't know quite how to interpret this. He debated to himself—whether the older man meant to mock the Kaiser or to mock the Jew who sat here at the table before a bowl of pea soup; he wondered whether the count had made a comment on the state of politics or the economy, or—God forbid—on race. Then he thought to distract himself by starting his soup. But he couldn't. Because there, in the middle of the bowl, he noticed a fat piece of bacon.

Now, it wasn't that Magnus had never been served pork. He wasn't religiously observant, and he always remembered his father invoking the Talmudic saying, "The way of the land before the Torah." But here, in this house, he sensed ... what? He sensed ... a provocation! He had come more than seven hours from Berlin on a very cold early March morning; he had agreed to ignore his business for the better part of two days. Yes, he had done this for his friend, Henning von Ehrlingen. For Henning really *was* his friend and practically a fixture in his household! He had come all the way to these sandy plains of Western Pomerania, to the home of a provincial nobleman whose circumstances were hardly worthy of deference, but rather of pity! And all this, only to be affronted?

These Boenings, Magnus thought, were nothing more than conceited mud-farmers, possessing an oversized house, and oversized pride in their feudal pedigree. Granted, the Boening patent of nobility was ancient. But what special privileges would it lend the young Wilhelm in the modern world? The privilege to an officer's commission, to backwater prominence, and to the vagaries of a calling card reading, "Employed at the Foreign Office!" All of these honors were very expensive, and all of them contributing irredeemably to the Boening family's impending insolvency!

Magnus absently poked at the offending pork.

"Vietzke!" Schwabacher's ruminations were interrupted by Wilhelm's voice. "Bring Herr von Schwabacher a bowl of soup without bacon."

"*So fort, Herr Graf.*" Vietzke swept the soup from the table so quickly that Magnus barely had time to leave his spoon on the plate.

"I must apologize, Herr von Schwabacher. I told *Mam'selle* not to serve pork. But I am afraid she failed to understand my directions."

A new bowl of soup appeared almost immediately. Wilhelm raised a wine glass to the banker and wished him "*Guten Apetit.*" Then he continued, "You looked through the books, I trust."

"I glanced at them, yes."

"And?"

Magnus hesitated.

"You may speak quite freely in front of my friend, Ehrlingen. I can't think of anything I might have kept from him," Wilhelm said.

"Well, we must take a look around, *Graf* Boening. We must. But, from what I see so far, you would absolutely need to consolidate and restructure your debt. Something I could possibly help you with."

Helmuth interjected, "You mean to say that you would pay off our present loans, and would then extend us credit on more favorable terms?"

"Exactly. If I can. I think it would be to your advantage. But then, we must see what you have in mind for the place. That is, we must discuss what you have in mind in terms of modernization. The idea of moving into more livestock production is a good one. So would be the purchase of modern machinery, if you don't already own it. The tariffs having been lifted, you cannot expect cereals to yield what they once did, and you seem to have many mouths to feed on this property."

"With regard to the tariffs," Wilhelm stated, "the Agrarian League will soon be organizing some effective opposition."

"Well," replied Magnus, "I hardly want to predict the future, but I would discourage you from relying on what might be, at best, a temporary return of the old tariffs. German industry is growing. We shall soon be—we already *are*—an industrial giant. We must have free trade to realize our nation's industrial potential! But that shouldn't prevent profitability in agriculture, providing you keep abreast of modern farming methods. One must allow the winds of change to carry one forward, because, in any case, they cannot be stopped."

The other men at the table were silent. Magnus knew his words were unwelcome. He sipped his soup and inquired casually of the younger man, "*Graf* von Boening, I noticed an intriguing portrait in your study—*Salome with the Head of John the Baptist*. Is it a new painting in the old style?

"New?" Wilhelm looked bemused. "It's an Onorio Marinari of the seventeenth century."

"Ah! Well, I thought it looked to be seventeenth century—in style, that is. But the colors are so vibrant, and the oil sheen."

"I restored it, Herr von Schwabacher."

"Ah! You had it restored …"

"No, *I* restored it. It's a hobby of mine. And the picture is a favorite. Given my financial situation, I shouldn't admit this to you, but I bought it at auction in Italy five years ago for a pretty penny, and I originally hung it in this room."

Magnus could not help but chuckle. "In the dining room, *Graf* Boening! Salome, with the Baptist's head on a plate?"

Henning laughed. "It hung here for several months. But curiously, no guest of this house ever commented on it. It was the servants who complained. Vietzke shielded his eyes and grumbled every evening, until his master removed it. Right, Vietzke?"

The pot-bellied servant nodded enthusiastically. "It is a horror and not to be taken with food, *Herr Baron*. I told my *Herr Graf* that he should put his angel up in the dining room instead."

"She is too small for this room, Vietzke." Wilhelm answered.

"But *Herr Graf* could paint her larger," Vietzke insisted.

Wilhlem smiled a wry half-smile. "I am afraid that our Vietzke has an exaggerated opinion of my artistic talents." And then turning to Magnus, he explained, "I happen to have a small Carlo Dolci portrait on copper, which the painter titled, *Head of an Angel*. Vietzke is in love with her, and wants me to copy her."

"Yes, I saw her," Magnus said. "She is quite charming."

"I purchased the Marinari and the Dolci portraits at the same time. And though it may sound odd, I have become convinced they are of one and the same model, just painted from different perspectives and in different light.

"The same model?" Magnus exclaimed. "Impossible!"

"Why impossible?"

"Well, if you must know," Magnus answered, "I was compelled to look quite closely at your *Salome* because she happens to bear an uncanny resemblance to my daughter. Whereas, your *Angel* does not."

Wilhelm leaned forward in his dining chair and looked intensely at the banker for a moment before replying, "Your daughter, Herr von Schwabacher, must be very pretty."

Then he leaned back and returned his attention to his soup. "But the fact is," he replied, "Marinari studied with Dolci and shared his studio. They were cousins. And the women, if you study them, have practically identical features. Naturally, the *Salome* is more compelling because of her insolent expression."

"You find the expression insolent?"

"How would you describe it?"

"Direct, unapologetic, candid, but in no way insolent. Salome is so often portrayed as an evil murderess. But she was no such thing. She was an innocent. And Marinari seems to have perceived that."

"Do you mean to say that she cannot be blamed for the Baptist's beheading?"

"I mean to say that, according to the Gospels, she danced for Herod, and when offered anything for that dance, up to half his kingdom, asked her mother what she should request. The Baptist's head was not her idea."

"You seem to have familiarized yourself with the New Testament, Herr von Schwabacher," Helmuth interjected. "Are you baptized, then?"

"No."

"Really! Then why study it?"

Magnus smiled at the old man, and wiped his mouth carefully with his napkin. Then he replied, "*Graf* von Boening, the Chinese have a very wise saying: 'If you know yourself, and know the enemy, you need not fear the result of a hundred battles.'"

# CHAPTER III

IT WAS DECIDED THAT MAGNUS WOULD, INDEED, refinance the Boening debt at the modest rate of three percent. He also agreed to extend two separate shorter credits—for livestock and for the purchase of farm machinery—at two and a half percent. From Henning, the banker would take nothing, of course, and though the Boening loans were certainly not a preferred or very profitable business endeavor, Magnus took the attitude that sometimes good will made the best business sense of all. And if Ehrlingen was happy, and a *Junker* family grateful to a Jewish banker, at least two things were right with the world.

It was an unusually warm mid-April day when Henning and Wilhelm next met, on the boulevard Unter den Linden. Both happened to be expected at their favored club, the Casino-Gesellschaft, for lunch and a round of cards, when Wilhelm spotted Henning in front of a fabric store window, staring intently. The elder, when greeted, seemed preoccupied.

"Ah, Boening!" Henning came to himself and smiled.

"Are you on your way to the club?"

"Yes. But thinking of going inside here for just a moment …"

"I can wait."

"Well, then …" Henning opened the door and followed his friend in.

A dark-haired and elegantly dressed woman was in conversation with the proprietor. She was examining several damask samples laid out on a table. As the gentlemen entered, both she and the proprietor turned toward the door, and she instantly smiled—a flash of warm recognition crossing her face.

"Baron Ehrlingen!" The voice was a melodious one, with a slightly exotic inflection. "What a happy coincidence! Because you might be helpful to us!"

"Glad to oblige, Frau von Schwabacher. Very glad, indeed." Henning took her extended hand and brushed the gloved knuckles with his lips. May I present my friend, Graf Wilhelm von Boening …"

"Delighted." The woman extended her hand to Wilhelm, who bowed over it. "But, Count von Boening, aren't you Prince Egon von Wittenbach's brother-in-law?"

"Yes." Wilhelm nodded politely.

"He is a very good friend of ours, and a fine musician. Are you musical, Count Boening?"

"I'm afraid not very," Wilhelm answered.

"What a shame!"

She smiled and turned to Henning. "I am thinking some shade of green for Magnus' new office drapes. And the pattern must be very plain. Naturally, he will not be consulted, no matter how much I beg him. I sometimes think that he would be happiest in his office with a military cot and a single, solitary candle. Herr Goldmann thinks this damask the most neutral of the blue-greens, but I feel it's a bit dull. What do you think?"

The proprietor interjected that he thought the lady and gentleman might like to take a sample or two to the window to observe the play of sunlight on the fabric.

"That's not a bad idea," said Henning. "Although I cannot guarantee I would have any preference, even in the sunlight."

"Well, Baron Ehrlingen, I can tell you are determined to make yourself useless then, as most musicians are in matters of the decorative arts. I think, Graf von Boening,"—and here she turned to Wilhelm—"that if we were to divide humankind into two distinct races, there would be those who are all ears, and those who are all eyes, and both types completely helpless to get one another out of scrapes."

Wilhelm smiled a half-smile. Susannah von Schwabacher at that moment seemed to him a quite striking example of *her* race—a Jewess whose Viennese-accented German sounded just slightly Hungarian. Her hair was black, her eyes olive-green, even slightly olive-shaped. She had a translucent complexion and a regal posture that made her seem tall, when she was only of average height. Her smile seemed to reflect perfect contentment. And so far, her conversation was of such easy flow that Wilhelm guessed her manners had to be the product of tireless study. Her light brown wool suit, with its enticing bustle and its tastefully embroidered bolero jacket, was stunning; her coiffure, perfect. He had heard it said that the wives of Jewish bankers competed with each other with regard to the lavishness of their *toilette*, a few spending as much as fifty- or sixty-thousand gold marks a year. Well, if they did, Wilhelm thought, the results were plainly magnificent.

Despite the fact that Henning had conclusively proven his uselessness in the matter of interior decoration, he and Susannah continued to discuss the damasks, with Herr Goldmann pointing up the advantages and disadvantages of a few more patterns and colors.

Wilhelm, who was getting hungry, was left to consider whether to excuse himself or to continue to wait for his friend. But he was soon diverted, for the door opened and a young woman of around twenty years of age entered, breathless and exerted. She carried a small parcel of what had to be books, wrapped in paper and tied neatly with string. She was small and slightly fleshy; and though beautifully dressed, she gave a curiously tousled impression. Her wild strawberry-blond curls looked like they were exploding from under a small, boat-shaped hat, and her large round eyes, of a very dark blue, and framing a long nose, were so deeply set in her face that they gave a waifish impression. She glanced at the couple deep in consultation with Herr Goldmann, and shrugged her shoulders in a gesture of irritation. Then her eyes scanned the shop, settling finally on a young man who stood on a ladder way in the back, replacing fabric bolts on shelves.

She walked rapidly toward him, and as she did, Wilhelm noticed that the back of her skirt was badly soiled.

"Herr Paul," the young woman whispered.

Herr Paul, a young man not much older than the girl, turned around rapidly, and recognizing her, was all attention. "*Gnädiges Fräulein,* how may I be of help?"

"I'm afraid I've slipped into something disgusting." She nodded toward the back of her dress, indicated her shoes, and then turned slightly so he could see. "Would you have a rag, and might I wash my hands after cleaning myself off?"

"*Ach, mein Gott! So fort!*"

He disappeared and was back in only seconds with two hand towels, a bowl of water, and soap. But having presented one of the towels to the girl with a quick bow, he then stood awkwardly by, presumably thinking himself precluded from aiding her, in as much as the souvenirs of her fall were caught in an area of her skirt just under the bustle.

Unfortunately, these same remnants of droppings were also in an area not easily seen by the girl; and Wilhelm watched as she attempted valiantly, but without success, to wipe them away.

"Fräulein," Wilhelm said, walking toward her, "will you allow me?" He removed his gloves, and stretched out his right hand for the towel.

"I wouldn't think of imposing ..."

"It's hardly an imposition. It's more of an emergency, don't you think?"

She handed him the towel. He knelt down behind her, stretched the material of her skirt well away from her body, and began to make quick work of an unpleasant task.

"I can't thank you enough, Herr ..."

"Graf Wilhelm von Boening at your service, Fräulein. And, if I may ask your name?"

"Elisabeth von Schwabacher." The girl turned her face, with its huge dark blue eyes, toward him, looked at him searchingly and smiled. "And though it's not exactly a proper introduction,

37

Count von Boening, I should let you know that your brother-in-law, Prince Egon von Wittenbach, is a friend of our family and has even told me about you."

Wilhelm did not reply to this, because when he had politely raised his own eyes to meet hers, he was completely distracted by the intensity of expression in her face, and the directness of her gaze. He had never seen a face quite like it. It was a veritable kinetoscope of rapidly changing images—perhaps reflections of rapidly passing thoughts. And in those frames, he saw someone he thought he knew, but fought to recall who that someone was.

Wilhelm having not responded, she continued with a mischievous smile, "Prince von Wittenbach warned me that you were the handsomest man in Germany. But somehow, I didn't envision you as you are."

She turned away again, and suddenly Wilhelm came back to himself. "What do you mean?"

"I mean to say that I didn't imagine you, in my mind's eye, kneeling at my feet and scraping excrement off the back of my skirt."

Wilhelm had an irresistible impulse to laugh at this, and knew the girl meant him to think it amusing; but for propriety's sake, he suppressed the laugh and replied only, "I am afraid that even the most fastidious young ladies run into bad luck at some point."

The girl turned and looked at him again, and as she did, he was struck, yet again, by the liveliness of her face. "I wonder, Graf von Boening," she said, laughing, "why people like to blame luck, or even fate for things like this; when stupidity and clumsiness can always be more easily verified."

Wilhelm allowed himself a quiet chuckle here, as he folded over the soiled part of the towel, placed it carefully on the counter, and washed his hands.

"I am afraid the rest will have to be brushed dry, Fräulein."

The girl nodded. "Are you waiting for Baron Ehrlingen?"

"Yes, but no matter! ... I see you have bought a few books. Entertaining novels, I hope?"

"Two novels by Herr Fontane, along with some social politics: *The Origin of Family, Private Property and the State,* by Friedrich Engels."

"Engels ... Isn't he a socialist?"

"A very prominent one, though he *is* no more. He is recently deceased."

"Fräulein von Schwabacher, I hope you are not a socialist!"

"I honestly don't know what I am, Graf Boening. I expect one of the virtues of reading, if one does enough of it, is that one never can make up one's mind in a permanent sense. One can read Edmund Burke at night and wake up a conservative in the morning. And the same goes for Karl Marx. Only that one wakes up a socialist instead. At any rate, one comes to sympathize with many different points of view ... Do you read?"

"Not much," Wilhelm replied. "And probably for the very reason you so wisely point up—namely, that reading does tend to cloud the mind!"

"But certainly you read some ... *Horse and Hound* magazine, for example." She looked directly at him and smiled openly at her own joke, exposing a dimple in each cheek. But her smile was not mocking. Rather, it had a quality of tenderness that unsettled Wilhelm, and prompted him to turn away from her.

"Well," Wilhelm answered, taking out his pocket watch and studying it assiduously, "my familiarity with *Horse and Hound* magazine is, in this case, to your great advantage, as I can assure you that you have landed in hound and not in horse, and to judge by the mere volume of it, a Shepherd or Boarhound."

She was quiet for a moment, and then said, "I think your friend Ehrlingen is keeping you from your lunch; but perhaps you have lost your appetite anyway." Here her voice was strangely muted, and when he looked back at her, he could read something in her eyes that made him feel he had slighted her.

Wilhelm smiled at her. "I have never once lost my appetite, Fräulein."

"I wish I would lose my appetite. I'm being dieted, and won't get any lunch."

The girl's candor shocked Wilhelm, and he hesitated before replying, "Ah! But that is a shame! I am very sorry to hear that! I, myself, am not a believer in diets. They invariably ruin the stomach. And if I may be permitted to say it, well-fed girls tend to be prettier than slender ones."

"Well, no doubt they are happier," Elisabeth replied, with a sigh.

Just then, Susannah appeared with Henning behind her. "Lisi, my love! You've been waiting, I know!"

"Mami, you mustn't delay these gentlemen. They want their midday meal. And you should know that Graf Boening has been incredibly kind, and cleaned me off from a fall into unmentionable things." She turned and showed her mother the back of her skirt. Then pointedly to Henning, she said, "Baron von Ehrlingen, we seem to meet practically everywhere lately. It's as if you are following us! So Mami, have you *finally* made your decision?"

"No, it's truly vexing," Susannah said. "It will be one of the original two patterns I was considering … But how kind of you, Graf Boening! How very chivalrous! Truly above and beyond!"

Wilhelm smiled a half-smile. "If I may be helpful, Frau von Schwabacher, the first damask you looked at had gray tones that in natural light might have too static an effect. So I would advise the second, deeper toned green, which is much livelier."

Susannah responded with a wide, genuine grin. "I am very grateful. Very grateful indeed. And if you happen to enjoy Brahms, you must come to our home in Lichterfelde West next Thursday evening. Your brother-in-law and the Baron will both be playing, as will my Lisi."

"Mami," Lisi interjected, with a frown, "Count von Boening may not be a music lover…"

"And yet, he may be!" her mother answered sternly.

"He doesn't even *read* much, Mami! And you mustn't go around proselytizing our music evenings!"

"And yet," Wilhelm said, with a nod to the girl, and a chastising half-smile, "Despite reading little, I am not quite an unwashed beast, Fräulein."

Susannah's eyes registered some perturbation at this exchange. But she smiled a very graceful smile and continued, "It's all quite informal. We entertain *en famille,* and you needn't reply now. Here is my card. You may drop me a note as late as Wednesday, and only if you plan on coming."

ORDINARILY, BOENING WOULD HAVE IGNORED AN invitation given so casually, and by a Jewish woman, for a chamber music evening he wasn't even sure he would enjoy. But there was something not quite definable that tempted him to go—something about the young girl that made him want to see her again. It was her openness and seeming lack of guile, he finally decided, that was compelling. It was as if she were fully taken up in an inner life, and didn't care at all what effect she produced. Well, it would do no good, he decided, if the Schwabacher home was not frequented by his kind of society.

"Who attends?" he found himself asking Henning, as they approached the Casino-Gesellschaft.

His friend demurred. "Who attends what?"

"The musical evenings."

"Which?"

"The Schwabacher soirees …"

"I, for one."

"But you play. Who goes to listen?"

"Nobody of your ilk, as the girl so clearly reminded her mother."

"What does that mean? *You* are of my ilk. We are of the same ilk."

"Not quite," Henning replied. "For example, you ask who goes there, because you wouldn't consider going if you were the only *Junker* there."

"And you?"

"I will go to any rich man's house that offers good music— without reference to the names of the other guests."

"But the other guests—or at least the host—would have to be rich."

"A man has to have some standards, Boening!" And then Henning changed the subject.

It was clear from this exchange that Henning was putting Wilhelm off. So that Wilhelm resolved not to attempt to return to the subject of the musical evening, even though he was spending the better part of the afternoon in Henning's presence.

There were, of course, others whom Wilhelm could lobby for information about the Schwabachers. Just after lunch, he was able to corner one of the officers of his regiment and a preferred partner at cards, Baron August von Hennholz.

Hennholz was something of a celebrated gossip. So Wilhelm felt no compunction launching a straightforward request for information about the Schwabacher family.

"Magnus von Schwabacher is a Jew." Hennholz replied, somewhat dismissively.

"I know very well he is a Jew. He is my banker. I was wondering what sort of people go there."

"Your brother-in-law goes every week. As well as our friend, Ehrlingen. Say, Boening, have you noticed Ehrlingen doesn't look at your dirty pictures anymore?"

"I hadn't noticed."

"Well, I find it alarming."

"How so?"

"When a man is no longer interested in pornography, it can mean only one thing—that he is in love."

"With whom?"

"He plays quartets with Monsieur. But they say Madame is his muse."

"I see."

"But you were asking who else goes there? And of course, other people of our sort do go in and out very occasionally—more diplomats than army officers ... But I gather not many are invited. Your banker is an ambitious businessman, but not a social climber. I think he mostly sees other Jews. It's a shame really. Because if he saw *only* other Jews, he probably wouldn't be playing the cuckold, presently. But then, one never knows. Maybe Madame would take a Jewish lover.

"Anyway, they have chamber music. And chamber music tends to preclude truly lavish dinners and entertainments ... But why do you ask? I cannot imagine their evenings at home would be much to your taste!"

All of this information came as a great disappointment to Wilhelm. First, there was the matter of Henning's attachment to Susannah von Schwabacher, which, while it should not have upset Wilhelm, being none of his business, was nevertheless somehow distasteful to him. Then there was the news that his brother-in-law, Prince Egon Senbeck-Wittenbach, was often among the Schwabachers' most frequent visitors. Prince Egon was a man of unassailable social position—the scion of a prominent South German family of mediatized nobility. He was also a devout Catholic as well as an intellectual and aesthete. Wilhelm disliked him heartily, and studiously avoided his company, even when visiting the man's home.

Wilhelm thought a moment and then asked, "What about Fräulein Schwabacher? What do you know about her?"

Hennholz looked surprised. "Well, Boening, I would hardly go there for her. She has certainly been kept out of view, which is never a good sign. And she has something of a reputation as a *lusus naturae,* having audited mathematics lectures at university as a very fat fourteen-year-old girl. Schwabacher is likely going to have to offer up a pretty sum to marry her off, though she is an only child and one day will be worth at least sixty-million marks. Of course, they say she plays like an angel. But then, isn't that what they always say about Jewesses that no self-respecting Christian would take to bed?"

# CHAPTER IV

THE SCHWABACHER VILLA, A STONE MANSION ON
the Kadettenweg in the new development of Lichterfelde West, was
Magnus' present to his wife, Susannah, on the occasion of their
twentieth wedding anniversary, in 1891. It was two years in the de-
signing and building, and Lisi (despite desperately missing Vienna)
loved every inch of it, from the marbled columns that framed
an elevated front portico, to the French windows that looked
out onto a generous back garden. Five ornamented stonework
balconies trimmed the edifice, and in the spring and summer,
when flower pots were on display, the house, despite its grand
size, made a warm and friendly impression. The public spaces—a
dining room, drawing room, music room (this fitted out with
two concert grand pianos), and a two-story library holding more
than twelve-thousand volumes—were brilliantly lit with great
crystal chandeliers, and sumptuously furnished with colorful fab-
rics, wall tapestries, and paintings ranging from the Old Masters
through the Impressionists. (At Susannah's insistence, Magnus

had been one of the first collectors to bring a Claude Monet into a Berlin home.)

For Susannah, the home's chief charm was its distance from the center of the city, in the quiet suburb of Steglitz-Zehlendorf. Here she could breathe fresh air, enjoy the respite of trees and flowers, and even cultivate a small vegetable garden. Here one could hear snow fall. The cobble-stoned streets, the wrought-iron lampposts, and the varied architecture of this quiet neighborhood offered some of the same charms as the outer districts of Vienna, where she had grown up.

But for Lisi, that same quietude, that very remoteness from the bustling streets and the crowded cafes of Berlin-Mitte magnified feelings of deprivation. Yes, she had her music and books, and relished the many hours she spent in solitary pursuit of her interests. But there was not a day she didn't wake up longing for more intelligent company than her mother would manage to provide for her; and not a day that her mother's preoccupations with dressing, housekeeping, and the serving of fancy dinners failed to irritate her. The Vienna home of Susannah's brother, the obstetric specialist Siegmund Weingarten, may have been small and crowded, but it was also lively and stimulating. None of the six members of the Weingarten family, three of whom were doctors of medicine, could manage to think a banal thought, much less express one. And, true to Lisi's own domestic priorities, the only strict household regimen centered on the punctual serving of hearty midday and evening meals. No one was particularly zealous about straightening up or cleaning. It was all the two servants (a cook and maid) could do to keep up with the family's appetite—the *Knoedeln, Nudeln, Strudeln,*

*Schnitzeln, Braten, Kuchen,* and *Keks* that emanated from *Tante* Anna's kitchen.

Susannah, of course, was a meticulous housewife, who expected the best and never settled for anything less. Every piece of furniture in her home—both new and antique—was kept in pristine condition. The surfaces in every room gleamed with polish. There was order everywhere. And her interior decoration was a model of the finest taste. Family dinners in the Schwabacher home, far from hearty, family-style affairs, were quite formal. And at this point in time, Lisi hardly looked forward to them. For while she was consigned to a diet of jellied broth, eggs, and almonds, she was made to watch a parade of Lucullan delicacies pass over her table setting on a nightly basis: *foie gras* in aspic, *quenelles, canard a l'orange,* Beef Wellington, *Opera* cake, profiterole. The list of Frau Bries' triumphs went on and on, and Lisi was allowed none of it. It should be mentioned that while Magnus—a small, nervous man with a very active metabolism—enjoyed his meals at home thoroughly, Susannah never took more than a few bites of the dishes she served, as she was permanently watching her figure.

The truth was, Susannah's epicurean repasts were more often than not rehearsals for the suppers she served at her Thursday "evenings at home." And they signaled much larger social aspirations than merely hosting a few musically interested friends on a weekly basis. In fact, Susannah would have liked to preside over a bonafide salon. Her husband's first cousin, the Countess Babette Meyer von Kalckreuth was a renowned hostess, whose position in Berlin society was exalted, despite the fact that her origins were Jewish. Susannah often dreamed of reaching the countess' heights—namely, that rare position in German society where Jewish birth was largely overlooked.

Magnus, however, had no such ambitions. He was determined to live quietly. So Susannah had to be content with her weekly chamber music evenings. At least they featured a convivial group of cultivated amateurs—even occasionally (thanks to her *impresaria* friend, Luise Wolff) a renowned concert artist. And they managed to attract a happy, if small, group of aristocrats, academics, and professionals who had become close to the family, and who came to appreciate Susannah's finely conceived French suppers every bit as much as the beautiful music performed.

Most people who came to the Schwabachers on Thursday evenings knew what to expect. One arrived between half past seven and seven forty-five p.m. and passed through the drawing room, where there was a choice of tea or sherry. By eight p.m., one had already taken a seat in the music room.

But Susannah's reply to Wilhelm's note of Tuesday morning, being a hasty, "So glad you will be joining us. We start our music at twenty o'clock—Su. v. Schwabacher," the count found himself slipping into a chair just as the opening strains of the Brahms Piano Quintet sounded. As he took in his surroundings, he breathed a short sigh of relief that he was in evening dress. Susannah's description of her gatherings as *en famille* had almost set him on the wrong course. And there was the lady of the house semi-reclined in a white brocade chair, wearing décolleté tulle over olive silk, large diamond drops hanging from her ears.

Of the guests (twenty-four in all), Wilhelm recognized immediately the presence of Prince Egon Wittenbach's sister, the Princess Edith von Schwarzenau, a sylphlike brunette who looked stunning as ever. Wilhelm had heard she was in Berlin visiting her brother. There was also a young diplomat from the American embassy, along with the handsome Countess Babette Meyer von Kalckreuth, whom Wilhelm had known since her visit to Pulow the summer of his tenth year. Then there was the impresario couple, Hermann and Luise Wolff (affectionately referred to in Berlin as the *Musik-Wolffs*). And finally, there was a very old professor of mathematics at the University of Berlin, whose name Wilhelm couldn't quite recall, but whom he had met at the Countess Kalckreuth's—Haber, he thought it was. His banker, his brother-in-law, and his friend, Henning, were among the performers, along with Fräulein Schwabacher and a distinctly Jewish looking woman violinist, whose expression struck him as unaffectedly refined and modest, in contrast to the lady of the house. This violinist was later introduced to him as Gerda Lilienberg, wife of the architect who had designed the Schwabacher villa.

It occurred to Wilhelm, as he was drawn into the music, that he had never heard Ehrlingen play the viola before, though he had heard him play the piano often. Nor had he quite appreciated Wittenbach's violin playing. And there was no mistaking Elisabeth von Schwabacher's musical expertise. She played with masterful clarity, and her interpretation of the slow movement was exquisitely sensitive. Having the opportunity, as he listened, to study her, her head slightly tilted, her eyes half closed, all the muscles of her face still and poised in concentration, Wilhelm realized why it was that he had the feeling, when looking up at her in the fabric shop, that her face was familiar to him. Because she could have been a double for his Carlo Dolci model—in those moments, every bit the *Head of an Angel*.

When the final rush of chords came at the end of the four-movement piece, the small audience applauded enthusiastically, and the mood was unmistakably jovial. It was clear that the performance had impressed. The assembled group rose to chat in anticipation of being called to the dining room.

Wilhelm had barely stood up when he found himself looking directly into the sultry brown eyes of Princess Edith.

"This is a pleasure, Graf Boening. I was hoping to see you somewhere, but not expecting it would be here." She extended her hand to him, which Wilhelm, in a cursory gesture, took and kissed.

"My brother says he rarely sees you," she added.

"I'm sorry for that. We never seem to be in the same place at the same time."

"Well I cannot say I'm surprised, and I am sure that Egon regrets it, even if you might not. But here you are, by happy coincidence! Or should I compliment myself for bringing you here? Perhaps not ...," she added quickly, seeing that a look of very slight annoyance passed over Wilhelm's face. "Perhaps your wild oats are finally sown. Perhaps you are engaged." She smiled at him with what looked to be a tinge of regret.

Wilhelm obliged her inquiring gaze with the brusque remark, "No, not engaged. But looking. And so, I have sworn off married women ..."

"I see. Your hint is gracefully taken. But then, you intend, presently, to live like a monk?"

"When one is looking for a wife, any other way of life would be immoral, wouldn't it?"

The Princess Edith laughed. "In bad taste, perhaps, but hardly immoral! In any case," she continued, "if you are wife hunting here in Lichterfelde West, you will have to wait in line, as I believe my brother has developed a serious infatuation with the daughter of the house ... But I hope that news doesn't upset you!"

"My sister is gone almost two years now. A widower with children as young as Egon's would have to be looking to provide them with a mother."

"I'm relieved to hear you say so."

At this moment, Magnus Schwabacher came up to them and, with a bow to both the Princess and Wilhelm, offered his arm to the Princess.

"I am surprised to see you here, Boening," an older woman's voice said behind him. "I didn't know you were acquainted with the Schwabachers. And I thought you had abandoned the city."

Wilhelm turned toward the tall, stout woman who had addressed him, and bowed. Whenever he was with her, he never failed to reflect on how much her looks had changed over the years. In her slender youth, she had been regarded as a dark, fiery beauty. But the graying of her hair and the aging of her figure had turned the fearsome impression she had once made to one of a subtler, friendlier dignity. "*Gräfin* Kalckreuth. A pleasure to see you. And I haven't abandoned Berlin; only there has been a lot to attend to in the country. My father is not as energetic as he once was."

"He must look out for his heart, Boening. I hope you are a help to him."

"I try to be."

"Your father's heart," she added, with a note of weary knowledge, "was *never* what it should be."

"Perhaps not." Wilhelm answered absently; for he had been looking around, hoping that there would be an opportunity for him to address Lisi, and perhaps even escort her into dinner. But Lisi was chatting warmly with the old Professor, who with exaggerated gallantry had offered her his arm, and then when she took it, had patted her hand.

Wilhelm offered his arm to Babette, who accepted it with a friendly shake of the head and the observation that he seemed "preoccupied."

"And what do you think of your surroundings, tonight?" she inquired. Then, answering her own question, she continued, "Quite opulent, wouldn't you say? And every bell and whistle modern in the extreme. Incandescent bulbs, everywhere! And did you know that Magnus has an automobile? A Daimler!"

Wilhelm knew she was thinking of her own staid life and her stubbornly old-fashioned, if palatial home on the corner of Viktoriastrasse and Bellevuestrasse in the center of Berlin. The house had not changed one iota since the fifties.

"It's truly impressive, *Gräfin*. The paintings especially."

"And what do you think of the girl?" she asked casually, as they crossed the foyer from the music room into the dining room.

"Very talented."

"I've known her since she was in diapers. And believe me, it has been a great temptation to display those talents, as they were prodigious. I can only give Maggi and Susannah credit for not making spectacles of themselves, and of her also. She's just back from Vienna, you know, where she studied piano with Theodore Leschetizky. And now I suppose they will try to find her a husband, if such a thing is possible."

"Why shouldn't it be possible?" Wilhelm asked, as they approached the table. He helped the countess into a chair to his left, where she was to sit next to Wittenbach. "After all, she's not only gifted, she is charming looking."

Babette glanced up at him in a way that struck him as maternally fond, and then replied, *sotto voce*, "Is she? Charming looking? I hadn't thought about it! One doesn't think of looking at her, really! But you are a true painter, Boening. Always looking!"

She laid a hand gently on Wilhelm's sleeve, and remonstrated. "And I wonder why I see you so seldom!"

Wilhelm could not have placed the countess more advantageously, for when he took the chair beside her, he realized that Elisabeth was sitting on the other side of him. She briefly glanced at him, smiled, and then turned back to Professor Haber, whom she proceeded to engage with intense queries regarding the work of the mathematician, Gottlob Frege. As the soup was served and Babette chatted with his brother-in-law, Prince Egon von Wittenbach, Wilhelm was left to eavesdrop. But he caught very little from the Frege discussion other than the fact that the girl seemed determined to get the Professor to admit the timeliness of a logical analysis of language, now that it seemed that Frege was moving in that direction.

Babette soon claimed Wilhelm's attention once more, turning suddenly to him with the monition, "I hope you haven't stayed away from this year's exhibit of the Association of Eleven?"

"Somehow, Gräfin, I knew that dreaded question was coming."

"You'll have to get out of the seventeenth century sometime, and the sooner the better."

"I'm afraid I like it there."

"Look here, Boening! They used to say that Berlin was a city of soldiers, not art. Yet, it's simply not the case anymore. Say, you'll no doubt have heard the very salty tales of your regiment's officers. What is it about the subject of homosexuality, nowadays?"

"I beg your pardon?"

"Don't be coy, Boening! We are adults, aren't we? And I have a theory about the recent popularity of that subject!"

Wilhelm laughed. "Homosexuality? I am dying to hear it! But tell me first where that scientific sounding word came from so suddenly. We used to say 'inverted.'"

"Well, thank God we have a new word. When we give a phenomenon a brand new name, we tend to view it differently!"

"You mean we encourage it?"

"No, indeed. It was always there. But we suddenly *see* it. With new—hopefully more tolerant—eyes!"

"Tolerance! Good Lord, Gräfin! I will leave tolerance to others!"

"All right, Boening. Let's leave off with that and turn to a subject more interesting to us both—namely, painting! Certainly you've come to know the work of Max Liebermann."

"For whom you claim great admiration. And I agree that he is a good painter. But I think his teacher, Millet, was the better artist."

"You find the subject matter too prosaic, I expect." Babette interjected.

"As long as we are on the subject of my regiment, and if you insist on knowing my uncensored opinion, I will tell you that the theme of naked boys—that is, boys undressing at swimming holes—makes me very nervous."

"Boening!" Babette laughed. "Can you tell me why pictures of naked women can be displayed with impunity in the most conservative milieu; but put a naked man in a painting, and it's like setting off a bomb!"

"It is indeed a major problem for your beloved naturalists. But the fact is, women are pretty, and men aren't. Of course, there are a few Adonises in this world, Countess. But most nude men are, frankly, unaesthetic ..."

"Unaesthetic?" she interrupted. "Or *unerotisch?*"

"Both, perhaps. And most especially when portrayed in everyday surroundings."

"Really? I think females would differ on that point. Perhaps our problem is that the art critics are all males. If I were still painting, which I am not, I would endeavor to change the critics' minds by painting up a storm of very wholesome male nudes engaged in ... Well, I would have to decide what to engage them in ... Perhaps military exercises!" She smiled at her own joke.

"But I would make sure everyone liked them, even if they weren't particularly handsome! Frankly, I don't see that a man needs to be dressed in a military tunic in order to appear on the wall of a decent home."

"Gräfin," Wilhelm said, smiling a mischievous half-smile, "I hereby challenge you to get out your easel and prove your pudding."

The conversation continued like this, and as Wilhelm savored it, he also stealthily observed Lisi leaving her soup, her fish, and her sorbet almost completely untouched. And he saw also that the girl's mother signaled her repeatedly with a frown.

Suddenly, just as the veal was served, Lisi was facing him, and it struck him for the second time that she had an unusual transparency of expression. He even felt he could read her thoughts, which were telling him that she was struggling hard for an opening line of conversation.

"Count Boening ... *Ja* ... Well, first I must tell you that it was kind of you to come tonight. I hope it wasn't a sore obligation. And I also hope you weren't thoroughly bored by our music. Brahms isn't everyone's taste."

"I enjoyed it greatly. And you play beautifully, if I may say so. But tell me, which do you prefer to leave untouched, your food or your wine? Fish or meat?"

Elisabeth laughed and tossed back her head, a red-blond curl or two shaking itself free from her hairpins. "I am afraid I'm only allowed symbolic portions. My mother holds the key to the pantry. When I returned from Vienna three months ago, she found I was twice the girl who had left Berlin. But for some reason, she only wants one of me."

"Well, you have to eat and drink something more substantial, Fräulein. Or you'll be like *Suppenkaspar,* who 'ended up a little thread / and on the fifth day, dead!'"

Lisi laughed again. "I am nourished by good discussions, like that which I have just had with my very dear mathematics teacher, whom I haven't seen for over three years. And that information, Count Boening, is by way of offering you an apology. My mother will certainly lecture me later for ignoring you. And I want to thank you, again, for rescuing me from my embarrassment the other day."

"My duty and pleasure, Fräulein." There was then a silence between them, and to fill it, Wilhelm said, "I hear your father has a very large library."

"You are welcome to peruse it after dinner. Many people accuse him, quite erroneously, of purchasing the entire contents. But the fact is, most of the volumes are inherited. The Schwabachers have been inveterate bookworms for many generations, and to the point where there was often little space to move in their dwellings. At any rate, I warn you that my father's quite extensive collection of periodicals contains not one issue of *Horse and Hound.*"

"I wouldn't need to see one, since I have every issue of *that* publication in *my* library. But does your father approve of *your* reading habits, Fräulein Schwabacher—namely, of Friedrich Engel's ruminations on the origins of family and private property?"

"Actually, my father recommended it to me."

"Really!" Wilhelm raised his eyebrows.

"I suppose that my father, in his subtle way, wishes to prepare me for the possibility of being pursued by gold diggers."

"Well I hope that you will not allow Herr Engels or your father to make you into a cynic so early in life. You will surely have suitors whose motivations can be trusted."

"I actually don't think I am in any danger of being taken advantage of," Lisi replied. "In fact, if I continue to slip in muck every time I venture into town, I doubt even the most desperate fortune hunter will take a second look at me."

She cocked her head, and continued, "But *you,* Graf Boening, have an unnerving habit of staring at me. Can you tell me why?"

"Forgive me. When I met you, you looked somehow familiar to me. And now I realize you remind me of a girl in a painting."

"Really?" Her deep blue eyes searched his face. "And of what provenance might that painting be?"

"Italian, Fräulein. It's an Onorio Marinari of the late seventeenth century."

"I don't know him." She paused, in thought. "But I hope the girl would be … not too horrible."

"She's very pretty. At least, I think she is. Very pretty, but unfortunately, in the painting, she has done an evil thing."

"And what is that?"

"She has killed John the Baptist."

"I see ... So she is a Jewess." Lisi suddenly grimaced, and her cheeks colored highly in what seemed like a rush of anger; but just as suddenly, it was as if a curtain descended on her face, and her features came to rest. Wilhelm watched her open a small, delicately formed mouth as if to say something, but she closed it again without speaking. Then she smiled and asked in a muted tone, "And where do you stand, Graf Boening, on the question of Wagner versus Brahms?"

"I am not a fan of Wagner. And you?"

"My parents are taking me to Bayreuth for the new *Ring* cycle production this summer."

"I'm sorry for you."

"Don't be. I love Wagner. And why do you prefer Brahms?"

"I find the music of Brahms *far* more pleasing."

"Papi," the girl raised her voice slightly, and laughed lightly as if preparing to tell a joke. Her father, at the far end of the table, and deep in conversation with the Princess Edith, raised his head.

"Yes, Lisi, *Liebchen*."

"Papi, Count von Boening says that he stands with Brahms against Wagner. And do you know why?" And here she enunciated emphatically, "Because he *likes* the music of Brahms more."

A shocked Wilhelm looked over at Henning to see his friend frown angrily. But Magnus seemed not the least bit perturbed by his daughter's rudeness. He merely smiled and replied with good humor, "And why not, Lisi, dear! Many people like the music of

Brahms better. If you think it is a matter of education, you might endeavor to enlighten the count; and then perhaps he will teach *you* a thing or two about the visual arts!"

And here Susannah spoke, "Frankly, Lisi, I don't see why the first criterion of aesthetic judgment should *not* be that a work of art pleases. Not that everything which pleases can be art, but art that doesn't please..." She shook her head.

"It would seem," Prince Egon interjected, "that all other criteria would stem from that first one, and isn't that Aristotle's first criterion in the *Poetics*?"

"*Durchlaucht*," Luise Wolff replied, chuckling. "To judge from some of the newest Berlin painting exhibitions, Aristotle would have been very disappointed."

"I don't follow the visual arts anymore, Frau Wolff," laughed the professor. "Considering my failing eyesight, your report comforts me greatly."

"Still, to say something pleases," offered Gerda Lilienberg, "is only the beginning of an answer. Not to put you on the spot, Count Boening, but can you describe what it is in Brahms that you like, and in Wagner that you don't like."

Perhaps, after Lisi's calculated insult, Gerda Lilienberg's question should have annoyed Wilhelm. But he was not a man to be put off balance in any company. And the question was offered in a tone of such earnest curiosity and kindness, that he found himself relishing the thought of attempting to answer it. "Well," he said, "I am not a musician, so I can only convey my unschooled impressions. In Brahms I hear orderly development, but in Wagner I hear only endless and irritating repetition."

Here, Egon ventured, "My brother-in-law is very conservative in his tastes. And what he means, I think, is that he cannot trace a line from Bach to Wagner. But Boening, while some people criticize the music of Wagner for being rhetorical, others see it as organic, and therefore ideally dramatic."

"Wittenbach, if by 'organic' you mean close to the realm of instinct, that is precisely why I find Wagner so off-putting. I'm afraid I find his music intolerable. And that's to say nothing about the so-called poetry which goes with it."

"Which is …?" asked Lisi, turning a cold gaze on him.

"Which, in my humble opinion, has the very rare distinction of being at the same time portentous and inane."

"But of course," Lisi said impatiently, "because it's comedy!"

"Is it, Fräulein? I mean to ask, is it intentionally funny? Or was the man, himself, a clown? In fact," he continued, looking straight at Lisi, "with all due respect to present company, I would bet a good portion of the Bayreuth audience goes there for the sake of that man's imbecilic politics. And another good portion are simply impressed by the scandal that was his personal life."

"Here, I am afraid I must agree with Count Boening," Princess Edith interjected. "There is nothing more tantalizing to an audience than contemplating how celebrities bring their pile of illegitimate children into the world."

The entire company laughed, and Hermann Wolff said, "Well, Count Boening, you seem to have put Wagner in his place! And did you hear Herr Mahler's Symphony in D Major last month?"

"Who is he? I'm sorry to say, I have no idea who he is."

Henning chuckled. "You haven't missed a thing, Boening. Speaking of a surfeit of the rhetorical …"

"I don't agree," Elisabeth interrupted. "I think Herr Mahler's D Major symphony is beautiful."

Hermann Wolff spoke. "Well, being, myself, a slave to everything that is music, I must say I thought it good enough. But many people find it too sentimental."

"Do they?" asked Lisi. "I was completely carried away by the first movement, which is so happy and full of the sounds of nature. It reminded me of the very precious mornings I spent hiking with my cousins in the meadows of the Rax, near Vienna. And as for the third movement, *lieber Onkel*," and here she looked directly into the friendly, bearded face of Hermann Wolff, "can you tell me why it is that Brahms can write pages of Hungarian melodies, and everyone swoons over them. But if Mahler colors eight measures of a folk tune in a way that sounds the least bit Jewish, it's labeled vulgar?"

Babette leaned into the table to look past Wilhelm and address Lisi. "Well, Lisi dear," she said, "Isn't it obvious? When Wagner wrote his essay, *Jewishness in Music*, everyone was embarrassed for him, because they knew the article was only a jealous rant on Mendelssohn, who could hardly be accused of writing anything sounding the least bit Jewish. But in Herr Mahler, we are faced with a composer who writes music that in places has the echo of the *Schtetl*. It's all potentially quite humiliating. Because one almost expects your beloved Wagner to burst forth from his grave and point to it, and say, 'There it is! There it is! You see? You … you … you see? Jewishness in music!'"

Babette's delivery of this last line was so aptly performed, down to Wagner's childlike stutter and choking noises that everyone at the table, including Lisi, burst into laughter.

# CHAPTER V

*Kadettenweg 9, Gross-Lichterfelde*
*April 16, 1896*
*Liebste Klara,*
*How I miss you and Uncle Sigi, Aunt Anna and Lene and Martin,*
*and even (truth to tell, especially!) my little, very annoying Isabel,*
*who climbs into bed with her cold feet and grabs all the blankets and*
*begs for stories and tickles me until I promise to tell her more.*

*And speaking of Isi, you must tell her that Mami has barely al-*
*lowed me anything more than jellied consommé and almonds for*
*more than seven weeks now and that I am ravenously hungry. (I am*
*dreaming of Esterhazytorte and can even taste the cream filling in*
*my sleep!) So she'd better hope I won't return soon to Vienna, because*
*I am preparing to eat her up when I do.*

*Klara, I am so sad to hear of Bernhard's illness; and frankly, I*
*don't wonder that he thinks it an inappropriate time to marry. But*
*in your case, a wedding must be, because you are physically married.*
*And if the worst happens, dear Klara—if he dies—where will you*

*be? Will you want to live the rest of your life alone? But then, you are always so sovereign, and so be sovereign with him and tell him the wedding must be on, if only because he will need you desperately in the coming months if he is to recover at all. And because if he does not recover, how will you possibly get a second husband if you haven't actually wedded your first? Dearest Cousin, how well I wish you and your irreverent fiancé, who makes everyone he comes into contact with, even his patients, ache from laughing.*

*You ask how your little "princess" is faring up north … Well, your "princess," now back in her very lonely castle (no cousins to torment her!), tries her best to keep busy—that is, without eating. Papi comes to me every morning to chat and to make sure I am not a "lie-a-bed." Naturally, I practice every morning for several hours. What else is there to do? No doubt, you will ask to what purpose, then? For my own enjoyment and edification, of course! (And now Klara frowns in scorn as she reads how Lisi wastes her days fingering the piano keys, while Klara is all up in ladies' blood and mucous!) Of course, there is always shopping with Mami, whose new project is Papi's office, which she delights in calling his "barracks." (You know Mami and her affectations!) And there are the tennis lessons, which are simply the best part of a very bad bargain, by which I mean, of course, being back here in Berlin, bereft of the company of you and all the other interesting and vital young people who make me happy!*

*Today, Mami insisted I accompany her to the Schleslischer Bahnhof, where I helped with some charity work for the refugees. They pile out of trains daily again and are so frightened and pathetic. I have a lot of trouble understanding them, as most speak only Yiddish, and the Ukrainian version of it. Mami thinks it's quite hilarious that a Jewish girl who speaks five languages can stare so helplessly at these poor people. And I must admit I find them mystifying, and even a bit frightening. But Mami says I should refrain from harsh judgment, because these ghetto Jews, despite their downtrodden aura, have energy and discipline. She insists that many will, in less than a generation, be ladies and gentlemen, and as German as the Kaiser.*

*Speaking of immigrants, Mami has managed to find me a French maid. I know what you are thinking as you read this: I've gone back to being very spoiled. And I wouldn't mention it at all if this young woman weren't as gifted with a needle as Tante Anni, and if it weren't curious to me that she claims to be a Jewess and insists she is relieved to have found work in a Jewish house. Her name is Susannah, just like Mami, but, of course, she is called "Suzette." And there is an air of mystery about her, as well as a touch of impudence. Last night, as I was dressing for Mami's evening at home, Suzette suddenly asked me if I were to marry soon. And when I said, "I hope not," she said that Jewish men were no good and Christians even worse. And she warned me, as only a French woman can, I expect, to avoid "les histoires d'amour."*

*I wonder, Klara, what you would think of the cast of characters who have come to frequent our home? It strikes me that you have never met Papi's cousin, Babette Meyer. The gentiles call her Countess von Kalckreuth—though I suspect that even Papi doesn't quite understand the very short episode in her life that was her marriage. She is a very fine lady, a salon Jewess in the truest sense. A lot of what goes on in her living room on Tuesday evenings involves political discussion. Remarkably, it seems she is able to gather together aristocrats (at least those not hopelessly conservative), journalists, men of industry, and politicians, as well as a number of poets and philosophers. She was once an intimate of Bismarck's house, but that was long ago, and they have been enemies for quite some time. I think you would find her wonderfully intelligent, although her views on music are very old-fashioned. Papi says she was quite a beauty in her day. And she still dresses grandly. Does it ever strike you as odd that so many of our relations are complete strangers to us? For example, you know almost no one in my father's family, when you might get along famously with several of them!*

*Anyway, it's another world, Berlin! Last night, Mami had one of her music evenings. Prince Wittenbach came, naturally. (He comes at least two afternoons a week to play. And I am so grateful for it, as he provides the only stimulating daytime society that I have.) And Baron von Ehrlingen was here—a man who, I have to admit, is so very musical and sailed through our reading of the* Brahms Piano Quintet in F minor, *though the viola has to be his fourth or fifth instrument. But I continue to hate him, because it has gotten to the point that he follows Mami around like a little lap dog. And she positively encourages him! He might as well move in! I'm beginning to think you are right about Mami, that she is susceptible to temptation because she longs so for admiration. And I wonder that Papi doesn't see that he is being played for a fool.*

*At any rate, Ehrlingen is now suggesting that Mami and Papi take a place in Borkum in August and that he will arrange it all. Borkum! Where no Jew has ever been seen! I truly wonder that Papi doesn't at least put a stop to* that *plan. But he seems to be perfectly sanguine about it, and even suggested last night to Ehrlingen that he come with us to America. His plan is that Ehrlingen will accompany Mami and me to the American Southwest, so that we can see the Grand Canyon. I was livid, Klara, and asked Ehrlingen (and right in front of Papi!) if he could be expected to save us from the wild Indians, because he really wouldn't be needed for anything else!*

*Oh, and Count von Boening, Prince Wittenbach's brother-in-law, was also here. You must remember Prince Wittenbach speaking of him in all the very amusing terms that befit a* Junker *caricature. And truly, last night it was as if he had arrived fresh from Nowhere, East Prussia, dressed to the nines and all stiffly starched. And although he is quite friendly with Ehrlingen, I think he must have wondered throughout the entire evening what he was doing here. The awkward truth of it is that perhaps he didn't want to come at all, but felt an obligation to come, because after he was kind enough to help clean me off from a fall in the street, Mami gave him her card and said he must come for a chamber music evening. Well, he sat next to me at supper and stared at me the entire evening as if I were some sort of freak; and aside from pronouncing that I reminded him of a Jewess in a seventeenth-century Italian painting (and imagine which Jewess: Salome!), he proved to be as dull as one could possibly expect. He's the handsomest man I have ever laid eyes on, though, so I had no trouble staring right back at him.*

*By the way, it turns out Mami knows about Prince Wittenbach's visits to me, because Uncle Sigi wrote to her how the Prince charmed you all. Honestly, Klara, I don't know what I expected her reaction would be. Whatever I imagined, and I imagined many things, her behavior was anything but exaggerated. She just smiled enigmatically, as only Mami can, and said, "How very nice of him! And besides being everything an aristocrat should be, he is such a lovely looking man, with intelligent brown eyes, don't you think?"*

*I just hope that she doesn't think she is dieting me for him, because Papi wouldn't approve, no matter how outwardly magnificent such a marriage would be, and I don't know if I even want him, although I am getting the feeling he could want me. He has taken to bringing me books of poetry. And as of last week, by his request, I am no longer allowed to address him as "Durchlaucht," but rather simply as Prince Egon. Imagine!*

*At any rate, if he did want me, I wonder if he could accept me fat, as I will be that again. You see, he's remarked so many times on the weight I am losing. And last night, he even took my hand as he was leaving, and whispered, "Fräulein Elisabeth, I treasure our memories of afternoon sweets at Demel in Vienna, but I do so like you looking delicate, as you do right now."*

*And speaking of self-denial, Gerda Lilienberg has lent me Gabriele Reuter's book,* From a Good Family, *which she insisted I read right away, as she feels it gets to the core on the subject of the condition of women in Germany. I'm wondering if you've read it. Of course, there are a few short but exceedingly nasty lines about Jews in it. (Sometimes I wonder if there is even one gentile writer in Germany, presently, who isn't an anti-semite!) But even aside from that, I don't really think much of the book, because the main character is so constrained and prudish, so completely banal and devoid of imagination, so stupidly obedient and pious, even for a middle-class girl trapped by social convention. And though there is some pathos about her, I just don't like her, and shouldn't one at least* like *the heroine of a novel? But the reason I mention it (beside the fact that you probably should read it, because everyone is talking about it): it reminded me of when you told me about that patient who confided in you that she had self-pleasured, and asked if it were true her babies would be stillborn?*

*Mami expects me downstairs now, so I will sign off with many loving embraces and kisses to you and the entire Weingarten household, and ardent requests, also, for more letters from Vienna!*

*Deine,*

*Lisi*

WILHELM VON BOENING WAS HARDLY A MAN TO dwell on the particulars of social evenings. But for days after his visit to the Schwabacher home, he could not rid himself of a certain, specific memory of that evening. It was the image of Elisabeth von Schwabacher pressing her lips to the hands of Professor Haber as he took his leave, her voice entreating him to "come again soon … please, please, even though we are so far out of town. Papi will always be happy to send a driver for you. And if he lets me learn to drive the Daimler, I will come for you."

For the next two or three weeks, upon dressing each morning in his modest rooms in the Regentenstrasse, Wilhelm found himself unwittingly contemplating the splendor of the villa on the Kadettenweg, along with the alluring small family of very fine Jews that lived there.

At first, his most frequent thought was a deep regret that Lisi was so obviously of superior intelligence and education, and so very rich. Because her looks alone were enticing enough to him that, had she been selling gloves on the Leipzigerstrasse, he was sure he would have been on top of her the very evening of the day he met her. But that thought was soon followed by the realization that it was the whole package she delivered that unnerved him—namely, that he couldn't call up her image without feeling the attraction of her wealth as well as the power of her intellectual energy.

He would not have been able to pinpoint the moment when he first conceived the idea that Lisi should become his wife. But it didn't take long for the two major temptations to which all men ripe for marriage are subject—sexual and material—to conflate into a single desire that was increasingly hard to suppress.

It wasn't that he gave up immediately on the possibilities of Helge von Schwerning. Not at all. The thought of a Jewess as the future Gräfin von Boening was as discomfiting as it was piquant. Indeed, for a while, Boening devoted the few precious moments of the day in which he could allow himself the indulgence of unrestricted thoughts to constructing a dual scenario of future events in which, on the one hand, he married and deflowered Helge, and, on the other, went through the same motions with Lisi.

It probably need not be said that Helge came to great advantage in imagining the wedding—a joyful union of two families sharing a social class, similar values, and identical interests. But in contemplating the marriage, Lisi came out the far more appealing choice. Wilhelm found his fantasies lingering more and more on Lisi's searching round eyes, her untamed hair, her ample décolletage, and her passionate and unconventional conversation. These things were undeniable attractions! And added to them was the dowry she would bring; at the very least four- to six-times what Helge was worth. Wilhelm found himself picturing the luxuries he would enjoy as a man liberated from worries about money— the many horses and dogs, the art auctions, the trips to exotic lands. (What would it be like, he wondered, to return a Jewess to her native Jerusalem?) And then there was the mental image he found himself calling up most—of quiet evenings at Pulow, listening to Lisi play the piano, Aldo and Hexi lying at his feet.

Slowly but surely, his daydreams of marriage with Lisi came to assume a regular shape in his daily routine, completely crowding out any thoughts of Helge. So much so that by early May,

Wilhelm found himself etching those daydreams on the real world. While dressing one morning, for example, he asked his young servant, Hans Dolwitz, what he thought about his master getting married in the near future.

Hans smiled broadly. "But high time, Herr Graf. And who would be the *wertige Dame?*"

Now Wilhelm had the opportunity to try the thing on for size and effect. He smiled, and said very lightly, "*Sie wäre eine Jüdin.*"

Hans seemed stymied. "A Jewess, Sir?" And then he looked as if something occurred to him suddenly, and he asked, "Is she very rich?"

"Very."

"And is she very pretty, Sir?"

"That as well."

Hans was silent for a while and then asked, "But is she very ... foreign, Herr Graf?"

Wilhelm laughed, "Not a bit foreign, Dolwitz! As German ... as ... well ... as much a Berliner as you are a Pomeranian."

"I see, Herr Graf. But surely you will have her baptized first?"

---

A FEW DAYS LATER, WILHELM WAS AT HIS CLUB and at cards with Ehrlingen, Hennholz, and other *Junker* noblemen from his regiment, several of whom were unmarried. The talk, as it often did, turned to eligible girls, and he suddenly heard Elisabeth von Schwabacher's name referred to by the Baron Botho von Flenheim, who had seen her at a concert.

"What do you think she will bring, Ehrlingen?"

"No idea. Why?"

"But you must have some idea. It has to be a fortune. Two million? Three million? Four million?"

"She won't marry out of her faith. Why should she?"

"Her father wants to keep his fortune in Jewish hands, eh?" asked a bachelor named Axel von Arnhelm.

"That's ridiculous!" Flenheim countered. "Schwabacher will be as hungry for a title as any other rich Jew."

"I think not," Henning replied.

"She's not such a dog," said Flenheim, "considering she takes after her father in looks. For four million, I would agree to take her."

"She's a lot more than *you* could possibly manage," said Henning.

Hennholz, completely misunderstanding Ehrlingen's meaning, observed, "I've seen her at the opera, and she's slimmed down considerably. But even so, Schwabacher will have to offer at least three to four million. He's worth sixty, if not eighty. Right, Ehrlingen?"

Henning dissimulated. "I have no idea what he's worth. But it seems his fortune grows in the mouths of the people who discuss him."

"But he knows what you are worth." Hennholz laughed.

"And so he should. He's my banker."

"Well, I can tell you this," Axel von Arnhelm stated. "The girl may no longer be fat, but *I* couldn't sleep with her. Not for the whole sixty million. She's not to *my* taste."

Hennholz turned to Wilhelm and asked mischievously, "What about you, Boening? I hear you've been to the banker's home. What do you think of her?"

Wilhelm did not look up from his cards. "I would take her to bed immediately, and without demanding anything up front."

Then he faced his cronies, smiled a half-smile, and pointedly declared, "That having been said, when I ask for her hand, I intend to suggest the number three. I am not as greedy as Flenheim. For the rest, I can wait until her father dies."

Six of the eight men present laughed at this. But Wilhelm could not have anticipated the effect of his words on the normally sanguine Henning, who looked and acted for the rest of the evening as if he were about to jump out of his skin.

As he was leaving the club, Henning caught Wilhelm roughly by the arm. "Boening! What in hell do you mean by what you said about Fräulein Schwabacher at the card table?"

"I said I intend to marry her, and I will, if her father approves and if she'll have me."

"How dare you!"

"Ehrlingen, why are you angry? My intentions are perfectly honorable."

"That girl is not for you!"

"Really? Whom is she for, then?"

"I don't know whom she is for. Perhaps for nobody! But most especially not for you. She belongs no place in *your* corner of society."

"Ehrlingen, calm down. You may not like her, but I do."

"*I* may not like her, but I certainly won't let *you* abuse her!"

❧ ———— ❧

IF, WITH HIS REMARKS OVER CARDS AT THE Casino-Gesellschaft, Wilhelm had finally charted his course to marriage, he had also set sail directly into the wind. A man cannot make declarations about a woman in the casual company of other men and expect they won't be repeated in some form or another. It wasn't long before the Gräfin Emilia von Schwerning, Helge's mother, suspended her dinner invitations, nor before Magnus von Schwabacher had a short discussion with his wife.

"Susannah, *Liebchen,* you haven't invited Count Boening again, have you?"

"No, but why dear?"

"He's a very poor man. I've lent him money, and although I am sure he would want to pay it back, I can't be sure he will be able."

"Yes, well, Baron von Ehrlingen mentioned Boening is looking for a rich wife …" She looked up at him over her needlepoint. "I would hate to refuse my home to anyone who has already been here. And he *is* remarkably handsome. But I suppose we wouldn't want to tempt him."

So there was Wilhelm's situation. The Schwabachers had quietly resolved to close their door to him, and Henning had made it clear that he was against this suit. And yet, Wilhelm had declared his intentions in company, so he wasn't giving up without first making an honest effort to court the girl. And in this effort, he thought he could count on at least one ally—his friend, the Countess Babette Meyer von Kalckreuth.

He telephoned the countess on a late May Wednesday afternoon, and she seemed delighted to hear from him, even asking if he might like to come to dinner that very evening. She would round up some company, she said. Boening politely declined, saying he wouldn't impose, and that he even preferred to see her alone.

"Of course, come right away, if you wish!" was her answer.

Entering Babette's palace near the Tiergarten park was something like entering a museum. Each room was outfitted in a different prevailing color, and the furnishings, while distinguished, were very old fashioned. Everyone respected Babette, and many people even loved her, but no one had the least compunction about poking fun at the *démodé* of her surroundings. With the exception of her brief marriage, Babette had lived in the same home her entire life, yet there was nothing in this home's vast and numerous chambers that bore anything of her imprint. Babette, everyone knew, had been the painter Gustav Graef's most promising art student, yet not even one of her paintings was on display in her home.

Hennholz had once joked to Wilhelm that Babette had left everything intact from her parents' residency so that the ghosts of Herr and Frau Meyer could come out to play at night. "If Kalckreuth spent any nights there," he chuckled, "it's not a wonder his marriage was so short!"

Wilhelm arrived at four o'clock and found the countess in the "green room," which looked out directly onto the opulent spring flora of the Tiergarten park. As was her habit, the sturdily built woman came toward him extending both her hands, her pince-nez bouncing off the V-shaped lace frontage of a brown silk blouse.

"So good to see you, Boening! We'll have some tea. Have a seat." She rang for a servant.

"I hear you've gone to see my old friend, Prince Bismarck. How is he?" she asked.

"Desolate, I'm afraid. But putting up a good front."

Babette looked thoughtful as she sat down, and after a pause said, "If ever there was a happily married man, it was he. Frankly, I never understood it. I never liked his wife. Probably because I prefer that sort of religious passion in men. That is, I think that faith somehow tends to harden the female sex and soften the male. But never mind that. I hope you will be a very good friend to him, because he is desperately unhappy, and I'm afraid he hasn't much longer to live."

"We spoke of you."

"Really …?" She sat up straighter and was silent again for a moment. "But that can't possibly be why you insisted on seeing me alone."

"No, Gräfin." Wilhelm smiled. "But I cannot resist telling you that when I did mention you, he got very angry—red as a beet from the forehead through the cheeks …"

"And cursed me to the heavens, I am sure."

"Yes. He swore and even raised his voice. It was hard to keep a straight face." Wilhelm looked at Babette and smiled a conspiratorial smile.

"Was it, Boening?" she answered impatiently. "You don't give the man enough credit, I think. The Prince is old and very sick, but he's not senile, and it would be a mistake to laugh at him!"

Wilhelm ever so slightly flinched at this scolding. "It wasn't my intention to insult Prince Bismarck, Gräfin."

"Of course not," Babette answered, as the butler set down the tea service. "I am an old lady now and perhaps overly sensitive. But I must tell you that it upsets me when young people think strong feelings unfitting in their elders."

They were both silent for a moment, and then Babette asked, "Have you brought some sketches, then?"

"No … I had actually come to beg an invitation," Wilhelm said. Then he added tentatively, "But I am afraid I've upset you."

"Not at all, Boening!" Her voice was warm again. "But why beg for invitations? You are always welcome here—as you are everywhere else in Berlin! There cannot be a man whose company is better tolerated." She smiled, and handed him a cup. "And yet you seldom come. Probably because you're not always sure you will like the company here."

"What I mean to say," Wilhelm responded, passing over Babette's gentle provocation, "is that I thought you might have music sometime. And if you do, I would particularly like to come."

"Really? Why?"

"Your young cousin is a very gifted pianist."

"Elisabeth von Schwabacher? You are interested in her playing?"

"I am interested in her entire person."

"I see … Well, Boening, you are full of surprises today, but I would caution you right away to give it up."

"Why?"

"For one, because she's a Jewess. What would your father say? Your friends and relations …"

"Who could blame me for marrying her? She's rich as Croesus!" Wilhelm exclaimed.

"My dear young man, people think because I rattle around alone in this mausoleum and because I am sixty-one years of age, that I have little or no knowledge of the ways of the modern world. But I can tell you that a marriage with that girl, even for a pile of money, would be unwise in the extreme, and not the least reason being the very unfavorable political climate!"

"Gräfin." Once again, Wilhelm felt chastised. "I am afraid I gave the impression of wanting her *only* for her money. That's not the case at all."

"Boening, I have known you long enough to know you are the soul of decency. And as Miss Austen so wisely said, 'The handsome ones must also have something to live on, as well as the plain.' But think on the virtues of your class: Christian piety and domesticity—qualities honed by generations of living on modest means. A marriage with my cousin would on these bases alone be a moral catastrophe for you. Not to mention what a catastrophe it would be for her. Because like many prodigious intellects, that girl is far more innocent of life than she lets on in conversation. You, of all people, would not want to offer her up to a sham conversion and tepid marital relations. No Boening, you must find one of your own to marry—preferably a girl who has grown up in the country and likes it there. A girl like that will be easier to love in earnest."

"So ... it seems I'm not to be invited when Fräulein von Schwabacher plays?" Boening joked.

The countess laughed. "My purpose is not to censure, but to warn," she answered. "You are a grown man and will certainly find your own way."

In fact, Wilhelm and Lisi would have had the opportunity to meet at Babette's home several times in the few weeks that preceded the summer. Only that three days after Wilhelm's visit to the countess, Helmuth von Boening suffered a heart attack, and Wilhelm was called to Pulow. There he remained for five weeks until his father had recovered enough to resume the responsibilities of his estate.

# CHAPTER VI

*Kadettenweg 9, Gross-Lichterfelde*
*June 8th, 1896*
*Lieber Fürst Egon!*
*This morning, two pieces of mail from you were delivered, both evoking exclamations of delight. I will let Mami reply to your very generous invitation to visit Kleinneubach on our way to Bayreuth, but as to the score of the César Franck Violin Sonata, I really cannot thank you enough. I heard it in Vienna and ever since have been longing to play it. I want you to know that I went straight to the piano and sang the violin part while playing through the piano part. So you may be sure that I have familiarized myself with the more treacherous passages.*

*Now, to answer all the questions you asked me in your very kind accompanying letter, and in the order you asked them:*

*1. Yes, I am now allowed salad, and 100 grams of lean meat or fish at dinner, as well as the consommé, eggs, and almonds; so while not being as hungry as before, I become ever more "delicate" (as you would put it) each day and may even disappear entirely before I see you next. And while I no longer yearn for truffle cake and whipped cream, a decent serving of pureed or fried potatoes would be very welcome.*

2. *Yes, I am learning to drive the Daimler. It's not easy, and I hope I don't break it.*

3. *Yes, you are replaced, but unhappily so. Papi has found a Herr Doktor Rheinberg, apparently a specialist in skin diseases, to play second fiddle. He makes a great mess of double and triple stops, so that the endings of some movements sound like a dinner plate has been thrown onto the dining room floor. And his vibrato is very unsteady. All of which means that Gerda Lilienberg must play first violin. And you know how she has always lacked confidence, despite her musicality. Well, to get back to the infamous Herr Doktor Rheinberg: It probably goes without saying that he can sight-read nothing more complicated than Haydn or Mozart. Baron von Ehrlingen, who should be terribly frustrated, never shows it and patiently cues this hapless fiddler, while Papi shakes his head and swears under his breath. It's not a pretty sight, and it's an even less pretty sound. You are greatly missed, and you mustn't stay away too long, as next week the Musik-Wolffs have promised to send us a* real *violinist, namely, from the Philharmonic. And, as you probably are aware, no one on this earth is irreplaceable.*

4. *Yes, I have a new tennis serve. That is—you had better sit down for this news—I have a gentleman's serve. Herr Leitner was very reluctant, and if you had anything to do with his surrender in the matter, I am forever indebted. Why an*

*overhand serve should be considered "unfeminine," I will never know. But from now on, I will never again know an underhand serve. I think if I ever learn to ride, it won't be in a lady's saddle. It has occurred to me that men (recipient of this letter excepted, of course) like to design ways in which to preserve a fiction of superiority over women and that an underhand serve and sidesaddle probably could be placed under that particular category of swindle.*

5. *Alternately rainy and rainier.*
6. *My answer to that question is that I refuse to answer the question!*
7. *Verlaine,* Romances sans paroles, *which I hope we will talk about sometime when we are together. I know no German poems that can compare.*
8. *"Death and the Maiden" Quartet. The final movement. But you* know *that! It's a splendidly tragic story but ends so happily!*
9. *You are truly an excellent friend, Prince Egon, and I send you, again, my profound thanks and very fond greetings, and without having even asked Papi, I know he would want me to say "Return!"*

*Ihre,*
*Elisabeth v. S.*

*Pulow*
*June 10, 1896*
*Fräulein von Schwabacher!*
*I hope you are well, that you are watching your step when crossing into the street, and that you have kept your clothes clean for the many fortune hunters whose hopes you are determined to dash.*

*I have thought often of our conversation during supper at your parents' home and am concerned that you may have taken amiss my words about your resemblance to a pretty young woman in a painting I own. In fact, I am looking at that painting as I write. I only wish that you could see it. I think that you would also be struck by the similarity in features, as was your father, when he visited my estate. And just remember that although the biblical Salome might indeed be the theme of the painting, the girl pictured is nothing other than an artist's model—and so, in all probability not even a Jewess.*

*Your cousin, the Countess von Kalckreuth, might have mentioned to you that my father suffered a heart attack two weeks ago. The doctors are very hopeful as regards a complete recovery. The old man has a strong constitution, so I have little doubt that he will be as good as new in a few weeks. Still, he needs care and supervision, as he has a habit when in recovery from illness of taking on too much too soon. All of which means that I have left Berlin for a time and must postpone a planned June visit to Schloss Wittenbach in Kleinneubach. I travel there each year to check up on my little nephew and niece, who seem to have been left to languish in the care of surrogates.*

*But I am now led to believe that we have a good chance of being in Kleinneubach at the same time—namely, in late July. You will no doubt be charmed by the place, which is one of the finest examples of baroque architecture in all of Germany. And I will look forward to possibly seeing you!*

*Have you been to your cousin's lately? And have you played? I particularly asked for an invitation from the Countess Kalckreuth to hear you, though, thinking it through, I can imagine that you would want to play Beethoven or Chopin or Liszt there. All fine music to be sure, but I feel the keyboard works of J.S. Bach have been unduly ignored.*

*And that there is no better music. Indeed, I would be very grateful to hear you play some Bach at Kleinneubach, if you are so disposed.*

*Please remember me to your kind parents.*

*Most Sincerely,*

*Wilhelm v. Boening*

*Gross-Lichterfelde*

*June 19, 1896*

*Herr Graf von Boening!*

*It is kind of you to write to me, and though our acquaintance is so short! I am very sorry to hear of your father's recent illness, and I wish him a speedy recovery. I wonder that you don't bring him to Berlin to consult a heart specialist. But perhaps the incessant rain prevents you, or you don't wish him to travel at present.*

*Yes, I am now watching very carefully where I walk. And yet, no fortune hunters have darkened my door. Apparently, even a wealthy girl has to have something to offer aside from clean clothes.*

*And yes, we will be in Kleinneubach next month. I believe my mother arranged that we arrive on the 23rd. We are to attend the Ring cycle starting on August 2nd, but I know you won't want to hear about those particular plans.*

*I think it does you credit that you want to visit your niece and nephew regularly, but I seriously doubt they aren't being raised properly!*

*And yes, I have been at Cousin Babette's, and naturally I played, because I'm always asked to. The fact is, I am not allowed to refuse, even though it's Cousin Babette's ancient piano, which is barely adequate to squeeze out Mozart or Mendelssohn, and perfectly hideous for Beethoven, Brahms, or Liszt. To propose an analogy fitting to*

Horse and Hound, *Graf Boening, playing Cousin Babette's piano is probably like taking out an old nag for a hard ride. I say "probably" because truth to tell, I don't know a thing about horses.*

*And now, in the matter of your "Salome": Perhaps someday I will have the opportunity of seeing the painting myself and will even perceive something of my image in it. And if my father also claimed, when he visited Pulow, that there is a resemblance, then so be it. But really, I wonder why you persist in this direction. Usually when offense is taken at something one has said, one endeavors to pretend it hasn't been said.*

*Now, apropos the discussion of music in your letter, I must say that, although I would hate to indulge your prejudices, I also think that the keyboard works of J.S. Bach are unjustly ignored. So yes, it would be a pleasure to learn two or three that I could play for you at Kleinneubach.*

*With best regards,*
*Elisabeth v. Schwabacher*

*Kleinneubach*
*July 23, 1896*
*Lieber Maggi!*
*We arrived at Schloss Wittenbach at 4:00 pm after a harrowing trip. Someone threw himself under a train in the station at Frankfurt am Main. Imagine, Maggi! A young man. Perhaps twenty-five years of age! It was so upsetting! We saw the whole thing, even the covered body being taken away in pieces! And so there was a lot of commotion in the station, and a long delay leaving Frankfurt, as well as getting to Aschaffenburg. And the result is that one of the trunks has gone astray—Lisi's, would you believe, with all the new evening dresses!*

*Suzette and Princess Beatrice's maid are busy whipping up something for her to wear to dinner. Princess Edith has left some things here, but she is, as you will remember, taller than Lisi and narrower in the chest, so you can imagine the alternations that have to be made and the time in which they must be finished.*

*Lisi insists she would be happy to stay in her room and sleep through dinner. She has had a wicked headache all day, as have I. But you know all about my headaches. And though she hasn't complained too much, I know she is perfectly miserable, because she's been very quiet—even before Frankfurt she was quiet—and hasn't read a line. And she was positively morose at tea, although she tried very hard to smile. It's really exasperating about the trunk, with all those lovely new things in it, and all those fittings behind her. Of course it will be found and returned, but when? His Serene Highness Prince Maximilian is making inquiries. Oh well! The things in trunks are, after all, just things, and I must remember that! I wonder truly why anyone would want to take his life in such a violent way. What misery can prompt a man to do such a thing?*

*Her Serene Highness Princess Beatrice received us warmly and couldn't have been more charming. (She insists she will send a dressmaker to us, if need be.) And Prince Egon was also here to greet us. His jaw literally dropped when he saw Lisi. You didn't believe me, but slenderness really does become a small girl, and especially one with such lovely round eyes as our Lisi has.*

*Baron von Ehrlingen, as you predicted, is already here, as well as Count von Boening, the latter having gotten some color this summer and looking breathtakingly handsome. I can't say I know what to make of him. He's very correct. But he steals a lot of glances at Lisi, as though he is trying to find a way to pick her up and swallow her without anyone noticing. So I suppose he really is after a rich wife, and I'll have to watch him. On the other hand, he was very sweet with Prince Egon's children at tea, and when we arrived, he was unfurling a kite for them in the garden. Whereas, Prince Egon barely seems to notice them.*

*Maggi, my love, you must come as soon as possible. Don't delay for long. Prince Maximilian is apparently also a very accomplished violinist, like his son. And remember that the gentlemen want their cellist. But more importantly, I won't have it any other way!*

*Your very loving,*
*Zsuzsan*

*July 24, 1896*
*Kleinneubach*
*Lieber Maggi!*
*I didn't hear from you today, and so I suppose you are not anywhere near to being on your way. Will you telegraph me when you leave? Because I feel very silly writing letters that you might not receive. Or you might telephone Frankfurt and leave a message for the operator to call Schloss Wittenbach. Frankly, I'm getting anxious that you won't come. I actually have a feeling that you won't, Maggi, and I would like to have you here. You know I've not been feeling quite myself. My hip is bothering me again, and the train travel did it absolutely no good.*

*The trunk has been found. It was unloaded in Frankfurt, but probably because of all the commotion, never made it onto the train to Aschaffenburg. Lisi, it turned out, looked quite charming in Princess Edith's clothes, if a bit provocative in the region of the upper torso. Your daughter, you should know, is really a fine little girl. She felt so ill last night and even threw up just after dinner. But when Count von Boening asked her if she would play Bach, she managed a ravishing performance of the* Italian Concerto. *You should have heard the second movement, Maggi. It was so affecting! One could see that on the men's faces especially. We are so blessed!*

*It turns out that Prince Maximilian speaks Hungarian! It was odd how the subject came up, but he asked how Elisabeth got her name, and when I told him she is named for my dearest Queen, the Empress Elisabeth, and that I was born and spent my early childhood in Budapest, we were suddenly speaking Hungarian! Maggi, you cannot imagine how charming their Serene Highnesses are. They are very good, very generous people, I think. And how grand this place is! A late baroque gem! It reminds me so of Belvedere; and the chapel is truly exquisite! You'll be upset to hear me say it, but I wouldn't so very much object if Lisi were to become a Catholic. It's my love of the Baroque, as you know, and my envy of religious art. But I can see you scowling as you read this, so I will say no more on that topic.*

*Your devoted,*

*Susi*

*Kleinneubach*
*July 28, 1896*
*Liebste Klara!*
*Forgive me for not answering your letter of the 18ᵗʰ. We were busy making "preparations" for our trip—by which I mean that Mami was busy making herself unbearable about the evening clothes and getting me stitched up to within a millimeter of my skin. And since arriving in Kleinneubach, I've been sick and upset and so really not in the mood to write. Sick, dear Fräulein* Doktor, *at first with nasty menstrual cramps … (Is there help for that?) And then, it turns out*

*that just when Mami allows me to eat again, I can no longer digest anything! It all either comes up or goes out the other end within an hour or two of being consumed. The food is very rich, here—everything done in butter and cream sauce, and the first courses generally served with that mouth-parching Franconian wine.*

*But neither the food, nor the wine, nor Mami, nor my long past menstrual cramps would matter right now if I weren't so confused and angry at everyone and everything around me. Your "princess in a palace" is not much enjoying this "very grand" place (Mami's words), nor the "very grand people" in it.*

*Not that the Wttenbachs aren't considerate hosts—even lending me something to wear to dinner when my trunk went missing for a day. In fact, HSH Prince Maximilian is a jovial, humane sort of person, and his wife, Princess Beatrice, who is Italian, is quite elegant and "simpatico." Of course, when I say simpatico, I mean it in that extremely reserved way the upper-class Italians have cultivated.*

*But I am terribly disappointed in our friend, Prince Egon. There has to be something wrong with a man who shows absolutely no interest in his own children, especially when their mother is dead. I think if I were a widowed parent, I might be distracted for a short time by the César Franck sonata and the poetry of Verlaine. But the eager smiles of my own flesh and blood would soon tempt me once again. Yesterday at tea, his four-year-old boy (also named Maximilian) placed a hand on his father's sleeve. And Prince Egon, our very charming, always kind Fürst Egon, flicked it off without even looking at the child—as if those sweet little fingers were unwanted insects crawling on his cuffs! And, Klara, he has the most adorable little two-year-old daughter, named Cecilia. She has fat cherubic cheeks and enormous hazel eyes; but it's as if he is pretending she doesn't exist!*

*As to the continuing saga of Baron Ehrlingen: It has been clear to me for a long time that he has set himself up as Mami's inamorato. But lately, he has also taken to playing the father with me. He constantly tells me what to do and how to behave. It really isn't to be stood for! "Fräulein Elisabeth, won't you fetch your mother her book from her room?" Or, "Fräulein Elisabeth, you must play more Beethoven and less Liszt." Or, "Fräulein Elisabeth, I find you awfully fresh with your elders!" I think at this point, he is beginning to annoy even Mami.*

*In fact, I know Mami is getting impatient with him. We took a walk the other day; that is, Mami, Ehrlingen, Count Boening (who is also here, and whom I will get to in a minute), and I. Boening and I walked ahead of Mami and Ehrlingen. And when I looked back, Mami was talking to Ehrlingen in a very serious way, and he was looking as if his mood was about to be thoroughly spoiled.*

*It serves him right. The other day we played tennis. Count Boening, being the best athlete among us, was my partner against Ehrlingen and Prince Egon. When I went after a few overhead smashes that should really have been my partner's, Ehrlingen wouldn't stop lecturing me, e.g. "A young woman shouldn't be so aggressive on the tennis court." Graf Boening never once complained, so what business was it of Ehrlingen's? All right, Klara; it's true that I went for Ehrlingen's privates with a few of my volleys, because he needs to be discouraged in that area. But I had to run for my life every time Ehrlingen got an overhead smash!*

*And now to Count Boening—a story of its own: Klara, he is devastatingly handsome, the very picture of a fit Prussian officer and nobleman. I could sit and look at him all day. And most of all because there is something about his expression—a bravely borne sorrow in his eyes that seems to spill into small creases in his cheeks. He looks as if he's lost something precious, but doesn't want to let on that it's gone.*

*And he's an awfully good chess player; which I take as an indication that he is not half as stupid as he appears to be at first glance. In fact, chess has brought us into frequent contact. And although I find distressing his habit of talking to me while I deliberate my moves, our conversation hasn't been uninteresting.*

*The night Mami and I arrived, I was quite shaken. I told him that we had witnessed a suicide at the Frankfurt-am-Main train station. Yes, it was terrible, Klara, and I can't stop thinking about it. I tell you, it doesn't matter how many Russian novels one reads; there is no preparation for that experience! And I wondered aloud what someone could be thinking as he throws himself before an oncoming train, and what could make a person so desperate as to take his own life! But Count Boening contended that he could think of several scenarios in which a person might rationally and honorably contemplate ending his own life, and that he saw nothing awry in that, if the person had thought it through. The question, he said, was why a human being who had rationally thought through suicide would be so rude as to disrupt a major transportation hub for several hours, when he could simply hang himself in the privacy of his own bedroom, or put a bullet through his brain in the bathtub.*

*But, of course, for many people, he said, it isn't a rational decision. Rather, it is purely impulsive. And in those cases, therefore, not worth dwelling on, because acts of madness do not yield to logical explanations. And then he told me something quite shocking: that both his mother and his sister had taken their own lives soon after bearing their second child. So there; we have solved the mystery of Prince Egon's wife's death. And isn't it sad? By the way, there is a* portrait of her in one of the drawing rooms, and it's not hard to understand how Prince Egon could have fallen in love with her. She was a great beauty.

Anyway, to get back to Boening: Mami has warned me that he is a desperately poor man, and in search of a rich wife. And it is becoming increasingly obvious to me that he is vetting me for the role. I wasn't here a day before he suggested, knowing Prince Egon and I are on fairly familiar terms of address, that I call him Graf Wilhelm.

And while in company, he remains the formal Junker par excellence—the very model of buttoned-up protocol—in private, he has become disarmingly personal in his addresses. After dinner, the night before last, we both repaired to the terrace where, looking out onto the grounds, I remarked how much I love summers and that gazing on an orange evening sky and breathing in the odor of honeysuckle was always enough to bring my worst temper into equilibrium. "Fräulein Elisabeth," he responded, "I think you have had a happy life so far. And I congratulate you for it. I am gazing on the very oak tree on which my sister, Fredericka hung herself. And every time I am forced to behold that tree, I become freshly angry that your dear Prince Egon refuses to destroy it."

And then he looked around as if to see if anyone was watching, smiled sadly at me, took my hand, and ran his fingers lightly over the inside of my wrist. "Fräulein Elisabeth," he said, shaking his head, "you are very pretty and don't seem to have even the smallest notion of it." And then he took my face in his hands and kissed me. It was a very deep, voluptuous kiss that quite frankly undid me and—apropos the patient you called a "dumb goose" last year—made me begin to understand how a woman might find herself compromised by someone she's known barely a week!

*During our walk with Mami and Ehrlingen, somehow we lost them, and Graf Wilhelm pulled me very close and started kissing me quite passionately. Well, you know what I want to say without my having to say it. And even now I can feel him leaning hard against my body and his lips on my lips.*

*Well, at that point, I thought it was really high time to discourage him. So I mentioned that while I absolutely enjoy the kissing, I don't really see marriage and children in my future. I prefer my freedom, I told him. And then he asked what sort of freedom did I mean? And I said, the sort of freedom my father's cousin, Babette Meyer von Kalckreuth has: freedom to pursue my art and to cultivate friendships with interesting and accomplished people. The kind of freedom that means not having to answer to anyone as regards my actions or future plans.*

*Did I really think Gräfin Kalckreuth was free, he asked? On the contrary, he insisted. Single women, and especially rich ones, are constantly derided. And they must watch their behavior at every turn. A married women, he said, is always freer than a single woman—freer than even any man could be. Because usually she is given to a husband who loves her and will cater to her every desire, rather than being consigned to submit to a superior whose only objective would be to abuse her. Because, he said, I must remember that not even the Emperor of China is truly sovereign—not at least, if he is married.*

*So I responded that a woman could be married and still lonely. And many married women are objects of public scorn when they are married for their money. And I pointed out what happened to Else von Bleichroeder, the banker's daughter. Shortly after her wedding, it became obvious that her husband wanted nothing from her aside from her dowry. I tried to make it clear that I could think of nothing worse than to marry a man who might be in love with my fortune, rather than with me. And then he said, "Fräulein Elisabeth, I have never met Else von Bleichroeder, so I cannot speak to her charms or lack of them. But your fortune is as much a quality of your person as your wild red-blond hair or your very deep blue eyes or your contemporary opinions or your musical gifts. Why shouldn't you trust a man to love you for these as well as your money? Or perhaps you think a man should love you for everything but your money?"*

*And now, to last night, a miserable night: There was a ball at the Johannisburg Palace in Aschaffenburg, and naturally the entire house party attended. It's at least twenty-five kilometers from here, so it involved travel. Which is why you will understand if I seem a bit incoherent. Because I've had very little sleep.*

*Well, you know what I think of those types of entertainment. That is, you know how much I relish languishing, with a perfume-induced headache, in hot, noisy, and crowded rooms; how much I enjoy Mami hovering over me and bending my ear about the lives of ladies and gentlemen who would be of no interest even to her, had they not a "von" before their last name. And really, Klara, what do people see in dancing? Dancing alone, maybe. If I could decently master the movements of a mazurka—dance it the way I can play it—I would choose to dance it by myself, rather than with an overstuffed, sweaty old man snorting in my ear. Balls mean less than nothing to me, and my first impulse in entering any ballroom is to throw my dance card right into the nearest waste basket.*

*But to get to the point: I was cut by the regiment. I bet you can't guess why, Klara! The ostensible reason (Isn't there always an ostensible reason?!) had to do with Captain Dreyfus, and Colonel Picquart's audacious investigation into the possibility that Dreyfus just may be the unwitting victim of vicious anti-semites. Surprise, Klara! Because of Dreyfus, Jewish girls were not wanted as partners for Bavarian officers last night.*

*Of course nobody objected to the officers' behavior! When I went to the ladies' room, I heard one young woman whisper how mean she thought the officers were being. But another shushed her and said, "That Jewess is in the toilet stall. And I think she's being sick." Which, of course, I was.*

*The entire thing was so embarrassing! And it need not have been at all. Because there is plenty to do at the Johannisburg Palace. I would have been happy to disappear into the collections for the entire rest of the evening. In fact, it is a wonderful place, with an impressive number of navigation instruments and telescopes. And being uninhabited at present, one can wander all the many rooms to one's heart's content. Which I resolved to do!*

*But wouldn't you know, Prince Egon came after me and, without quite admitting that I was* persona non grata *as a dance partner, suggested I play for the company! And so I played. I know you will say I was wrong to agree to do it in that hostile environment, Klara. But I had to! I couldn't disappoint my host, and my mother would have been livid had I refused. But I played something quite short—the posthumous Chopin* Nocturne in C-sharp minor. *And I played it well. I am sure I did! But when I finished, nobody even had the politeness to acknowledge it. I looked out into the room and saw nothing but little groups of people in still poses, grimacing at each other. Not one person was facing me, not one looking at me, the performer! And the silence was so deadly that the gas-lit chandeliers sizzled in my ears. I honestly felt I would faint from humiliation.*

*Maestro Leschetizky likes to say that an artist can spend his whole life preparing something for an audience, and when he finally preforms it, chances are that people will only want to spit on him and call him a swindler. Once, in my lesson, when the Maestro made me repeat a melody until I wept in frustration, he laughed and said that the best end a musician can ever hope for is to be struck through the heart with a stiletto and put quickly out of his misery.*

*But you know, Klara, I think of everyone in the world, I still love Mami the most passionately, despite her vanity. Because when I got up from the piano and went to her, she looked at me so sweetly! She grabbed my hands and kissed both of them and said, "That was sublime, Lisi. Every note in its place!"*

*And then suddenly, Count Boening was standing next to me, holding out his hand and saying, "Fräulein Elisabeth, I want you to dance this next waltz with me." Well, of course, I said no, and that I had thrown away my dance card. But he said "I insist." And he literally grabbed me and started me to the dance floor. Baron Ehrlingen tried to stop him, saying "Boening, she's been cut by the regiment." But Graf Wilhelm said, "Not my regiment!" If I hadn't gone with him, I would have had to fight him off in front of several hundred people! He is a strong man, whose physical presence I can feel even when he is not touching me, and he was practically carrying me!*

*So there we were on the dance floor. I begged him not to, but he dug his fingers into the small of my back and said, "Look at the tip of my nose and nowhere else until the music stops. Be brave, Fräulein Elisabeth. This cannot be the first time you have experienced anti-semitism."*

*And then we were dancing alone. Alone! Can you believe it? Everyone left the dance floor! It was ... I can't describe it! I begged him to stop and to let me go, and he just held me tighter and said, "Let those damned papists have their pathetic demonstration. They aren't fit to kiss the hem of your skirt." And we kept on dancing until the waltz ended. It seemed like an eternity.*

*Klara, I can't help but think he's abused me terribly, and when he brought me back to my mother, I made sure to tell him so. He hates the Wittenbachs and detests Catholics, and he's using me to insult them all. Of course, he is also after that big dowry, and he thinks if he champions me, I'll fall at his feet. I have never understood why men think they have to fight women's causes, when we are perfectly capable of defending our own honor, and without their help. And really, Klara, he's a* Junker, *which means he is probably a worse anti-semite than any Bavarian officer could possibly be.*

*At any rate, he will have his own rude awakening. It's raining cats and dogs right now, with loud, nasty claps of thunder. He sent a note to my room saying he would wait for me at the chessboard in the east wing drawing room. But I won't go down, and I won't have a thing to do with him again. I'm done with him! And while his kisses were amusing when I thought they were only a game, I know now they are no longer a game.*

*You know, Klara ..., I don't think I agree with you that physical impulses can always be kept under control. It seems to me easy enough to lose oneself when things get going. At any rate, you should see that man all dressed up in the formal uniform of the* Gardes du Corps, *with his embroidered white tunic and his eagle helmet. He could not be more ludicrously beautiful were he stark naked, which is how I really would want to see him, if I weren't a girl from a good family.*

*I desperately miss you and all my Vienna relations! Please send me news of Bernhard. I want to know that his health is improving.*

*L*

*July 28-*

*Papa,*

*I'm sorry we had words last night. I am a coward not to walk up the stairs, embrace you, and tell you face to face how I feel about the girl. You would never wish to pursue a frank discussion of my first marriage. Suffice it to assure you that it is the failure of that marriage—because it had failed long before she took her life—that drives my choice more than anything else.*

*You know as well as I do that what happened last night was extraordinary in every way and also unnecessarily aggravated by Boening, whose behavior I will never understand and will find hard to forgive. How could such events possibly be repeated? And especially: how could they be repeated if Elisabeth von Schwabacher were to become my wife and a Catholic, enjoying all the protections of a great noble house?*

*Papa, I know you appreciate her. I saw your face when you listened to her playing; she is so cultivated and so tender! I know I can love her in a way it was not possible to love my first wife. And there can be no drama with Elisabeth, because there is nothing fragile about her.*

*I am confident you will not persist in your objections.*

*Your loving son,*
*Egon*

*Kleinneubach*
*July 28, 1896*
*Vater,*

*I hope you are well and that you are not exerting yourself too much. You are not to ride. I have given the servants clear instructions in that regard. I hope you are not sneaking around them and tacking up your horse.*

*I thank you for your letter, which I received this morning; and I will be sure to convey your greetings to the entire Wittenbach family, and of course to the children. When the children are old enough to travel, perhaps in a year or two, I shall bring them to Pulow for a short visit. God knows, at Pulow they will receive more familial attention in a week than they get here in an entire year.*

*I want you to know that I have met a young woman of stunning wealth, not yet twenty-one years of age, and impressively educated. She is the daughter of Magnus von Schwabacher, the banker who holds our mortgage. Not everyone would think her pretty, but I do. I expect you will object and that you will protest that we haven't come to this, yet. But we would hardly be the first noble family to admit a Jewess, and we won't be the last.*

*Father, I want you to understand that we could be quite profligate and never exhaust the resources Fräulein v. Schwabacher would bring into a marriage. To be honest, I don't know if you will like her. She is very modern, even irreverent, in her views. But I think you would be quite taken with her piano playing.*

*Ever your devoted son,*
*Wilhelm*

*Kleinneubach*
*July 28, 1896*
*Maggi,*
*Today, both Ehrlingen and Fürst Egon received telegrams from you, and about the sale of a stock position. A stock position! Maggi, what are you thinking when you ignore your wife and let your host and hostess wait for you in vain? Can business really be so urgent?*

*You cannot imagine the farce that is playing itself out here in Kleinneubach! Last night, we went to a ball in Aschaffenburg. Our Lisi was cut by the Bavarian regiment. Apparently, the officers are convinced the Jewish Captain Dreyfus is guilty of treason, as if they could care less about the honor of the French military! And what do you think Prince Egon's reaction to that was? He put Lisi on the stage! Oh, Maggi, it made me sick to my stomach to see him do that! And how she played! It was as if she had been carried away to her own private heaven—or at least to a better place, one where people aren't so capriciously hateful. And when she finished, nobody moved for at least a full minute. There wasn't a dry eye anywhere I looked. And then the orchestra conductor put his hand to his heart and bowed to her.*

*Of course, to add insult to injury, Count von Boening insisted she dance with him. I can't go on, Maggi, because the image of them dancing alone—everyone leaving the floor—drives me to distraction. And let me tell you something: That man has been on her like a vulture ever since we arrived. There have been tête-á-têtes over the chessboard; he has taken her outside into the gardens to sketch her; and there have been a hundred stolen kisses; I'm sure of that. How am I supposed to stop this without your help!*

*Oh, Maggi, I am so angry with you! And I have some more news you are not going to like, so I might as well tell you in a letter, as you refuse to appear in person. There is something I noticed last week on my breast. At first, it looked only like a shadow. But now it is taking a raised and very irregular shape. It can only be something very bad.*

*I just wonder how you can leave me like this … Tomorrow, your daughter will be celebrating her twenty-first birthday in a strange house. You were to play Schubert for her. When you gave me the necklace to put in my jewelry carrier, I never dreamed you wouldn't be here to give it to her.*

*-S*


*July 28, 1896*
*Frankurt-am-Main*
*By Telegraph*
*An: Madame Susannah von Schwabacher*
*c/o Schloss Wittenbach*
*Kleinneubach, Deutschland*
*Mami,*
*Arrival late afternoon. Cello in the violin maker's atelier until yesterday with hairline crack. Something wrong with automobile. Useless toy. Kiss my little one. I will wake her on her birthday!*
  *Don't be angry, Zsuzsan. You are my one and only!*

*Papi*

# CHAPTER VII

MAGNUS SCHWABACHER NEVER RECEIVED HIS wife's letter of the 28th, because at the very moment of its writing, he was on his way to Kleinneubach. Nevertheless, he hadn't ensconced himself at Schloss Wittenbach a full forty minutes before he was brought up to date on the status of his daughter and his wife.

The result of this debriefing was that when Schwabacher presented himself for dinner, he seemed unusually subdued, even dour and distracted. Moreover, he looked disheveled. His white tie was crooked, his face was bandaged from a razor cut, and his curly hair was in such disarray that it was as if he had fought off his barber and valet. His eyes were so very red that it was impossible to think otherwise than that he had been weeping.

Prince Egon had harbored great hopes for Magnus' arrival: hopes of stimulating conversation, hopes of satisfying chamber music, and—most of all—hopes of a convivial meeting between the banker and Egon's father, Maximilian. Despite differences of class and religion, Magnus and Maximilian had similar tastes, similar liberal politics, and similar upbeat dispositions; and Egon hoped that these commonalities would smooth the way to a pleasant relationship between the Wittenbach and Schwabacher families. But upon receiving the banker in the main drawing room before dinner, Egon despaired that anything good would come of this particular evening, least of all the engagement to Elisabeth that he so desired.

The evening did pick up, however. As often happens after a profound social embarrassment, everyone was determined to put things right. And so, the entire party endeavored to be of good cheer at dinner. There was a long conversation about the pleasures of touring in northern Italy and the right hotels in which to stay. And then Henning and Lisi kept the company amused with talk of music personalities—Henning with observations about famous conductors (his imitation of Arthur Nikisch giving cues with his eyes eliciting much laughter), and Lisi with stories of her studies with the notoriously witty Theodore Leschetizky.

And then Prince Maximilian asked Magnus several provocative questions designed to extract an economic forecast. After avoiding most of them, Magnus' face suddenly lit up with an impish smile, and he declared, "*Durchlaucht*, one must never predict in decades, but solely in millennia. That way, it's impossible to be proven wrong—at least in one's lifetime. And so I will gladly make one incontrovertible prophesy: that the final victory of American over German industry, or vice versa, will, in the year 3000, hardly matter to any of us sitting here at this table."

By the time dinner was over, everyone had laughed and the whole party was much more relaxed. The gentlemen even resolved to read through a Beethoven quartet, and the ladies, along with Boening, listened appreciatively. When they were done, Wilhelm suggested that perhaps Fräulein Elisabeth would play some Bach, whereupon Lisi replied reprovingly that as string quartets were the purest and finest music of all, she had no intention of competing with the gentlemen, and therefore would absolutely have to refuse.

When everyone finally started for their bedrooms, Henning stopped Wilhelm in the stairway, and said, "I think Wittenbach expects an apology from you."

"You must be joking."

"You can't have missed the fact that both Madame von Schwabacher and her daughter have gone out of their way to avoid you today."

"I had noticed. But I'm not a bit worried."

"Boening, Fräulein Elisabeth just told you off!"

"Not at all. She has refined sensibilities where the performance of music is concerned; and I stood to be corrected."

"It hasn't occurred to you that the girl might actually marry Wittenbach? Because he has every intention to ask her father for her hand."

"It has occurred to me that he will ask, but she will never marry him. I heard him this afternoon reciting French poetry to her. *'Au calme claire de lune triste et beau, … fait sangloter d'extase les jets d'eau, …'* Jets of water weeping their ecstasies in the moonlight? Only a simpleton like my sister would think Wittenbach was anything but sexually inverted. Oh …, excuse me. Should I say, instead, 'homosexual'?"

"So if a man quotes French poetry, he must be assumed a homosexual?"

"Do you have proof he isn't? Look how he behaves with his children! Fräulein Elisabeth has lost respect for him on that basis alone."

"I think he is acting very much like a man in love."

"Is he? Then why has the girl been exchanging kisses with me, and not with him—fervent kisses! And I can tell you, Ehrlingen," Wilhelm whispered, giving his friend a playful shove of the elbow, "that I am looking very much forward to married life with her."

"You're very sure of yourself, Boening, but I will let you in on a little secret. Magnus and Susannah von Schwabacher are circling their wagons, as the Americans would say. However, where Fräulein Elisabeth and her fervent kisses are concerned, be warned: she has only been amusing herself with you."

⁕

AS HE PROMISED, MAGNUS AWAKENED LISI EARLY the next morning, opened her drapes, sat down on her bed, and instructed her good naturedly to be downstairs at nine o'clock for breakfast, as a little surprise had been planned.

Lisi sleepily stretched out her arms to his affectionate embrace and then turned over. "But you'll let me snooze just a little bit more, Papi, won't you?"

"I won't leave until you are up. You have very bad habits, Lisichen. Reading through the night. And now you've trained your maid not to bother you, and at an hour when decent people have long been up and dressed."

"Professor Leschetizky plays billiards until four a.m. and doesn't get up until ten. At noon he looks out of the window to see who his first student of the day will be, and if he hasn't liked that student's last lesson, he runs back upstairs and refuses to come down."

"When you are Maestro Leschetizky's age, and have his reputation, you may do as you like. But until then, you will lead a respectable existence, if I have anything to say about it. Anyway, my dear, you know that you aren't a child anymore, and life, even for young people, can suddenly and unexpectedly get serious. So we must be prepared for it."

Lisi sat up. "Papi, you are very dark this morning. And when you came downstairs for dinner last night, you looked desperately sad!"

"Lisi, there will be some changed plans. I think you should know that."

She started and grabbed his sleeve with both hands. "We're not going to Bayreuth?"

"Yes, of course, we are. I didn't mean that. Only that afterward, Mami wishes to go to Vienna to see a specialist about her headaches. She hasn't been feeling well, and I think it will be a comfort to her if Uncle Sigi has the oversight. And ..." he paused, "we won't be going to America. I haven't yet told Baron von Ehrlingen, and I think he will be very disappointed, as I know *you* are." He took a deep breath, and clapped his hands over hers. "But, in the meantime, your birthday is to be celebrated, and I have something for you that I hope you will like."

"Papi, have you made a failed investment? Has the bank gone under?"

Magnus smiled. "No, my dear ... That is, I took a risk recently that I probably should not have taken. The American stock market is very troubled right now. However, I managed to unload that burden, and in the nick of time ... But I will tell you this,

Lisi: Money isn't everything, and you mustn't take anything for granted, especially the things that really matter. And now, I want you to open this little package."

"Papi, are you telling me that Mami is seriously ill?"

"We aren't sure yet, Lisichen. But it isn't like Mami to complain about her health, is it? And she has been complaining a lot. So we must assume it to be real."

"Papi ..." Lisi reached out her hand in a gesture of comfort.

"Lisi, you are always the first to want verification for all theories before calling them facts. So let's not worry until we know there is actually something to worry about. And now, please open your gift!"

Magnus pushed forward a small box wrapped in gold paper and tied with red ribbon.

Inside, Lisi found a ruby pendant in the shape of a treble clef. It was set in gold and attached to a delicate gold chain, the angular cuts of the jewel giving it the effect of a prism in the morning sunlight that poured through the bedroom windows.

"It's beautiful, Papi! Thank you." She wrapped her arms around his neck and kissed his cheek.

"Well, you have finished your music studies and fully deserve it. I had it cut specially."

"I will wear it to breakfast."

"Perhaps you shouldn't do that, Lisichen. It is really meant for evening wear."

"But it's my birthday present, and I want to flaunt it this morning!"

LISI REACHED THE BREAKFAST ROOM AT NINE a.m., only to find that while the table had been laid, nobody was to be seen. But there was music to be heard; and she was left to follow the excited strains of the final movement of the "Death and the Maiden" Quartet. They led her into a small drawing room in the eastern wing of the house, where her father, Prince Egon, Prince Maximilian, and Henning von Ehrlingen gave an enthusiastic, if not quite technically perfect performance.

A little table in that sun-filled room was laid with a cake and three presents. From Baron Ehrlingen, there was a copy of Mark Twain's *Life on the Mississippi;* from Fürst Egon, a first edition of Robert Browning's *Men and Women;* and from Graf Wilhelm, a miniature traveling chess set, in which the wood pieces were set on small pegs that could be inserted into a square board with holes.

Lisi thanked all three gentlemen warmly, observing that considering the books she had received, Graf Wilhelm would have done better to make his gift an English dictionary.

"Lisi!" Susannah interjected, adding "The chess set is absolutely charming. Wholly unnecessary, Graf von Boening, and so thoughtful. Where did you find it?"

"It's mine." Wilhelm answered. "I've had it for many years. But I knew your daughter would appreciate it. Now, Fräulein Elisabeth, you must let us all admire your pendant. Is it a birthday present?"

Lisi smiled. "From my parents, in case you haven't guessed. And perhaps you shouldn't have mentioned it, because from the looks my mother has been giving me, I know she would rather I hadn't worn it to breakfast."

Susannah patted Lisi's hand, and remonstrated with a smile, "You are correct, my love. It was not to be worn to breakfast."

"'A woman of valor, who can find? For her price is far above rubies ...' Do you know it?" Wilhelm asked Lisi.

"Yes, unfortunately," Lisi laughed. "The woman of valor is the biblical saint who rises before dawn, spins wool, plants her vineyards, and brings food to the hungry. And all before lunch! And then in the afternoon—probably exhausted by it all—she laughs at death. I hope I am never expected to live up to her standards!"

"Well now," Fürstin Beatrice said, "Our charming young lady having been duly feted on her birthday, shall we all go in to breakfast?"

ON THE 30TH OF JULY, A BALL WAS TO TAKE PLACE at Kleinneubach. And on the 31st, the house guests were to depart. As their visit drew nearer to a close, the Schwabachers found themselves much in demand. Lisi had to acknowledge both Egon and Wilhelm's competing requests for companionship, namely at the piano and the chessboard. Magnus was at the beck and call of the Princes Egon and Maximilian, both of whom sought him out on a variety of subjects, not the least of which had to do with a possible union of the princely house of Wittenbach and the banking house of Schwabacher. And Susannah had to carefully manage Henning, a man as confused as he was disappointed in what he rightly perceived to be his very sudden banishment from favor.

It was a relief to Lisi that on the morning of the 30th, she was required to have yet another fitting for the ball gown her mother had planned for her to wear that evening. (Owing to her persistently uncooperative stomach, she had shed another kilo and a half since her arrival at Kleinneubach.) Indeed, she was happy to have time to herself to think. And one of the first thoughts she had was how happy she would be when Kleinneubach and Schloss Wittenbach were behind her. Perhaps at Bayreuth she would be able to digest some food.

But meanwhile, she must have a plan for the evening, for it had to be assumed that she would once more be consigned a wall flower. She would, of course, shorten that torture by waiting as long as possible to join the party. And when her dance card was handed to her, it would go straight into the waste basket. Why not spend most of the night in the garden, she thought to herself, as the weather was warm, and the less time spent near the dancing, the better!

Once having resolved on this plan, Lisi didn't even venture out of her room to go downstairs until ten thirty p.m. But things were not to turn out quite as she had anticipated, because when she entered the ballroom, just after throwing away her dance card, she was approached by a young Bavarian lieutenant.

"Fräulein von Schwabacher, please allow me to introduce myself ... I had the pleasure of hearing you play at Schloss Johannisburg and wish to ask if I may have the honor of a dance."

"That's very kind of you," Lisi answered. "But unfortunately, I seem to have misplaced my card." She went to move past the young man, when suddenly Wilhelm appeared.

"Fräulein Elisabeth" he said, bowing and handing her the jettisoned dance card. "I believe this is yours. I hope you don't mind that I took the liberty of putting my name on it." He nodded toward the Bavarian officer and then disappeared into a crush of guests on his way out of the room.

Lisi tapped the dance card on her wrist, and by looking around her, tried to avoid eye contact with the young officer. But he remained rooted in place, his eyes meeting hers expectantly as she inadvertently turned back toward him. "May I, Fräulein?" the young man asked, reaching for the card.

"Count Boening is a handsome man, don't you think, *Herr Leutnant?*" Lisi said quickly. "Probably the handsomest man here. And though I don't really care to dance tonight, I'm tempted to follow him."

As the lieutenant's eyes widened, she turned away.

IT TOOK LISI A WHILE TO LOCATE WILHELM, BUT when she found him—sitting quietly on a stone bench on the marble terrace outside the ballroom—she was disappointed in her welcome.

"Fräulein Elisabeth, did you refuse that nice looking Bavarian officer a dance?" he asked, as she approached him.

"I did."

"If it is anti-semitism when soldiers refuse to dance with a pretty young Jewess, what is it when she returns the insult by refusing a perfectly decent Christian officer?"

"I don't think there is a name for it."

"Well, we must create one, then."

"'Anti-Aryanism' perhaps?" Lisi flopped down beside him on the bench. "But I've always hated dance parties. Even when not attended with political demonstrations, they are humiliating social rites."

"Humiliating because …?"

Lisi looked sideways at Wilhelm. "Oh don't be disingenuous! And by the way, if I were pretty, the regiment never would have cut me, and you know it as well as I do."

Wilhelm stared straight ahead and seemed to be deep in thought for a moment. Then he replied, "I remember reading once that the ancient Babylonians, when they wanted to marry off their young women, would line them up—rather like we do in ballrooms, today. But they would sell them off one by one. The prettiest was sold first, and then the next prettiest, and so on. The best-looking maidens would go to the rich Assyrians, who would travel great distances to get at them. But some of the money fetched for those beautiful girls would then be given to the plain and crippled ones for dowries …"

"It appears you have actually read Herodotus, Graf Wilhelm. I won't pretend I'm not shocked."

Wilhelm turned to Lisi and smiled wryly. "Fräulein Elisabeth, you have a dangerous habit of underestimating my erudition, most particularly in the area of romance. When a boy gets to a certain age, he finds himself suddenly with an urgent interest in the kind of stories *Horse and Hound* magazine is not likely to cover.

"But never mind all that. My point is: What a generous idea to provide the ugliest women with the profits from the most beautiful ones! Because it evens out the competition, and everyone goes away satisfied. And if there is a socialism I can support, that is it."

Lisi looked at him and laughed. "A socialism you can support? I think someone will have to awaken me from this dream."

"It's no dream!" he replied. "You must not consider this observation a dream, but rather an earnest mental exercise in which I am asking you to participate. I would like you to consider seriously which girl you would rather be: the beautiful one who is bought, or the plain one with the power of purchase."

Lisi looked at him skeptically. "I don't believe it worked quite like that in ancient Babylonia, since the girl never really had any power to choose!"

"But here, in present day Germany, she does, providing only that she is rich enough."

"Yes," Lisi sighed. "It's a plain fact of life that German husbands are bought."

"Fräulein Elisabeth, when I think that my sister had nothing to offer but her beauty, and how miserably it all ended for her. While you could marry any man in the world who pleases you. Yet no one is likely to please you. Because you think that any man who could benefit from your money cannot possibly be worthy of you."

Wilhelm smiled a mournful half-smile. "Now, go inside and dance. There are men in that ballroom who have sinned and wish to make it right. Allow them. It's the Christian thing to do."

"Ah … But I'm not a Christian!" Lisi replied, playfully.

"Of course. How silly of me … Look! Your father is coming. And he seems profoundly displeased." And truly, Magnus Schwabacher approached them in rapid steps, bent forward and bearing a frown.

"Herr von Schwabacher!" Wilhelm stood. "Have you come for a breath of fresh air? It's too lovely a night, I think, to stay inside, no matter how enticing the dancing."

Magnus nodded and bowed, but said very coldly, "I've come for my daughter, Graf Boening. Hopefully, you won't mind relinquishing her company. Lisi, if you aren't engaged to dance in the next few minutes, your mother and I would like to have a word with you. She is waiting in the east wing drawing room, where we played for you yesterday morning."

Wilhelm glanced at Lisi's face, on which only a moment before he had seen an open, warm expression. But now, her features had suddenly frozen in what looked to be a combination of embarrassment and defiance.

Magnus took Lisi's hand, put it through his arm, and said sharply, "Shall we, Lisi? You will excuse us, Graf Boening." Lisi allowed her father to lead her away, but she briefly looked back apologetically.

"What is this all about, Papi? Why were you so rude?"

Magnus turned on her. "Is that a joke, Lisi? I wonder you think I owe that stuffed military tunic any deference at all."

"Papi, I have never seen you this way. Is something wrong? Should I be worried?"

"Nothing to be alarmed about," Magnus answered stiffly. "Only that we do need to talk to you, and before you see Prince Wittenbach again."

The door to the east wing drawing room was no sooner closed than Susannah exclaimed, "Lisi, how pretty you look in your new gown and your necklace! Slenderness becomes you so, my love! Come and take a seat by me. Doesn't she look lovely, Magnus?"

Magnus did not answer this. He simply said, without ceremony, "Lisi, Prince Wittenbach has asked for your hand in marriage. I have to admit, this was totally unexpected. Apparently, he visited you in Vienna! I was not aware that you had contact with him outside our home. But Lisi, I want you to understand, my dear, that I am not in a position to refuse that man. So I gave him my approval."

Susannah took Lisi's hand. "It's, of course, a great compliment to you and to our family, my love. But it goes without saying your father is not enthusiastic about the idea of you marrying a Christian. And I think—and Papi doesn't quite agree with me— but I think that Fürst Egon is perhaps not capable of making you happy. I have no particular grounds for thinking that at all. And of course, he is a charming, cultivated man. A fine friend and everything a nobleman should be. Only that I have this feeling—in part, perhaps because of what happened to his wife, and in part because of the way he is with his children."

Magnus continued. "In any case, he would want you to become a Catholic, which I would not. And I think that you probably would not want to become Catholic, would you Lisi? And there we at least have a graceful way out of our predicament; if you tell him that you cannot in good conscience abandon your faith ..."

"What faith?" Lisi erupted. "I have no faith!"

"Of course you do, Lisi!"

"What *faith*, Papi? You want me to lie to him and pretend I'm religious? He knows me very well—too well for that!"

"Lisi, my love, do you want to marry him?" Susannah asked.

"No. But he is my friend, and I won't lie to him. However I answer him, it will be truthful."

"And what truth will you tell him, Lisi?" Magnus frowned. "That you don't love him? That you love someone else? Maybe even that you love that Lippizaner stallion, Count Boening?"

"Maggi …"

"Susannah, I've had enough! I've just brought her inside from a *tête-á-tête* with that man! Now look here, young lady! I have given you every advantage a young woman could possibly have! And I do not appreciate, nor do I intend to tolerate your vulgar flirtation with the likes of Graf Wilhelm von Boening. Or have I raised a complete fool? Do you really think that a man like Boening could be after anything, where you are concerned, aside from your fortune? If you *are* so naïve as to think so, I would advise you to take a good look in the mirror! And I would also like to remind you that I am not in the business of buying titles!"

Susannah shook her head. "Maggi … stop! I think Lisi will know just what she wants to say to Prince Egon, and that she will manage to always be friends with him. Won't you, my love?"

"Yes, Mami." Susannah stroked Lisi's cheek gently and then took her hand.

"And with regard to Count Boening," she said softly, "I think you know where we stand, Lisi."

"Yes, Mami."

"And now, Maggi, I think that we have had our discussion, and that perhaps Lisi wants to go back to the party."

Susannah left the room quickly, but Magnus stayed behind and watched his daughter, who sat very still on the couch, looking away from him, her hand absently passing over the area where her mother had been sitting. He walked over to her and lifted her chin. "Lisi, dearest … I am sorry I lost my temper. You know I love you. And it's because I love you that I want to protect you from men like Boening. And there are many of them, who are simply desperate for money, and arrogant and unimaginative enough to think they can marry for it, rather than working for it more honestly. So they ensnare women they cannot possibly love and, what is even worse, Lisi, whose children they could not possibly love. Lisi, take a lesson from Else von Bleichroeder. When that episode was all over, she married a Jewish man. And that's what I want for you: a Jewish man who can love you. But if we don't find one, the world won't come to an end. You are an accomplished young woman! And we are living in a new epoch. There is nothing that might prevent you from learning my business, and one day even taking over the bank! Look at our friend Therese Simon-Sonneman, a woman who is the brains behind two very fine newspapers! Lisi, the possibilities for you are limitless, and an appropriate marriage is just one of many!"

Magnus exhaled sharply. "Now then, young lady, let's go back to the party, shall we?"

"You go, Papi, and I'll be there soon."

After Magnus closed the door behind him, Lisi rose from her seat fighting tears, and without thinking much about it, she went to the piano. She had the habit, on the rare occasions she was preoccupied with negative thoughts, of improvising harmonic progressions that came to her; and these tended to lead naturally into the playing of a piece that would lift her spirits, or at least bring her back into emotional balance. This time was no exception. Before she knew it, she found herself in the opening aria of Bach's Goldberg Variations. And when she had finished it, she looked up from the piano to see that Boening had entered and had taken a seat in an armchair near the instrument.

"Fräulein Elisabeth," he said, "you stood me up for my dance. I hope you are ashamed of yourself!"

"I'm afraid I got distracted, Graf Wilhelm."

When she looked at him, there was still enough distress in her face that Wilhelm found himself asking, gently, "What was that piece?"

"The theme from the Goldberg Variations, of which there are thirty, but I only have four by heart. Learning all of them is quite a project, and I've only just begun it."

"Look!" Wilhelm said impatiently, after a moment of silence passed between them. "You have evidently decided to hide out here with your Bach. But there is a rumor circulating in the ballroom that you are engaged to my brother-in-law, and that it will be announced tomorrow. I even heard a woman say, 'His first wife was a Protestant, and the second will be a Jewess.' Is this true, Fräulein Elisabeth?"

"If it were true, it would be highly irregular, as I have been kissing *you* all week. Perhaps Fürst Egon *intends* to propose to me, but he hasn't, as yet."

"I am glad of that, because *I* intended to propose to you first, though my offer perhaps cannot compete very well." He rose from his chair and sat next to her on the piano bench.

"Fräulein Elisabeth, if you married my brother-in-law, you would undoubtedly have a great deal of time to devote to your thirty Goldberg Variations. You would have, in addition, every fine thing that is possible to have and could spend your entire life in the city—in a multitude of cities, going from concert hall to opera house, as well as to any court ball you chose. And once there, far from being cut, you would be invited, and in the most obsequious manner, to dance with all the important men." He turned to her and studied her face for a moment.

"And I wonder, Fräulein Elisabeth, if that isn't the life you properly deserve."

"On the other hand, if you marry me, you will have to make yourself happy in the country, where there are fields and woods and gardens to tend, and a lake too—a lovely lake with a spit of sand beach I would be so happy to show you, because it is my favorite place on earth. But no theaters or concert halls. And even trips to Berlin will be few and far between.

"There will be a court ball, but only once a year—at least for as long as the throne of Imperial Germany continues to be occupied by that sorry excuse for a man, our dear Kaiser Wilhelm. And while there might be a few officers there who will happily flirt with you, because you *are* pretty, invitations to dance will be rare. People will think it doesn't really matter how they treat you, since your husband certainly married you only to save his encumbered estate."

At this last remark, Lisi looked away from him. But Boening took her face in his hands, turned it to him, and continued, "But you won't care what people think, because you won't have time to care. Your children will occupy you, as well as your dogs, your horses, and your chickens." He smiled and caressed her cheeks with his fingers. "You will be surprised how intelligent and friendly chickens can be."

"Graf Wilhelm, if that is a proposal of marriage, you haven't exactly made it irresistible! ... But even were it irresistible, I couldn't marry you. My father doesn't *want* me to marry."

"You will have to marry, Fräulein Elisabeth. You are too rich not to marry." Wilhelm smiled and kissed her—a deep kiss that undid her.

"Graf Wilhelm ..."

"I think you should call me 'Willi.'"

"Willi…" And then he was closing in on her, and pulling her to him. And out of his embrace she found herself saying, "Do you know if that door can be locked? If it can be locked, will you please lock it?" Wilhelm rose and did as she told him, and then came back to her.

And then he was drawing her to him again, and he was asking her to say she loved him, because he loved her.

She didn't stop him, but said, in between embraces, "Willi, if you really love me, would you be willing to prove it?"

"What does that mean?"

"Would you make me your mistress?"

He opened his eyes wide at this and laughed softly. "What are you saying? You don't even know what you are suggesting!"

But she pulled away and looked hard at him and said, "I mean it, Willi! Because there won't be another way for us."

And then, he seemed to understand. Because suddenly they were on the couch, his gloves were off, and his tunic, the *Waffenrock* of the *Gardes du Corps*, had been removed, and his hands were everywhere, as were his lips, searching out her lips, her neck, pushing into her chest. All was confusion and heightened sensation, and she found herself reaching for the few parts of him that were unclothed—for the nape of his neck, for his hands and cheeks and ears, any touch of his skin—and sighing all the while from his touch. And then, suddenly his hands and mouth were under her dress and on her thighs, and from her undergarments, she could feel him expose her sex, and suddenly his lips and tongue were there, and she was mortified; but she was holding his head though she was anguished, and she was sighing, and from the center of her body there was a spreading chaos.

And then he took her head in his hands and kissed her lips and said, "You are so quick, you are like fire!" and he was on top of her, pushing and whispering for her to let go, let go, relax, because it will be over in a minute. The part that hurts will be over. So don't cry out! From now on, it will only be good ... Here, don't you see how good it is now ... how good it is now ...? And if women didn't want it just as desperately as men, and if they didn't enjoy it just as much, who would speak of love?

◦⁓————⁓◦

IT WAS AN ETERNITY BEFORE LISI COULD RISE from the couch where they lay, and when she did, she was so unsteady that Wilhelm said, "You need to find your land legs, my love." And he caught her and held her close for a moment. And then he said, "We need to leave here. You will go before I do; but first, let me help you straighten your hair." And he kissed her cheeks and forehead and said, "Lisi, you were an angel and you are now *my* angel, and we will be together again, later. I will come to you, later. Wait for me in your room."

And then she was in her room; and it was so long after midnight, perhaps almost two o'clock, that when she asked Suzette to prepare her bath, it was evident that Suzette was annoyed, but she prepared her bath without delay and left Lisi to linger in it. And then Lisi was in the bath, and her hand went to her sex, which felt somehow wetter than the water, and where she touched a streak of blood which floated to the surface of the water. And she was just contemplating the streak of blood when suddenly she started, because Suzette looked into the bathroom and said plaintively, "*Mademoiselle, voulez vous besoin de quelque chose plus?*" And she answered, "*Non, merci, Suzette. Vous pouvez aller au lit, maintenant.*" And Suzette looked relieved. And Lisi smiled and thought of Suzette's warning her to avoid "*les histoires d'amour,*" and then thought of the paintings she had seen in which women were being ravished; and she lay back in the water and wondered, did they feel what I feel in the nether regions of my body, and will he ravish me again? And a while later, her bath done, her skin still moist and fragrant from the fresh lemon she used on her arms and legs, she put on her nightdress and brushed her hair, and when she came into the bedroom, he was already standing there waiting for her, and she flew to him.

It was much later when they were locked in each other's arms, and she knew sleep was overtaking him that she whispered, "Willi, why did you want to hurt me?"

Suddenly he was wide awake and put his hand on her cheek and looked her in the face, which he could see very clearly in the moonlight that shone through her bedroom window, and where he saw a variety of changing expressions, which he decided, right then and there, were in themselves a kinetoscope of pictures with all the passing images of tenderness in the world.

And he asked, "Whatever do you mean?"

"You said, 'I want you to cry out for me!' and then you hurt me."

"*Ach Gott, Lisi!*" he said. "Forgive me! I was carried away, and I wanted you to be too."

And then they were silent. And he pulled the coverlet over them and gently tucked her in, and folded her against him, and said, "Lisi, I wonder how is it that you can play the way you do? It's as if you shut out the world entirely."

And she waited a moment, because she wasn't sure she really wanted to reply. But then she said, "I go to another place."

"What place is that, my love?"

"The place where the music is."

And then she turned to him and smiled and said, "It's never easy to find. But once I'm there, it's as if I cannot ever leave."

# CHAPTER VIII

IF WILHELM HAD EXPECTED THAT ON THE MORN-
ing of July 31st, 1896, he would wake up to find his romantic
and financial stars aligned in perfect harmony, he was to be sorely
disappointed. As soon as his eyes opened and he trained them on
Lisi, it was apparent something was wrong—very wrong. For she
sat on the bed beside him, and what he read in the kinetoscope
of her face this time was every imaginable variation of agitation.

And then she began to pace. Did he know that she couldn't
sleep for contemplating the very wanton things she had done, she
asked? So she watched him sleeping. He was particularly handsome when he slept, she said. But he probably knew that. And
from the window of her room she had watched the guests leaving
Schloss Wittenbach, and all looking relatively unscathed from the
evening before, the women's dresses barely wrinkled. (Here she
chuckled a bit.) She didn't know how some girls did that, looking
fresh after an entire night in the ballroom, since she was always a
complete mess after only three hours in a ball gown. (At this, he

drowsily smiled, remembering the state of her dress as she left the east wing drawing room the previous evening.)

But at any rate, she had listened to their voices, she said. The *tessitura* of the women all a half octave higher, and the men half an octave lower than they would normally be, probably because their throats were parched from champagne and coated from the breads and cold cheese and sausage they had been served for breakfast. Yes, they all sounded even more exhausted than she quite evidently was.

And now he must go, she said, because her father would come. And would she see him again? She wanted to know if she would see him again. And no, it was not a silly question. She pounced on the bed and grabbed the sleeve of his nightshirt. Would she see him again? And yes, she said, she loved him. Really, she did. Or at least she thought she did. Either she was madly in love with him, or she was a nymphomaniac. Hopefully, the former … And why would that be a silly thing to say? And how could he be so sure she really loved him? How could she know she loved him? She loved her parents—that she knew! But she had lived her lifetime with them. They had given her life! And what did he mean? No! No! He would not talk to her father this morning. He mustn't talk to her father, now or ever! And what did he mean, put things in order? He could never put anything in order, today or ever. There was nothing to put in order. Nothing! What would he say to her father? That she had been whored last night? Oh, she was sure her father would like to hear that! And what way would he put it, then? What way could he possibly put it? What did Wilhelm think her father was made of? What did he think *she* was made of? He must stop this nonsensical talk now, because there could be no marriage. Marriage was not in the cards, and she had never meant marriage when she said there was no other way for them. She had never at all meant marriage. And she was sorry if he thought that she had referred to marriage.

A monstrous idea? To be his mistress? How could it be monstrous? He had agreed to it! She had meant it! But then, perhaps she *was* monstrous, if that's what people said. And if he thought she was a freak of nature, then good, she was a freak of nature! But she had taken a lover last night, not a husband. Hadn't *he* had lovers before? *Many* lovers? In the *dozens*, she would guess. At any rate, plenty, and none whom he had evidently felt a need to marry, or he would be married already! Of course there was a difference, because she had money. But she was sorry; he would never see that money. He had said he *loved* her, and that it wasn't about her money! And now he must go! And why was he following her? He must go now, because her father was coming, and she must wash. And why was he shaking her? It would do him no good to shake her! He must stop shaking her and go! He must get out!

And then, suddenly, there was the image of Magnus von Schwabacher, who stood at the door of Lisi's room as Wilhelm opened it to leave, shaking with fury. And the two men looking at each other, just looking … in silence and horror. Which of the two men was more horrified? But certainly Magnus von Schwabacher! Blanching, it was he who turned away first.

And then, for Wilhelm, there was the long hallway to his bedroom, the grimace frozen on his face, along with the tears of rage and humiliation that gathered on his cheeks. He threw open the door of his room, calling "Dolwitz, run me a bath! Now!"

"*Jawohl, Herr Graf! So fort!*"

Because he will wash her away, he thought. Her blood and her sweat and her mucous, and the smell of salt and fresh lemon and woman. And everything he had planned and hoped for—everything that was now utterly destroyed by that conceited girl, that arrogant *lusus naturae* who had taken a lover, not a husband! And after all the women he had made love to, and to whom he could promise nothing! Nothing!

"Dolwitz!" he called, impatiently. "Is my bath ready?"

*"Jawohl, Herr Graf!"*

Damn that woman! And to think he would have given her his name! His title! Only she didn't want it. It wasn't good enough for her. She was out for her "art"; and he, apparently, was nothing but an adventure for her—his honorable marriage suit a mere game! That Jewess, with her pile of money, thought she could play him like she played the piano!

And then, as he fairly stomped into his bath, Dolwitz looked in, asking, "Herr Graf, I have found a pendant in the pocket of your robe. How shall it be returned to the lady?"

"Leave it, Dolwitz! I will deal with it in my time." Or not at all, he thought. Why should she have her damned pendant! It could even have its uses. He could ruin her with it. He could let it be known in the Casino-Gesellschaft that she had taken a lover. And that her lover was Graf Wilhelm Anton Leopold Herbert von Boening, who didn't even want her now! See if she is so arrogant when it is known all over Berlin that she has taken a lover! A girl who plays at cultivation, but who is nothing but a fake! A swindler! A cheat! A rich, arrogant Jewess, too smart for her own good, and the whore daughter of a dirty, cheating, money-lending Jew!

Ha! He would destroy that place she goes, where the music is! Because he would destroy her! He would trample her!

———

MAGNUS VON SCHWABACHER WAS THE FIRST TO take leave of the house party on the 31ˢᵗ of July. He was gone by seven thirty a.m., leaving alone, after having directed a servant to get a carriage for him. His destination, of course, was not Bayreuth, but rather Frankfurt-am-Main, and then Berlin. He would not go to Bayreuth. No, he would never go to Bayreuth.

And all the time, Lisi was waiting in her room, wondering why her father didn't come to her. When it was finally well after the time her father should have come, she resolved to dress. Suzette appeared and began to prepare Lisi's things for packing. And as Lisi's gaze passed over the dresser, she wondered what had become of her pendant. She could go downstairs to breakfast without her pendant, certainly; she wouldn't have worn it again to breakfast. But she could not leave Kleinneubach without her pendant. And suddenly she remembered the necklace being lifted away to make room for Wilhelm von Boening's hands and mouth, and she knew where it was. It was in the east wing drawing room. And so she turned to Suzette. "Suzette, will you run to the east wing drawing room, please, to see if my necklace may have fallen on the floor? The catch was weak, and I am afraid I have lost it."

"*Oui, Mademoiselle. Tout de suite.*"

And when Suzette returned, Lisi had finished dressing by herself, but no ruby pendant had been found in the east wing drawing room. *"Non, Mademoiselle. Je n'ai rien trouvé,"* Suzette had said.

And so something caught in Lisi's stomach, and she ran down to the east wing; she flew there! She searched the tables and chairs and the couch. She moved each cushion and even ran her hand over the place where it seemed a cushion had a small stain. In the place where she and Wilhelm von Boening have made love, she thought she saw a small stain, perhaps a stain of blood and the mixing of body fluids. No, she was only imagining it ... But, yes, it was there for anyone to see! *Ach, Gott!* And suddenly, there was a pounding in her ears, the pounding of her heart; because she was hearing the even-toned voice of Fürst Egon, and he was walking toward her, still in evening dress.

"Fräulein Elisabeth! I looked everywhere for you last night!" His arms were outstretched, and his face, despite lack of sleep, radiant with pleasure. As he neared, she noticed a blue shadow where he was normally so cleanly shaved. And for some reason, it jolted her. Because he was so finely dark, such a lithe contrast to her muscular, blond lover.

"I'm so sorry ... I went to bed early, Fürst Egon." And the pounding of Lisi's heart in her head was growing louder as he approached.

Then he was suddenly beside her and taking her hand. "Well, never mind. But you are leaving after lunch today, and there is something very important I have to say."

"Fürst Egon!" She could barely hear her own voice, her heart was pounding so loud, and now it seemed her heart was in her throat, and she even heard a slight whistle, a whoosh of white sound in her ears, accompanied by a slight dizziness ...

"Fürst Egon, I seem to have misplaced the pendant my father gave me. The catch was weak. I would be so upset to lose my father's present to me."

He saw the tears in her eyes. And his expression grew properly concerned. And he said, "But of course it will turn up, and we will question the servants as to whether someone has seen it. But Lisi, I will call you Lisi now, because I have spoken to your father, and I had hoped, I have hoped for a while now that you would soon be my wife. May I mention that you are looking very pretty today, although a bit tired?" (Here he smiled and gazed at her affectionately.) And then he was drawing her to him, and her heart was pounding so loudly in her ears that she thought she might lose consciousness at any moment. He kissed her, a chaste kiss, a gentle kiss, but a sensual kiss, nonetheless. And then he smiled and said to her, "Your soul is the choicest of landscapes."

And this paraphrase of Verlaine's *Clair de Lune* landed on her like a shock of cold water. Grasping at it through the white noise in her head, she recovered her balance and answered, "We are such good friends Fürst Egon. And I want us always to be good friends. But it cannot be. It absolutely cannot be."

His eyes registered surprise and disappointment, even sadness. And he said, "Somehow, I was afraid of this. But Lisi, think of all we have in common—our love of music and poetry, and think how much we have to say to one another—a lifetime of things to talk about. Because I have wanted so long to find a real companion and am so very sure now that I have found her." And then he stopped and inquired, softly, "But perhaps, after all, you feel you cannot become a Catholic?"

And after a short silence, she responded, "No, that is not the reason." She had no religion—no need, really, for religion. But he knew that about her. He knew that for her, one religion was as good as any other. They were such good friends, so he must know that! He had to know that if she truly worshiped anywhere, it was at the altar of music!

The reason she couldn't marry him, she said—and here she placed her hand on his sleeve to steady herself, because she was suddenly feeling very faint again and would have fallen if there had been nothing to hold onto. The reason, she said—the pounding in her ears growing louder and more distracting with every breath she took—was that she belonged …

*Ach, Gott!*

"I belong," she said, "body and soul … to another man."

And Fürst Egon went white. Every speck of color drained from his face. His eyes widened, and his mouth opened, but he was silent. He was silent for what seemed to Lisi a very long time. And Lisi knew that she was fainting because she could feel her legs begin to soften beneath her. And then, just as the veil of darkness set in, just as she was going down, Prince Egon caught her gently where her arms met her shoulders, and he whispered, "Who knows this, Lisi?"

"Nobody. Nobody knows this. Only you know this." Her voice was small and weak.

And he nodded and held her firmly, and gently led her to the couch, where he waited for her to recover her senses. And then he said, slowly and sadly, "But surely you love this man. And he will marry you."

And she answered, "No. I have sent him away."

And Fürst Egon nodded, and took her hand in his and put the hand to his cheek, and said, "We will always be friends, Lisi, and we will never speak of this again."

IT NEED HARDLY BE MENTIONED THAT LISI NEVER got to breakfast. What, if anything, could she digest from breakfast? Rather, she resolved to return to her room to rest until lunch. But once there and lying on her bed, she found she couldn't sleep. So she went in search of her pendant again, and then in search of her mother and father, and failed to find them, not even in their rooms. No, there was no response from their rooms. Perhaps they were sleeping, she thought, after the long night. So she wandered the *Schloss*, so silent after the party, the servants tiptoeing so as not to disturb the *Herrschaft*, all now resting from their gaieties. And then she roamed the garden in solitude, watching the servants take down torches and remove garlands from the railings of the great marble terrace, where she had sat with Graf Wilhelm von Boening last night. It was hot. It could not have been later than nine thirty or ten a.m., but she could feel the heat of the sun sticking at her head and shoulders, and wondered that she was stupid enough to forget her sun hat in her room.

No, she said to a servant who approached her and bowed. She needed absolutely nothing, but it was kind of him to ask. And she looked at the sculptures of naked-breasted sphinxes that bordered the terrace, and the gods and goddesses—Hera and Venus and Hercules and Mercury—that lined its balustrade, and thought of Fürst Egon, her very august friend, whom she had cruelly disappointed, and then, of course, of Boening, her lover, who should have known what she meant when she said that there was only one way for them. Because why would a woman take a lover when she could have a husband? Could he really be so stupid as to have thought otherwise? But perhaps he was. Though Boening was hardly the beast her father thought him—there was nothing bestial about him, but rather an artless civility, a conscious earnestness of bearing that was strangely touching—perhaps he was, finally, just a dumb *Schegetz* ...

Dumb ... and maybe sly enough to think he could force the issue of marriage by sleeping with her. And then it occurred to Lisi that perhaps he hadn't loved her at all, because Klara had said that most males were hardly particular where intercourse was concerned, and any female with the requisite female parts would do. And how did Lisi think it worked with prostitutes, Klara had asked, authoritatively. Lisi had forgotten this. She had completely forgotten this. And when it occurred to her, she felt an ache in her lower abdomen, a deep longing. And she suddenly remembered the feel of him naked, and she remembered the chaos, and the exquisite sensation of penetration, and sighing, and the press of his kiss. His kiss! She heard in her head that melody from Schubert's *Gretchen am Spinnrade* (*"Ach, sein Kuss!"*), and smiled and remembered that though Goethe's Margarete was a real woman (not like the proverbial Woman of Valor, who could not possibly have been a real woman), Margarete also had held a spindle. But in this case, the spindle was not a symbol of godliness and virtue and good works, but rather of Faustian seduction and corruption. And though a lot of people now laughed at Schubert's melody, thinking it maudlin, it was haunting, and it would always be haunting. The only thing wrong with it was that it had become too famous, too ubiquitous, so that people were embarrassed to love it the way it should be loved.

Well, if *Wilhelm* didn't love her, she thought, then she still had come out ahead. Because surely he wanted to marry her, if only for her money. And she had sent him away without that. And now she was free. No man would have her for a wife, and she needed no man for a husband. And hopefully nobody would join her in the garden, and she would be alone at least until lunch. Oh, how she dreaded lunch!

⁓————⁓

AT LUNCH, THERE WAS MOSTLY SILENCE. WILHELM stared into nothingness, and Fürst Egon was singularly muted. Ehrlingen carried much of the conversation, and Lisi learned from her mother that her father had left Kleinneubach. There was some business he must attend to, which required that he return to Berlin immediately. What a shame, said Fürst Maximilian, that he will miss the new *Ring* cycle at Bayreuth. Life is always presenting surprises, mused Susannah, and smiled. But honestly, *Durchlaucht*, sometimes I think that my husband is overly zealous in his work!

And now, it was time to take leave, and the Wittenbachs came outside to bid Madame von Schwabacher and Elisabeth farewell. Susannah was elegant in her summer traveling coat, and there were warm speeches and good wishes all around, and Susannah gently prodded Lisi to mount the steps of the carriage, all the while smiling her smile of perfect contentment.

And then they were off, Lisi thinking how tired she was, how every muscle in her body felt both abused and curiously insensible, and that if she could perhaps sleep a bit, she would then have the courage to tell her mother that the pendant was missing. Yes, she was tired in her entirety, and her eyes were closing now, their lids so heavy; but from under them, she suddenly saw her mother's hand, which looked oddly fat. And as she followed the contour of Mami's wrist, resting on her lap; and as she traced Mami's forearm up to the shoulder, Lisi became wakeful once more, thinking that Mami wouldn't like the look of her own arm today, because it was quite swollen. And it suddenly occurred to her that ... Mami your arm looks swollen, lately. I have wanted to mention it. Did you injure yourself?

And then, that very arm, that swollen arm and hand flew to Susannah's mouth, and there was a cry. It was a long, shrill cry, a primal cry, but followed by a storm of words. OH! HOW we are ALWAYS punished in this life for our VANITY and AMBITION! LISI! What have we done to you to DESERVE this! We have only LOVED you, CHERISHED you, and PROTECTED you from the moment of your birth! What have we done to DESERVE this? Why have you DONE this to us? Why, why, why have you RUINED US! WHY?! And now Lisi was being shaken, and Mami was slapping her hard on her cheek, once, twice, and then on the head and arms. And Mami kept slapping her, and it would not abate. And from out of the chaos of Mami's repeated blows and screams, Lisi felt her eyes stinging, and the ache in them peeling away with salt tears. And there were hands on Lisi's shoulders, and suddenly Mami's face at her face, so close she could smell her mother's breath. "LISI,

WHY HAVE YOU DONE SUCH AN EVIL, UNGRATEFUL THING? WHY HAVE YOU RUINED US?" Mami was screaming. And how Lisi's ears hurt, because the cries would not abate, and she was feeling now both dulled and repeatedly stung by her mother's physical force, which was a violent tempest assaulting her ears and shaking her face and upper body!

And suddenly Mami took Lisi's head in her hands and cradled it, crying, "Lisi, I am DYING! I will die soon! And your father! Your father cannot face this! Where will he be when I DIE, and now that you have betrayed him! Where will *YOU* be? LISI! LISI!" And Mami was weeping and still calling out, "WHY?" And Lisi calling out, "MAMI, MAMI! ..." and choking on her tears, which were hot streams from her eyes, and her sobs came from her throat and from her chest and her stomach, and she was reaching for her mother, reaching for her embrace. "... *Et fait sangloter les jets d'eau,*" she was thinking, and her sobs kept coming with jets of tears accompanying them. "Mami, I am so sorry! I am so SORRY!" she was calling. And reaching for her mother's embrace. And they were like this for many minutes, crying and sobbing uncontrollably and reaching for each other's embrace.

And after a while, her mother became calmer and suddenly whispered, "Lisi, did Count Boening force himself on you? Is that what happened?"

"No," Lisi answered.

And her mother sighed, and then asked, all the while weeping, "Then why?"

And Lisi was silent, and then through yet another sob she answered, "Mami, if I tell you, I don't know what you will think of me."

And her mother said, weeping all the while, "You are in love with him."

And Lisi answered through her own sobs, "No, I really don't think I love him, Mami. Only I had such a longing …"

And her mother whispered, "Lisi, what do you think being in love *is!*"

# CHAPTER IX

*Hotel Imperial, Vienna*

*August 19, 1896*

*Maggi,*

*If I knew how to begin … You are angry with me, I know. But I am just as angry with you. What a scene, Maggi! How could you! To want to make me choose between my husband and my child! And to hear nothing from you now for over three weeks! To send the letter of credit to Sigi, without a word to me! Without writing or cabling! It's intolerable! You should have come to Bayreuth with us! You should be here with me now! If you had come, we could have been a comfort to each other! But no, you prefer your office barracks, and the company of your papers and your cello to that of your wife, who has loved you and cared for you for twenty-five years. But what can I do about it! You are not to be changed, are you?*

*The* Ring *was just as the critics contended—namely, a very stiff production, and cast with morbidly obese women. Cosima Wagner is all too wedded to the way that her husband wanted everything and refuses to move with the times. But you don't need me to tell you these things. You read the papers. Only to say that she is perhaps the ugliest woman on the face of the earth. I hadn't realized that before seeing her in person—that she so resembles her father, Liszt; and yet makes the opposite impression. He was so charismatic, and she is so off-putting. And to contemplate her with that hideous dwarf, Wagner, is to have a good laugh, and you can bet Lisi and I had one at her expense—Lisi even saying, "Mami, can you imagine that couple talked of nothing but how repulsed they are by Jews? Did they never once see themselves in a looking glass?"*

*You won't like this, Maggi, but I have forgiven Lisi. Bayreuth may have been a disappointment to us, but not because we couldn't find peace with each other. We had our row, and it is over now, and I do not want to live the rest of my life denying myself the company of my dear daughter. I know what you will say. You will say I forgive much too easily, and I know I do. Amen.*

*You need to know that Lisi's ruby pendant has gone missing. She is desperately sad about it and is very afraid of what your reaction will be to its loss. She says the last time she saw it was our last night in Kleinneubach. She had it on when we all sat together in the east wing drawing room and had our talk. Just after we left, Boening joined her there and, as things progressed, removed it. The Wittenbachs have questioned the servants. Nobody seems to have seen it. Maggi, I think it very probable the jewel is in Boening's hands. What he will do with it, I cannot begin to guess. Certainly he has no intention of keeping it, as that would be theft; and he is surely no thief. So he will be devising a plan for it on the way to its return. And whatever that plan is, it will mean nothing good for us. I have told Lisi that if it comes to any form of threat, you might decide to go to the police, or even to hire a lawyer. And there could be a legal process in which she will have to say that she never gave him the jewel. She understands well enough that this could involve testimony as to the entire circumstances.*

*The fact is, the morning you saw him coming from her room, he had insisted that he would see you. But she told him to stay away, because there could be no marriage. And then, she says, he became at once weepy and enraged. I suppose he thought he had won the lottery! I am telling you this because if he comes to you, and especially if he comes to you in possession of the pendant, you will have to consider how you want to answer him.*

*Maggi, she admits what she did was beyond the pale. Still, you mustn't abjure her, for what good can that do any of us now? We have to pick up and move on! She is not the daughter you thought she was, but you have always had a blind spot where Lisi was concerned. You savor her talent and intellect, yet you ignore her willfulness.*

*I have now seen all the best doctors and have consulted with my brother. Sigi says that an American surgeon, William Halstead, has developed a procedure in which the breast, the lymph nodes, and the entire pectoral muscle are removed. It's called a radical mastectomy, but in effect, it is a maiming; and it would do me no good at all. The doctors all agree from the nature of my symptoms that the cancer is metastatic, already rooted in several places, and in principle, inoperable. This, apparently, is how they explain the upper abdominal pain, the pain in my hip, and my persistent headache.*

*So you see, Maggi, there is nothing to be done. Nothing at all. They have given me nine months, perhaps a year if I am very lucky. The tumor on my breast is growing rapidly, and they surmise that the one on my hip is also fast-growing.*

*I am not coming home without Lisi. You may be sure of that. We are here and await correspondence from you. Lisi spent the past*

*week in Bad Ischl with Klara and Martin, and with Klara's fiancé,
Bernhard Levin. I would so have loved to go, but I wouldn't impose
on the young people. She claims the weather was glorious, with the
Katrin peak visible every single morning but one! They rose early
and hiked, so far as Bernhard was able; and in the afternoons they
made the obligatory pilgrimages to Zauner's pastry shop for "Jause";
Lisi says she barely enjoyed the hazelnut cake. I don't think she will
ever be fat again, Maggi. And that is a great relief to me. Naturally,
Franz Josef and his entourage were to be seen daily at Zauner's—the
emperor always ordering his favorite lemon cake.*

*Lisi tells me she played for Leschetizky in Bad Ischl. He refused
payment because, he says, she is an old friend now and no longer a
student. He has even asked her to play Lizst's* Un Sospiro *for his master class, should she be in Vienna this fall.*

*Maggi, my love, please do not disappoint me—*

*Your Zsuzsan*

*P.S. You will notice I wrote a check to Maestro L. in support of
two young students (One is Polish, the other, American) who presently cannot afford tuition.*

*Behrenstrasse 8, Berlin
August 24, 1896
Zsuzsi, my own!
I haven't known what to write. And when that happens, I don't write.
But you must come home now. You must be with me! And I am sorry
we fought and that I said unconscionable things to you. I am very
ashamed of myself.*

*And if you must bring Lisi home; if you need her, so be it. I don't
find it as easy to forgive as you do. I don't think I will ever be able to*

*forgive her. On the other hand, being a rational man and knowing my duty as a father, I know that I have no choice but to continue to give her a home, whether in my home or elsewhere. What should become of her otherwise?*

*But Zsuzsi, Lisi and I will never be as we were.*

*With regard to the missing pendant, and Lisi's version of things, I must admit I feel strangely relieved. Because I waited for Boening to come to me. And frankly, I even began to hope that he would come and, with an arrogant reference to his title, tell me that the whole thing is a* fait accompli, *that the girl belongs to him, and that it only remains for me to cough up a dowry. When he didn't come, I began to think the worst—that he had taken her and been thoroughly unsatisfied with what he got. And it was killing me.*

*Because there is something I didn't tell you about him. As if the shock, simply the shock of seeing him leave my daughter's room wasn't enough, I read the expression on his face. It was indescribable, but I read it to be disgust. I understand now that I read it wrong, and that it was wrath.*

*Of course he is not a thief. He is holding the necklace hostage out of anger. And now, the question is: How long will he hold it, and whom will he show it to when he has decided on his revenge? Let us only hope that he is both angry and dissolute. Because if he is, he will come to me first before he creates a scandal, and I can buy him. I tell you, Zsuzsi, he is in a tight financial situation, and there is an advantage to that for us. I won't be tortured, like Bleichroeder was at the end of his life. I won't be sending regular payments to silence talk. But I will offer him one chance, one payment to disappear. He can have his estate free of encumbrance, provided he never mentions my daughter's name.*

*Zsuzsi, you of all people know what a circumspect life I have lived. I have done everything I could to avoid even a whiff of impropriety. I have not compromised one principle I hold dear—not ever. And this is my reward: a wayward child who has whored herself to an officer's tunic!*

*And now, what? Are we to be exposed to mockery and disdain? Are we to be fodder for the Jew-baiters?*

*I wanted a Jewish husband for her. A quiet marriage. But Susannah, who will take her now?*

*Maggi*

───

SUSANNAH VON SCHWABACHER DID NOT KEEP the contents of her husband's letter to herself. In fact, the same day she received it, she read every word of it to Lisi in the living room of their suite at Vienna's Hotel Imperial. It was almost nine p.m., and the setting sun was spilling a pinkish hue over Susannah's olive-green dinner gown. The two ladies were on their way downstairs for a light, cold supper; the day had been sweltering hot. As she finished reading, Susannah slipped the letter back into its envelope and looked earnestly at Lisi.

"My dear girl, I don't think it's prudent for you to return to Berlin with me. I want to give your father a little time to adjust to the new lay of the land. What do you say to remaining here with your uncle and aunt and cousins?"

"I don't want to."

"Well, I am afraid you will have to."

"Mami, you will need me! Papi cannot possibly take care of you. You know he won't!"

"I won't need the kind of care you are referring to for quite a while yet. And frankly, if I did need it, I wouldn't want it from you in your present dampened state of mind. I want you fully recovered from your adventure. I want your presence to be a cheerful one!"

"I know I have been sour, Mami. But I haven't felt well. I didn't want to tell you, because my health complaints are so minor in comparison to yours. My stomach is permanently upset. But it's not as if I am emotionally unfit. I am over what happened. I never *really* cared about Count Boening. I think you want me to have cared more than I did."

"Are you truly over it, my love? I seriously doubt it. But even if you are, I don't want you home with us right now. I think it would be too much for your father to handle."

Susannah rose to return the letter to the top of the desk. Then she turned suddenly, and said, hesitantly, "But there is one thing …"

"What, Mami?"

"Only … that I hope you will eat sensibly while you are at your Aunt and Uncle's. Not too little … but not too much, either. I don't want to see you fat again. And of course, you are so easily influenced by Klara, who could stand to lose more than a little weight."

It was hard for Lisi not to laugh at this last remark. Her first thought upon hearing it was that if her mother harbored one dying wish, it would be that Lisi remain slender. What a waste of energy and native intelligence her mother was! Obsessing on things of so little import in life—on all the minutiae of appearances—and when she was terminally ill!

Susannah's preoccupation with looks was the first subject Lisi turned to the night she returned to her relatives, knowing how critically disposed her cousin Klara was where Madame von Schwabacher was concerned.

But her cousin Klara's reaction to her remarks, as they were making ready for bed, surprised her.

"Of course your mother is obsessing over your eating habits. She is feeling guilty. She's ruined your digestive system, the fool! When you aren't having diarrhea, you're throwing up. You are skin and bones. Nothing left to you."

"Then why do I feel so full? And why are my clothes so tight?" Lisi asked as she got under the covers.

"Perhaps you are getting your monthly. In any case, it takes time for the system to recover from starvation. And sometimes that involves bloat."

Lisi moved close to Klara as her cousin sat down on the bed. She put her arm through her cousin's and teased, "Klara, do you wish that it was Bernhard here in the bed with you?"

"No."

"You know, I am really beginning to think you are not the marrying kind."

"We are not on that subject. We are not, in fact, on any subject, because I do not wish to continue talking. I'm exhausted, and I want to sleep. I delivered a breech this afternoon."

Klara exhaled liberally. "It was a piece of work, if I do say so myself." She then got into bed, turned away on her side, and placed a pillow over her head.

"Klara, I am thinking I might come into the practice ..."

"Come in to what practice?" Her voice was muffled under the pillow.

"To yours. Your father's ..."

"What on earth for?"

"To be examined."

"We're very busy. Go to a general practitioner. One for princesses."

Lisi laughed. "I wouldn't have the name of a doctor for princesses."

"Papa will give you the name of someone—someone bound to find enough things wrong with you to pay for an addition to his summer house."

⌁————⌁

SIEGFRIED WEINGARTEN'S GYNECOLOGIC PRAC-tice was just across the hall from his apartment. And yet, in the three years Lisi had lived with the Weingartens, she had never once entered its offices. Nor had she ever seen her cousin in a white coat. A few days after their bedtime conversation, the full-figured, black-haired Klara—dressed in a white coat, and looking thoroughly preoccupied by medical thoughts—emerged from one of the two examining rooms to find her cousin, pale and worn looking, in a waiting room chair.

"You're serious, then! You want to be examined? Perhaps even need to be ..." Klara's brown eyes opened wide with concern.

"I can't keep anything down today."

Klara approached the chair. "You look a wreck. But you hardly need a *Frauenarzt*. Why don't we call a general practitioner?"

"There may be things ... Klara ...," Lisi whispered, "that I haven't told you yet ..."

Ten minutes later, Lisi was in possession of a diagnosis, in the form of the wry observation by Klara that her cousin was "*Pumperlgesund*."

"If I am fit as a fiddle, why do I feel so horrible?" Lisi sat up on the examining table and drew the covering sheet to her.

"You have a six-week pregnancy."

"That can't be! That's impossible!"

"Lisi, you aren't going to tell me, now that I have thoroughly examined you, that you have no idea how this pregnancy occurred." Klara put her hands on her hips and looked critically at her younger cousin.

Then she exploded. "How could you *be* so stupid! Who is the father of this child? Wait … is this your soldier in the white tunic? The blond *Junker* you insisted that you wanted to see naked? And I thought you were joking! I thought you were laughing at him!"

"Klara, calm down please! And don't mock me! Help me! It goes without saying that I cannot have this child."

"Really? I'm sorry to hear that! Especially since I don't perform that sort of operation! But as money is no object for you, my dear princess, I will give you the name of someone of impeccable medical reputation who will be more than happy to perform it!"

"Klara, don't be mean!" Lisi's voice broke.

"Mean! Is that what I am? Because I happen to find abortion objectionable?"

"You're not religious! Don't pretend you *are!*"

"What has religion got to do with it?"

"What are my alternatives?" Lisi could feel a hot tear descending down her cheek.

"One might be to write to the gentleman you slept with."

"He hates me."

"He *slept* with you!"

"Only for my father's money!"

"And so, perhaps he shall *have* your father's money, along with your child!"

"I don't want him, Klara!"

"You should have thought of that before you went to bed with him. Now you're with child by him! Don't you think he has every right to know it?"

"If I did write to him, I wouldn't know what to say."

"I would advise your being direct. From your descriptions of this man, he has proven himself more virile than perspicacious."

"Well that settles it, because I could *never* be direct. He might have taken something from me."

"Something other than your virginity?" Klara asked sarcastically.

"A pendant my father gave me has gone missing."

"Are you telling me you *slept* with a man who may have *stolen* something from you?"

"Stolen is not quite the right word. He may have decided to keep a pendant that he removed from around my neck."

"Why would he do such a thing?"

"Because he's angry."

"Lisi, I don't know what to say to you … I think you should go home now, and we'll put our heads together tonight."

It took several hours of putting their heads together for Lisi and Klara to come up with the following letter, which—it probably need not be said—was not wholly satisfactory to Klara:

*Servitengasse 10, Alsergrund*
*Vienna*
*September 19, 1896*
*Graf Wilhelm,*
*Since our stay at Kleinneubach, I am missing my treble clef pendant.*
*Fürst Egon has made inquiries with the household staff, but nobody*

*seems to have seen it. If you remember seeing it, or have any knowledge of where it could be, I would be grateful for the information.*

*I am extremely sorry for the way things turned out. If I could see you, speak with you, I might make you understand how very sorry.*

*I may be contacted in care of* Familie Priv.-Doz. Prof. Doktor *Sigmund Weingarten at the above address in Vienna.*

*Elisabeth v. S.*

The answer to this note came fairly promptly, arriving with the morning postal delivery of September 27th.

*Pulow*
*September 23, 1896*
*Fräulein von Schwabacher,*
*Your pendant is in my possession. It will be returned when I am done with it.*

*I never want to see your face again.*

*W. v. B.*

Upon opening this hostile reply at the Weingarten breakfast table, Lisi, already in a weakened state, stood up from her dining chair and passed out cold.

# CHAPTER X

AND SO, IT WAS MADE CLEAR TO THE Schwabacher family that Wilhelm von Boening was indeed in possession of Lisi's pendant, and that he was likely to be up to mischief with it. But the truth was, Boening had no idea what he would do with it. In the hours he spent alone at Pulow or in his rooms in Berlin's Regentenstrasse, he could work himself into a proper state of rage and make plans for the jewel. He would consider what subjects he could exploit among his colleagues at the Foreign Office or at his club. He would prepare delicious innuendos on the subject of his lover and her ruby necklace, verbal arrows that wouldn't miss their mark. He even mentally practiced the tones of voice he would use and the facial expressions he would bear when the right subjects were brought up—Berlin's richest unmarried girls or the Jews, in general. Yes, the arrows would fly!

But it turned out there were hardly ever suitable opportunities for launching those arrows. And in the rare case there was an opportunity, he couldn't bring himself to exploit it. Because on the shadow side of his mountain of hot anger, there was the knowledge that were he to try to hurt the girl in this way, he would be revealed both a blaggard and a fool—that is, a man far more contemptible to himself than he could possibly be to others.

So there the pendant lay on his bedroom dresser, weeks long. There it lingered in his pocket as he traveled from Berlin to his estate. Every so often his young valet, Hans Dolwitz, would mention it, always with a sad look of reproach. "Herr Graf, you will want to return the jewel, won't you? The lady will certainly be missing it." And Boening would answer, "Yes, Hans. All in good time." Until one day, as Dolwitz brushed Boening's evening coat, he turned suddenly on his master, clearly agitated, and said, "*Euer Hochgeboren*! If the necklace is not returned, the lady will surely consider it stolen!"

"I have thought of that, Dolwitz," Boening answered. "And certainly, I had no intention to steal it."

"Then why do you keep it, Herr Graf, if it isn't yours? It isn't an honorable thing to do!"

"If you insist on knowing, Dolwitz, I thought the girl would be my wife, and I feel she cheated me."

"Herr Graf, to see that girl's face and to hear her play … I would sooner believe she is an angel sent to test you than a devil sent to torment you."

"*Na gut,* Dolwitz. Not that it's any of your business!"

"No, Herr Graf. None of my business, Herr Graf. Only that …"

"Only, what?"

"That she could have had her reasons, Herr Graf …"

"And what would those be?"

"Herr Graf, I have cousins at Libnow. They've served the Counts von Schillingen for—well, it's been long before anyone can remember that they've raised the best pigs and geese on the estate. But Oskar, he was one of seven and wanted to go to sea. So he joined the navy. And what do you think became of him, Herr Graf? He lives in Shanghai! And has a Chinese wife and three Chinese children! And I have to believe that he loves those children, just the same as if they were German. But he can't bring them home."

———

AS SOON AS THIS CONVERSATION HAD TAKEN place, Boening began to feel uneasy. Because it suddenly occurred to him that the girl perhaps did have her reasons for rejecting him. And that these reasons had less to do with distrust of his motives for marriage than with the same peculiar alienation toward his origins that he had to admit he felt for hers.

But then, why the plaintive tone in the letter she had sent to him? Could it have contained a message that hadn't been spelled out? Could she be pregnant? And if she were, had he cavalierly repudiated his own child, and destroyed his single hope to reunite with her?

And yet, he had replied with that hateful note. How could he have thrown her over with such contempt? For, after all, he had seduced her. Of course, she had suggested making love. But only after a week of calculated efforts on his part to get her to want him. She hadn't been the first girl he had seduced. There were plenty of them. He knew how the drill went. He was a handsome man. And he had perfectly mastered that drill.

And no sooner had that thought occurred to him than it became an obsession, a kind of constant and enervating *Leitmotif* that played on him while working and while riding, while idling, while playing cards with his *Junker* friends at the Casino-Gesellschaft, and especially while in church on Sundays. She was likely pregnant. He had made no effort to prevent it, though he knew well enough how to do that. So that he was, in any case, a blaggard: an unwashed beast, in fact, whose subtlety of understanding was just good enough for the perusal of *Horse and Hound* magazine, and no better. And the haunting image in his mind of the monstrous Fräulein Elisabeth von Schwabacher, his cruel and wanton Salome, who had taken a lover, not a husband, was overtaken by one far more disconcerting to him—the angel-faced Lisi, who flew into his arms and cried out as he ravished her.

It wasn't until mid-November that his worries were quieted. The familiar group of cronies were at cards in the Casino-Gesellschaft, and Botho von Flenheim mentioned that Magnus von Schwabacher was to receive a medal from Kaiser Wilhelm II.

"They've had one designed, you know, especially for Jews like Schwabacher, who won't wear a cross. It's an oval, or a circle—something in that vein."

Everyone laughed at this except Ehrlingen, who said, "Cross or oval, Schwabacher read the American market like a prophet. He has made even the Kaiser a great deal of money, and has saved a lot of other German skin as well. Why shouldn't he be recognized for it?"

"They say his wife has cancer," Hennholz observed. "Is it true?"

"There have been no Thursday music evenings of late."

"It's a shame. She's a beautiful woman," Hennholz replied.

On the way out after cards, Wilhelm took his opportunity. "Ehrlingen, has Fräulein Elisabeth returned from Vienna?"

"She was at the Philharmonic with her father last week, looking very thin."

"I have something to return to her. I want to know if you will take it."

"Look here, Boening. I never thought I would say this to *you*, of all the men I know. But I think you've behaved like an asshole."

"I won't disagree with you. Will you take it, then?"

———

THOUGH HE CONSENTED TO RETURN THE PENdant, Ehrlingen knew it wasn't said and done that he would even gain admittance to the villa on the Kadettenweg. Nevertheless, he tried.

*November 17, 1896*

*Susannah,*

*I came to Lichterfelde West earlier today, and, as I feared, I was told yet again that you were not at home. I know you were at home; you are always at home on Tuesday afternoons. I even saw your purse and gloves on the center table in the foyer.*

*So I am leaving this note and the enclosed small packet, which is from Graf Boening. You will, I expect, know what is inside. You need no longer fret about him.*

*There are things I need to say to you; and yet, you don't allow me to come to you and say them. I brought Boening into your home. And while I can promise you that I never encouraged him, I feel some guilt for the suffering he has caused you.*

*But other things, also. That I behaved miserably because I thought your husband had rediscovered you, as if it weren't his right all along to do so!*

*Susannah, if love and destiny had been aligned, how happy we could have been together! And you would let me comfort you now, as I so wish to do.*

*Just let me know if there is anything, anything at all that I can do for you.*

*Always,*
*Henning*

He received the following answer the next day:

*My dear Henning,*
*Do not be angry or hurt that you were not admitted. I don't feel well. And when I leave home, it is usually to see a doctor. So you see, I am no company anymore. I walk with a cane, and I spend a lot of time lying down. Luckily, I have a few very tolerant female friends who refuse to blanch at the sight of me, and who insist on coming to visit, even though I have become a complete bore.*

*And of course, there is Lisi who, while not always cheerful or patient with me, remains attentive and always amusing. She is the light of my life!*

*That the pendant has been returned is a great relief, especially to Magnus. You know what a worry wart he is. But with regard to guilt: Who is without guilt in this life?*

*There is something you can do for me, Henning. It's very possible we won't see each other again. I hope you will continue to be a friend to my husband, who thinks so highly of you.*

S.

From the point in time that she returned from Vienna, Susannah's illness had begun to manifest itself in ways that restricted her movements and sapped her energy. And it wasn't only her spreading cancer that took its toll. Her fears that her daughter would be the subject of salacious gossip precipitated somatic symptoms that had nothing to do with her cancer: She suffered from stomach pains and heart palpitations, and there were panic attacks. At times, she thought she would go mad with sadness and anxiety. So that each week, she admitted fewer and fewer visitors to her once open home, eventually restricting her company to a small circle of female friends.

Luise Wolff had for years been in the habit of having either lunch or tea with Susannah at least once a week. Susannah and she had known each other as teenage girls in Vienna, being only a year or so apart in age, and had both grown up loving the theater (Luise had been an actress). And both, having settled in a city they considered a cultural backwater, had from the moment of their marriages and migration north nursed ambitions to make life in Berlin more like life in Vienna. Luise, however, had actually realized those ambitions in a way that benefited the entire continent of Europe. With her husband Hermann, Luise had, within a decade, secured Berlin's place as a major cultural center for music and the home of one of the great orchestras of the world.

At the Wolffs' legendary Sunday afternoon dinners after Berlin Philharmonic rehearsals, Susannah and Magnus had met Brahms, Tschaikowsky, Anton Rubenstein, and many other great artists.

Luise was a straightforward woman, and at times she could be brutally witty. And between the two friends, there had never been artifice. So that when, on one cold and rainy late November day, Susannah looked over tea and cake at her friend and broached the subject of her abbreviated future, Luise made no effort to offer the standard platitudes of comfort.

"Do you remember, Susi, how, in the early seventies, we used to despair of living well here?"

"Living well? There was never a question of living well. Even living decently was a challenge! Berlin was a rat's nest—surely the filthiest city in Europe! I remember there wasn't a public toilet to be found anywhere in the center of town. And that I would always remove my shoes before entering our apartment. They were so disgusting from traipsing through waste water."

"You see, then, how things are improved. The rest of your life may be short, but it will be very pleasant. Look around you, and especially at your lovely home."

Susannah had to laugh. "But I do worry about Magnus and Lisi. That they won't ever be on good terms, and that they will live here together unhappily, and both grow old and bitter. And that he will always be angry with her."

"Has the necklace been returned?"

"Yes."

"There, now! You see? All's well that ends well. All that *Angst,* all that energy expended over something that could have barely touched you, anyway."

"You think the whole thing a bagatelle! Hardly!"

"You know, Susi, the other day a young pianist came to me with the best recommendations—glowing reviews! He asked that Hermann and I listen to him play. Well, I looked through the notices he brought, and I told him that of course we would hear him and that we are always looking for new talent. But I warned him that no true artist can garner only positive reviews, and that if he were as great as he probably would like us to think, he wouldn't hesitate to include a negative one."

"Luise, you cannot be suggesting …"

"I am suggesting only that your daughter will one day be one of the richest women in Germany. And if the rich cannot break the rules and carry on, I don't know who can. Why work so hard to keep her love affair a secret? These things tend to make young women more, not less, desirable. Do you actually believe no man who loved her could forgive it? You and Magnus are much too conservative. And much too conscientious—too worried about what the gentiles will think. You become more and more each day like your cousin Babette Meyer, who has cut off her Jewish nose to spite her German face."

"Oh, Luise, how wrong you are! You simply don't appreciate Babette, or how good and true she is! Now, there is an example of a woman who should have had an affair and left it at that, instead of marrying the man she thought she loved."

"Well, I can't speak to Babette's love life, but I know what I see when I encounter her. And it's a woman who does nothing but play to the demands and expectations of people she has convinced herself are her betters, however dignified she makes it all appear."

"Luise, if you had known Babette when she was young! So passionate and confident. There was no girl in Berlin so magnificent! Magnus says she was all thunder and lightning—just waiting to break! She kicked him where it counts once, and so hard he hurt for weeks! And she boxed the Gräfin Marie von Arnim-Kröchlendorff on the ear the very first time they met!"

"But that's exactly my point, Susi. The countess and Babette have been the best of friends ever since. So the Gräfin von Arnim-Kröchlendorff probably deserved it, and it was the right thing to do. But then Babette turned from all that and began her campaign of self-denial—and long before her Count von Kalckreuth came into the picture. For thirty years she has thought of nothing but how others will judge her. She has done nothing but allow her own gifts to tarnish, while polishing other people's metal. And when she dies, what will have been left of a remarkable woman? Nothing but a shadow!"

"Luise, that's cruel! What do you know about her! You know nothing of what she may have suffered!" Susannah glanced at her friend meaningfully.

"Oh, now I get it!" Luise waved her hand impatiently.

"What women who love must suffer for their reputations, Luise!"

"Oh, come now, Susannah! If a shop girl terminates a pregnancy, do you really think she is heartbroken? My dear, there are likely as many lower-class babies *aborted* in this country as born. Virtue is a privilege of the well-heeled, as poor Wozzeck would have observed. But if a lady has an abortion, well! She becomes a martyr forever more. And why? Only because she can afford the guilt, as well as the psychiatric treatment for it.

"The truth is, Susannah, that love and all its messy consequences are as common as table salt. But art is not! So before you vanish on your daughter, you must allow her some bragging rights. You must give her permission to own how exceptional she is!"

---

*Gross-Lichterfelde*

*January 14, 1897*

*Liebe Klara,*

*I've heard nothing at all from you, and I am wondering how you are, and especially how Bernhard is doing at the Göbersdorf Sanitorium. I hope he is keeping his spirits up, as well as the other patients amused. Martin wrote me that you paid him a visit over the New Year holiday.*

*Klara, I want so much for everything to clear up between us, and for us to be as we once were. But I fear it won't happen because it's as if we are moving in opposite directions, though we have been so intimate, and once agreed on so many things. And yet, I still need a friend; that is, someone who really knows me and accepts me the way I am, and loves me, even if she doesn't like me much.*

*It's hard at home now, with Mami's illness. She's a wonderful sport, laughing about her walking stick, and ordering pastries every day with whipped cream so that she is not swimming in her clothes. But she is in excruciating pain and won't take morphine, because the doctor says that once she starts, there will be more and more of it needed, and she doesn't want to live the rest of her life in a fog.*

*She loves it when Fürst Egon comes to visit me and we play together. And when he does, she has the door open in the library and listens from there. But she refuses to see him or anyone else at all except Tante Luise, cousin Babette, and Therese Simon-Sonneman, who each come by once a week. Tante Luise and Frau Therese have taken me under their wing, and both have separately told me they are worried that I don't get out much, and that I should play more, especially at their evenings at home. Babette says she has purchased a new piano, so that I will have no excuse not to come. Tante Luise insists I attend the Philharmonic more with Papi, and even suggested that I should play a benefit recital for the refugees.*

*But I don't stay close to home for the reason you think. I stay close to home because I don't want to leave Mami alone to morbid thoughts. You have never appreciated how very loving Mami can be! She would lay down and die a thousand times for me. So shouldn't I try my best to be entertaining to her? At any rate, we play duo pianos together (She never had a decent technique, but she is so musical and never neglects to make a melody of the simplest scale passage); we play chess and cards; and when all that becomes too strenuous, we raid the library and read together.*

*We've just read* Daniel Deronda, *staying up many nights when she has been too much in pain to sleep. And there have been great debates. You would think that Mami would be on the side of love, rooting for a marriage between Deronda and the glamorous, if dangerous, Gwendolen. And that I would be on the side of politics, hoping all the while that Daniel will marry his shy little Jewish singer and go off to Zion to build a nation.*

*But now that she has read* Der Judenstaat, *Mami thinks the idea of a Jewish state is not so preposterous—provided that "all the gentlemen who settle Palestine are as dashing as Theodore Herzl." So a good Jewish marriage, apparently, is no longer too parochial and middle-class for her taste. While I, for my part, and under the present circumstances, am no longer in a position to even think of getting a Jewish husband!*

*The truth is, we both think the character of Deronda quite absurd. How could a fully formed man, raised a Christian, suddenly discover he's Jewish and then embrace it, as if rendering some concealed expanse of his inner being to the light of day? But that seems to be the way gentile authors want things. They want there to be something bred in the bone that is specifically Jewish. It's their excuse, Mami says, to argue our segregation, though heaven knows what we have done to deserve it. At any rate, we both agree that Eliot, whatever her intentions, bought into theories that are a slow-acting poison on the intellectual community. And Mami even insists she is glad she will be dead before a critical mass of the so-called respectable elements of society get it in their heads to simply round us all up and shoot us.*

*Not to accuse George Eliot of an inhumane perspective on the Jews. She was hardly plying the blood libel, or inciting street riots. But in the end, she was preoccupied enough with the "Jewish Question" to have written a very long and philosophical novel about it. Which means she thought the Jews were a problem to be solved.*

*Did you know that in Berlin, it's gotten to the point where the police won't approve the public performance of any play with a Jewish character in it—whether 'good' or 'evil'? And not because anti-semitism has become official, the way it threatens to become in Vienna, but simply for fear of exciting yet more public conflict, which is all too perversely and violently focused on the Jews.*

*Well, enough of that! In fact, it's all by way of informing you that I no longer disagree with the world according to Mami. Perhaps I am wiser than I was only a few months ago when we were together in Vienna. Or perhaps illness has matured my mother. Who knows?*

*At any rate, I am with Mami constantly, so very much under her influence. And with Papi spending his time increasingly at the bank and in his office, Mami would have no real company if I weren't with her. And you know how she needs people—how she loves being admired, and also how she loves admiring others.*

*But all this will change eventually—I mean my being at home constantly. Although I hate myself for having the thought, I know that when she is gone, it will be caution to the winds for me; and I will go anywhere I please, and do and say anything I please, and I will play where and what I please for whomever I please. I will be a true eccentric and the sworn Enemy of Order! And I relish at least that part of my future!*

*And now, where am I, having started this letter in a mood of contrition? Klara, you are right in that the world is not what I think it is. You are correct that I am spoiled and have unlimited funds to both pursue and then to bury my indiscretions. But is the world really what you think it is? Because we all see such a small piece of it and then form our opinions, which we jealously guard and cultivate. And remember what Papi always says about opinions: namely, that one should always be of two opinions on every subject. But, truly, why should your view of the world—the view from female parts, and from a "decent Jewish family"—be the final truth? I'm not saying this because I'm ungrateful, nor to challenge you. I'm saying it because I want you to appreciate that I had no choice but to take my child's life. And I want you to forgive me. Because if Mami knew, even she would come to understand. Only that I couldn't put her through that—not now.*

*Please give my love to everyone. You think me heartless, but I think of my Vienna family all the time, and I especially think of Bernhard.*

*Deine,*

*Lisi*

# CHAPTER XI

IN FEBRUARY, MONEY BEING EXTREMELY TIGHT, Boening relinquished his Onorio Marinari *Salome* to the auction house of Lempertz in Cologne, pocketed a sum that would bring him at least one more relatively comfortable year in the Regentenstrasse, and paid a visit to the Schwerning home. Though Babette Meyer von Kalckreuth strove to get him to her Tuesday evening soirees, he didn't go, fearing he might encounter Elisabeth von Schwabacher there, and preferring, in any case, to visit the older woman when they could be alone, and he could discuss sketching and painting with her.

As winter plodded on, Wilhelm's disposition started to regain its previous equanimity. And he even began to think that a marriage with his distant cousin, Helge von Schwerning, might be desirable after all. There would be no bridges to cross, at least—no very contemporary ideas to negotiate, no mocking of his staid *Junker* values and habits, and certainly no talk of female emancipation. Husband

and wife would each fall easily into their roles as master and mistress of the estate at Pulow. They could even thumb through the pages of *Horse and Hound* together. And most importantly, Wilhelm would be moving forward with his life.

But it seemed the Fates were against him. That is, the shadow of the Jewess Elisabeth von Schwabacher still cast itself across his path. One evening at the Royal Court Opera, he was sitting in the parterre with Henning von Ehrlingen and Botho von Flenheim. Flenheim fingered his opera glasses and then focused them on one of the boxes above.

"Say, Boening, how did you fare with the Schwabacher girl?"

"I beg your pardon?"

"During cards one night last spring, you declared you were going to apply for three million marks and the lady's hand."

"I don't remember that."

Flenheim looked skeptical. "Well, they say she's had a lover."

"Really? Well, Flenheim, you can't believe everything people say, you know."

"Yet, somehow I *do* believe it. She's certainly not pretty, but she has something—a *je ne sais quoi*. She looks like she has had a lover. "In fact," and here, as he trained the opera glasses, he chuckled, "It's all over her face. Was it you, Boening? Were you her lover?" He continued to train the glasses, paused, and looked through them intently.

"Don't be absurd, Flenheim."

"The thing is," Flenheim said pointedly, "she's certainly got a nice pair up front … and one can almost imagine her all exerted, *en déshabillé.*"

He offered the glasses to Wilhelm, who ignored him.

"Well, then, if she has had a lover, and the lover wasn't you, then it's got to be Wittenbach, right?" Flenheim continued. "He's the only one who goes there now, and he's the only one, aside from her father, who is seen with her."

"Flenheim, I can pretty much assure you that Wittenbach would sleep with a woman only by necessity—and, it goes without saying, only with the blessing of the Pope."

"But you, Boening," Flenheim whispered, smiling at Wilhelm sardonically, "You'd jump her by choice, wouldn't you! Come on, Boening! Everyone in Berlin knows you got between her legs at Kleinneubach."

"Really? And who exactly is this 'everyone,' Flenheim?" Wilhelm replied evenly. "Because I wish to know precisely whom I need to thrash for saying that."

<hr />

IN MID-MARCH, BOENING RETURNED TO PULOW, having been absent for the better part of eight weeks. His father was, for the first time since the heart attack, completely himself. And he let his son know it by interrogating him on his marriage prospects.

"I thought we were to have a rich Jewess in the family," he said one night at dinner.

"That didn't work out, *Vater*."

"You wouldn't have her in the end, or she wouldn't have you?"

"The second."

"Well I made some inquiries about that girl, and I am told that while she is not beautiful, she *is* quite gifted. She's apparently one of those *learned* Jewesses, the type for whom people of our ilk would be viewed as rather raw. So I find it curious you thought you could keep her captive in the very untamed environment of Pulow, and for the purpose of raising your Christian children and supervising washing day. It shows you have a lot of imagination, if not much sense."

"*Vater*, there would have been nothing wrong with bringing some culture into the family. Not to mention brains ..."

"Perhaps not, seeing as you are so plainly lacking in these things ... And where are you with the Gräfin Schwerning, a girl certainly more on your level socially *and* intellectually?"

"I intend to marry her."

"When?"

"When it's time."

"Hopefully before I'm dead, or before she is. She's come down with scarlet fever. I had a letter today from her father."

Hearing this, Wilhelm resolved to write immediately to Count Schwerning, who replied that the girl was indeed seriously ill, that she had picked up the disease while helping to nurse her niece and nephew, and that it had gone into rheumatic fever. If all went well, she could be expected to travel in April. The doctor had prescribed a spa cure at Bad Homburg vor der Höhe.

As he could hardly impose himself on the Schwerning family at Bad Homburg, and as he didn't have the funds to set himself up in a spa town, Wilhelm refrained from replying to the count's letter. But as fortune would have it, he received a note from Henning von Ehrlingen right before returning to Berlin. Henning was to be taking a suite at Ritters Park Hotel in Bad Homburg for two weeks in April. Would Boening consider keeping him company?

WHAT EHRLINGEN DID NOT CONVEY TO BOENING in the context of this very generous invitation was that Madame von Schwabacher and her daughter had arranged to take a villa in Bad Homburg for the entire month. It was thought that the *Kur*, if not of any use in stemming the progression of Madame's disease, would distract her from it; and that the baths would help ease some of the acute pain in her spine and hips. So long as the headaches remained manageable, said the doctors, a decent quality of life could be expected; and Frau von Schwabacher was certainly not yet in danger of the worst. Yes, Bad Homburg in a quiet spring month would provide a relieving change of scenery.

When, on the 13th of April, Wilhelm had settled in at the Hotel Ritters Park, he sent a note to the elder Countess Schwerning, asking her if he might visit on the following day, a Wednesday afternoon. The countess replied immediately that the Schwerning family would be happy to receive him, so long as he promised to come shortly after lunchtime. Later than three would not be suitable, she wrote, for the family were to attend a music gathering that evening at the Empress Friedrich's retirement residence in the town of Kronberg im Taunus.

Naturally, Boening and Ehrlingen had also been extended invitations to this concert and reception—a spontaneous affair the empress (mother of Kaiser Wilhelm II) had conceived after hearing that a talented young pianist, a former student of Maestro Theodore Leschetizky, was presently staying in Bad Homburg.

Wilhelm arrived at the Schwerning residence in the Kisseleffstrasse promptly at two the day of the concert. He was taken immediately into the drawing room where Helge and her mother awaited. The girl, tall and disposed to be muscular, was slenderer than Wilhelm remembered her; and if her face was a bit wan, it had acquired a delicacy that Wilhelm had not seen before.

"You are so kind to come, Cousin Wilhelm."

"I hope you are better now."

"I'm told I shouldn't have contracted it at all. Or at least, not as badly as I did. I'm not a child, after all. And now I've caused so much worry for my parents and so much inconvenience for everyone. Not to mention all the pleasures I have missed." She smiled at him. "I'm itching to ride again and to go to parties!"

"Well, I am sure that you will soon be restored to yourself completely. And that your parents will no longer worry about your health. They will worry instead that you are wearing out your horse and have too many dance partners on your hands."

The Countess Helge smiled again, and her eyes told him that he would undoubtedly be her most desired partner for dancing and for riding.

"Will you be going to Schloss Friedrichshof tonight?" she asked.

"I will."

"My parents are not very anxious to go, it being a piano recital of serious music, and surely a bore. But they say we must. They say that though the Empress Friedrich is one hundred percent German by blood, her heart has always been in her place of birth—England. And that if her husband had lived, we would all be squeezing German feet into English shoes, and there would be Jews in charge everywhere—even in the officer corps and in the civil service."

"The empress always was liberal in her politics. In this, though, perhaps she conformed to her husband's views, as a good wife should." Here Wilhelm was lying, knowing full well that every view the Empress Victoria of Germany had ever expressed was her very own, and that many of her husband's views were actually hers before they were his.

"But," Wilhelm added, "She has always been known as a brave and kindhearted woman."

The conversation continued in this vein. There was nothing in it that Wilhelm could particularly savor, or likely even remember later; but he found it satisfactory enough in that it was gentle conversation, certainly inoffensive; and Gräfin Helge was still young enough, at nineteen, that one could hardly hold her lack of inspiration against her.

Wilhelm left the Schwerning home at exactly three in the afternoon, feeling that perhaps it had not been a mistake to come to Bad Homburg, that Helge was certainly an attractive girl, and that should the girl's mother ever leave the room, he would attempt to kiss her and see whether that led to firmer resolve on his part. At any rate, he would see her again in the evening at Schloss Friedrichshof.

⌘

THAT EVENING, UPON ENTERING FRIEDRICHSHOF Palace's "*Grüne Salon*" a few minutes early, Wilhelm found himself face to face with Elisabeth von Schwabacher, who was just getting up from the grand piano. She was painfully thin and dressed in a diaphanous light-blue chiffon gown that made her dark blue eyes and her shock of red-blond hair appear almost disembodied.

"Graf Boening!"

"Fräulein von Schwabacher. What a surprise to see you."

"Really? You didn't know I was to be in Bad Homburg?" Her face was a kinetoscope of barely concealed turbulence.

"No."

"Your friend Ehrlingen did. And I think you must have come with him."

"I did."

"Well, then, Graf Boening, can you really expect him to be loitering more than fifty meters from my mother?"

"I hope your mother is finding some relief here in her treatments, Fräulein Schwabacher."

"No, but thank you for the kind thought. And now I must go … and … and put my hands under warm water."

This encounter, the first since the final lunch at Kleinneubach, deeply unsettled Boening. For several minutes after it, he felt a dull heat rising and falling in his innards, as well as a mental haze so acute that he was beset with the impulse to shake his head free of it. It wasn't until he had taken his seat next to Helge, and indulged in some small talk with her, that he felt relief.

For her part, Lisi was also unnerved. But, having sought the refuge of a lavatory where, to her surprise, she found herself weeping copiously before disposing of her negligible breakfast and lunch, she was also able to regain her composure. When called to the keyboard half an hour later, there was a resolute calm in her expression that hadn't been there when she spoke with Wilhelm. She smiled graciously at the empress and curtsied low with requisite dignity. The empress asked what she would play.

She answered, "Your Imperial Majesty, I thought I would play Mendelssohn, as you have done so very much for his reputation.

Ever since your wedding, he has been the undisputed favorite of brides and grooms; and that may very likely go on until 'Kingdom come.'" The audience chuckled appreciatively and settled in for a spirited and sensitive performance from the *Songs Without Words*.

Lisi played for a good three quarters of an hour. And when she finished, there was thunderous applause. The empress, who had been visibly moved throughout, opened up her arms and motioned to the girl to come to her. Then she embraced her, kissed her on the cheek, and whispered some things that were quite obviously affectionate.

The Gräfin Helge von Schwerning, sitting next to Wilhelm, joined politely in the audience approbation. But she also turned to him, laughed, and raising her voice just slightly above its din, said, "Imagine kissing that ugly little Jewess! I wonder that such people are even allowed in Bad Homburg. You know, Cousin Wilhelm, my father says that in Austria, they will soon be eliminated from all the decent spa towns. Their reservations will no longer be honored."

At this very casually given remark, Boening was seized by a wave of revulsion so powerful that he caught himself lurching forward in his seat. "Cousin Helge," he replied, in the steadiest voice he could manage, "it's a riddle to me that Fräulein von Schwabacher's playing has left you so completely cold. Do you think your problem is your recent illness? Or is it simply craven envy of another woman's gifts?"

The Countess Helge looked at him dumbfounded, and her eyes filled with tears.

<hr />

IT PROBABLY NEED NOT BE SAID THAT WILHELM resolved to excuse himself from the Countess Helge's company as soon as practicable; but as he rose from his seat, he realized that Ehrlingen had disappeared. It immediately occurred to him that if he did not act quickly, he would be facing the unhappy fate of escorting the entire Schwerning family to the supper table and attending them there. Offering an abbreviated bow to the girl and her parents, he declared his intention to pursue his friend, who, he said, had undoubtedly gone to congratulate the artist.

He found Henning in the *Speisesaal,* where a great table stood laden with cold meats, fish, and salads. He could see through the scores of guests that Ehrlingen was indeed in conversation with Lisi, a conversation which, considering their history, looked oddly intimate, even friendly. It seemed as though Lisi were requesting something, and Ehrlingen was nodding his head in a reassuring way.

A moment later, Henning was at Wilhelm's side.

"Boening, do you think the Schwernings would bring you back to Bad Homburg?"

"I do not."

"Well the fact is, there has been a misunderstanding. The empress believed Fräulein Elisabeth would spend the night here, which she on no account wants to do. I have explained that her mother is gravely ill, and that I am expected to return her tonight."

"And where does that leave me, Ehrlingen?" Wilhelm snapped. "Shall I walk back to Bad Homburg?"

"Well, Boening," Ehrlingen answered pointedly, "I suppose you'll have to buck up and tolerate the ride back with us. Madame von Schwabacher has taken a turn for the worse in the last two days. The girl is quite exhausted and will probably sleep the whole way home, so she'll likely be no bother to you. We will leave as soon as the empress allows. *Ihre Kaiserliche Majestät* requested to see Fräulein Schwabacher once again in private. After that the girl has to eat something, and we will be off. You'll excuse me while I have a plate prepared for her." At this, he turned on his heels and went straight to the buffet.

Barely thirty minutes later, Wilhelm, Henning, and Lisi were ensconced in the carriage that would take them back to Bad Homburg, Elisabeth holding in her hands a small cloth drawstring purse she had received from the empress. And she was smiling broadly enough that her dimples appeared.

"Did you receive a gift?" Henning inquired.

"A bracelet, which she took off her own wrist, and pressed into my hand. It's very pretty, but much too big for me. Baron Ehrlingen," Lisi continued, unashamed relief in her voice, "I really don't know how to thank you for interceding on my behalf. What an impossible woman, and how good to escape her passionate declarations and very confident opinions. She went on so about my being too thin. She even insisted on feeding me from her own hand! I felt like a bird in a cage."

The men were silent at this outburst, Ehrlingen looking amused. But after considering for a moment, Wilhelm countered, "I would think, Fräulein Schwabacher, that you would be a bit more generous in your judgment of the empress. They say she is a great friend of the Jews, and she is certainly an appreciative audience to *your* talents. I cannot think of a greater compliment than an invitation to be an overnight guest in her home."

"Oh! Thank you for reminding me that I am a Jewess, Graf Boening. I might have forgotten, and as one of that reviled people, not been properly grateful for Her Majesty's regard."

"It wasn't meant that way …, and you know it."

"… And I didn't mean to imply that Her Majesty isn't good and kind. I merely said she is impossible. So obsessed with Mendelssohn, when I begged her to let me play a little Brahms. And Brahms hardly cold in his grave. I think she's very conceited."

"You think the dowager empress of Germany conceited, do you?"

"I was not referring to her position, Graf Boening. Of course, she has a perfect right to be conscious of her position. But about her intellect … which I imagine is not much greater than most other people's."

"Certainly not half *your* intellect, you mean."

"If you insist on putting it like that … But perhaps I am being too hard on her. Because when I explained about Mami, and that I am her only child and had to go home tonight, the empress insisted that my mother must be very proud of me—that of her own eight children, only two had more than a thimbleful of natural gifts, and both were lost to her as young boys."

Elisabeth paused, and then said, "I will never marry, Baron Ehrlingen."

"No?"

"No. And do you know why?"

"Why, Fräulein Elisabeth?"

"Because I will not run the risk of bringing fools into the world."

"Where is your music, Fräulein Elisabeth? I hope you haven't misplaced it!"

"The empress asked to borrow it. She insisted she wants to study my markings, and has promised to send it along ... When she's done with it, of course ..."

"But" she continued after a long, marked pause, "I must admit there is something cozy and friendly about the Friedrichshof palace, something along the lines of my fantasy of a Scottish castle. The piano is beautiful, and the empress, in her own overbearing way, a motherly type. So perhaps if it weren't for worrying about Mami, I might even have *wanted* to stay."

❦

LATER THAT NIGHT, OVER SCHNAPPS IN THEIR rooms at Ritters Park Hotel, Boening learned from Ehrlingen that the Countess Babette Meyer von Kalckreuth had accompanied the Schwabacher women to Bad Homburg. And that it was she who had suggested to the empress the concert reception in the palace. She had become very concerned for the girl, who hadn't gotten out for an entire two months, and was very low.

"And it worked, didn't it, Boening! I mean to say that the girl really came back to herself tonight, in all her wit and insolence!"

"Ehrlingen, why didn't you say they were here in Bad Homburg?"

"Would you have come then?"

"Of course not."

"I thought as much. Even with the temptation of Helge von Schwerning, you wouldn't have come. And yet, it was essential I have company."

"The Gräfin Helge is no longer a temptation."

"Ah, well. Back to the drawing board, eh Boening?"

"Ehrlingen, would you think it impertinent if I were to ask you if you loved your late wife?"

"Very impertinent. But I will answer. Not as a man should."

"And that's just the thing. I will have to love my wife. Life is too long for any other way …

"Why isn't Schwabacher here?"

"You are asking *me* that question?"

"It's not normal."

"No, it certainly is not!"

"Can you explain it?"

"Boening, when it began … between Susannah and me, he hadn't touched her in fifteen years."

"A *mariage blanc.*"

"Fräulein Elisabeth was a twin. The boy died during child-birth, and there were other medical complications. Susannah came very near death. Perhaps he was afraid should she conceive another child, he would lose her. At any rate, he seems never to have explained himself."

"Maybe there was another woman. Maybe a Christian woman."

"Schwabacher? You must be joking! That man is so upright, I would bet he barely shits in his own toilet. And that scrupulous-ness, by the way, is the primary reason why I think the girl's affair with you was so diabolical."

"Yet, you brought me here, as your company."

"Boening, in comparison to most swine of our class, you qualify as a rare half-swine. And when I said diabolical, I believe I meant on *her* part, not yours."

"I don't know that she is diabolical. I think she is sensitive, and that makes her prone to resentment."

"Boening, you won't tell me that you haven't closed the book on that girl? Because you must!"

"Not until I marry, Ehrlingen. She's very rich and very pretty and very talented. And a man can dream."

"Well, at least you admit now that she's too fine for you. Think how she plays! She belongs on the concert stage! She finds all the little provocations in those pieces of Mendelssohn—all the eccentricities, and then she brings them out and lingers on them. I have never heard 'Confidence' played so wistfully, and I wanted very badly to run off and weep."

# CHAPTER XII

APRIL 16ᵀᴴ, 1897, WAS GOOD FRIDAY, AND AT three thirty-six a.m., Susannah von Schwabacher died in her bed at the villa she had rented in the Kaiser Friedrich Promenade. It wasn't clear to anyone, least of all the spa doctor who was brought in to issue the death certificate, how this could have happened so quickly. Usually, he said, in cases of metastatic cancer, the patient was taking much more morphine near the end and was complaining of excruciating pain. He guessed that the tumors were more advanced than Madame von Schwabacher's presentation had indicated.

A cable to Berlin could not be sent until seven that morning; and to complicate things, Susannah, in the last hour of her life, had said that she wanted *Tahara*, the Jewish ritual purification. So the Burial Society would also have to be notified, as well as arrangements made for receiving the women who would prepare the body. Lisi had gotten no sleep for several days; nevertheless, she insisted she be the one to telegraph her father and arrange for the women, and that Cousin Babette sit with Susannah's body.

At six forty-five a.m., Ehrlingen was in Boening's bedroom.

"I have a favor to ask."

"What?" Wilhelm shook off his sleep.

"Susannah von Schwabacher has passed away. Perhaps you'll meet Fräulein Elisabeth at the telegraph office and be of help to her, if you can. She's had a long night. Gräfin Kalckreuth suggested she take a short walk in the Kurpark after cabling. Perhaps you'll accompany her."

"I doubt she will relish seeing *me* in her state."

"Still, you might help. She's all alone, Boening. Gräfin Kalckreuth must stay with the body. You will know what to say to her. You always know what to say."

"Are you going to the villa?"

"Yes."

"I see. I am to be your decoy. Well, I hope for your sake that your plan works."

EHRLINGEN TOOK CARE NOT TO ARRIVE AT THE villa before a few minutes after seven, so as to avoid a meeting with Lisi. It had been his dearest wish to visit Susannah once more before her passing, and though it pained him deeply that this had been denied him, he felt grateful that he might sit with her body and see her face one more time.

He was to be disappointed. He was admitted into the house immediately and shown to the room where the Countess Kalckreuth awaited and Madame von Schwabacher's body lay. But when he entered that room and turned toward the bed, it was empty. Susannah's body was instead on the floor, feet pointed toward the door, a sheet covering her entirety. Her head had been propped on a pillow, and a solitary candle lit behind it.

At first, it wasn't clear to Ehrlingen that his paramour hadn't died on the floor and been simply left there. His facial expression must have conveyed this confusion, because Babette immediately said, "Susannah has asked for a ritual cleansing and burial. So we have done things according to Jewish tradition."

Henning nodded and moved toward the body. "May I be alone with her for a few minutes?"

"I'm afraid not, Ehrlingen."

"May I ask why?"

"Because you might be tempted to lift the shroud. And if you did, I could never forgive myself."

"Do you mean to say I may not look at her?"

"Absolutely not. It is not allowed. And even if it were, she wouldn't have wanted it."

Ehrlingen found it hard not to hide his distress and shifted his feet, not sure whether to remain standing, to take a seat, or to go.

"Ehrlingen, you begged to come, and I could hardly refuse you. I'm sorry if you find it awkward." Babette said. "But you will have to make do."

"Is it because I'm a Christian?"

"No Ehrlingen. This is the tradition. Only the women who prepare her body for burial will see her. It's the way things are done. And we really must not talk. If your intention is to stay a few minutes, take a seat. But please be silent."

Ehrlingen sat and heaved his shoulders in a sigh. "Gräfin Kalckreuth," he asked softly, "Where is her husband?" It wasn't truly a question, and Babette knew this. So she didn't feel the obligation to answer.

WILHELM HAD DRESSED QUICKLY AND SET OUT immediately for the post office. But when he arrived there, Lisi was nowhere to be seen. So he started for the Kurpark, a sprawling complex of trees and grass and fountains, accented in this season and on this very bright morning with great flower beds of spring bulbs—daffodils and tulips in profusion. He found the girl sitting on a bench in the graveled Brunnenallee. Directly in front of her was the graceful pink, domed rotunda of the Elizabethan Fountain. She made a disheveled impression. Her legs were sprawled apart, her elbows on her knees and her chin resting on her fists. Her hair was partially unpinned and noticeably uncombed, and as he approached her, Boening saw also that there was a large tear at the neck of her blouse.

"Fräulein Schwabacher, I don't know if my presence is welcome, but your cousin thought there might be some way I can be of help …"

"That's kind of you. Thank you, but I really don't need any help," she replied, staring straight ahead.

Wilhelm remained standing by her long enough that Lisi felt compelled to break the silence between them.

"Graf Boening, I know very well that you have been asked to distract me while Baron Ehrlingen makes his clandestine visit to my mother. But you needn't stay, because I have no problem with it. It even allows me a brief respite. I will just sit here and listen to the water for a while. The sound is so comforting. It really is a lovely park. Everything measured and civilized. One thinks of the poet's words: 'Tall slender water jets sob their ecstasies among the marble.'

"Do you know the poem, Graf Boening?"

"*Claire de Lune.* I know it's one of your favorites. Fräulein Schwabacher, I am very sorry for your loss."

Lisi lay back on the bench, stretched out her arms and kicked her feet out. And then, in a voice that was surprisingly strong for a girl who had spent the last several nights sleepless, she said, "I think I would have liked to come here to recover from some fairly negligible illness, like your friend, the Gräfin Helge von Schwerning, who looks so very delicate in her robe at the baths, but is already eating like a horse and is probably strong as an ox ... It would have been so nice to be here on a different basis, and promenade from fountain to fountain in the afternoons after playing a little tennis."

"Fräulein Elisabeth, the young Countess von Schwerning is recovering from rheumatic fever—not exactly a negligible illness. But she is, thank God, on the mend. You, on the other hand, have just suffered a tragic loss. And it will take a long time before the pain subsides. You must be patient. Let me take you back to your villa ... Did you know your blouse is torn?"

"Intentionally. It's a Jewish custom."

"I see ..."

Lisi laughed softly. "I don't know why I did it, exactly. Because when I telephoned the Rabbi, you would have thought my mother died just in order to inconvenience all the Jews of Bad Homburg at Passover. Mami would certainly have been amused by that."

Wilhelm, who was still standing, leaned in and said, "Fräulein Elisabeth, it should be a comfort to you that you have known a mother's love. Not everyone has."

Lisi didn't reply for a while. And then she said, "Well of course I know you say that to comfort me. But unfortunately, it's no comfort at all. You didn't have a mother, so you cannot possibly know what it is to have a mother and to be horrible to her, as I was horrible last night. She wanted something from me every minute. A pillow, a back rub, a lozenge, a cool towel, and then a warm one … And more and more laudanum. She was very restless and in terrible pain, and I was so longing for sleep. So that when she asked for water at three fifteen in the morning, I said … I said— and very impatiently, I must tell you—I said, 'All right, Mami, but it's the absolute last thing I am bringing you, because I must sleep. You have to let me sleep!' And then I brought the water to her, and, of course, I had to hold it while she drank, because she was so weak. And she whispered, 'Thank you so very much, my love.' And then she seemed to catch her breath and swallow hard. And then she was quiet … and I found myself wondering how many more nights I could do this and even working up an anger. And all before I realized that she was already gone…."

Lisi looked straight up at him through tears, her voice breaking with barely concealed anger. "Wilhelm, if you hadn't written that ugly reply to my letter from Vienna, I would be just about to bear a child of my own, who would no doubt sorely disappoint me in precisely the ways I disappointed my mother. But there would at least be some solace in knowing that the same misery I visited on my mother would be visited on me someday."

Boening did not reply to this, because he felt a sudden crushing in his chest, and a dark veil descending on his head. And the idea occurred to him that this was how women must feel when they are about to faint.

He turned away from Lisi and suddenly felt his legs moving under him—moving away from her, and away from the wickedness of her revelation. That he had been callous and self-absorbed, he thought, as his legs propelled him forward, he must acknowledge at once. The whole episode had been his fault, and he knew it. His footsteps quickened here, and fearing he might break into a run, he found himself consciously expelling breath after rapid breath in a bid to control his feet.

It was hard to slow down while tackling the plethora of unpleasant thoughts that assaulted him. Because if a man planned to marry and had a child in the world somewhere, well that was one thing. He could tell his intended wife, "I have a child in the world, a child of another woman whom I loved before I loved you." But if he had taken the life of his child, or let it be taken on his watch, well that was something entirely different. That wasn't just ordinary human weakness; that was sin.

He had seduced Elisabeth von Schwabacher, and in seducing her, he had thrown both of them off the rails of an ordered life. He had destroyed her innocence. He had shattered her soul! How could he possibly find a wife, now? How could he approach a woman who was untouched? How, more importantly, could he atone to the Jewish woman he had corrupted—with a black stain impervious to any cleansing but through the intercession of Christ!

Why, he asked himself, as the street pavement spread under him with ever more dizzying speed, had he gone after her? Why had he consigned this gifted, passionate girl to waste?

It was his situation, he decided, as his body fairly heaved in a frontal direction. The impossible circumstances of his life! His life had dictated it! His life! A long trail of shameful transgressions and humiliating compromises forced upon him in order to protect his family name! A contemptible succession of abuses perpetrated on innocent people for the sake of his family name! A set of chains bound to him in service to his class and his Kaiser, and all for the preservation of his family name! A heap of gratuitous destruction for his family name!

When would it end? Likely never. Not, at least, until his life ended.

Oh, yes, he would marry—someone whom he didn't love, and whose children he couldn't possibly love, and all for the sake of his family name! It was what his father expected from him, a father whom he certainly didn't love, and who in all probability didn't even love him!

He wondered, would his mother have loved him, had she recovered her sanity and lived? Ha! What a joke! Seven weeks after his sister's birth, his mother had come into the nursery while he slept and tried to set him on fire!

How odd these Jews were who loved their children with a fervent love!

He stopped in his tracks and gulped the air in front of him, because it seemed the ground beneath him was swaying, that his head was reeling, and that he must endeavor to regain his balance.

But he must think no more of the Jews and especially not of Elisabeth von Schwabacher. He must be rid of her! He must strive to think of himself *without* reference to her! He must give up on her once and for all!

He could sense the muscles of his face twitching, and feel the stinging in his eyes that always preceded weeping. The wind had come up, and a few stray magnolia blossoms gently floated by him as the first tear descended down his cheek.

No! There was nothing for it, he thought, as he picked up pace again, except to buck up and do his duty! And even if his duty meant a future repugnant to him—a continuing vicious cycle of unwelcome obligations!

Unless … unless … unless he abjured the future wholly!

Unless … unless … he shot himself! Yes, unless he shot himself!

And at this thought, the ground beneath abruptly braked, and a strange calm settled on him. Because it was a realistic option, wasn't it? Putting an end to it all! For wasn't he, in any case, finished? Wasn't he bankrupt? Wasn't he an abject failure at the Foreign Office? Hadn't he betrayed and destroyed the only woman he had ever loved? And wouldn't his bathtub at the Ritters Park Hotel be the perfect place to end his hell of an existence?

And then he laughed, a helpless howl of a laugh, and one that lasted several seconds. Because he knew that he was not a madman, and that his friend Ehrlingen would hardly appreciate the inconvenience of finding him in a pool of blood in his bathroom. And that Elisabeth von Schwabacher was doubtless a very resilient young woman who may be laid temporarily low, but whose music—not to mention her many other talents, as well as her bottomless financial resources—would not fail to buoy her.

Tragedy is never well served when followed by despair. Rather, hope is what is needed; and Wilhelm had learned *that* lesson early in life. He needed to be in church, today. It was, after all, Good Friday, and the Eucharist would be offered. He knew also that he must confess, and that somehow he must repent for the senseless killing of his unborn child.

# CHAPTER XIII

*Bad Homburg*
*April 18, 1897*
*Lisi!*
*I am told by Gräfin Kalckreuth that for your mother's sake you will
observe seven days of ritual mourning. So I will not expect an answer
to this letter until that period of time is over.*

*Until now, you have borne the entire burden of our wrongdoings.
But the greater guilt was certainly mine. If it had not been for my
initial impositions upon you, my impatience and rashness, and then
my vindictiveness! I think if I were to attempt to explain myself, I
would say that it started with desire, then grew into passion, followed
by anger, and then deliberate misunderstanding. In short, the course
of love affairs with tragic endings.*

*I have gone to confession. And I suspect from your many expres-
sions of impatience with your faith that you may be near to becoming
a Christian. But Lisi, consider that even if we put our transgressions
away, and even if we are both absolved of them, there are sure to be*

*new ones if we cannot make order of the bedlam between us. We are both of us free to marry, our path is wide open, and I cannot help but feel you still love me as I love you. What is preventing us from finding peace together?*

*Can you make your father understand our situation? And can you could arrange it so that I may speak to him?*

*I anxiously await your answer.*

Wilhelm

*Gross-Lichterfelde*
*April 28, 1897*
*Wilhelm,*
*You have a way of making an argument that refuses all argument. I don't know that I can live with that three days, much less the rest of my life. But I suppose I must try. My father will be expecting you at our home in Lichterfelde West on Sunday, May 2nd, at 3 p.m.*

L.

*Gross-Lichterfelde, Berlin*
*May 3, 1897*
*Babette,*
*Your friend, Graf Boening, was here yesterday to ask for Lisi's hand in marriage. You, of all people, must know what transpired between the two young people at Kleinneubach.*

*I believe I have never found myself in such an absurd situation. He entered my study in full attack mode—declaring that I must know the object of his visit, and that to avoid further embarrassment between us, I should state my intentions at the outset.*

I *should state* my *intentions!*

*And when I told him that I had no intentions, that it was his intentions we were ostensibly to deal with, he answered only that there could be no way around a marriage, that it must take place as soon as possible, and that it had to be obvious to me that the matter of my daughter's dignity and comfort as the future Countess Boening was in my hands.*

*I answered him that my daughter is hardly in a position to make a decision as to her future at this of all times. And that while I had agreed to see him, he should appreciate how she is sick with grief at her mother's passing, and not really in her right mind.*

*And imagine what he said to me: He said, "Precisely. Because if your daughter were left to make a decision when her so-called right mind is restored, she would reject me once and for all and never marry. Consider, Herr von Schwabacher, that you might want grandchildren someday."*

*I must admit, this stopped me in my tracks. The truth is, I've never thought much about grandchildren, probably because the world is such a relentlessly fiendish landscape. But Susannah would have wanted them. And if I got one or two, even from a man like Boening, how could I possibly avoid loving them?*

*So I wished him luck with her, since she cannot be given to anyone else. And I told him that I would agree to support her requirements.*

*No number was mentioned, and he seemed perfectly satisfied not being offered a number. He only said that he trusted I would be generous with her, and that I wouldn't punish her for his own imprudence.*

*But Babette, he wasn't out the door two minutes when I started wondering how this marriage could possibly work? To support it goes against every scrap of sense in me and against all my instincts!*

*Are you home this evening?*

*Maggi*

*Behrenstrasse 8, Berlin*
*May 10, 1897*
*Graf von Boening!*
*I have had my lawyer draw up a contract, which you will find enclosed. I realize that these matters today are often settled with handshakes. But I have no intention to leave my daughter's fate, not to mention the fate of four million gold marks, to the tenuous recall of an oral agreement. I take this position less from distrust of your person than from my conviction that neither you nor my daughter have an inkling of the difficulty of the path ahead. You will see, also, that I am settling on my daughter the same sum, which will remain hers, and wholly separate. She has consented to let me manage it.*

*I draw your attention to the fact that, according to this agreement, should the marriage end in a divorce in which you are declared at fault, you renounce all rights to retain any portion of the dotal property. I am hoping, as your banker, that you will seek my advice as regards investment of the dowry, and that as a husband, you will also not be averse to consulting your wife.*

*I remain most respectfully yours,*
*Magnus v. Schwabacher*

*Regentenstrasse 12*
*May 11, 1897*
*Herr von Schwabacher!*
*Thank you for sending the marriage agreement along with your very edifying letter. I wonder, Herr von Schwabacher, if you think there are no laws at all in Prussia to prevent my abusing your daughter's fortune? I seem to remember some from my study of law at university. But I could be mistaken.*

*I will not let it disturb me that in creating parity between Lisi's property in marriage and her property outside of it, you may have sown the seeds of a vicious competition in which I cannot fail but to take second place. But then, I suppose that you and your lawyer will also have thought through that eventuality.*

*And now, Herr von Schwabacher, that I have signed and notarized your document, may I ask that the announcement be placed tomorrow? And may I be admitted again to the villa in Lichterfelde West for the purpose of visiting the future Countess Boening?*

*Respectfully yours,*
*Wilhelm v. Boening*

*May 14, 1897*
*I wonder if you will appreciate these lilacs. I thought them beautiful and am told they symbolize new love. Now, you have kept me too long in suspense. So when will we be married?*

*W.*

*May 15, 1897*
*The lilacs are charming, and their scent, wonderful! But Willi, how is it you can't have guessed, when I gave you so many hints on the telephone, yesterday. Because you know it must be July 30th, and no other day! I won't have it any other way! (Well, maybe July 30th of next year or the year after, but only July 30th!)*

*L.*

*Berlin*

*May 16, 1897*

*Vater,*

*I write to tell you that I am engaged to be married to Fräulein Elisabeth von Schwabacher. We have set a wedding date—the 30<sup>th</sup> of July. You will be pleased to know that the dowry is very generous—four million gold marks. This is as it should be. As you no doubt found out through your inquiries, the bride has known only the finest of everything. We will have to do a considerable amount of work on the Gutshaus in order to receive her in any semblance of the style to which she is accustomed to live. We will also need to purchase two new grand pianos. You can well understand that I want her to have every comfort and stimulation possible in the country.*

*All that aside, however, I can assure you that our financial worries are at an end. Fräulein v. Schwabacher is an only child, and upon her father's death will inherit at least 50 million marks, if not more.*

*You will be relieved to know that she is attending instruction for baptism in the Marienkirche, where we will be married. That is, provided the pastor does not send her away. I have told you that her ideas are very contemporary. Unfortunately, she is no friend of religion. I have asked her to keep herself in line, to learn the catechism, and to refrain from asking provocative questions. To which she only replied, "Is there any other type of question?"*

*I tell you this so that you are duly warned. Fräulein Schwabacher will in no sense be the daughter-in-law you expected—not, at least, if you expected a Helge von Schwerning. But she is a good young woman who will love me, and I intend to make her happy.*

*I hope you are well, Father. I will be back at Pulow by the first of June.*

> *Your devoted son,*
> *Wilhelm*

Wilhelm was hardly the effusive type. Yet he sailed through the latter weeks of May and could not recollect having ever felt the kind of sustained elation that gripped him during these days, which were filled with plans and projects. He had never been lazy but now awakened each morning with a renewed sense of purpose, the kind that comes to a man when the burden of an uncertain future is lifted and when his personal and financial life begin to take a shape he recognizes as the shape of his ambitions.

Indeed, Wilhelm was so happy that he found himself immune to the knowing and slightly cynical, even sometimes pitying looks he received from his Foreign Office colleagues and Casino-Gesellschaft friends as they congratulated him on the announcement of his engagement. Because he didn't care what they thought. Why should he? He was to be a rich man—richer than all of his friends and colleagues. And he was to marry a girl who … Well, he would defy any of them to find a wife who could fuck like Lisi had at Kleinneubach. No, he wasn't thinking about what *they* thought. In every sort of company he found himself, he was only thinking about Lisi, longing to see her, making love to her in his imagination, mentally composing letters and even little epigrams for her.

Of course, he never ventured to write these letters and epigrams down on paper. First, because there was usually a telephone at his disposal, and this made letter writing seem superfluous;

and second, because there was something about Lisi—something both alluring and off-putting—that made him fear to indulge in the standard script of betrothal. Each time he imagined penning epistolary declarations of his love, he also imagined Lisi reading them and either recoiling or smiling in the sovereign, yet not unkind way she smiled when she referred to *Horse and Hound* magazine. "After all," he thought to himself, "I am not a Heine, nor a Shakespeare; and a girl who reads as much as Lisi does could just as well laugh at my sentiments as think them touching."

If Wilhelm had been more honest with himself, he would have admitted that his so very voluptuous happiness during these May days was like the euphoria of a man drunk on good wine—not wholly *compos mentis*. The truth was that he felt more comfortable with his fiancé contemplating her from afar than in her presence, more confident with his decision to marry Lisi when lounging in the privacy of his Regentenstrasse rooms than when sitting in the salon of the villa in Lichterfelde West. If the visits he made to Lisi's home were replete with highly charged moments, some of those moments were as alarming as they were gratifying. Lisi was always stimulating company to her fiancé, but her expressions of affection were few and far between. Even where she offered playful anecdotes and observations to make Wilhelm smile, the overwhelming majority of them seemed to be tainted either with bitter irony or the pathos of fresh grief. And she refused to accept any of Wilhelm's statements of warm feelings at face value. She always presented questions and possible objections.

And then there was the plain fact that during the meals Wilhelm shared with her (and only very occasionally in the company of her father), Lisi refused almost all food and drink, letting course after course, plate after plate be removed from her place at the table practically untouched.

Wilhelm told himself that all of this was nothing to worry about. That the little strains he felt in Lisi's presence, and that she was evidently feeling also, were due to the fact that as an engaged couple, they were forced to deny the intimacy they had shared as lovers, forced to retreat to an earlier stage of social intercourse from which they had long since graduated.

But one evening, when they were alone in the glittering drawing room of the Schwabacher villa, their challenges appeared suddenly in relief. Wilhelm had pulled Elisabeth toward him with the light remark that he longed for her, but she was getting so thin that he feared she would disappear before his very eyes; he hoped she would not vanish, like *Suppenkaspar*, before their wedding day. As usual, she yielded to his kiss but then broke away saying, "Willi, I wonder that I can't get over you, though I absolutely have tried, and it all seems so wrong."

To which he replied, after kissing her again, "My love, our marriage will start soon, which is all for the best, because our courtship was something of a shipwreck. And if it all seems wrong still, though we have reached this point safely, it's because you are starving yourself and lingering in the past, instead of embracing your future. You will soon be a *Gutsfrau*, a lady of the manor, with all the blessings and responsibilities that will give you an active and useful life. And I wish you would look forward to it."

"An active and useful life? As opposed to what, Willi?"

"As opposed to the life you lead presently."

"Which is perhaps not active, or not useful?"

"Lisi, I didn't mean that. But your present life is lived as a single woman, without a husband and children to love you … And if I may be permitted to say so, it's a life you lead as a Jewess, which you will no longer be when you marry me."

"I see … Well, then, Willi. I suppose it's all clear, isn't it? To you, at least. But I should probably warn you that whether or not I can be active and useful in my future as the Gräfin von Boening, I promise you that I will never be anything in the eyes of the world but a Jewess. That can never change."

And truly, Wilhelm was made to realize this as well. Because the very next morning, as the devil would have it, he received a letter from his mother's brother, Graf Herbert von Finckenburg zu Lothau. It was a friendly letter, gently questioning Wilhelm's choice of a Jewess, and a Jewess of very recent wealth and ennoblement, as a bride. The letter continued with an assurance that while the Count Herbert certainly appreciated the Boenings' urgent financial situation and would endeavor to make the young couple welcome at the Finckenburgs' smaller estate (the *Nebengut* at Hohenwald), if not at their residence in Lothau, other members of the family—in particular those on the von Lutzpoggen side—would likely not be so generous spirited. They were to meet to discuss the issue of whether to receive the future Countess at all. Wilhelm, he wrote, should be advised that the Boening line would not be easily wiped clean of the black stain of racial mingling. For *Onkel* Herbert had heard that the girl, although blond, looked somewhat semitic; and on these grounds alone it would likely take several generations to recover the full dignity of the Boenings' *Uradel* heritage.

Contrary to his habit of allowing letters to sit one or two days before replying, Wilhelm found himself at his writing desk within minutes and at the post office within the hour:

*Berlin*

*May 26, 1897*

*My dear Uncle!*

*You are very kind to remember me, and may I assure you that the future Countess von Boening and I will be delighted to avail ourselves of your hospitality at Hohenwald (if not Lothau) when we are married.*

*I much appreciate your concern for the continued social standing and racial purity of the Boening house. But occasionally, miscegenation must be. And let us be fair. It does tend to freshen the bloodlines, even if the progeny of such unions suffer some loss in conventional good looks. But in respect to Fräulein von Schwabacher's Jewish appearance, you may rest assured that I would be reckless, indeed, were I to marry a woman whose features (Jewish or otherwise) I would be loathe to see in the faces of my children. And on that same point— namely, the point of producing children—I do not hesitate to remind you that not a single daughter of the Finckenburg house (in the past five generations, at least) has failed to take her own life after her second or third child. And that sort of madness, while rather common among German aristocrats, seems to be missing in Jewesses.*

*Perhaps you forget that in the year A.D. 1136, when serving Albrecht the Bear in the struggle against the Slavs, my paternal ancestor, Ritter Adelbert of Bonige was badly wounded at Pulow. And there he was tended by a beneficent and beautiful West Slav woman named Genowefa, who was the daughter of the Polabian knight who held the estate at the time. Ritter Adelbert fell in love with her, had her baptized, and married her—thus establishing the noble Boening line at Pulow out of just that sort of racial co-mixture which seems to be so fearsome to you.*

*760 years later, I find myself in a similar situation. Although I have not been wounded in battle, I have managed to fall in love with the daughter of the banker who holds the encumbrance on Pulow. I don't know what her nursing gifts are, but I can tell you that her piano playing would soothe the sorest heart. And so I find myself, far from regretting the mésalliance, quite looking forward to it. One might see the entire thing in the following way: That it is the happy fate of the Boenings to marry into Pulow twice in a single millennium. For we could just as easily have never acquired our beloved corner of the world; or having acquired it and tended it for several centuries, we might have been forced to relinquish it.*

*I send my fond greetings to the entire Finckenburg family and hope this letter finds you well.*

*Your devoted nephew…*

*Wilhelm*

Unfortunately, Wilhelm was not allowed to bask in the satisfaction of this smart reply. For the very same day he posted it, he was passing a tobacco and newspaper store on the Leipzigerstrasse, and his eye caught an illustration on the cover of the satirical magazine *Simplicissimus*. It featured a bridegroom in the shape of a tall, thin, blond, and mustached *Junker*, smartly turned out in formal military attire, and seated at the side of a banquet table. On his lap was a small, buxom, and highly bejeweled bride. She had a grotesquely long nose and light, kinky hair; and she looked at him flirtatiously, her china doll lips pursed vulgarly in a kiss. She was feeding the *Junker* with her fingers from a plate of gold coins, and he was smiling at her lasciviously as he opened his mouth. The caricature was labeled, "A Nobleman's Wedding Feast," and it was fully evident to Boening which nobleman had been singled out.

*May 28, 1897*
*Lisi!*
*Why was I turned away, today? You were home. I heard you playing. Why did you leave me standing at the door of your father's house? And why did you not even pick up the telephone? I leave for Pulow tomorrow for three weeks!*

 *Explain yourself!*

*W*

*May 30, 1897*
*Willi!*
*Perhaps you have seen the cover of* Simplicissmus. *My father brought it to me. I am not sure it resembles us so very much. At least, it seems to me a rather gross exaggeration of our respective physiognomies. But isn't it really amusing, because in its own way, true?*

 *And to think I was on my way to being baptized. But it must be over between us. And I am sorry for that. Really I am. But Willi, think what a misery a marriage to me would be for you. To be the butt of that kind of humor, and regularly too. Always to be believed a dishonest man who cannot love his wife and children.*

 *And it's for the best, because I think my entire motivation to mar-riage was that I miss my mother so much. I will never love anyone the way I loved my mother. My longing for her is crippling, and the only thing that makes the sadness go away, even temporarily, is playing the sonatas of Haydn.*

*Willi, there was always inspiration for Haydn, and all that musical wit and happiness, even bliss, seems to have come from the power of prayer. So perhaps, in the end, when I know all the Haydn sonatas by heart, I will have been comforted and will have even found some religion. But I doubt I will have found the Protestant religion.*

*Forgive me!*

*L*

Reading that letter shortly after arriving in Pulow, where he had gone to start preparations for receiving his bride, Wilhelm von Boening was shaken to the core. All the happiness he had so thoroughly trained himself to feel in the weeks that had passed since his engagement to Elisabeth von Schwabacher drained from him.

# CHAPTER XIV

UNDER THE CIRCUMSTANCES, THERE WAS NOTH-
ing left to Wilhelm but to seek the counsel of a mutual friend.
On the first of June, he wrote the Countess Babette Meyer von
Kalckreuth, hoping for the best and resolving to be undeterred in
starting the renovations at Pulow.

*My dear friend,*
*Your cousin tells me she wants to break our engagement. There are a*
*number of ostensible reasons, only one of which I find even remotely*
*convincing. It seems she is reluctant to be baptized. I thought you*
*might be able to help.*

*v. B.*

Several days later, he received the following reply:

*Berlin*

*June 6, 1897*

*Boening,*

*I am very glad you came to me and wish I could have written sooner. I know you have been beside yourself. I can report that all is well, though I really did have to force my way in. The thing is, Magnus v. Schwabacher does not spend a lot of time at home presently. And that has left Lisi to her own devices, so that she has been practicing twelve hours a day, but eating almost nothing.*

*I am with her as much as possible now, and I think we will have restored balance very soon. I am being very strict with her, as must you be when you are married. She is taking nourishment three times a day, and I am bringing her to religious instruction. She has asked me to be her godmother. So, you see, we are on the right path.*

*You mustn't delay your return, and if you could take as many meals with her as possible, and make sure she eats (You must tell her to eat, and even find ways to punish her if she does not!), that would be best. It's a shame that the wedding is not until the end of July. She would need to be released from Lichterfelde West and its memories earlier.*

*Your devoted friend,*

*Babette M. v. Kalckreuth*

*June 6, 1897*

*Magnus,*

*I have had quite enough of the Schwabachers! In fact, I have been thoroughly exhausted by all of you. Where Susannah was concerned, there were extenuating circumstances, and why should I have felt burdened, when she was dying and so convinced it should not be in the Kadettenweg!*

*But you need to get hold of yourself now, and you need to get hold of your daughter, and see to her future. She has had a very nasty episode. You can believe she got a hard slap across the face from me the other evening. It's your job, and always has been, to shape her to the world around her. And all you've done is build a wall between her and the world! She must now go out into it! She will be a countess and a Christian, and will have to know how to manage an estate household!*

*With regard to Boening, you should know that he has been sick with worry, and that I hear from him every day by mail. When he gets back, I expect you will open your house to him day and evening, no matter what Lisi's state, or yours. He will marry her no matter what, so the sooner he is exposed to all your eccentricities, the better.*

*Magnus, Boening is a Junker, but he is a kind man and hardly as stupid as you seem to think. You mustn't alienate him. Lisi could have done much worse. You must grow up and realize that it will all be up for the Jews—and most of all the rich Jews—if we do not conform!*

*Babette*

*Lichterfelde West*
*June 7, 1897*
*Babette,*
*Though I truly think the world of you, you and I see the world so very differently. One doesn't turn a Jewess into a Christian by slapping her in the face; on this point, I am in absolute agreement with the so-called anti-semites. Before she became sick, Susannah might have agreed with you that religion is merely a question of conformity—of aesthetics, and not of principle. But, in the end, I think she knew this cannot be true, or why would she have asked for* Tahara!

*And so, Lisi also knows very well that what she proposes to do is a travesty of conscience. I cannot help her with that. She must come to terms with it alone. You are right in that she made a decision and now must endeavor to follow it through. But there will be consequences that perhaps she would rather not face, and they are becoming clearer and clearer to her. It's nice you are so confident of her future as the Countess von Boening, but I am not sure at all yet that I am to see my daughter married in the Marienkirche. Only this morning, she came to breakfast panicked from a sleepless night and begging me to call the wedding off.*

*I am relieved you think that Boening is kind. Whether he is kind or not, I have the strange impression that he loves her. Though how this would have happened to him, I cannot imagine. Perhaps he isn't the most egregious of the mud-farmers who are threatening to drive this nation to ruin.*

*Magnus*

*Pulow*
*June 8, 1897*
*Ihre Hochwohlgeborene Fräulein v. Schwabacher!*
*I am valet to Graf Willhelm v. Boening.*

*Please do not mention to my Count that I have written this letter to you. But his entire hapiness [sic] depends on your becomming [sic] his wife. I know this for a fact, I can promice [sic] this. And so you must not dissapoint [sic] him. Because he suffers to think you may not love him enough. And we all of your servants at Pulow will look forward to receiving you as our Gutsfrau and Gnaedige. I have told everyone how you will bring beautiful music to us.*

*Your humble servant,*
*Hans Dolwitz*

*Gross-Lichterfelde*
*June 12, 1897*
*Wilhelm,*

*Baron Ehrlingen was here today about the pianos and your other preparations at Pulow. You are far too generous with me, and I absolutely don't deserve it. Well, the pianos, perhaps, I must deserve, or else I'll only get on your nerves, not knowing what to do with myself in the country. And, of course, it would be lovely to have Bechsteins. Really it would. I will try a few out; Ehrlingen has promised to go with me.*

*I don't like it that you are so far away right now, and that I cannot feel your presence. It makes me fear I am planning marriage with a man who is a figment of my imagination. But Ehrlingen insists you do exist. And he tells me that you must love me too, or how could you possibly entertain the idea of marrying me, since I am, according to him, everything insurgent that a woman can be—"Queen of the Night," he says, and "Insolence Incarnate."*

*Deine,*

*L*


*Pulow*
*July 6, 1897*
*Babette,*

*Presumably it won't be a surprise to you to hear from me once more. You can well imagine that, due to the upcoming marriage of my son with your cousin's daughter, I find myself pretty severely inconvenienced. Pianos are being purchased. Rooms are being renovated. Book shelves and music cabinets have been ordered. And a tennis court will be installed!*

*The young countess will be kept amused and well exercised. But tell me this: Will she prove at all useful?*

*Your old friend,*

*H. v. Boening*

*Berlin*

*July 8, 1897*

*Helmuth,*

*I suppose she will prove no more useful than I was in my youth.*

*Babette M. v. K.*

*July 10, 1897*

*Well then, Babette, I expect they will have a glorious honeymoon. But after the honeymoon, I don't hold out much hope.*

*H.*

*July 12, 1897*

*You are absolutely right. After the honeymoon, it will be the clash of civilizations.*

*B.*

*July 14, 1897*

*I expect I will see you at this wedding?*

*H.*

*July 16, 1897*

*Yes, Helmuth, but you must perhaps adjust your expectations. I am a stout old woman now.*

*B.*

*July 18, 1897*
*But do you still have your wicked temper?*

H.

*July 20, 1897*
*Quite possibly.*

B.

*July 29, 1897*
*Gross-Lichterfelde*
*Liebe Klara,*
*Today, Graf Wilhelm v. Boening and I had our civil marriage cere-*
*mony. And I must say, there were elements of hilarity. First, there was*
*the clerk who, before the ceremony, asked Wilhelm to state his religion*
*and then that of the* "hochwertige Dame." *And when he said, on my*
*behalf,* "Auch Christ, auch Protestant," *the man looked thoroughly*
*skeptical! Of course, he went through all the documents, and when he*
*came upon my baptismal certificate, he couldn't resist muttering,* "The
*ink isn't dry on this one."*

*Then, there was Baron Ehrlingen, whom I so detest, and whom*
*Willi brought as his witness (Cousin Babette was mine), and who*
*looked the whole time as if he wanted to raise his hand to stop the*
*proceedings. Ehrlingen brought me flowers and took the four of us out*
*for lunch and champagne at Hiller's. And I have to admit, it really*
*was a happy and easy party; mostly, I think, because we all felt better*
*that the marriage was now a* fait accompli.

*Tomorrow, of course, is the church wedding, and I've gotten over*
*that—or at least I hope I have. Because the whole thing is a lie—that*
*is, my white dress as well as my conversion from Negro to White. Yet,*

*none of it can be helped. Just looking at Wilhelm is a love potion, and having already been a mistress, I would so much rather be a wife.*

*We will leave straightaway after the wedding breakfast for Dresden and spend our wedding night there. Willi spoke of nothing but the Sistine Madonna all through lunch today, and how he is looking forward to spending the entire "morning after" with her. It really did make me wonder ...*

*I will write to you from Italy.*

*You have been very good to me over the past few weeks. And I have been intolerable. I am going to try to be happy, Klara. But if I'm not, I think my husband will understand. At least that is what he tells me—that I'm grieving, and so don't want to believe that there is happiness anywhere.*

*But I do want everything happy and good for you. I want you to be married soon, also!*

*Love to all,*

*Lisi*

*Part II*

# CHAPTER XV

*By Picture Postcard from Dresden*
*July 31, 1897*
*Liebe Klara!*
*Here it is! The much celebrated Sistine Madonna! What should a*
*bride think when, not yet an hour out of the marriage bed, her hus-*
*band stands transfixed at the feet of this woman for a full ninety*
*minutes? Is he taken by the sublimity or the irreverence? That's what*
*I want to know, and am afraid to ask ... Note, please, the brooding*
*Holy Mother, the anxious Baby Jesus, and the two very bored little*
*cherubim ....*

*Deine,*
*L*

*Hotel Helvetia and Bristol*
*Florence, Italy*
*August 18, 1897*
*Ehrlingen,*
*Received your very kind inquiries and wishes yesterday, relayed them immediately to Lisi, and asked her how I should answer. She said I should say that I am perfectly thrilled with my new wife, and so—this being very true, and I being an obedient husband—I promised her that I would say exactly that.*

*As I write, it is 8:30 in the morning, and my wife is sleeping. We took a train right after the wedding breakfast, and weren't even quite past Birkengrund before she began to organize her married life exactly to her taste. That is, she promised if I let her sleep "just until 9:00 a.m." every day, that she would be the best wife a man could ever ask for, and "for all intents and purposes" my "slave." Of course, making an agreement with Lisi is like making one with the Devil, as you know. For although she hasn't exactly refused me anything I have wanted from her—not yet, at least—by now she has managed to push it until 9:30, and it will soon be 10:00, I am sure. Because according to her, "Professor Leschetizky never gets up before 10, and his playing never suffered from it."*

*Which reminds me that you were the subject of conversation last night, and I was surprised to hear how highly my wife thinks of you as a musician. She says you are far more talented than she and can play anything at sight, though you seldom practice.*

*Well, Ehrlingen, a man couldn't wish for any better company than Lisi when she is awake, though she is also very pretty when she sleeps. In fact, I have taken to sketching her while she is sleeping, so as to memorize the structure of her face, my* Salome *having been long since sold to a Swiss collector, and it being impossible to capture where the bones of my wife's cheeks sit when she is animated.*

*But you cannot imagine how affectionate she is, so very tender, so open to all things beautiful—whether in the museums and churches, or in the countryside. So erudite, and I hadn't realized the amount of poetry she knows by heart, which is truly astounding—especially Heine, whom she is always quoting. When I asked her how it is that she memorized it all, she said that it was a habit ingrained in her by her father, who told her that the foundation of all original thought is poetry, and that anyone who doesn't have poetry at his fingertips cannot think outside of his own narrow milieu.*

*But you know how constantly amusing she is; nobody has ever made me laugh so much. Her mind is a plaything, and though she often gives the impression of a want of seriousness, even an enmity to order, I've come to realize that this disguises a strange sort of moral urgency, the foundation of which, I think, is despair that the important things in life never quite yield to our understanding. And she is completely devoid of faith. So you see, though she is baptized now, I have serious doubts she will ever be a good Christian.*

*On our wedding night, there was a nasty storm, and as we lay listening to the thunder, I asked her if it disturbed her. And she replied, "Not at all, Willi." So I volunteered that these things seldom bother one if one's soul is at peace, at which point she asked me where I thought my soul was, and if I could point to it. And then she started pointing to various places on my person. Was my soul there, in my head? Or there, in my breast? Or there—I will let you use your imagination ... And I have to admit that I got annoyed. If she didn't believe in the soul, I asked, how could she play the piano as she did, because things are always more than the sum of their* parts; and did she think her playing could be reduced to a series of vibrations?

Or how could she love me? And then she told me that she thought what was between us was purely physiological. And if it wasn't purely physiological, it couldn't be defined anyway, so there was no point in dwelling on it. Things that didn't yield to logical analysis didn't bear ruminating over. And hadn't I said exactly that to her once at Kleinneubach?

And then she said that it was such a shame she is a woman, and not a man. For were she a man, her life's mission, starting in our Dresden hotel room that very night, would be to write a scholarly work that would once and for all expose the sheer vagueness and meaninglessness of words like "soul" and "love." It would be a work that would crush German metaphysics once and for all. And there would one day be a plaque on the outside wall of that very hotel which would mark her contribution to the end of the hegemony of German philosophy, as well as mentioning that she stayed there on her wedding night. But as things are, she being a woman, nothing whatsoever would come from her wedding night, except perhaps a baby, and what was that in comparison to a great work of scholarship that would make heads roll ... (So you see, she is my Salome!)

I honestly don't wonder that her parents protected her so zealously, but they made a great mistake in not accustoming her at all to the world, because she's so like a hothouse grown plant, all too vulnerable in the garden. And though she would scarcely admit it to me, even now, when we are so intimate in all things, I think all the time she resented that protection, and was even hoping her father would find us out at Kleinneubach. And now she suffers for what she did to him. She had a letter from him a few days ago, which arrived just as we were leaving *our hotel for the Uffizi Gallery. And so she stopped to read it, and there was so much sadness in her face, I thought my heart would break for her. So I asked her what he had written, and she said, "Willi, it's not what he writes, which is all sweetness and light—what he can do for me, and what he* will *do for me—it's the overlay of anger and hurt."*

*"For example?" I asked. And she said, "For example, the salutation reads, 'My dear Gräfin Boening,' as if I weren't the seed of his loins."*

*So I told her that perhaps he is proud she has a title now. And even if not, she can't let his attitude distress her, because women are meant to marry. And then she said, "But not meant to marry you, Willi. Because if I were a seamstress in a novel by Fontane, I would, of course, never have refused the very handsome Graf Boening his share of my body; but then we would have had only a few days and weeks together, and you would have been gone. And though I would never have gotten over it, I also wouldn't have become a Christian or have left my father for you. But I'm not a seamstress; I am a rich Jewess. So it seems I am allowed a fighting chance of getting over you, since marriages are usually measured in years, rather than in days or months. In the meantime, though, my father is a very lonely man in that enormous house in the Kadettenweg, and I have abandoned him to it."*

*And then on the way to the Uffizi she said to me, "Willi, you know I don't mind how long you want to stay, nor what we look at. Only let's not see Rembrandt's* Self-portrait as an Old Man *today, because I don't think I can take it." I suppose that when she looks at that painting, she sees something of her father's suffering. But it could be otherwise for him. Yes, he is a widower, but a very rich one. And he could at least be enjoying his money, were he not the very paradigm of a rancorous Jew.*

*Ehrlingen, I think that I truly suffered in not having a mother. At any rate, I find those small, secret rituals women have all the more charming to me—the way my wife scrubs her face in the morning with a certain cream, or binds her very wild hair back, or applies lemon juice to her arms and legs at night, or takes care never to let her bare feet touch the floor. But I suppose I will never know which of these rituals all women have, and which ones are Lisi's only. Except one, which is the way she tilts her head when I give her what she calls my "very facile lectures" at the Uffizi, "as if I didn't have eyes of my own, Wilhelm."*

*Yesterday, as we were leaving the hotel for the Accademia, we ran into Lenzdorf and Witznowsky and their wives. They seemed pleased to see me and were not at all unwelcoming to Lisi, but she took offense at something Lenzdorf said about it being a shame her mother passed away, and what a beautiful woman her mother had been. She said, "I wonder if ugly people are mourned as deeply as beautiful ones?" which, of course, made everyone chuckle a little in that way people have of chuckling when they are uncomfortable. Lenzdorf suggested we join them on a trip today to the vineyards, but Lisi said, "But Wilhelm, Liebchen, aren't we already committed tomorrow?" So, of course, I said, yes, that we were already committed, though we weren't.*

*The thing is, Ehrlingen, I was actually well-disposed to spend the afternoon in the vineyards with those people, if only because I want Lisi to come along socially and to be able to live comfortably in the circles she is to inhabit. And Lisi must have sensed that; because later she confessed to me that it makes her jealous how much people seem to like me, and she asked me if I was disappointed we weren't going to the vineyards. I said no, I wasn't. And that I took it as a compliment that she didn't think me too boring to be alone with for days and weeks on end. And then she answered, "Willi, you are frightfully boring, but you are so kind and so good to me. And you love me, I know. I even have it in writing. So I have no compunction about entertaining both of us. But the others—Witnowsky and Lenzdorf and their wives—are probably not very kind and certainly cannot ever love me. They are just boring. On the other hand, I suppose I mustn't deny people the chance to feast their eyes on you just because they can never take to me the way they take to you."*

*Truly, I think Lisi is far more interesting than Lenzdorf or Witznowsky (or, to put a fine point on it, almost anyone) could ever be. So it's nothing to me that we didn't spend the afternoon with them. But we won't be able to live forever in isolation.*

*Which reminds me of the original purpose of this communication: Regarding Herr Schleemann and the pianos, make any arrangements that suit your convenience. I hope that my father is a decent host to you.*

*Well, my very good friend, my wife is stirring, and it isn't even 9:40 a.m. And I have imposed upon you enough. Now I shall go and impose upon my wife!*

*Be well,*

*v. Boening*

*Pulow*

*August 23, 1897*

*Wilhelm,*

*I trust you are enjoying your honeymoon, and that your bride has proven everything you had hoped. We've come along well at Pulow as regards preparations for her arrival, and you may tell her that her pianos are here, along with Herr Schleemann and Baron Ehrlingen.*

*The weather has been very bad—nothing but rain—and the harvest will reflect it. It's good you've married money.*

*I enclose a letter to you from Prince Bismarck, as well as one to your wife from her piano teacher, Maestro L.—who seems to me overly generous with marital advice, considering he's working on his third wife.*

*Take care not to spoil that young woman, or she will be completely useless at Pulow.*

*Yours,*
*Father*

*Friedrichsruh*
*August 10, 1897*
*My friend, Boening!*
*I am afraid I missed your wedding announcement in the papers and am only glad my son happened to mention it to me. I offer sincere, if belated, congratulations and hope this small gift will please your bride.*

*You may be aware that I have energetically advocated for such unions. I hear the new Countess v. Boening is quite pretty, and gifted too. You must bring her to meet me soon. I look forward to hearing her play.*

*It goes without saying that I was sorry to hear of your resignation from the Foreign Office. Though not surprised. The principled men are disappearing. Eventually, only the sycophants will remain....*

*Yours,*
*v. Bismarck*

*Bad Ischl*
*August 8, 1897*
*My dearest Countess von Boening!*
*I've just gotten wind of your marriage from our young friend Artur Schnabel!*

*I wish you all the best in your new life. But he evidently wishes he had been born a few years earlier, and talks of nothing but his determination to go to Berlin. I wonder if that could actually have something to do with you.*

*At any rate, I hope you are not so madly in love as you were when I last heard you play. You will remember what I always say: A marriage for love is the end of the comedy of life. So you must keep it light, my dear.* Legere e animato! *But then, you must always think of that first passionate romance whenever you play* Un Sospiro, *because you captured the mood exactly.*

*Now, don't neglect your music for domestic duties! There is no art without life, but there is certainly no life without art!*

*Your old teacher,*

*Th. L.*

*Gritti Palace*
*Venice*
*August 30th, 1897*
*Liebste Klara!*
*I assume you will want to know all about my honeymoon, which is almost over. At least, I hope it is almost over, because if I don't get to a piano for some serious practice soon, I might forget altogether how to play. This morning, I awakened my husband and told him that I had been thinking I want to go home now; and he gave me the strangest look—a shaken look, actually, as if he had been hit in the head with something very bulky. Then it occurred to me that he thought, when I said "home," that I meant my father's house. So I immediately said, "I mean to Pulow, Willi. The pianos have arrived, and I can't be wandering and idle like this for much longer." Because it*

*really is unsettling, Klara. Not for him, because he wanders so happily anywhere and everywhere. All he needs is a sketchbook and pencils, and me on his arm. And if there is a museum or renaissance church within 50 meters, he is the happiest man on earth—surveying all the Venuses and naked personifications of Spring, and all the Salomes and Judiths, not to mention the ever abundant Holy Families, and Stations of the Cross.*

*This afternoon, when we were in St. Mark's Basilica, I told him that if one were to judge by his obsession with Italian painting, he should really have been a Catholic, that it would have been easier for me if he had been, and that I would have liked it far better than this so-called conversion to the Protestant cause. Whatever the contributions of Bach, I told him, I'm on the side of the Catholics. And he smiled and said, "Lisi, I won't be provoked by that remark, as it at least indicates that you are making some effort to take your baptism seriously. But as regards our ongoing discussion of art, I will say that if we could have stayed in Florence for just a little longer, and if I could have fed you just a little fatter with pasta and Florentine steak, you would be the spitting image of the* Venus of Urbino, *and I would love to paint you exactly that way." Of course, I told him that he must have noticed my bosom is at least twice the size of the* Venus of Urbino's, *if not three or four times. And that the difference can only exaggerate itself on canvas, so that the painting would actually be very vulgar. To which he answered, "Not if I could learn to paint like Titian."*

*But I would venture to say that Wilhelm is altogether too invested in the painting of breasts, and even insists that one can tell much about the technical mastery of an artist by the breasts of his naked ladies. Wilhelm says that breasts are quite individual, and though they can be always reduced to certain geometric shapes, they should probably never be perfectly matched. The other day, he indulged that sort of talk so freely that I finally said, "Willi, I wonder if you will be a faithful husband. You are much too interested in women's parts to be happy to live with just one exemplar of them." And then I told him on no uncertain terms that I couldn't be with him if I thought he had penetrated another woman—that I had to think away his love life before me, and less from moral considerations than because I am so put off by the underside of women's bodies. Then he said, "But I'm not." Nevertheless, he claimed that given all the other duties of a "useful" life, he didn't think there would be much time for* Seitensprünge, *especially if I were a "good wife" to him.*

*So you have a relatively complete picture of what we have been up to as regards tourism, and where it all leads ... In Rome, we hardly got out of our hotel bedroom where, as Willi says, we had our fill of bread and circuses. One wonders about this custom of honeymoons ... This "crazy carnival of love / this frenzied rapture" will so obviously have to end sometime ... And wouldn't* that *be the time for sightseeing—when "sobered, we yawn at each other?" But no! One is forced to cram all the pleasures and sensations of a lifetime into one's honeymoon ...*

*Anyway, we had both been to Rome before, and it turns out that beyond the Sistine Chapel, neither of us really thought much of it, other than the pleasure of wandering the hills and piazzas in the late afternoon. Even the Moses is a disappointment, since one must think away the horns.*

*Klara, the best parts of Italy are not the museums and churches, as so many insist, but the narrowest and sleepiest streets. The quietest corners of Siena and Ferrara, the deserted canals of Venice—these are* the impressions of Italy I think ultimately prove irrepressibly memorable. Yesterday, we took a gondola ride late at night, and it was just like the Venetian Boat Song in Book I of the Songs Without Words—all awkward tenderness and tipping to and fro and little splashes. And I think it's by far the most pleasurable thing we have experienced here. Because of the Italy of the indoors—that is, of the beaux arts—there is really so much that it actually hurts, because one cannot get at even one percent of it. But in the relatively silent moments outdoors (perhaps one or two voices break through the quiet alleyways on a sultry afternoon), one feels Italy.

It does make me a little sad to give up and go home, to start my life as a lady of the manor, when all magnificent things are waiting to be discovered. But I'm very nauseated the last few days, and threw up even before breakfast this morning, so you have some idea of what's coming, and the worst thing would be to make myself a burden while traveling. But we will see, because Willi is the designated tour guide. I promised to let him make all the decisions, if only he let me sleep in mornings; and he has not disturbed me once before 9:30 a.m.—not unless there was a train to be caught.

And, yes, I have heard from Papi, and it's a sore point, because Cousin Babette thinks that there must be some way we could set up household in the Kadettenweg, although she's not entirely sure how that would work and neither am I. Perhaps she thinks Papi should have smaller quarters now—or at least something closer to the city center—but she doesn't want to say it. At any rate, I cannot imagine my husband and my father in the same house. And yet, Willi would not really be there much at all—only once in a while. And it would be a comfort to my father if I were to be there somewhat regularly. At any rate, we *will be mainly resident at Pulow, because Willi has resigned from the Foreign Office—I hope not wholly because of his marriage to me.*

*I expect not, as he wasn't getting along very well there. He has been telling me things about the haphazard aggressiveness of current German diplomacy. Apparently, there is a coterie around the Kaiser, led by the ambassador in Vienna, that inveterate anti-semite, Count Eulenburg. These men have plans to remake the world in their image of German domination, and they are increasingly influential in decision making. They are a tight group, passionately in love with each other, and they share a sort of occult bond—meeting for secret ceremonies that are meant to seal their physical and spiritual unions.*

*For all their sexual eccentricities, many remain married. But Willi tells me they refer to intercourse with their wives as 'Schweinerei,' and that they have been known to put bowls of water in their marital bed to prevent their wives' advances. The upshot is that Willi is thoroughly disgusted, although he has refused to mention the anti-semitism—either because he accepts it, or because he wishes to avoid the subject with me. It's strange how one can be so intimate with one's spouse in some matters, and then live as complete strangers in others.*

*But Klara, my husband harbors an unshakeable conviction that while the things we do together when we are alone (things I cannot have imagined doing only a month ago, much less imagined liking to do) are holy script between men and women. But that if men do them with men, or women with women, they constitute abominations.*

*Well, I don't think I agree. If these physical acts are not acts of prostitution, then they are acts of love. And it seems to me that to denigrate the expression of physical love between any two people, regardless of sex, would be cruel.*

*Of course homosexuality is disgusting when proselytized by a po-
seur like Eulenburg, who, aside from his obsessive vanity and racism,
composes the most imbecilic drawing room music to be heard on our
side of the Rhine. But I would venture that people like Eulenburg only
lend homosexuality a bad name, in the very same way that some Jews
give Jewry a bad name.*

*Klara, I know things are difficult for you. And you are in my
thoughts.*

*Deine,*

*Lisi*

# CHAPTER XVI

WILHELM VON BOENING COULD NOT HAVE KNOWN but might have guessed the subject of conversation at cards in the Casino-Gesellschaft on the late afternoon of July 30th, as his train pulled out of the Anhalter train station in a southerly direction.

"So, Ehrlingen," Botho von Flenheim began, "You've been to Boening's wedding, have you? Then it was Boening all the time who was her lover. But what a con artist! And what a straight face he has!"

"I don't know what you're talking about, Flenheim. I highly doubt she had a lover. And now she is married, and to our friend Boening. So I hope she will no longer be the subject of this type of conversation."

"Well, if it wasn't Boening who was her lover, he should be finding out about it in a matter of a few hours." Flenheim teased.

The others at the table, all except Ehrlingen, laughed at this.

Then Axel von Arnhelm said, "He will be kept active tonight. They say the Jewesses can't get enough."

"Of what?" asked Ehrlingen.

"You know exactly what I am referring to."

Hennholz interjected, "Ehrlingen's right. She's a countess now, and Boening is a decent man, so all this talk is not in the best of taste. Every man has his weakness, and I have a feeling that Jewess is his. And Flenheim, if you are jealous and want a Jewess of your own, along with four million gold marks, I challenge you to find one. I think you may not be up to the task. You are not half as handsome or courtly as Boening. I know several *men* who would like to get into his trousers."

"But that's just it, Hennholz," Flenheim answered. "Boening would have been better off to have fucked one of the Kaiser's happy crew of homosexuals—a Kuno von Moltke or a Philipp zu Eulenburg—rather than a Jewess. I won't say that the girl is wholly unattractive—for a Jewess. But it would have got him farther at the Foreign Office. And let's face it: Sooner or later, it will all come home to roost with the Jews, and they will be sent away or destroyed. And then where will Boening be with his Jewish wife? And his children, who will have inherited the black stain. She may have made him a rich man, but he might as well hang himself ..."

And here Axel Arnhelm interposed, "Flenheim, that's all just empty political talk, about destroying the Jews. No one will ever have the courage to do it."

A man named Olmannsdorff, who had taken Boening's place at the card tables, observed, "In the end, there are only two ways we can possibly neutralize the Jewish menace: We can either destroy them or marry them. And in my humble opinion, the latter option is the far more pleasant one, and perhaps even the more economical one. Because it means we can save our bullets for the English."

Hennholz replied only, "Well, I think it is a very good thing when looks marry money."

"Really?" said Ehrlingen, "That's how you would put it? I might have put it differently. I would say it is a fine thing when form marries substance."

⸎

THE BOENINGS ARRIVED AT PULOW ON SEPTEMBER 14th, a warm and bright day. And their welcome was an auspicious one. The entire *Gutshaus* staff, as well as the estate workers and their families, had lined up to bow and kiss the hand of their new *gnädige* Frau Gräfin. Lisi was as much embarrassed as gratified by these provincial gestures of fealty; and it immediately struck her that managing the servants at Pulow would not at all be like managing the household staff at the villa in Lichterfelde West. These people would be far less efficient and far more obsequious.

Nor could the graceful villa in the Kadettenweg be in any way compared with the clumsy *Gutshaus*. Lisi was struck immediately by its awkward balcony and its muddy driveway, where fattened white geese roamed aimlessly on this late summer day. But on the other hand, the back lawns shimmered with wild violets and buttercups, and she could see behind them a leveled grass tennis court, and beyond that, gentle rolling fields and pastures, recently cut. The air smelled sweetly of hay. And when she entered the house, the effort that had been made for her welfare was immediately apparent, Helmuth von Boening pointing up all the newly installed comforts she might have overlooked, as well as remarking that "Your father, young lady, has sent a lot of music, and I have seen that it is organized alphabetically according to composer."

On one of the new Bechsteins, arranged facing one another in the salon, there was a note from dear Herr Schleemann, the piano technician, reading,

*Hochgeborene Gräfin von Boening!*
*I have spent two days at Pulow, in the presence of your father-in-law and Baron von Ehrlingen. I hope I have finished the pianos to your general expectations. There will be a good deal of tweaking, I am sure. I leave here a pictorial exemplar of the keyboard so that you may note those pitches which will need more voicing. Pay attention also, please, to the weighting of the keys, and be sure to let me know if there is something that disturbs you. In any case, I will be back in four weeks for tuning and adjustment and look forward, as ever, to hearing you play.*

*I harbor the fondest memories of you at the keyboard as a child and wish you all good things in the years ahead.*

*Your most devoted servant,*
*R.K. Schleemann*

It was an unexpected tone from a man under whose legs Lisi had crawled as a child—a man who had often promised to take her to the opera and then, in the same breath, threatened to leave her there. And Lisi, as she fingered the letter, remembered that once, when she was around nine-years old, Herr Schleemann had shouted at her. She had purposely scuttled a pencil onto the sound board so that he would have to open up the piano action one more time.

Now, it seemed Lisi Schwabacher had grown up and become a countess. And Herr Schleemann was to be her humble servant, trekking himself seven hours from Berlin to the wilds of Western Pomerania for the sake of her pianos, and subjecting himself to dinner and breakfast in the servants' hall.

Lisi hadn't much time to dwell on this, however, nor even to do so much as run her fingers over the keys of both pianos before Wilhelm solicitously took her by the arm and offered to show her to their bedroom upstairs.

"Bedroom, Willi? Are we not separate?"

"For dressing, but not for sleeping, Lisi. Did you want to be separate? I honestly never thought of it."

"I'm very sloppy, and you know I am up all night, and there will be books everywhere."

"But there is something you don't know about me."

"And what's that?"

"I sleep with my dogs."

"The dogs will share our bed?"

"Yes, so you see, your books are a trifle in comparison with two Weimaraners, who will push as close to us as possible."

"I hope they aren't jealous dogs."

"If they are, you may throw them out of bed."

So this, Lisi thought, was not anything like her parents' life. And it didn't seem very aristocratic, either, not to have separate sleeping arrangements, and to share the marriage bed with two hunting dogs. But when she saw the enormous and ornate pol-ished-walnut bed, and the rather cavernous room that housed it, she understood.

"Willi" she said, "You won't be able to find me in that bed."

"It's large, I know. But I am large, and frankly, at the time I bought it, I thought I would get a larger wife."

"I see."

"You think it's grotesque."

"It's certainly baroque. I've never seen so much *Schnitzerei*. Talk about sleeping amongst the angels! There must be thirty of them carved into the headboard! ... And we could house an entire pack of dogs in that bed."

"All the better. Dogs procreate as do people."

And then she laughed and fell backwards onto the bed and held out her arms to him and said, "I don't suppose it can be a bad thing to have the entire heavenly host watching over us as we sleep."

———

WILHELM AND ELISABETH VON BOENING HAD AR-rived home just in time for harvest celebrations. So that Lisi's initial introduction to Pomeranian rural life was one that highlighted all the charm of its customs. The Sunday of October 3rd was the official *Erntedank,* the harvest festival. It began with a gay procession that led from the village church to the front steps of the *Gutshaus.* There, the families of the estate employees gathered in a semi-circle, the *Inspektor* holding the harvest "crown," an arrangement of the grains that he presented to the lord of the manor. A solemn poem was recited by a young girl, the daughter of one of the estate farmers. "Look upon your harvest wreath, your lordship ... He is a good lord who also harvests his field; and he is indeed a poor lord who cannot bind to his field."

A hymn of thanks was sung by all the estate workers, after which there was a recitation of couplets for each of the members of the noble household. Graf Wilhelm was wished (to the amusement of the entire company) "a table laden with a well-fattened goose / a fine wine and a warm bed always." Graf Helmuth was wished "the peace of a full house / good health in old age," and the Gräfin Elisabeth "the pleasure of plenty / the sound of children's voices." After this ceremony there was considerable feasting, drinking, and dancing, with Lisi, the lady of the manor, dancing the first dance of the evening with the *Inspektor*.

Any fears Lisi had with regard to initiating good relations with the estate workers disappeared that evening, lost in the general spirit of jubilation. As she observed her husband drinking freely with his dependents, and yet preserving that necessary distance of *noblesse oblige,* Lisi even made up her mind that life at Pulow might actually be manageable. And if it were not, there would be Wilhelm to help her negotiate it.

It was lucky that her initial residence at Pulow could boast that happy note. Because the next several weeks passed mainly in a scramble of unpleasant tasks. First there was the absolute necessity of altering Lisi's clothes which, owing to a burgeoning pregnancy, were getting tighter by the day. Suzette, however, who had arrived shortly before her mistress, was unhappy at Pulow, where the low German dialect was completely inscrutable to her. The result was that the fittings took ever longer each day, owing to Suzette's many tears and lamentations; and Lisi had never had patience with fittings.

Then, there were menus to plan—a task which became a source of constant strain on the new Gräfin, not only because

*Mam'selle's* disposition was stubborn and taciturn, but also because Lisi had observed on the sixth or seventh night of her residence at Pulow that *Mam'selle* slept in the old Count's bedroom.

Indeed, the manor house cook was a thorn in Lisi's side, because food, though she ate little of it, was of huge importance to her, and the less it pleased her, the more it obsessed her. Added to the tensions of dealing with *Mam'selle's* wooden demeanor and peculiarly elevated status at Pulow, the natural constraints that country life lent to culinary ambition were very irritating to Lisi. Meals at Pulow were not like meals in the Kadettenweg; for practically everything consumed at Pulow was made from scratch—either with raw, seasonal foodstuffs, or with things grown and preserved there. If *Mam'selle* indulged any creative impulses at all, they were in the direction of feeding many mouths with limited resources.

Aside from supervising the planning of meals, the *Gutsfrau* of an estate such as Pulow had a number of responsibilities: She was expected to pay bills, take inventories of household items, make necessary household purchases, and tend to sick estate dependents. She tended the vegetable and fruit gardens, was expected to husband the small animals, and oversaw the planting of formal gardens. She was furthermore to oversee the servants in their household chores—most especially, the dreaded "washing day"—a day, once every month, devoted to the strenuous tasks of washing and ironing all the manor house clothes and linens.

From watching her mother in the small garden in Lichterfelde West, Lisi had some familiarity with the cultivation of ornamental flowers, as well as herbs and vegetables. But she had never been exposed to chickens and geese. Nor had she ever done washing, not to speak of providing medical attention to souls who lived in very primitive conditions.

Finally, the *Gutsfrau* was the patroness of the village school, which meant meetings with the pastor and the teacher, two people whose narrowness of vision was apparent to Lisi within minutes of introduction, and who made no pretense of considering her presence anything more than purely decorative.

But not even the worst of her responsibilities could be compared, in its power to elicit discomfort, to the riding lessons which—Helmuth von Boening having procured a gentle mare and a side saddle—began her first week at Pulow. Every day of lessons, Elisabeth endured at least one tumble from the horse, and at one point Wilhelm became irate, accusing her of purposely leaping from the animal.

Thankfully (or at least thankfully in *her* mind), Lisi had a short episode of bleeding at the end of her first month at Pulow. Her pregnancy and its sudden vulnerability having been confirmed by the local Doctor Hasslinger, the Boening men were forced to suspend the riding lessons.

"Look here, Wilhelm," Helmuth said one brisk day in late October during an early morning ride with his son. "You have quite a useless young woman there. If you had wanted a concert pianist at Pulow, you could have hired one a few nights a year; but you would have needed a decent wife."

"I like my wife quite well, thank you."

"She can't look at a blood sausage without retching and running away."

"She's expecting, *Vater*. That sort of sickness will be over within a few weeks."

"I fear she will never learn to ride, and she is not firm with the servants. I've never heard so many pleases and thank yous to servants."

"Well then, she won't learn to ride, and I will speak to her about the servants."

"And there is something else."

"Yes, *Vater?*"

"She has no respect for the pastor. Last Sunday, she smirked through the entire sermon."

"She thinks he's a fool."

"You make sure to tell her he is not."

"*Vater*, with all due respect, Lisi cannot be told things like that. It's not in her to be instructed in things like this. She will have to find her own way through Pulow, the same way she finds her own way through a new piece of music."

"Well, *mein Sohn*, I see she has you all wrapped up in her Jewish sophistry. While you are married to her, you had better watch that you remain a man and a Christian."

———

THAT NIGHT, AS HE PREPARED FOR BED, WILHELM resolved to broach with Lisi at least the subject of the servants. But he found himself asking her instead what she thought of going to Friedrichsruh the following week.

Lisi, who was reading, looked over her glasses, and closed the book on her index finger. "To Prince Bismarck? Next week? No, I truly don't want to."

"I think he would like to meet you. He is anxious to hear you play."

"But that's just what I cannot do right now."

"Lisi, don't be ridiculous. You play beautifully. You played so very beautifully this evening."

"What do you know about it? You know nothing about it, Willi. I haven't practiced in months. I can't cobble together a half hour around here to even think about music!"

"Do you really feel so burdened here at Pulow?"

"Let's put it this way: I am beginning to understand how a woman might be very happy living in a polygamous union. So long as she's the head wife, of course."

Willhelm smiled. "I'm glad to hear you are losing your aversion to sharing your husband. But seriously, Lisi, what if you had nothing to do but practice for a week?"

"For a month, you mean. Or for three months."

Wilhelm smiled again. "Then we will go next month! Because Lisi, if you can just be firmer with the servants, you won't need to expend so much energy to see that things run smoothly around here."

"What does that mean?"

"You are too solicitous, my love."

"Because I don't bark at them? Because I say '*bitte*' and '*danke*' and treat them like human beings? After all, Willi, they are barely paid."

Wilhelm frowned. "Lisi, people here in the country are very simple. They understand the order of things only if it's a clear-cut order."

"I see. And Willi, will you do me the favor of explaining to me the order of things? Because I'm not sure I know what it is. But certainly *you* know what it is, because you were born to rule. You think people owe you unfaltering allegiance merely because you exist."

Wilhelm felt his anger rise at this. "Lisi, I know my duty as well as any other man. And as my wife, you should know yours. Now, if you cannot ..." he paused, "If you are unwilling to do your duty, even in these very small things, I wonder how we will live together happily."

"Unfortunately, Willi, the matter of how I treat people of the lower classes is not a small one to me. I realize, of course, that this makes me a problem at Pulow. But I cannot help it. And I will tell you something else, something you are not going to like. You are under a sad illusion if you think that in making Elisabeth Schwabacher into the Countess von Boening, you have brought me from the darkness into the light."

Now Wilhelm was livid, and it took all his self-control to reply as deliberately as he could muster, "I was all set to make love to you, Lisi, but I've lost my appetite for it, so I will say good night."

His hand was on the door handle when he heard his wife inhale a sob, and so he stopped and said with only the slightest impatience in his voice, "Why do you cry, Lisi, when you behave in such a vile way?"

"I was thinking that if you asked me to walk over hot coals for just one kiss from you, I would do it. I would do it ten times over. And that's why I am in this godforsaken place where I am completely at a loss."

Wilhelm walked back to the very baroque, polished-walnut bed and lay down with his wife to comfort her.

# CHAPTER XVII

IN THE LAST WEEK OF OCTOBER, 1897, LISI HAD A
letter from her father suggesting she come to Berlin for a much
anticipated concert of the Venezuelan virtuoso, Teresa Carreño,
who was to play with the Philharmonic on November 6th. The
"Valkyrie of the keyboard," as Carreño was known to the music
world, would perform three *concerti*: the *Emperor*, of Beethoven,
the *Capriccio Brilliante* of Mendelssohn, and McDowell's *Second
Concerto*. Naturally, Lisi resolved not to let this cup pass, and
not least because if she was to meet Bismarck and play for him,
she had to find a few days to devote to practice. And what better way to assure that than going to visit her father, since life
at Pulow was hardly conducive to any prolonged concentration
on music.

Though Wilhelm was manifestly unenthusiastic about her
leaving, and her father-in-law openly scowled, Lisi obtained their
good will by promising to remain in Berlin for only three days
and to shop for Christmas gifts while there. But once ensconced

in the villa in Lichterfelde West, Lisi prolonged her visit. Wilhelm received the following letter on November 10th:

*Lieber Willi,*

*Don't be angry with me, but I will stay in Berlin a while. My father is being all kindness and sweetness, and we are really as we were before, which I cannot resist. He even came home early today, just to hear me practice. Last night we had a quiet evening at home and read through three of the Beethoven cello sonatas. And then we had a wonderful talk. He says he will take me to the theater; although I wonder if we will have time for that. The fact is, he has accepted engagements for us at the Fürstenbergs' and the Israels', and to Therese Simon-Sonneman's this week, added to which he has promised he will also invite the Lilienbergs, Ehrlingen, and Wittenbach, as well as cousin Babette for a music evening.*

*By the way, he insists that I see a specialist just in case there is anything to be known. But I don't want you to worry. I haven't had any more bleeding, so I don't believe there is any cause for concern.*

*Willi, I hope you will like me plump as well as you like me slender, because I am gaining weight every day, though I'm really trying not to and eating next to nothing.*

*La Carreño was magnificent. Nobody can play a faster scale, and I despair to ever play as well as she does, because everything that should be fast in Beethoven is faster than one would ever think possible, like a gale ripping through the sails of a ship, and yet so cleanly expressive, the important things salient, like hearing the individual drops of rain in the middle of the storm. And then, how she can allow herself the great expanse, and we breathe with her into a* ritardando, *all anticipation! You cannot imagine it! It's very discouraging to me, but wonderful, nonetheless, to listen to. Perhaps exactly what you feel when looking at a Titian …*

*But you probably don't want to hear about the passionate* La Carreño, *except that I must mention that we had Sunday afternoon dinner at the Musik-Wolffs with her. And though she talks of nothing but the importance of sacrificing oneself for love (not art!), she has already rid herself of three husbands, and Luise Wolff says she even gave away her first born. So I expect she will not have been as patient and well-behaved a wife as I promise to be.*

*Which leads me to the greetings sent to you by both Hermann and Luise Wolff, who told me they think you are very handsome and charming. To which I answered, "Handsome, always, and charming, perhaps intermittently." I shouldn't have said that. It just came out, I suppose. But you yourself know that you are hardly charming. Rather, you are irresistibly attractive—and in a way I could easily come to resent, because I know that I can never be as attractive as you are, even when you are not trying to be attractive at all. And I truly wonder that everyone is so prepared to like you from the start. How is it you never manage to turn people away? And even when they really should have their grievances against you?*

*And now to Christmas (You see, I haven't forgotten about that): I have picked up some cookbooks for* Mam'selle. *Perhaps she won't appreciate receiving them; but really Wilhelm, there must be something besides bacon, boiled beef, and smoked goose at Pulow. And let's face it: she can't pull together a sauce of any refinement. Anyway, I am watching Frau Briess here and learning a little something about French sauces; and I will stand with* Mam'selle *in the kitchen at Pulow, and will advise if need be. I've decided also to show* Mam'selle *how to prepare some warm Austrian desserts.*

*Oh, but naturally, I found nice leather gloves for her and a very fine wool scarf; so the books aren't really an official Christmas present, but rather only a vocational offering.*

*Incidentally, for the pastor, I thought a first-flush black tea, because any worthwhile book would be totally lost on him.*

*But Willi, please don't rush me back to Pulow, because I really must practice, and if the truth be known, would be perfectly content to stay here indefinitely, if only I could hold you at night.*

*Ewig Deine,*

*Lisi*

*P.S. Suzette refuses to return to Pulow, so I must find a new maid. That may take a few days, also.*

It perhaps need not be said that aside from the reference to warm Austrian desserts, there was hardly a line of this letter that did not either worry Wilhelm or aggravate him. His first thought upon finishing it was not flattering to him. It involved the fear that Lisi was all too quickly resuming life in the social circles that characterized her days as an unmarried Jewess, circles Wilhelm considered completely inappropriate to the wife of a *Junker*. For every home she mentioned visiting was a Jewish home and, with the exception of the Musik-Wolffs', one distinguished by unreserved opulence.

Indeed, Wilhelm frankly didn't know which was the most repugnant to him—the idea of his wife being received by the department store Israels, by Therese Simon-Sonnemann, owner and publisher of the liberal *Frankfürter Zeiting*, or by Frau Aniela Fürstenberg who, during her first marriage, had been the reputed mistress of perhaps a half-dozen noblemen of Wilhelm's acquaintance before finally settling down with the banker Carl Fürstenberg. Granted that all three hostesses were reputed to be lively, intelligent, and very attractive, and there would likely be a few aristocrats, as well businessmen and artists, at their gatherings. But these ladies were, finally, Jewesses and not even baptized!

But even more distasteful to him than the thought of Lisi consorting in these fashionable Jewish homes was the notion that she should be seen at the theater, as well as in other public places (perhaps even restaurants!) in the company of Jews who didn't even have great wealth to recommend them: Jews like the Musik-Wolffs or the Lilienbergs. And this, before she had a proper introduction to court society as the Countess von Boening!

As was typical of him, Wilhelm refrained from rushing off to write while in an unsettled state. Rather, he waited a day to calm down before answering.

*Pulow*
*November 11, 1897*
*Lisi, my love!*
*I am to some extent gratified that you have reconciled so nicely with your father, though you should remember that you have a husband too, who might be very annoyed with you that you have left him indefinitely, and under the pretext of going away for a mere three days. There is no reason in the world you would need to live with your father in order to be able to practice. You have two Bechsteins at Pulow that are brand new, were very expensive, and are meant to be played. And speaking of expense, I will begin this letter exactly in your spirit by getting at least one or two unwelcome notices out of the way: Lisi, we at Pulow are not rich Jews; and the very idea that the pastor*

*should be presented at Christmas with a first-flush Himalayan black tea—of which any amount to speak of would probably cost what would be very near half a month's salary for him—is preposterous. Buy him a book, even if you think it too intelligent for him.*

*I'm sorry you are unsatisfied with the cooking at Pulow. My father, however, is very satisfied, and though I have no objection to an attempt to expand Mam'selle's repertoire, within reason and without offense to her, I honestly doubt that your father-in-law will relish French sauces any more often than very occasionally. Remember, please, that he has a heart condition.*

*Lisi, it truly alarms me when you claim you are not eating anything in your father's house, though you insist the food is so superior. Should it not be superfluous, as well as maddening, to have to tell one's wife that pregnant women are supposed to gain weight?*

*I suppose you have already seen Wittenbach. But when you see him again, please give him my and your father-in-law's regards.*

*Finally, Lisi, if you truly wish to embrace me at night, you will come home, and soon.*

*Ewig Dein,*
*W.*


*November 13, 1897*
*Willi,*
*I didn't say "Lieber Willi" in my salutation, because I didn't like your letter. You are impatient with me, but I have to practice if I am to play for Prince Bismarck. And I've decided to play the "Waldstein" Sonata, because everyone tells me the Prince's wife loved Beethoven.*

*In the Kadettenweg, I have no responsibilities. Did you think you have a wife who can just get up and play? Not even La Carreño can*

*do that, as witnessed by the disappearance of three husbands and who
knows how many lovers! Perhaps you are thinking that Ehrlingen can
just get up and play. And it's true, he can. But I will remind you that
he has the wrong equipment to bear your children!*

*I am trying to please you. Really I am. And I desperately miss holding
you. But I won't leave here until I can perform the "Waldstein" Sonata.*

*Lisi*

*Gross-Lichterfelde*
*November 14, 1897*
*Liebe Klara!*

*You must think me either dead or the rudest cousin in the world for
not replying to you in so many weeks, but it was enough to write
Onkel Sigi and Tante Anna a proper thank-you note for the lovely
Herend bowl. I couldn't bear to write to you, also. At least not until
now, when I'm back in Berlin and in Papi's house for a few weeks.*

*First off, I didn't know for a long while what would become of my
pregnancy, as I had bouts of bleeding, and you know exactly what I
was thinking—namely, that I would be punished for ending the first
pregnancy. But the bleeding seems to be over now, and the pregnancy
is holding. So if I am to be punished, it will be later on or in some
other way.*

*Secondly, I have scarcely been able to write anyone from Pulow.
It's hard to write from a place one wants to escape, and I wonder
whether I will ever feel at home there. Perhaps you will get a sense of
my desperation if I tell you that at breakfast early this fall, Vietzke,
the butler, came in with the mail and said to my husband, "Herr
Graf, there is a letter, from Vienna addressed to the Wohlgeborene
Gräfin. It is from a Fräulein Turner. I have not yet opened it. Shall*

*I?" (Yes, Klara, the servants here open the post before they lay it on the breakfast table. It goes without saying that they also read it and very often comment on it!)*

*Well, my reply to Vietzke was to tell him to hand the letter to me, upon which he gave me a doubtful look and turned immediately back to my husband.*

*"The letter," Wilhelm declared, "is improperly addressed, Vietzke. It is to be returned unopened!"*

*As you probably know, Klara, Frl. Turner is the American piano student for whom my mother paid two years' tuition last summer. So naturally I wanted to read her letter. And just as naturally, I was fully sympathetic to the poor girl's confusion with the somewhat arcane customs of German styles. I explained to my husband that it might be very easy for a young American to confuse* Wohlgeboren *with* Hochwohlgeboren, *or even* Hochgeboren.

*But Willi would have none of it. I pleaded a second and third time that this was undoubtedly a letter of thanks for my family's support of the girl's music study, and that she would be mortified were the letter returned as "improperly addressed." And then he shouted at me! Shouted! "The letter will be returned unopened. And that is the end of it, Lisi!"*

*And so now you know what my husband thinks of his "Wohlgeborene" bourgeois wife, whose honor he must be very anxious to dignify; after all, we can't have a Jewess mistaken for a Jewess, when, in fact, she is a countess!*

*Klara, in all the years of my childhood, my father never once raised his voice to me. And this particular incident was in company! In fact, we were at the time billeting an officer on maneuvers. It was so humiliating! I was beside myself for hours and unable to muster a coherent sentence for at least half a day. Of course, Willi immediately felt guilty and tried to make it up to me. But that was even more humiliating. Because as I ascended the stairs to our bedroom in a state of perturbation, he stopped me within earshot of the officer and said, "Lisi, my love, I must go to Greifswald tomorrow and will be staying overnight. I wondered if you would come with me. It's early in our marriage to have to spend the night apart, don't you think?"*

*Truly, I love my husband, the very sight of whom makes me weak in the knees, and who is anxious to see me made happy. But his notion of my happiness revolves always on the axis of his own comfort and dignity.*

*Then there is my father-in-law—the true master of Pulow. He stares me down at dinner every night with his cold blue eyes, as if he cannot believe that his only son would be so imprudent as to bring the likes of a Lisi Schwabacher into the family. And really, Graf Helmuth von Boening is absolutely right. I don't belong in the country. I have nothing to lend it, and it has nothing to lend me.*

*I don't have half the comforts at Pulow that I have in Berlin—no electric light, nor inside running water (unless you count the pump in the kitchen). And where heating is concerned, the halls of the manor house were so bitterly cold on the fifteenth of October that I fear what they will be like in February.*

*And as for the* Stille Ort, *where I have come to be so fond of reading since returning home to Berlin (I know I'm terribly spoiled): well, there is a dignified little room at the end of the second floor hallway, which Wilhelm has painted very sweetly in bucolic themes. It features a rather tall platform with a commode chair shaped very much like a throne. Naturally, the servants always make sure to keep a large jug of water ready, as well as a hand basin and soap. But you* cannot imagine how awfully frigid that little place is. And when I complained (though I don't know what good I expected that would do!), my husband didn't even laugh at me. He tapped me on the chin, smiled, and suggested I could be kept warmer if we went together after breakfast each morning to the one on the first floor, where there are two seats, and we could even share the newspaper. Somehow, I didn't imagine marriage would mean that sort of togetherness!

But Klara, I have married six hundred fifty hectares of mud and sand, along with a village of fools!

You cannot imagine the willful ignorance of so many of our peasants—and especially the women among them, who typically do not marry until a baby is about to burst forth from their womb, and then raise five or six children in their dark, one-room cottages, where the little ones have one narrow bed piled high with an enormous feather duvet that is guaranteed to smother them, even in winter. It is a wonder that the infants survive, as they are left to melt in these beds day in and day out, are never separated from a sibling who is sick, and are mostly never brought into the open air. And indeed, many don't survive and not just because of those beds. Four weeks into my tenure at Pulow, I heard of a three-year-old girl on a nearby estate who died in circumstances that were perfectly avoidable—having suffocated from smoke inhalation after her mother lit a fire, locked her in the house, and went to work. This, though there is an older woman in the village whose job it is to watch small children while their parents are away.

You will be interested to know that although it is incumbent on the Gutsfrau to call on anyone who is sick, nobody takes seriously any medical advice, even when the local doctor is called in. And though there is a village school, and everyone is nominally literate, nobody would think of using a prescription according to directions. Rather, medicines tend to be taken all at once, or thrown out.

Perhaps it goes without saying there is nobody to talk to in the country, unless one counts cow dung and recipes for stewed bacon among subjects of vital interest. (Incidentally, I am expected, when I visit the cottages, to always taste what is on the fire. And that means considerable spoonfuls of stewed bacon on the days that Willi doesn't rescue me and sample them himself.) In any case, no one at Pulow has any conversation whatsoever that would inspire me. Least of all the people with whom I am expected to have conversations—for example, the Inspektor's wife or my father-in-law or the pastor or the schoolmaster.

Of the latter two, I can only say that the pastor—a tall, angular type with the longest chin and fleshiest eye bags I have ever seen on a middle-aged man—is a blithering idiot. His entire powers of exegesis consist of the repetition—always three times, always verbatim, and always in a booming voice—of favored passages from the New Testament. Every Sunday at church service, I am reminded of Heine's quip that if the Protestant Church didn't have an organ, it would be of no interest at all. And yet my husband never tires of reminding me that I need to be a better Christian. But how, being subject to those interminable hours in the damned church!

So much for the pastor. Now to the schoolteacher: a short, chubby young blond man, who looks barely older than twenty and seems always to be on the verge of bursting out of his jacket and sleeves. The last time I stopped by the school, an arithmetic lesson was in progress. Not to be embarrassed by his pupils' poor showing, he stopped the lesson and suggested that the children sing for me. Of the singing, I can only make one comment: that the children are in dire need of a decent music teacher—a post I intend to take up immediately when I return. (So at least I may prove good for something!)

All of which leaves me in the position, every day, of longing for the coming of evening and the going to bed with my husband. I tell you, Klara, if it weren't for the pleasures of the marriage bed, I would have left Pulow no more than three days after my arrival!

I haven't told Papi that I am unhappy in the country, because I know he would fear that I am unhappy with my husband, which I am not. So I have simply said that I need time to myself to practice, as Wilhelm will take me to meet Prince Bismarck next month. And I told Papi also that I was preparing a transcription from organ to piano for my father-in-law's seventieth birthday. Because I have nothing otherwise to give him that he would value. And he seems to love Bach so. Klara, you cannot imagine how simply the old Count lives. Aside from the fact that the cook shares his bed, he is an extremely pious man. Every meal at Pulow is served up with a prayer of thanks im Namen Jesu, though few of our meals are, in culinary terms, worthy of any such high praise.

But as regards Papi, I don't think he cares why I am here. He is just delighted I am, and it's so much like it was before that a great burden has been lifted from me. And giving Papi some much needed attention is worth even risking the anger of my husband, who really did expect me back in only a few days.

Because, in the end, Papi misses Mami desperately. And I have to admit that I become angrier with Mami by the day for robbing Papi of her presence at the end of her life—which I think she did out of sheer pride, rather than retreating, as I had once surmised, from frustration with him. And those days and months when he could have shared the end of her life, as I did, will always be missing, and *only because she didn't want a man to see her when she wasn't at her best.*

*I think about you constantly, especially now that I have so little female company. Women need each other desperately, don't you think?*

*Deine,*

*Lisi*

*November 15, 1897*

*Ehrlingen,*

*Wondering whether you wouldn't mind escorting my wife once in a while—anywhere, it doesn't really matter where to. Perhaps to the theater, or to the Philharmonic. Just so she isn't always seen with her father and the Wolffs, or other Jews.*

*She seems to have left me, and I'm not sure for how long.*

*v. Boening*

*Berlin*

*November 19, 1897*

*Boening,*

*I saw your wife at the Countess Kalckreuth's a few nights ago. She played some Bach she has transcribed for your father's upcoming birthday (the C minor Organ Passacaglia), along with the first movement of the "Waldstein" Sonata. But she didn't stay long. I'm afraid I won't be taking her anywhere, but you needn't fear her being seen in the streets in the company of Jews. At this point in time, she is doing nothing but practicing, and until all hours of the night, Schwabacher tells me. And when she is not practicing, she is studying the "Waldstein" score and working on her transcription. To be honest, Schwabacher is hard put to get her balanced in the last few days. He has invited*

*Wittenbach and me for dinner and piano quartets tomorrow, and that will undoubtedly help. She apparently is too preoccupied to eat. But she was quite charming at Gräfin Kalckreuth's; that is, in the blunt and willful way that only your wife can be charming.*

*Boening, you should have known your wife would find her way back to the villa in Lichterfelde West. I wonder whether you have any idea how big, how demanding her talent is. Did you think it could be stored in the closet like an ermine cloak—to be brought out as needed for parades before high society? Wittenbach would have been a better husband for her, and he knows it. I wouldn't say he is exactly resentful, but certainly very conscious of a superiority of claim. And he even said it to me the other night—that your seduction of the girl robbed her of any real choice in the matter of marriage.*

*Other than coming to Berlin and physically forcing her home, I don't see that you have a choice but to wait patiently until she has prepared the "Waldstein" Sonata for Prince Bismarck. She tells me you gave her a month. And that when she is prepared, she intends to return to Pulow.*

*If you need a distraction, there will be a hunting party at Eichenhohl, Klaus von Lehnau's estate in Brandenburg, from the first to the fifth of December. Several of our fellows from the Gardes du Corps are coming. I am not too sure of the complete cast of characters (which will probably number around twenty-five). And I must warn you that it all may get somewhat eccentric—in the way things have of getting eccentric nowadays. But there will certainly be a lot of good cards. Why don't you join us? You are rich enough now to let a little real money fly at the card table. And it can't hurt, under the circumstances, to keep your old comrades well-disposed toward you.*

*As ever,*

*v. Ehrlingen*

*Berlin*

*November 23, 1897*

*Boening,*

*I realize it is absolutely none of my business, but I do wonder why you haven't joined your wife in the city for at least a few days during these past weeks. It cannot have been a surprise to you that she would strain at the leash of country life. After all, she has a great gift and one for which an audience is necessary. At any rate, I won't believe that you have argued so early into marriage. At least, I didn't read that in Lisi's face, and my young cousin's face is eminently readable.*

*But in case you are inclined to stay away from the Kadettenweg, I thought I would assure you that Magnus Schwabacher has a way of making himself very small when necessary. His is the loveliest of any home in Berlin, and there is no reason, in my opinion, why the Count, as well as the Countess von Boening, should not take advantage of it occasionally.*

*Your devoted friend,*

*Babette M. v. Kalckreuth.*


*Pulow*

*November 25, 1897*

*My dear Gräfin v. Kalckreuth!*

*I fear you won't be satisfied with my answer to your letter. My wife wasn't at Pulow a full eight weeks before she absconded to her father's house. She has now been gone nearly a month! Am I really expected to chase her down there? What will people think?*

*Not that I care if people talk; they will always talk when a poor* Junker *marries a rich Jewess. But I do care what they say, and I fear right now that none of what they would have to say puts me in a good light, though I have done everything I possibly could to provide a welcoming home for the woman I have chosen to spend my life with.*

*Your young cousin has a way of continually pulling out the rug from under my feet. And there must be an end to it if we are to live together at all successfully as man and wife. And yet, I am told (and not only by you, Countess Kalckreuth, by others too!) that I must have forbearance, because she is an artist!*

*Well, I have no intention of offering myself up to Lisi's artistic ambitions. You, of all people, know that I have my own artistic aspirations, but I wouldn't think to make my spouse suffer for them. Because I am a nobleman and a husband foremost, and any other ambition must be tertiary.*

*And so, my esteemed Gräfin Kalckreuth, if you have any influence with Lisi, you might use it to explain the rules by which married people in our sphere of life are expected to live.*

*Yours,*
*Wilhelm v. B.*

*Pulow*
*November 26, 1897*
*Gräfin Boening,*
*Because you are so stubborn and refuse to come home to me, and leave me to sleep alone on your side of the bed, I will spend the first week of December at a hunting party in Brandenburg. May any sins I commit there be upon your head! I have postponed our trip to Friedrichsruh until the third week of the month but expect you home when I return on December fifth. And if you are not home, I will start throwing your belongings out, beginning with your shoes.*

*I include here a letter from the neighbor to which she will require a reply. She has been kind enough to invite you to a ladies' gathering on the sixth. I think it would behoove you to go. You cannot stay in Berlin forever and will want some society here in the country.*

*W.*

*P.S. I've forgotten what you look like and so am consulting my sketches.*

*November 28, 1897*

*Graf Boening,*

*May I ask, please, how it is that you and your father think you can send me open correspondence from third parties? If I change one thing at Pulow as* Gutsfrau, *it will be the vile custom of having servants open the mail!*

*And speaking of open correspondence, my cousin Babette came today to show me your letter to her, in which you complain that I am not pleasing you. When all I do is done to please you, Willi!*

*My love, will it appease you if I tell you that you may very soon "unloose my chain, and take me into your lap again?"*

*When I return, and I will be home by the fifth, I will do every-thing you wish, including attending what promises to be a very boring luncheon at the neighbor's.*

*And I will do all the other things that you like, just as you like them. (I will be your slave!)*

*But why can you not leave my mail alone?*

*And Willi, why do you care what people think, when people will always think the worst anyway? And let them; because it means they fear that* our *lives are more interesting than theirs.*

*But with regard to your consulting your sketches to remind you of what I look like: You needn't, Willi! From the neck up and from the waist downward, you may imagine me as you imagined me in Florence: as the Venus of Urbino. But in that space of canvas in between, you will have to forget me altogether; I am afraid I am looking rather vulgar.*

*L.*

# CHAPTER XVIII

COUNT WILHELM VON BOENING ARRIVED HOME, on the evening of December 5$^{th}$, 1897, in roughened shape. He was half-drunk. That is, three and a half days of wine and spirits had settled on him like an advective cloud of gas, dimming his sensibilities and agitating his nerves. The party at Eichenhohl—involving twenty-six guests, all of them present or retired officers in Boening's regiment, the elite *Gardes du Corps*—was a driving hunt. And Boening had bagged a fourteen-point trophy—an impressive kill. As the carriage rounded the battered mud driveway and pulled up to the Pulow estate manor house, the pungent smell of animal blood still stuck in Boening's nostrils. The sound of horns, gunshot, and deep-throated cheers still rang in his ears. He was ever so slightly sick to his stomach. And when he attempted to close his eyes, the inside of his lids kept registering a line of boar and deer carcasses, and he felt a muted pain at the crown of his head.

Indeed, as Boening neared home on icy dirt roads, he had re-viewed the events of the previous few days with trenchant regret: There had been a lot of card play. Ehrlingen was right when he predicted that. And though it had amused Ehrlingen to no end that Boening won a pot of cash simply by "letting money fly," that money, Wilhelm ruminated now, could have easily flown away forever. Of course, he laughed with the others when they joked that having married a Jewess, Boening had suddenly procured the Jewish knack for spinning money out of the air, and also for tak-ing it from innocent Christians. Yes, Hennholz said, money now streams in Boening's direction. Hopefully Boening will keep his wife, since she seems to be magic where money is concerned. And at this, the ever good-natured Boening laughed with Hennholz and the others, assuring them all that his wife was worth keeping even aside from the pile of money she brought into the marriage.

But at this point, he also reminded his friends that the real money he made off them had not turned on his Jewess wife, nor on his curious new-found luck at cards, but rather on his exem-plary horsemanship. Namely, riding that course bareback, with-out a bridle, and, need he mention, without a stitch of clothes on. He even thought to himself, as he laughed with his friends, "I shall buy my wife a string of pearls for Christmas, because I won my bet and almost dead drunk too."

Beyond the cards and the hunting and the riding naked, there were other things etched in Wilhelm's memory of the house par-ty. Absurd, farcical things, such as the two men who danced on the tables in tutus on Friday night. Disgusting things, such as the grotesque makeup Lehnau wore to dinner on Saturday, his lips red like raspberries, his eyelids blue, as he toasted his "dear" comrades, and kissed each one of them on the mouth. "Everyone will have something to his taste, tonight, my darlings," Lehnau had said at Saturday dinner. "For the men who insist upon it, we have women! And for the others, we have men!" And everyone laughed, because the champagne was flowing. Every officer could take home a trophy and even have his chance at a whore or two.

But while the women brought for the pleasure of the *Gardes du Corps* officers really *were* prostitutes, the same cannot be said of the men. Some were enlisted men, but some were mere boys, and a few of these looked to be innocents lured under false pretenses from the Eichenhohl manor village.

And here, as he descended from the carriage, and received Vietzke's welcoming words ("Herr Graf, the countess has arrived from Berlin, and may I say, looking very healthy!"), Boening stopped his thoughts forcibly.

It was nearly nine thirty p.m., and dinner had long since been served. Count Helmuth von Boening was in the study, sitting in his favorite fraying armchair among the many trophies on the wall. He was looking over the latest agricultural science journal. The folded pages of the *Kreuzzeitung* newspaper lay untouched at his feet, a glass of vodka on the small round table beside him.

As Wilhelm peeked in, his father looked up, and the elder's thin lips tensed into a half-smile under his mustache. Within a split second, they released to their former dour position, however, and he looked back at the journal, all the while saying to Wilhelm that he should know that his wife is back, and looking nicely filled out.

And then he picked up the glass of vodka and sipped, dropped the journal on his lap, and looked directly at his son with his piercing blue eyes.

"You know," he said with deliberation, "It occurs to me that my daughter-in-law is far more entertaining than my son—not to mention that she is more than charming looking, actually quite pretty, when one looks at her for long enough.

"And I think now that I actually don't mind you married a Jewess ... if only she could be more useful in the sort of way that good German wives are useful. However, she eats so little; it will be a wonder if she brings a fully formed child into the world.

"By the way, *you* look tonight like something the cat dragged in!"

Wilhelm nodded and answered, "Yes, *Vater*. I think I'm suffering from *crise de foie*, as the French would put it."

"So the hunting party degenerated into a bacchanal?"

Wilhelm, who was not feeling very tactful, replied, "Even worse, *Vater*, because there was more buggering than one could shake a stick at, and more men who wanted to bugger than men who didn't. It's an epidemic, and the entire regiment is down with it."

His father seemed unprovoked by this comment and merely looked at him and said quietly, "Well, it seems to me you have always had something of a fixation where the subject of buggering is concerned. And though I must allow that it does tend to undercut discipline in an army, if one must fear for one's nation, it's the Kaiser who's at fault, and not the buggering. It's the Kaiser who sets the tone! Maybe he's an effeminate; I don't know. He's fathered several children. But mainly, he's an ass. In any case, you have a very charming young wife upstairs, and she is waiting for you, so I suggest you go to her."

Having thus been dismissed with a wave of his father's hand, Wilhelm climbed the stairs, his legs heavy with exhaustion, but his arms and torso beginning somehow to prickle in anticipation of a return to wakefulness. When he entered his bedroom with the great polished-walnut bed, he noticed immediately that it was turned down enticingly, the sheets and duvet cover made glistening white on washing day. And for the first time in four days there was something that relaxed in him, and he felt a nearly irresistible impulse to reach out for those bedclothes and wrap himself in them. And then he heard his wife in her bath. And, listening to the sound of splashing water, he thought that the way Lisi had, when in her bath, of clearing her throat and then sighing was always so very soothing to him.

He took off his jacket and stood aimlessly a moment before his eye caught an open band of music on the bed. He walked over to the bed and picked it up, fingering back through the leaves until he came to the title page of the "Waldstein" Sonata. Wilhelm was a weak reader of music; but he was able still to muse the markings she had made everywhere in the score. There was not one measure unmarked. Indeed, he thought, she has burnt a hole in the music with her markings. She has taken the entire thing apart, every measure notated with fingering or some direction of dynamic or articulation or tempo, and sometimes a big circle with red pencil. And this amused him. But what amused him most of all was that at the very beginning of the first movement she had written a note to herself, "Play it fast; think it slow!"

And then, suddenly, she appeared out of the bathroom with her wild red-blond hair piled in a careless knot and her robe half open, and he could smell lemons; and he could see the shape of her breast peeking out of her robe and the arc of her expanding lower belly and her huge round eyes, which were the deepest blue, and her color high and complexion radiant; and she smiled at him, and her dimples showed. And he thought for one moment that she must be the most beautiful woman alive—not objectively, of course, but who could have a more angelic expression and a tenderer smile! His heart wanted to break when he looked at her, and something, some warmth came searing through the cloud in his head. And he thought to himself, "Where has she been?" And he felt, along with the warmth in his head, a sudden sting of anger just under the place where his ribs met his breast bone.

And she came to him and took his right hand in hers and kissed it; and then she lay her left hand on his cheek and said, "Willi we are both back from our adventures, and I hope you are glad to see me. I know I stayed with my father much longer than you would have wanted; but you must understand how much I needed that undisturbed practice. We *will* be going to see Prince Bismarck soon, won't we?

"… But you don't look well, Willi," she said.

And he answered, "But *you* look so pretty, Lisi!" And he unfastened her hair and kissed her mouth, a deep, voluptuous kiss that he knew undid her. And he opened her robe and said, "Now you are my Venus of Urbino."

And she smiled, a wry smile and said, "Maybe from the neck up and from the waist down, Willi, but in the place you are staring at, I am very vulgar." To which he replied that in that place, in that canvas space, she was magnificent! And he knelt and pushed his face against her breasts and then against her belly and then he began to make love to her with his lips and his tongue, and she said with a tiny spasm of laughter, "Willy!" And she began to sigh in that breathless way she had when he knew she was feeling the chaos.

And then he suddenly stopped and said to her as he moved her toward the edge of the bed and sat down, "Last night at the hunting party, they sent a Jewish whore to me, as a joke—or maybe not as a joke—maybe because they think I only like Jewish women. At least, I thought the whore was Jewish, but I didn't fuck her, and do you know why, Lisi?"

And Lisi whispered guardedly, "No. Why, Wilhelm?"

And Boening said, "Because I have a Jewish whore at home."

At this she tried to turn away from him, but he laughed and grabbed her, firmly but gently, at the hips, and continued to make love to her with his mouth. She looked down and took his head in her hands and raised his eyes to hers and whispered plaintively, "But you know, Willi, that I will never belong to anyone else."

And he looked into those eyes, at the kinetoscope that was her face, and there he saw frames of sadness and tenderness and hurt and even guilt. And the place just underneath where his ribs met his breastbone stung again. And he said, "Yes, perhaps that's true …" and began making love to her again.

"But," he continued, kissing her and caressing her all the while, and laying her out gently on the bed, "you are only waiting until you are over me to go back once and for all to your Beethoven and Schubert, and maybe even to your father's house, because you don't really love me the way a good German wife should love her husband. You would prefer to live with your father. Perhaps you would even prefer to take your Beethoven score to bed with you."

And now she was sighing again and catching her breath, and her sighs were deeper because the chaos was spreading, and he said, "Admit it, Lisi, you don't love me."

But she wouldn't admit it. She said instead, "I do, Wilhelm. Too much for my comfort."

"No," he said, "No you don't."

But he knew now what he would do, he told her. Because although she didn't love him half enough, he loved her to utter distraction. She was everything to him. And he would take her apart the way she had taken the "Waldstein" Sonata apart, every inch of her. He would burn a hole in her, the way she had burnt one in Beethoven, and he would make her submit to him!

❧————❧

THE NEXT MORNING, WILHELM ENTERED THE DIN-ing room, and as soon as his eyes met his father's eyes at the table, he saw his father's lips tense into a three-quarter smile, after which his father looked down at his newspaper and said, very lightly, "Shaking the leaves from the trees, last night, what?" And Wilhelm could not resist smiling himself, answering that he hoped his father was not disturbed. To which his father answered that the whole house was kept awake, and that he wouldn't be surprised if the coupling had been heard in the town of Wolgast. But hopefully his son's head was clear again, and the hangover from the hunting party, along with its more unpleasant memories, erased. At least, his son was looking quite a bit better this morning.

But where was his wife?

And just then, on cue, Lisi entered, a sweet picture in her boiled wool, forest-green skirt and jacket, and fur-lined *Trachtenhut*, with her red-blond curls exploding from under it, and her gloves in her hands. She was to be leaving for the neighbor's luncheon soon. But though she was exhorted to sit down for breakfast, she refused. She intended to practice a bit before she left, she said. And soon the opening phrases of the "Waldstein" Sonata filled the house. It seemed, for the next hour or so, that the Boening family was the most content on the face of the earth, the ungainly Pulow manor house a haven of warmth and happiness in the frigid Pomeranian landscape of oak and pine forest and sand dunes and cereal fields, now all laced with the early winter snow and ice.

And when it was time for Lisi to leave, Wilhelm was at the door of the salon, listening to her play. He made his way to the piano and sat down beside her on the bench so that she stopped in mid-phrase. It really was time for her to go, he said, and he knew that much of it would be a bore for her, but perhaps she would strike up a friendship with one or two of the women. To this, Lisi replied, "But Willi, I don't really strike up friendships with women. In fact, I don't believe I've ever had a female friend who wasn't a cousin or already a friend of my parents."

He took her face in his hands and kissed her on the cheek and said, "Lisi, will you promise me to keep yourself under wraps today; that is, will you promise to be a little less … a little less … Lisi? Because if you are, I am sure you will make friends in the neighborhood." And she answered, "Well, Willi, that is not exactly a compliment, but I get the gist of what you are saying, and I will try, I promise."

And Wilhelm kissed her quickly again, this time on the lips. Then he looked at her tenderly and said, "That is all I can ask, and you know how happy I am that you are home again."

THE BOENING COUNTRY BROUGHAM ARRIVED AT the Zehlenau estate at noon exactly, though Lisi was not quite sure how she had made it on time, since she had to awaken the coachman, Peter, twice when the horse meandered off the road. The Zehlenau manor house was larger than that of the Boenings and looked to Lisi's eyes more like a proper castle: the center of the structure markedly older, boasting turrets, and well-covered in ivy, all the way up to its roof. As the carriage pulled up into the driveway, Lisi noticed that a long northern wing seemed to spring up from a set of stone ruins. Entering the front hall, however, Lisi had the feeling of *déjà vu* when taking in the sparse and dowdy furnishings.

There were already a number of women in the salon. That is, Lisi heard a considerable amount of lady chatter even from the front hall. Upon being announced, she entered an enormous great-room, where an imposingly vast stone fireplace, perhaps four meters in height, was ablaze. There was an immediate hush, quite obviously because the neighborhood aristocracy all wanted a look at the Jewess who was now the Countess Boening. And suddenly, Lisi was very conscious of her frizzy blond hair and her long nose and that her pregnancy was showing, because all the women were looking her up and down critically from their sitting groups of chairs and couches. And curiously, not one of the women— not even the hostess—nodded, much less came to her to extend a hand. The Countess Zehlenau, an older woman with a wrinkled, pinched countenance and stringy gray hair tightly wound at the back of her neck, was seated on a faded mustard-yellow silk Recamier sofa near the fire, her cane draped over the lounge's raised end. She motioned for Lisi to take a seat on a couch at the center of the room. And there was utter silence, Lisi fighting to decide where to focus her eyes in this sea of north German faces, as all eyes focused on her.

The Countess Zehlenau made some introductions, and Lisi nodded from the couch. And then the Countess Zehlenau looked at her sternly and asked her how she found Pulow. Lisi immediately thought of something very amusing to say—that is, it was amusing to her, and no doubt Willi would have laughed to hear it, and no doubt her father, and Ehrlingen too, would have thought it hilarious—but it wouldn't be amusing, she was sure, to the Countess Zehlenau. So she fought it off, fought to be less herself, as instructed by her husband. And she found herself saying, "Well, I am not really very used to country life, and I would say I am a bit overwhelmed by all there is to do, and all there isn't to do in the country."

The Countess Zehlenau looked quizzically at her, as if she were speaking a foreign language. And then the elderly woman said, "But I cannot imagine that your people, who probably come from the east, have been long in Berlin?"

"Long?" repeated Lisi. "My father's family not longer, perhaps, than three-hundred-fifty years, which by a little quick reckoning cannot have been more than, well … fifteen or seventeen generations."

The Countess Zehlenau, conspicuously unimpressed, asked "And before that?" And Lisi answered dutifully that if her father was to be believed, his forefathers had settled in Frankfurt at the turn of the second millennium, coming by way of Italy. Of course, she added with an effort not to smile, "Who knows if they really came through Italy. Because people are always prone to glamourize their family history. Wouldn't you say, Gräfin von Zehlenau?

"And what use is it, anyway, all this family history talk? No matter who we are, we have thousands of generations behind us somewhere, and all of those ancestors had their adventures and their stories to tell."

The countess did not respond immediately to this, looking instead inward, as if she were struggling hard to understand the point. And then suddenly she raised her chin and said haughtily, "Certainly not!"

Lisi once more felt an irrepressible impulse to laugh, but instead, she tugged at her earlobe and looked down at her swollen belly.

But this particular mortification did not last much longer, because she was offered a glass of sherry by a servant, and it seemed that other ladies' arrivals were being announced. And the women around her soon began to chat happily with each other again, thoroughly ignoring her. Though she did hear someone directly behind her whisper to a newcomer, "That is the Jewess, Gräfin Boening, née Schwabacher, who has bought herself the handsomest man in Germany."

Lisi, grateful to be left to her own devises, sipped her sherry and decided to distract herself by rehearsing in her mind the little *ritardando* at the end of the first phrase of the "Waldstein" Sonata. But that led her somehow to rehearsing her husband taking her apart last night, and suddenly she felt an aching longing in a place deep in her abdomen. It occurred to her that she must be more madly in love with him than ever, if he can get her mind off Beethoven like that. Either madly in love or a nymphomaniac.

And the ladies surrounding her faded from sight and hearing in this lovemaking reverie.

But she was suddenly awakened to exclamations and joyful sounds. Because Caroline had arrived, yes, Caroline! Obviously, Caroline was someone who was—well, we don't know who she is, Lisi thought. But we know who she is *not!* She is *not* the Jewess, Gräfin Elisabeth von Boening née Schwabacher, for whom everyone hushes. And indeed, she was not; she was Caroline von Schillingen! Because she was nearly two meters tall, and devastatingly beautiful, with her silken blond hair and light blue eyes, with the cheekbones standing out under them, and Lisi could sense that every woman in the room wished to be graced by Caroline's exquisite smile. And Caroline, unlike but one or two of the other ladies, was wearing her riding habit, because she rode to the party from her estate at Libnow, much preferring horseback to the carriage.

The ladies' chatter was getting louder—to Lisi's increasing discomfort, because she had always hated ladies' chatter. She wanted to turn away from the clatter of that chatter, because some women's voices were positively grating. But when she did, suddenly Caroline von Schillingen was by her side and taking her hand and saying, "Gräfin Boening, I had so hoped you would be here! I had hoped to meet you again ever since we met at the Empress Friedrich's soirée last spring, where you played Mendelssohn so beautifully!"

Lisi returned Caroline's smile, but found herself answering, without thinking about it, "I'm afraid I have no recollection of meeting you."

"Of course not. Why *should* you remember me?" Caroline responded. "But I want you to know that your concert gave me such comfort at a time when I desperately needed comfort; and I heard afterward that your mother was gravely ill, and that it was a very difficult time for you also."

Lisi looked into Caroline's face, which was a stunning, confident face, but with an overlay of human empathy, even bravely borne pain, which seemed to spill from her forehead into little creases by her eyes. And this reminded Lisi a lot of Wilhelm.

"I hope you don't think me too forward, but I have asked everyone I could what they know about you. I'm told you are a creature of the city. How are you finding the country? Do you ride?"

"I'm afraid I don't ride at all, and to be honest, I recently ran away to the city for an entire month, and my husband wasn't very happy about it."

Caroline threw back her head and laughed, and said, "Well, it's important to remember that husbands don't always have to be kept happy. And you'll like the country much more when you learn to ride. Perhaps I can help teach you. And you might teach me to play the piano a little. Naturally I had lessons, only they seem to have done me no good. But what I really want from you, Countess Boening, is an invitation to play tennis when summer comes. Because I hear your husband has built you a court, and I am a passionate tennis player!"

And then Caroline turned to the Countess Zehlenau and said to her, "Will you do me the favor of seating me next to Gräfin Boening at lunch?"

The Countess Zehlenau looked surprised and a little put off by the request, but assented. And going in to lunch, Caroline took Lisi's arm and whispered, "I shouldn't have done it, but I've pulled rank because my mother is a very distant cousin of the Kaiser, and

Gräfin Antonie is so impossibly obsessed with pedigree that it's an irresistible temptation. Plus, she always puts me next to *her,* and she's a deadly bore!"

During lunch, Caroline entertained Lisi with a glimpse of future motherhood, telling Lisi all about her three "wild men" at home—that is, the men between three and eight years of age—who, in all probability, she said, were at that very moment pouring lentils into their ears and trying to shake them out the other side of their heads. And could Lisi believe that she had caught them yesterday in the freezing cold among the cottagers' children—all of them playing the parabola game with their manhood, trying to melt the newly fallen snow with their urine. And by the end of lunch, Caroline and Lisi were laughing together and on a first-name basis. And by the end of the week, they would be *per Du.*

So that when Lisi returned to Pulow, she had more to tell Wilhelm than, "Really, Peter should be retired as coachman, because he fell asleep two times on the way to the Zehlenau estate, and three times on the way home. We could have been stuck in a bog forever, because God knows I couldn't push a brougham out of a mud ditch, not even with Peter's help." And when Wilhelm answered, "But what should the poor man do when he is 'retired,' as you so euphemistically put it? Should he hang himself?" Lisi knew she had lost that argument.

"Willi …" she then said cheerfully, all the while thinking that she might someday meet her end in a Pomeranian bog, "Willi, you won't believe this, but I have made a friend today!" And Wilhelm smiled and asked "Who?"

"Countess Caroline von Schillingen. We sat together at lunch and couldn't have been better amused with each other. And do you know, she insists that the raising and breeding of chickens is a high art, and that there is nothing like the producing of a prized Polish hen, which is the most beautiful creature on earth! That's what she told me! She promised to prove it and has a book to lend me about hens. What would you think about my taking a little trip to Greifswald together with Caroline?"

Wilhelm looked extremely pleased, even delighted. "Caroline von Schillingen," he said, "is a very highborn woman and will be excellent company for you. And you for her," he added, as did she know that Caroline lost two sons last year from scarlet fever, and was in Bad Homburg in April, where she was recovering from depression. She had heard Lisi play at the Empress Friedrich's and was quite taken with Lisi's playing.

IN THE THIRD WEEK OF DECEMBER, THE BOENINGS finally made the trip to Friedrichsruh, a day trip each way, and with three nights spent in the home of the Iron Chancellor. Lisi was sick several times during the trip there; she couldn't seem to digest any food at all and arrived with a beastly headache. But after dinner, she played the "Waldstein" Sonata, and the Prince did not contain his delight. He even mentioned that it was a favorite of his wife's, and wouldn't it have been wonderful for Johanna to have heard it played like that—with as much feeling as technical mastery. For his wife thought the heroic Beethoven nothing; she was for the heartfelt Beethoven, the Beethoven that is *innig*.

Lisi played several times for the Prince during the visit: works of Mendelssohn, Schumann, Bach and Schubert, as well as Beethoven and Liszt. And the great man received it all with an unrestrained enthusiasm that was just short of passion.

Bismarck, Lisi decided, was not at all the man she thought he would be. Listening to him dissect the state of the world at meals, where she had expected bear roars and growls would be rising and falling at the table, she was surprised at the precision, youthfulness, and concentrated energy of the old man's voice, which, it seemed, was always under perfect control. Indeed, she had thought Bismarck would be a bass or perhaps a bass baritone. But Bismarck, it turned out, was a tenor and seemed never to quite match the tone of his voice to the tone of his rhetoric. It was hard for her to imagine him losing his temper. And as she studied him, she thought about her Cousin Babette, who was said to have been the most beautiful young Jewess of her generation, as well as brilliant company. She had been greatly admired by the Prince. What was it, Lisi wondered, that Cousin Babette could possibly have said so many years ago to have made the man angry enough to cast her from his house forever, and how would he have sounded as he did it?

Mostly, Lisi was quiet in the great man's company, taking in Bismarck's praise for her playing and listening to the other guests, who were worthies from the neighborhood and whose conversation was elevated enough, if unremarkable. Of course, she politely dissembled when the Prince asked her questions about her father that she was reluctant to answer; namely, why he left the banking house of Bleichroeder and went out on his own so early.

But then, on the third night at dinner, in a larger company of guests, Bismarck suddenly declared in an odd non sequitur that it was hard to believe men like Magnus Schwabacher could be so consistently, so damnably prescient in matters of money! For there had been a great deal of risk in the markets of late—risk that only the Jews seemed to take. Did the Gräfin Boening think it was genius or chance, what her father had accomplished, especially as regarded the financing of American industry?

And perceiving immediately that Lisi demurred to answer this question, he turned from her for a long while. Until much later, when undertaking the subject of the failings of the emperor, who had just been to see him, the Prince nodded meaningfully to Lisi before addressing the rest of the company with the pointed statement that "Beside the Kaiser's damned effeminacy, I haven't even touched on his anti-semitism, which is becoming a sickness."

And suddenly, Lisi found herself recoiling and then responding involuntarily, "Do you mean to say that he hates the Jews more than would be desirable?" At which Lisi saw Wilhelm go white. But the Prince, though silent, seemed not even mildly put off at this remark. He merely turned to her and in a slightly subdued tone asked, "What could you possibly mean by that, Gräfin von Boening?"

"Your Highness, you never acknowledged the passing of the great jurist Eduard Lasker and even returned the message regretting his demise to Washington. And though he worked himself to death, and all for your cause, the cause of the unification of Germany. Of course, I realize he had become your political opponent by the end, but it wasn't perceived as that kind of slight. It was perceived, at least by the Jews, as a nod to anti-semitism."

At this, Bismarck was quiet for at least a half a minute, taking several sips from his wine glass and cutting into his cheese with very deliberate motions. Then he threw back his head and laughed, fastened his eyes on Wilhelm, and declared, "Boening, your wife is very quick—too quick for her own good! Like her cousin, Babette Meyer, whom I knew all too well!"

And then he turned to Lisi, and said, "And while you don't have her height, Gräfin Boening, you certainly have her nerve. But you have given me great pleasure with your playing, and in return I have been very impertinent in my questions about your father. So you are forgiven."

And after a pause, he said, in a softer voice, "But Gräfin Boening, I worry that you don't eat enough to keep a bird alive, and here you are, expecting."

When they left the next day, one of the first things that Lisi asked Wilhelm, as soon as they boarded the train, was whether he was angry about what she said to Prince Bismarck.

He answered, "A little shocked at your candor, but not really angry, or would I have made love to you last night?"

"Perhaps … That is, I don't let anger stop me from holding you. But I sometimes can't keep myself from saying things I should know from the start people won't like."

And Wilhelm smiled and reached for her hand, bringing the palm to his lips, and said, "I am beginning to take you more in stride, Lisi, or perhaps it's just that this is the epoch in our married life when we live on love. But I do wonder if you will ever learn discretion."

And he looked at her and smiled again—a broad smile. And then, as he settled back into his seat and closed his eyes, he said, "Prince Bismarck told me he understands very well why I married you, because you are pretty and intelligent and rich. But he insists that I was wrong to do it, because I've stolen you from the concert stage."

Wilhelm was quiet for a moment. And then he said, "But the Prince doesn't know what I know."

"What is that, Willi?"

"Lisi, only three months on the concert stage, and you would have retched your stomach completely from your body. Six months, and there would be nothing at all left of you—maybe a shadow."

# CHAPTER XIX

*Pulow*

*January 7, 1898*

*Liebe Klara!*

*I was relieved to receive your letter of the 16ᵗʰ, and can only apologize a thousand times that it has taken me so long to answer, though I miss you as much as ever. But you can imagine that with the holidays, there has been a lot to prepare and attend to at Pulow, and it being my first Christmas as a so-called Christian, I was anxious to do right by it all, especially as we had a quite large gathering of neighbors and local notables here for dinner on the Second Day, because the 26th was also my father-in-law's seventieth birthday.*

*I must admit that I have thought many times over of how jealous Mami would have been that I now partake with impunity in these so charming Yule customs—the tree hung with candles, fruits, sweets, and little glass balls; the presents opened by its light; and the playing and singing of Christmas hymns for the members of the household. It is all so lovely that it makes up for the interminably boring*

Sunday sermons I must attend. I actually think that had Mami lived, she would have wanted an invitation to stay with us at Christmas. Perhaps you don't know that Mami had agonizing Christmas envy, and even used to stalk the Christmas markets, though all she could justify buying there—at least, for herself—was honey and Lebkuchen, and occasionally a cup of mulled wine. But she always sent something for the tree to her old friend Margit Novotny—as if there were no Christmas markets in Vienna!

Every Christmas, she used to complain to me that we were the only "sophisticated" Jews in Berlin who didn't have a Christmas tree, and that it was just one of Papi's "silly principles" not to celebrate, and to insist his refusal was so as not to offend the Christian community by abusing their sacred symbols. Because everyone knows, she said, that Christmas is a German holiday, and so hardly exclusively Christian. And that as Germans, we must participate. But I always pointed out to her that it was nice we could give the servants the day off, and Papi loved the idea that she would prepare and serve a small dinner all on her own, because Mami really did know her way around a kitchen and was even an excellent cook. Funny how I am just thinking of our first Christmas in the Kadettenweg, when Baron Ehrlingen showed up unexpectedly. It was the first time I ever heard him play the piano, and we read through perhaps a dozen four-hand arrangements of Haydn symphonies, along with the Lebensstürme of Schubert.

Of course, Christmas, when one celebrates it as a Christian, is not quite as romantic as Mami conceived of it. It's also a lot of time-consuming bother—most especially all the time spent at church, along with those parts of it that involve the hundreds of gifts to the schoolchildren and the estate employees, all of which have to be presented with so much ceremony and are so small and appreciated far beyond *their worth by people who have so little—not to mention that these people are objects of our generosity but once or at most twice a year. And in a way I resent how Willi always refers to those presents when he talks about creating the requisite* Weihnachtsstimmung, *as if his very precious "Christmas mood" were really all about giving, when it is clearly about* noblesse oblige. *But then, perhaps I am being ungenerous here, because when the Boenings were poor, before my tenure, all those gifts might well have been a terrible strain on their economy.*

*My father-in-law, who loves to lecture others, has cultivated a particularly high level of obnoxiousness at Christmas: As I handed our farmers and servants their gifts, he reprimanded each and every one of them for something he or she did this year to disappoint the* Gutsherrschaft *and the Lord God. For example, "Katharine would be a perfectly adequate kitchen maid, if only she weren't in such a hurry; for that is how the milk is spilled, the porcelain serving plate broken, and the silver spoons streaked with tarnish where they haven't been properly dried."*

*I truly wanted to strangle him, until he did the same to Willi and me. And then I just had to laugh. (My Christmas present from him, by the way, was a selection of Martin Luther's most important writings. Evidently, he had noted how much I like books!) But what do you think were his Yuletide admonitions to us? To Willi, he said that while he is not wholly insensitive to my charms, he hoped his son would take care not to be seduced by Jewish sophistry. And to me, he said, "My dear daughter-in-law, you are a young woman of truly unnecessary extravagances, starting with taking your tea with sugar!"*

*I bought Willi oils and canvas for Christmas, thinking to keep my giving modest, as I hear nothing but "We are not rich Jews" from my husband (echoed, in spirit, by everything my father-in-law says to me). And this, whenever I devise a way to spend even a little bit of money. I had the idea last month of having some of the drawing room furniture reupholstered, and perhaps some new drapes ordered. Well, you would have thought I had asked for the moon served up on a silver platter. I was summarily taken into that room and asked where the fabric was worn through. And when I suggested that perhaps a few warmer colors would enliven the place, I was told that if one was going to be a slave to fashion, there would be no keeping up and no end to renovations; and that my husband and father-in-law had no intention of waking up one day in a home they didn't recognize as their own.*

*But for all the talk of our genteel Christian poverty, the truth is that we are rich Jews—or at least semi-rich Jews, or rich semi-Jews, or half-rich half-Christians, or half-rich semi-Christians—because Willi actually bought me a lovely string of pearls for Christmas, which Ehrlingen picked up in Berlin, and which Willi claims to be expiation for the gambling he did at a hunting party in Brandenburg while I was at home in Berlin with Papi. Evidently my husband won a tidy sum at cards from the fellow officers of his regiment.*

*I can't help wondering what I would have gotten had he lost at cards.*

*In answer to your questions about Papi, I must make a shameful admission. I never mentioned inviting him for the holidays, figuring that it would mean so little to him anyway, and why turn the house upside down when it is so obvious to all concerned that there is no love lost between him and my husband. And what would my father-in-law do with Papi for two or three days—or my father with Graf Helmuth von Boening for that eternal amount of time? But then Willi asked me, and quite out of the blue, what my intentions were regarding Christmas and my father, because he supposed my father would be expecting to come, but perhaps not?*

*And so I had a very bad moment. And I asked him, point blank, "What do you mean when you say, 'But perhaps not?'" And he answered testily, "I mean exactly what I have said." And so I told him that it pleased me to inform him that my father had announced he would be spending Christmas with Ehrlingen. They would have dinner in the Kadettenweg and planned to play the Brahms cello sonatas together. And at that, Willi laughed in that peculiar way he has of laughing when he doesn't want to, and knows that it's mean spirited but cannot help it: It's a silent, open-mouthed laughter accompanied by an involuntary jerk of the elbows and a little skip. And then he said he thought it quite fitting that Madame von Schwabacher's "two husbands" would be making music together on Christmas.*

*Apparently, Willi had invited Ehrlingen to come to us, as he has no family of his own. (Or so Ehrlingen insists, even though everyone knows he's related to half the nobility in Brandenburg.) But he declined, as he always politely declines the Boenings' Christmas invitations, with the excuse that he has little use for holidays, especially religious ones. Honestly, Klara, it made me so sad to imagine my father and Ehrlingen all alone in the music room of the Kadettenweg villa—Papi at his cello, plucking at that sparse and brickly theme of the "Adagio affetuoso" in F-sharp major, with Ehrlingen accompanying him. I simply forced myself to stop thinking about it.*

*Klara, I am very big for five months along, and it worries me. I eat very little, but my belly is quite extended, and the only thing I can think is that either there is something very wrong, or I will have twins. The doctor here says he suspects twins, because if something were seriously amiss, he says, my legs and feet would be more swollen.*

*But I am beginning to look more like a barrel on sticks than a human being.*

*I'm not a very good sport about it either. A few days ago, Willi wanted to skate with me on the Pulowersee, which is, I must admit, so very lovely presently in its frozen stillness, all surrounded by the conifer woods. When we got down to the lake, one of our cottagers was sawing a hole for ice fishing; and, with the wind being quite still, this was the single sound we heard for several minutes, other than the occasional chirps of Bohemian waxwings. Well, we tied up our skates, but I didn't get very far on my own, as I kept falling over, so I stupidly cried and blamed my husband for being so tall and saddling me with a monstrous fetus that was keeping me in a preposterous state of imbalance. Of course, Willi just laughed and held me up and told me that I needed to eat more, and if only I had properly indulged in the Christmas lamb and goose, my legs could carry my belly, and I would also not be in such a bad mood all the time. We managed to cross the lake—that is, with me holding onto him for dear life and bobbing back and forth like a roly-poly. But really, if there is only one child in me, it is already half my size, and I will never be able to expel it without splitting in two.*

*I played my arrangement of the Bach* Passacaglia and Fugue in C minor *for my father-in-law's birthday, and it was really wonderfully received, Klara. Everyone loved it, and the Schillingens, neighbors of ours who were invited to celebrate, were especially enthusiastic. Graf Schillingen asked his wife, Caroline, what she was going to do for his birthday, and she said, "Lisi has set the bar so high ... I suppose I will have to train a horse!"*

*At any rate, I will always carry the memory of when I finished, because my father-in-law's arms and legs flew out from under him as if all his reflexes had been tested at once, and he said, "Wie schön,* Tochter! Und wie feierlich!*" Imagine he called me "daughter!" And I saw him grin for the first time! It looked a little unnatural, actually. So I am finally making headway with him, as he considers me otherwise a totally useless addition to the Boening household, and isn't afraid to tell me so. Even when I offer to take up tasks that would normally fall to the lady of the manor, he is quick to say, "Never mind. You needn't attend to that, my dear. Go and practice your piano. Vietzke will see someone attends to it." Because he knows I'm not up to any washing or cleaning or sewing or darning or fixing drudgery, and would die before stuffing a blood sausage. But I am getting busy in the kitchen and am trying to develop a rapport with* Mam'selle, *because we must improve her cooking. And I even did a little baking at Christmas. (You are smirking, I know, but I have learned a little something from watching Mami and* Tante Anna.*)*

*But I don't think I told you that I have a new friend. That is, I have made a female friend all on my own for the first time in my life—Caroline von Schillingen, who is by far the most beautiful woman I have ever met. And as good as she is pretty. We have become very intimate in a short time, mainly because although the Schillingen estate is about six kilometers from here, she is a passionate rider and enjoys coming to visit. She is not at all like you or like Mami, but she makes it easier that I don't have you or Mami here with me. It's clear she thinks me endlessly entertaining, and she can be also. And she is wise and socially adept, which I certainly am not. So you see, the relationship is quite similar. But occasionally she says something very peculiar which I find myself longing to repeat to you. For example, the other day, she said that it was obvious to her that I am not a good Christian yet. But that once my child is born, I will have to become a good Christian, because having a child will finally "bring me into the world." Isn't that an odd thing to say? But then Caroline, like my husband, says a lot of things that seem odd and perhaps a little simple-minded, but strike one also as somehow profound—though one isn't sure where the actual profundity lies.*

*I bet you didn't know you were making good Christians of all those mothers whose babies you deliver, or you probably would decline to deliver them!*

*Klara, you never really talk about the essential anymore in your letters, so I've pretty much given up asking for news of Bernhard. But if there is news, I would like to hear it.*

*I wish you and the entire Weingarten family all blessings in the New Year. And special greetings and a dozen kisses to Isi. You must tell her to write to me in English. In her last letter, she complained it's her most difficult subject at school and that she seldom gets a chance to practice.*

*Deine,*

*Lisi*

*Berlin*

*January 18, 1898*

*Boening,*

*Yesterday both Hennholz and I received anonymous letters and so, we must assume, did several others of our acquaintance. The subject was the hunting party at Eichenhohl. These letters contained threats, along with pointed references to the Friday and Saturday evening goings-on. Hennholz's was accompanied by lewd drawings, and mine came with a group photograph of all who attended, taken after the Saturday hunt.*

*It's clear enough to me that the author of these letters is one of us, or at least well-informed by one of us, because he seems to be very familiar not only with our movements, but also our individual financial situations.*

*I am not sure how to react, or whether even to react—having, like you, not been involved in certain events of Saturday. Yet, we are bound to be compromised by our mere presence at v. Lehnau's, and I fear that the organizer of what appears to be a fairly thorough blackmail scheme might have other evidence at his disposal that would implicate the three of us in reckless enough behavior.*

*Perhaps you have already heard from this person. If you have, I would appreciate your writing to me immediately, as I think it best that the three of us make a decision in concert.*

*As ever,*

*v. Ehrlingen*


*Pulow*

*January 25, 1898*

*Ehrlingen,*

*I received the letter you warned me of. And it brought back that very unpleasant memory of your appearing in my room in the wee hours of the morning—a memory I had managed to push away for two months.*

*My letter contained no drawings. But it did contain a photograph, which, if I were to be honest, I don't clearly remember having been taken. Because although I have a vague memory of a victory wreath and a camera flash, I do not remember having on an eagle helmet when I rode that horse.*

*With regard to the sum I have been asked to pay: It is simply absurd. I couldn't purchase this person's silence if I wanted to, because I would have to invade my wife's dowry to do it. And I have no intention to do that. So there is your answer; namely, that I will not respond. The only question in my mind is whether I should speak with my wife, should this break into the open, about the things I did and did not do at Eichenhohl.*

*Which leads me also to the question of the injured boy, and whether he or his family was compensated. Because, though it wouldn't be my business to do it, it probably must be done.*

*v.B.*

*Pulow*

*February 2, 1898*

*Cousin Babette,*

*I telephoned Papi the other day from Greifswald, and he mentioned you were down with influenza. I hope this letter finds you recovered.*

*I wonder if you would consider visiting Pulow. I would need some wisdom from my side of the family, and it would be so good to see you. I would come to Berlin to see you, but my husband refuses to come with me, and I'm not allowed to go alone, as he doesn't trust me to eat properly unless under his supervision. You wouldn't believe I've practically starved myself through this pregnancy, because I am insanely big with child and have at least three months to go.*

*Dear Cousin, can you tell me what you know about Caroline v. Schillingen? We have been spending a great deal of time together and have become very intimate friends. To be precise, she is more forthcoming with me than I with her—not because of any discretion on my part, but simply a lack of interesting tales to tell.*

*We were together in Greifswald last week. And while it was diverting to stroll in that pleasing Hanseatic town, and to be bowed and scraped to in the restaurant and stores, Caroline told me some deeply disturbing things that I truly wish I didn't know. And they are beginning to prey on me.*

*I send you affectionate greetings!*

*Your devoted,*

*Lisi*

*Berlin*

*February 8, 1898*

*Liebe Lisi!*

*You were a dear to have those tropical fruits sent. I cannot tell you how much I enjoyed them. I credit them completely for my swift recovery. I hope you haven't mentioned that extravagance to your husband, as I can only assume he would be apoplectic if he knew.*

*Now, my child, to the subject of Caroline v. S.: She has been looking for a friend for a long while now, and I think you have absolutely fit the bill. She is also badly wanting a divorce, and on her terms—something, under the circumstances, she richly deserves, and I hope she gets. Perhaps she will even have a second husband who is more her equal in looks and manners.*

*I have heard that unspeakable things went on at a hunting party at Eichenhohl in December. And I also heard that Alexander v. Schillingen and your husband were present. There seem to be no boundaries to behavior anymore; not, at least, among those who have inherited wealth along with social position. And Schillingen is a perfect example of a man who has shed all inhibition and principle. So whatever Caroline told you is, unfortunately, probably true, though I wouldn't worry too much that your husband partook in any savagery.*

*I know for a fact that his father raised him with the fear of God, and in very straightened circumstances, and he never had a mother to leaven that lump.*

*But if you want advice from an old woman, I would say you might approach your husband and ask him straight out what his part in it was. If he cannot set your mind at ease, you might as well know now, before the rest of the world knows.*

*My dear girl, the world is becoming a very nasty place, and it can all be reduced, I think, to a regretful lack of spiritual discipline. When I look around me, I cannot help but think that the most primitive impulses are everywhere being trotted out as grand and noble ideals. Not that vulgar and salacious behavior is new. But it used to be that when it reared its ugly head in the better classes, people were ashamed of it. And now it has been dignified, starting with our Kaiser. I keep thinking of Franz Grillparzer's warning:*

*"The way of modern culture, we see*
*leads from humanity*
*through nationality*
*to bestiality."*

*And all in one short century too ... At any rate, as your Verlaine might put it, the German soul can no longer boast the choicest of landscapes.*

*But to a far more pleasant subject: I was at Pulow many years ago. There is a corner, on the eastern side of the Pulowersee, where one finds a tiny, secluded sand beach completely protected by reeds and shallows. It's a sunny spot, but when the summer sun is hot, one can take refuge in a charming shingled lean-to. From that sweet little stretch of sand, one looks straight out across the very blue water to the thick woods beyond. I think you will enjoy that beach next summer,*

*especially at sunset, when the trees break and scatter the low, redden-*
*ing rays of sunshine. You must go there with your husband. I painted*
*it once and I have the fondest memories of it.*

*Your devoted cousin,*
*Babette*

*Libnow, Vorpommern*
*February 12, 1898*
*Meine liebe Lisi,*
*When you receive this, my three boys and I will have left for Berlin,*
*where we will be staying with my parents until my head clears. I have*
*been through my husband's letters and have found what I needed—*
*all the evidence I could possibly need. Lisi, you cannot imagine the*
*things that men have had to say to the father of my five children—two*
*of whom are gone from me and lying in graves! The passionate things,*
*the arrogant things, and in some cases the absurd and lewd things they*
*have written would make you blush were I to repeat them here. And*
*you cannot imagine the things those men have to say about women;*
*about me, Lisi, the mother of Schillingen's children, not to mention*
*about people like you! So you see the detritus that my once so happy*
*married life has become. A pile of "love" letters from men to men that*
*are nothing if not paeans to vanity and bigotry. But perhaps my mar-*
*riage was never happy, and I just imagined it so, because I was naïve*
*and was told by my parents that noblewomen marry noblemen and*
*live happily ever after.*

*Of course, I will bring copies of these letters to a lawyer. And*
*there is a man named Maximilian Harden, who I hear also collects*
*such things. Do you know him? He was in the theater but is now a*
*journalist and publishes a magazine called "The Future." He is on a*

campaign to clean up the political leadership of Germany, which he considers near completely corrupt. And if my husband is any example, he is right.

Of course, Schillingen was livid when I confronted him; he even threatened to take the children from me. But when I warned him that were he to try that, I would have no compunction about showing his collection of indecent letters to a judge, he got frightened. And there came a long confession that revolted me to the extent that I never want him to touch me again.

I told you in Greifswald that he and the other officers of the regiment are being blackmailed and that a thirteen-year-old boy almost died at Eichenhohl. My husband now admits to me that he was in the room and that he "saw" it happen, although he still cannot explain why this child would have been set upon by a dozen grown men.

Lisi, I asked him if Boening was also in the room. I know it wasn't my place, but I had to know. He said Boening was very drunk and had gone up to his bedroom, where a woman was waiting for him.

So you see, my dear friend, you are the lucky one.

Deine,

Caroline

Lichterfelde West
February 15, 1898
Lisi, meine liebe Tochter!
Your Onkel Sigi has written to say that Klara's fiancé, Dr. Bernhard Levin, passed away on the seventh of February. I am sorry to be the bearer of that news, as I know how very fond you were of him. I heard only good things of him from your Aunt and Uncle Weingarten, as well as from Mami, though I never had the pleasure of meeting him myself.

*But if that were the only bad news! I have received a threatening letter concerning your husband, with a request for payments. The letter came with a compromising photograph. I must tell you that I have turned everything over to the police, since I will not be blackmailed.*

*While you were in Berlin, your husband apparently attended a hunting party with fellow officers from the* Gardes du Corps. *I will not burden you with the sordid details, though you will have to face them at some point. Suffice it to say that the activities there involved criminal behavior, and a boy almost died.*

*Lisi, this will break and there will be a terrible scandal. There are journalists who lie in wait for something like this. I won't have you being a part of it, and so you must come home immediately, while you are still carrying your child. We will talk to a lawyer; it will all be resolved, and you will have your child for yourself. You mustn't fear you will have to give up your child. And if we have to pay your husband to let you go, we will do that. No price is too high.*

*I know you haven't felt well, that you have headaches and stomach pains. And probably the best way to go about this would be for you to simply say you wish to see a specialist in Berlin.*

*My dearest, I had hoped it wouldn't come to this. But it is just as I feared from the very beginning. People like Boening are what they are and have always been. It's in their blood. A man can be handsome and well-dressed, even have some education, and still he is a boor. And he doesn't even mind that he is. Quite the contrary, he is proud of it. These* Junkers *are a race of their own. They would never admit a Jew to the officer corps. And for a reason: Because they are savages, and they won't be restrained by more civilized men.*

*I will tell you something I have never told you before about your cousin Babette and that* Mamzer, Kalckreuth, *from whom she had no choice but to run away. Babette, the very finest flower of womanhood, admired everywhere for her beauty and cultivation! Well, of course, she had a past. What woman in middle age would not! But do you think Kalckreuth had any compassion for the embarrassments of her youth? Oh no! He was happy to take her money but was derisive of her sufferings and insanely jealous of her talent. Each day with him was an exercise in humiliation, and he wasn't satisfied until he had her prostrate before him. Yes, he broke her! And that is the way it is with our so-called nobility. That is how they treat the finely wrought Jewesses who marry them!*

*Lisi, my child! You cannot remain married to Boening! You must come home!*

*Your loving,*
*Papi*


*Pulow*
*February 20, 1898*
*Papi,*
*I honestly don't know how to answer your letter to me without creating unbearable tension between us. But I must write as plainly as possible. I am touched that you want to protect me and that you haven't forgotten to love me, though I certainly have betrayed you in every way a girl could possibly betray her father. So I thank you, and I am deeply grateful that, despite everything, you want to give me a loving home, should the heavens crash on my shoulders.*

*Put Papi, you have miscalculated in that you have forgotten that I love my husband. And I think I know him well enough by now to promise you that he is as far from victimizing me as anyone could possibly be. My Graf Boening may be a little rough around the edges intellectually; and he is a* Junker *to the tip of his toes—including per-haps a number of reflexive prejudices from which he will never loose himself. But he is hardly a savage. Consider that he tolerates my worst moods, my sharpest humors, and has allowed me to embarrass him countless times with my thoughtless indiscretions, and with only the gentlest reprimands. I think I probably test him every day. The truth is, Papi, that I really think my husband far kinder than either you are or I am; though, of course, as a man of distinct social advantages, he can well afford to be kind.*

*I had known about the hunting party before you wrote to me. My husband told me one or two things about it when I returned from Berlin. And I can only say that while I know Willi must bitterly regret his presence, I will not suspect him of participating in an atrocity. At most, maybe a* bêtise, *but not a bestial act. The question is when and whether he will get around to telling me all the things that happened at Eichenhohl, and what he did or did not attempt to do about them. Of course I am angry with him that he hasn't yet come clean with me, when it appears that the police are involved, and I know from other sources that journalists will soon be poking around. But to divorce him for that?*

*And when I'm expecting?*

*Papi, your letter has deeply upset me, but not for the reasons you think. I have the impression that there is something very wrong with my pregnancy. It has been confirmed that I am expecting twins. But I am much too swollen and enormous—not to mention much too tired, too breathless, and too achy—for things to be normal, even for a multiple pregnancy. And if anything frightens me, it's that. But now I feel I cannot even ask my husband for permission to stay in Lichterfelde West while I consult a specialist. Because if I came to you, you would only want to interfere in my marriage, which is my business and not yours.*

*I hope that you and my husband, with your conflicting world views and your contradictory demands upon me, are not going to set to rending me in two. If so, I will eventually retaliate; you may be sure of that. But right now, I have only enough strength to plead with you that you allow me the peace to see to my health and that of my babies.*

*Deine,*

*Lisi*

# CHAPTER XX

IT WAS NOT LONG AFTER CAROLINE VON Schillingen's arrival in Berlin that the papers were full of innuendos about a hunting party in Brandenburg at which the aristocratic participants, many from the best and oldest *Junker* families, had engaged in lewd acts. An editorial about the party even appeared in Maximilian Harden's magazine, *The Future,* pointing up the increasingly shameless decadence of the Berlin military elite—in particular, the circles around the Kaiser. Diplomats, army officers, and other national leaders, Harden wrote, were becoming increasingly vulnerable to blackmail. Their inexcusable lapses of judgment in entertainment, not to mention their eccentricities of sexual taste, were putting the security and prestige of the Imperial Reich at stake.

Lisi was relatively estranged from her husband's class, but these very active rumors still took their toll. True, at Pulow she was sheltered from the constant derision she would have faced were the Boenings living in Berlin—the smirks and rolling eyes, the cool insinuations. Nevertheless, on the few social occasions in which the Boenings partook in the country, there were invariably allusions, if delicate ones, to the winter party at Lehnau's estate. And these smarted—principally because despite Lisi's hopes and expectations, Wilhelm never came to her with a recounting of the events that had taken place. Indeed, as the days of February passed away, Lisi became increasingly concerned that no recounting was ever to be offered, and she began to think that the reason for this was that her husband's offenses at Eichenhohl had gone beyond what he could admit to her.

Unfortunately, this burgeoning scandal was not all that bothered Lisi. There was also the deterioration of both her physical and mental condition in pregnancy. Her face, arms, and hands were swollen. She was irritable, endured constant headache, and suffered serious lapses in concentration. It was obvious to her that her complaints were not normal ones. And it was obvious also to Wilhelm, who was solicitous to the extent of insisting that she rest frequently, eat (this, to no avail), and not spend too much time outside in the frigid winter air. But beyond that, Wilhelm offered nothing except regular visits from the local Doctor Hasslinger, who, though correctly diagnosing preeclampsia, seemed helpless to treat it.

"You see, Frau Gräfin, many doctors would take the babies as soon as possible, by Cesarean," said the doctor one wet and snowy early March day. "But I am afraid we will lose them if we try that too early. They are still very small. And the risks for the mother are also great. I would err on the side of caution ... Yes, caution. You must tell me if you have any disruptions in vision."

"And then what? Then what will you do?" asked Lisi.

The good doctor prevaricated. "Well, at any rate, we must avoid convulsions, Gräfin von Boening. At all costs, we must avoid convulsions."

It could not fail but to occur to Lisi, even in her hazy mental state, that this seemed an incomplete medical plan of action. So she broached the subject that very day at lunch.

"Willi, I don't suppose you would let me go to Berlin to consult an obstetric specialist."

"I would not. Not alone, at least."

"But you would come with me."

"If I had to. But I don't see the necessity. Not yet."

"Well, when then? When I'm lying unconscious? When I'm convulsing?"

"Lisi, don't you think you are being overly dramatic? Doctor Hasslinger's diagnosis is only an educated guess."

"But if you have no faith in his diagnosis, how is it you can have faith in his treatment, Willi? And frankly, I don't trust Doctor Hasslinger to be able to handle things if I do become very ill."

"Why, Lisi? Because Doctor Hasslinger is not a Jew?"

"Willi, what should that have to do with anything?"

"Well, certainly the obstetric specialist you'll see in Berlin will be a Jew. As well as the lawyer your father will have you meet with, as long as you are in town and under his roof. And God knows who else he will want you to see. Did I forget the journalist? Ah, yes, the journalist. The journalist who will call, with the object of getting you to dictate to him all the decadent habits of the *Junker* aristocracy to which your father so objects. Yes, you'll have plenty to tell all those Jews. Oh, and did I mention to you, my love, that I had a very unfriendly letter from your father yesterday, in which I have been accused, and hopefully only privately, Lisi, of a number of what he terms 'barbarities' that I never came near to committing. And in that letter I was even offered—and I quote him—a 'generous financial settlement' to divorce you, as well as certain arrangements for our unborn children that he seems to think would be mutually commodious."

Lisi didn't know where to begin with this. Through the fog in her head, she replied, "My father claims he received a letter of blackmail with a compromising photograph of you taken at Eichenhohl. Although, he didn't tell me what it showed you doing. But then, you must already know that, as the mail is always opened before I read it!"

"Well, I will tell you, my love, what that photograph showed me doing. It showed me on a horse, stark naked, with a bottle of vodka in my hand. Such behaviors may be stupid, and they may be cause for embarrassment where you and my father, sitting here, are concerned, and maybe even for your father; but I'm not sure they are sufficient grounds for divorce. And I have written your father to that effect."

"Willi, it was wrong of my father to accuse you of untoward things, and especially when I had already told him to stay out of it. But you can't blame him for being frightened. He reads the papers. He reads trusted people. Harden is a trusted journalist. Even Prince Bismarck trusts Harden, Willi."

"Does he? Well, if he does, the Prince is a fool. Because Harden is nothing but a sly, scandal peddling Jew-bastard, whose nerve and personal ambition know no bounds!"

Lisi didn't answer this right away. But after a moment she said softly, "I don't know, Willi. Perhaps Harden is an ambitious Jew, but not half as ambitious, nor half so Jewish, as your wife. Because I suspect his conversion to Christianity was more sincere than mine, since he claims to be a good Christian, and I claim no such thing. And I know for a fact that Harden didn't purchase a title of nobility for four million gold marks."

Helmuth von Boening started at this, and Wilhelm was very quiet for a minute. And then he said, in a whisper of resignation, "Well, then, we know where we stand, don't we? And you are released, Lisi." He stood up from the table, went to her, and grabbed her arm. "Yes, you are released, and you can go straight back to your father's house, where you may keep the title you bought so dearly, just like your cousin Babette did. And like her, you may then avail yourself of all the social advantages of that title, while maintaining all the Jewish doctors and lawyers that please you." And then he raised his voice to the bald, pot-bellied servant who stood in the dining room. "Vietzke, have the carriage brought around, because Gräfin von Boening is going to Wolgast this afternoon. And have her clothes prepared. We will send them after her." And here, he dragged Lisi from the dining room into the front hall and threw her fur coat and hat at her, her gloves and her purse.

And as he was pushing her out the door of the *Gutshaus* and into the driveway and onto the stone bench that stood in front of the manor, covered in snow, he said, "Because, Lisi, you've read a lot of books about social politics, without ever having understood what they are really about. You think your father is pure because he counts his wealth in stocks and bonds and gold and paper, and not in mud and men's sweat. You think, like the most primitive anti-semite, that he spins his money right out of the air, like the devil's magic. And that no human being has been injured or died, or even been the least bit exploited building a bridge or a railroad, or laying a cable or digging a coal mine. Well, you are a proper rich Jewess, and you should be returned to a properly Jewish home."

Only seconds later, when Wilhelm reentered the house, the door closing behind him, he saw that his father was standing at the dining room door, and Vietzke was in the front hall, looking alarmed, and wiping his brow and the tip of his bald head with his serving towel.

"Herr Graf" Vietzke said, nervously. "With regard to the carriage, perhaps the *Gnädige* …"

"Never mind the carriage, Vietzke. Naturally, I don't want the carriage!" Wilhelm answered. "But have the Gräfin's maid prepare a warm bath for her. She will want it after sitting in the cold."

Then Wilhelm went into the drawing room, where he stood before one of the large windows watching the late winter sun set, watching the wet, March snowflakes fall, and watching his wife shivering in the snow-covered driveway on the snow-covered bench, where she was waiting for a carriage that would never come.

Some minutes passed before he heard the voice of his father behind him.

"How long are you going to leave your wife out there in that weather?"

"I don't know. I was thinking perhaps fifteen minutes."

"And to what purpose? She won't be brought into line, so you will only make her sicker than she already is."

Wilhelm did not reply to this, but instead said, "*Vater*, when I was ten years old, we were in this very room one summer night, just after Fräulein Meyer and the Countess von Arnim-Krochlendorff had left us, and I asked you if Fräulein Meyer was to be my stepmother, which, I will freely admit now, was actually my greatest hope at the time. And you said no. And I asked you, why? Do you remember what you said?"

"I said, 'Because she is a Jewess.'"

"Yes. And that confused me, as she had gone to church with us that morning and was very earnest in her worship. And I pointed that out. To which you replied ..."

"To which I replied that she might pray as a Christian from now until the Second Coming, but that I would have to cut off her head at the neck and attach a new one if she was ever to be anything other than a Jewess."

"Then I remember the conversation verbatim."

"It has occurred to me that up until that night, you always called me "Papa," and thereafter I was '*Vater*' to you. And perhaps it was that night you conceived the notion you had to bring a Jewess into this house, come hell or high water.

"Well now you have your Jewess, my son. And if I may be so bold as to say it, she is an indulgence for which you are likely to pay very dearly. But she has now sat almost fifteen minutes in the cold, and it's obvious she isn't well. Surely, you cannot want her to collapse?"

"No," said Wilhelm as he turned to leave the room. "I'll fetch her now."

But outside, when Wilhelm approached the stone bench and tried to take his wife's face in his hands, she turned away from him and sobbed, angrily, "I hope you aren't going to make me walk to Wolgast, Willi, because I have an excruciating headache!"

And he answered, "I suppose we will have to get you looked at by a Jewish doctor."

⌖

KLARA WEINGARTEN ARRIVED AT PULOW LATE IN the afternoon of the 15th of March, and while her initial introduction into the Boening household had its rugged moments (the roughest being, upon exiting the carriage, her dressing down, in Austrian German, of the very sleepy Peter), it was clear she was to settle in with less difficulty than the Boening men had initially feared.

Wilhelm had come out to greet her as the carriage pulled in. And when an enormous trunk was brought up the entrance steps, Klara seemed to anticipate his surprise. He shouldn't think she was there to stay for good, she said immediately; rather, she was working on an article, and the trunk was filled mostly with the books and medical journals she might need.

"An article you say, Fräulein Weingarten?"

"Fräulein *Doktor*, if you don't mind Graf von Boening. But if your next question concerns the subject of the article, I think you would be happier if I weren't forced to say it aloud."

Klara was much taller than Wilhelm would have expected, and her full figure made her look older than her thirty-two years. Wilhelm mused—surprised at his own lack of prejudice—that she carried herself with an iron confidence that inspired immediate trust in her capabilities.

"I see. Well, on another subject, I am afraid I don't know whether my wife has given *Mam'selle*, the cook, direction for the eventuality you have …"

"I am an omnivore, Graf Boening," Klara interrupted, having somehow anticipated the question. "And the more of everything, the better. Where is my cousin?"

"She is resting."

"Good! … You do live at the edge of the world, it seems. Are you really fifty kilometers from the Baltic sea?"

"Yes. Perhaps we'll take you there after the delivery, when the weather warms up."

"You probably won't believe it, Graf Boening, but I've never been to the sea—any sea!"

"Well, I'll be glad if we are able to offer that diversion."

"And tell me, did that narcoleptic man who brought me here understand a word I said to him?"

"Probably not."

"It took me a full five minutes to recognize my name as it came out of his mouth at the station. They seem not to pronounce a hard 'g' here. It's as if they are talking while chewing. Will I be able to communicate with the servants at all? That is, do any of them speak *Hochdeutsch*?"

"They will do their best to understand you. Though," and here Wilhelm smiled a half-smile, "you do have a very strong Viennese accent."

"Well, I'm hoping the diagnosis of preeclampsia is wrong. If my cousin seizes, I might need some help from people who can understand what I am saying to them.

"If the truth be known, Fräulein *Doktor*, my wife is not at all herself, and I'm beginning to worry in earnest. She hasn't touched the piano for three days, and earlier today she complained she was seeing floating lights."

"Where is the nearest hospital? I mean the nearest university hospital?"

"In Greifswald."

Klara seemed to consider something a moment. "Is there a doctor close by who could sign prescriptions, if need be? I hope my cousin warned you that I am not certified."

"There is the local physician, Dr. Hasslinger."

"Good. If necessary, we will tell him I am a nurse and midwife. He doesn't need to know I have a university degree."

Then she asked, "Must I dress for dinner, here?"

"It's customary. But we are not so formal in the country as in the city."

"I'm afraid I have a rather limited wardrobe, Graf Boening. I am not an aristocrat, nor a Schwabacher. I am from the poor side of the family."

"I am sure you will do your best, and that your best will be good enough, Fräulein *Doktor.*"

Just as Klara was removing her coat and hat in the front hall of the house, Lisi appeared on the stair landing, calling to her cousin. Then she bounded down the staircase looking, Klara thought, something like a beach ball with wild curls. Wilhelm watched as Klara's facial expression rapidly metamorphosed from anticipation to shock, and then to clinical detachment. She took her cousin in her arms and said, "Lisi, I'm very happy to be here. Why don't you show me to my room? We will rest and visit. I will just bring my medical bag." Then she turned to Wilhelm. "And would it be possible to have a servant bring up some tea and a *Butterbrot?*"

TWO HOURS PASSED BEFORE DINNER, BUT WHEN
Klara appeared (in what was distinctly not dress for evening dining), Lisi was not with her. Her cousin's blood pressure, Klara said,
was dangerously high, and Klara had sedated her; Lisi wouldn't be
getting up for a while, perhaps several days or even weeks. She
would be having modest meals in bed, but these meals would be
vegetarian, and must contain no salt.

After reciting grace *im Namen Jesu*, Helmuth von Boening
gazed at Klara with unabashed curiosity, and continued to fasten
his blazing silver-blue stare on her throughout the entire meal.
After the soup, he began asking questions. And he pursued them
relentlessly during the meat course, attempting to penetrate the
great mystery of how a woman acquires a medical degree. Did she
actually matriculate at a University? But certainly not a German
University? Ah, Zürich. Well, the Swiss were always liberal in such
questions. As were the French. And how many such women were
there in this university? And were there Christians among them?
And while one saw no real contradiction in the idea of a woman
gynecologist—after all, a woman might know something about
women, by nature—were there any women doctors who actually
treated men? And what was the Fräulein *Doktor* going to do about
marriage and children for herself? Did she have a fiancé or an
admirer?

At this question, Klara put down her eating utensils for the
first time that evening, having indulged an exceptionally healthy
appetite. "If you must know, Graf Boening, I was engaged for
seven years. My fiancé passed away last month of lung disease."

Helmuth von Boening kept his piercing blue eyes steadily on
Klara and inquired, "Engaged for seven years?"

As if anticipating the next question, Klara replied, "We wanted to establish ourselves financially before marrying, and then he got sick."

"I am sorry to hear that, Fräulein *Doktor*, very sorry. But you mustn't give up. You must take heart. You are not an unattractive woman, although you seem to be educated quite beyond marriage!"

IT WAS ALMOST FOUR WEEKS BEFORE KLARA AL-lowed Lisi to spend any time out of bed. And when she did, it was not because she thought her cousin's blood pressure could be kept under control while ambulatory, but in the hopes that movement would stimulate labor. The longer one waited for delivery, the greater the risk of a difficult labor and the need, perhaps, for heavy sedation. It was now near mid-April, and Lisi's pregnancy was in the eighth month. The babies were mature enough to be born, and the easier the birth, the lower the risk of convulsions.

Lisi had been a cooperative patient these weeks, not even complaining about her inability to practice piano. One reason, to be sure, was that under Klara's care—and most especially under the sedation—Lisi had some relief from the headaches and swelling that had plagued her.

But another reason, as she told Klara, was that she found in her cousin's presence maternal comfort. Especially as Klara, anxious to taper off the morphine as soon as Lisi's blood pressure stabilized, largely replaced the drugs with warm baths, massages, and long talks in the darkened bedroom. When conversation lulled, and Wilhelm was not present for a game of chess, she brought her cousin scores to study and books to read.

"Do you know that the first evening I was here, when you were heavily sedated, you confused me with your mother?" Klara asked, when she was sitting by Lisi's bed one early April day.

"You won't have been pleased by that."

Well, beyond for my feelings about it, I'm not at all like your mother."

"You don't want to be, because you always thought Mami vain and superficial," answered Lisi. "But the fact is, you are very reassuring, just like Mami was, and you are also always dieting me, exactly as she did. When only my husband is around, I am forced to diet myself. But that's not easy, because he is constantly encouraging my appetites. In fact, Wilhelm discourages all physical self-control on my part. Sometimes I think he would have me fat as a pig, and as ruttish as a cat in estrus. And then he goes on about *Zucht und Ordnung*, as if order and discipline didn't apply to me as well as to everyone else. I think I will have to leave him every so often just in order to keep myself in line, or as my cousin Babette would say, in order to preserve some spiritual discipline."

"I wonder, Lisi, that you are a married woman and still so childlike, wanting a mother around and liking to be told what to do and how to live."

"Not what to do and how to live, Klara. You don't really mean that. But I often feel I cannot trust my instincts. And it's also true that I long for direction, only because I feel somehow so unformed. I think I will never know what I am, and especially now that I am supposed to be a Countess and a Christian, and am really neither of those things—certainly not by right. Do you think others have this sense—of being like a piece of music that's not quite ready to perform, because so many passages are still not free of wrong notes? And think how ironic that is, when one considers that there is a good chance I will die in childbirth. I wonder what will be said at my funeral? 'The Gräfin Elisabeth von Boening nèe Schwabacher was a young woman who had some potential, but she wasn't anything very particular, even in the end.'"

"But if she was nothing very particular, she was certainly something very peculiar," Klara interrupted. "I could write a very amusing eulogy for you, dear Lisi, but I have no intention of losing you in childbirth. Because if I do, it will be so humiliating that I won't be able to return home. But I think, if I may be permitted to say so, that you fell in love with the wrong man. And by that I mean that you might as well compare yourself to a cast bronze statue as compare yourself to your husband."

"Klara, don't you like my husband?"

"Like has nothing to do with it. He's handsome and certainly polite enough. But he's what my father would call a 'type'—a man fully formed, for good and ill, fit for a certain life and unlikely to make readjustments should they be needed. He certainly won't evolve, if we want to use Darwinian language. And so you will be forced to shape yourself to fit him, and I warn you that you may suffer for it." .

"I don't know that, Klara. Perhaps he will improve me … In any case, we are bound to each other now, and 'rushing to our end,' as the Norse God of Fire would put it.

"Klara, do you remember the postcard from Dresden I sent you last summer, with a picture of the Sistine Madonna?"

"I certainly do."

"After I mailed it, I asked my husband why he thought the Holy Mother—not to mention her child—looked so frightened in that painting. And do you know what he told me?"

"Of course not. But you are about to tell me."

"He said that the work was commissioned for the sepulchre of Pope Julius II, where it was to be hung directly across from the crucifix. So Raphael portrayed the Virgin Mary and infant Jesus in that very line of vision—that is, gazing upon the Crucifixion ..."

Lisi looked at Klara with a wry smile. "It makes one consider, doesn't it?"

"Consider what?"

"That whatever our hopes, we are always in clear sight of catastrophe."

Klara burst into laughter. "What a comforting thought for an expectant mother, Lisi! I shall share it with all my patients, especially the Jewish ones!"

# CHAPTER XXI

---

*May 1, 1898*

*Papa and Mama!*

*I know you have been anxious to hear from me, but I couldn't write again until I had all good news to tell. As you know from our telegram of the 13th, Lisi's twins were born on the twelfth of the month. They were very small, the boy, Helmuth, weighing only 2.1 kilos; but the girl, Fredericka, weighing a bit healthier 2.4 kilos. The boy had difficulty learning to suckle, and he's a very quiet baby. The girl is constantly hungry and does nothing but howl from sun up to sun down and longer; that is, when she is not chewing on her mother's breast! The infants were baptized today, the girl screaming bloody murder through the whole thing. It quite amused the congregation, and even the very dour pastor had to laugh, in spite of himself. And Lisi being Lisi, she whispered to me after the service that perhaps little Fredericka knows she is half-Jewish and was resisting her baptism. (Of the boy, she said, "I don't think he minds anything that's done to him. And I'm beginning to get the feeling that it's because he's a little dull between the ears.")*

*I have regrets that we didn't bring Lisi to the clinic at Greifswald. If I were to be honest, I would admit that we almost lost her. I allowed her out of bed for the first time on the ninth, thinking that perhaps the walk to church on Easter Sunday would get things moving, and knowing she would need a day to gather strength for it. However, on the first day up, her blood pressure spiked, so there was no question of a walk to services.*

*Still, she refused to return to bed during daylight, and so for the next three mornings and afternoons, she wandered the house—sometimes quite lucid, but other times in steep agitation and confusion. She did go to the piano while the rest of the family was at services on the 10th, and seemed to center herself there for an hour or so. But that quite exhausted her, and for the rest of that day and on the following one, she did little but roam. On the third night, she refused to go to bed at all, despite her husband's entreaties, and refused also any sedation, saying that if she slept, she was sure she would die.*

*Thank God, early on the fourth day, there was bloody show, and the contractions started. I ruptured the membranes and everything went very well until the expulsion of the placenta, at which point we had uterine atony, and she began to rapidly hemorrhage. Essentially, I had the choice of watching her bleed out, or administering ergonovine, with the associated risk of convulsions. So I prepared the ergonovine injection and called her husband in to take her hand, just in case. I will not forget the look on his face when he saw the pools of blood, but he immediately lowered her head without my telling him to do that. At any rate, the injection of ergonovine had the desired effect on the hemorrhaging, but naturally she convulsed, and it was not a pretty sight. She had three seizures in a space of twelve hours. Graf Boening was beside himself, although he tried hard to hide it.*

*And the third time, as he tried to restrain her, I saw his lips moving in prayer. I couldn't help thinking to myself, I hope it does him more good than it did me.*

*But by some miracle, she has recovered. Indeed, I almost feel I can't take credit. She is still very tired and spends much of the day in bed, but then, she is an aristocrat, so she can take all the time she wants to convalesce.*

*Lisi being Lisi, she has refused a wet nurse—even says the very idea disgusts her. She doesn't seem to care that she can never be finished with the feeding of twins. Her husband, however, is sanguine about it and even mentioned to me that it's gratifying to him that he is seeing her eat well for the very first time since their honeymoon.*

*I know you will want a report on Graf Boening. But other than the fact that he is remarkably handsome, there is not much else to say about him. He is pleasant company and seems a devoted husband. I honestly wonder what conversation Lisi has with him, though. He is no Fürst Wittenbach. But perhaps not all married people need stimulating conversation. Of course, they play a lot of chess together; and we all know that where conversation is concerned, Lisi has enough for at least two!*

*At any rate, the count is visibly enjoying fatherhood. He often sets the little girl, belly down, on his knees, and rubs her back to stop her incessant crying. He might actually turn out a better parent than our Lisi. Tonight at dinner, she complained that she was afraid her babies weren't half as pretty as some other infants she had seen, and then she fretted that if the boy turned out to be as slow as she feared, she didn't know how she could be a decent mother to him. And Graf Boening merely looked kindly at her and said, "Lisi, my love, I am very satisfied with my children, and find them thoroughly appealing.*

*And if it turns out the boy is deficient in some way, I am confident you will do your duty by him."*

*More interesting than Graf Wilhelm von Boening, in my estimation, is his father, Graf Helmuth von Boening, a man of seventy years who has a very dry wit and a blistering stare. He peppers me with questions of all sorts at every meal, ranging from medicine to politics to the bridges over the Danube. And he ends every conversation by telling me he fears I won't find a husband. Yesterday, I warned him that all his talk of a husband for me might give me the impression that he is working up to a proposal of marriage. And he looked at me very seriously and said, "No, Fräulein Doktor, though you are far from a useless woman, I am too old for marriage. You would need a much younger man, and one who is intelligent and energetic, or you will dominate him, and neither of you will be happy."*

*At any rate, Graf Wilhelm has offered me money for my medical services, which I have refused. I told him that I'm much too proud of my poverty to take money from rich relatives. Lisi has bought me a train ticket to Berlin, however. And I will accompany her and the babies on a short visit to Uncle Magnus as soon as she is able to travel. And when we return to Pulow, the Graf and Gräfin von Boening will take me to the sea. All of this by way of telling you that I intend to spend at least another six weeks in the north. I can use the time to review some things for the certification exam. (How good they will finally allow me, a "mere" woman, to take it!) And anyway, no sense coming home until I thoroughly understand Low German.*

*By the way, Lisi insists you should send Isi to visit. Not now, of course, with the babies so small, but perhaps next summer. She very much misses Isi.*

*Papa: There is a neolithic grave site on a small hill not far from the manor house; it's rather interesting. I've come to think that there is some significant pattern in the arrangement of the stones. And I've gone up there several times in the past few days to study it. It's a pleasant place to sit, as are, I expect, all grave sites to which one has no possible personal connection. All in all, it's probably a healthy thing to contemplate death in ways beyond caring and compassion. And humbling, too, to consider how the dead become a mere archeological curiosity once a few millennia have passed.*

*Incidentally, I must tell you that I ruminated aloud on that burial site at dinner last night. And what do you think? Graf Helmuth von Boening said, "Yes, Fräulein* Doktor, *there have perhaps been many before us at Pulow; but nobody will come after us, thanks to the marriage of your cousin with my son." Well, I am afraid I laughed out loud and said that the good count must have a very naïve view of history to say that. Whereupon he replied that his view of history was hardly naïve, but rather Christian. The Germans, he reminded me, had christianized the Poles of Pomerania. For Pulow to slip through the fingers of the Boening family, he said, there would have to be an apocalypse—a war and post-Christian era he would not wish to witness!*

*Now Papa, you will see I have enclosed the latest draft of my article on uterine prolapse. Please give some time to proofreading it. I am hoping to put the finishing touches on it before returning home. If you can think of any pertinent clinical examples you wish to add, I would want to know. You are good to spare me so long in the practice.*

*So, Mama, to answer* your *question, how can you possibly expect I am getting over it? And there is really nothing to say, is there?*

*Although you would probably say that some prayers are answered and others are not. Mine, evidently, were not.*

*But you must kiss Martin, Lene, and Isi for me.*

*Yours,*

*Klara*

*Heringsdorf, Usedom*

*June 25<sup>th</sup>, 1898*

*Lieber Papi!*

*I trust Klara is safely on her train to Vienna. And I didn't want to delay writing to thank you for setting us up so beautifully in the sea villa. I am so glad that you were able to come and enjoy it a bit. With Ehrlingen here, I think you managed very well to scrape through five days in the same house as my husband, and with nothing but pleasantness.*

*Though my husband would be reluctant to admit it, since he loves to complain about any place that isn't Pulow or, alternately, 50 meters from a Titian, he couldn't be happier. And you have seen how very comfortable everything is, now that we have brought in a decent piano, and we have a better cook. And we are so well-placed vis-à-vis the beach, with ample room for the babies and their nurse—and, thank God, some respectable distance at meals and at night from Fredericka's fits of wailing. I don't understand how little Helmuth can be so quiet while his sister screams. But they shared a womb and perhaps came to some tacit agreement that she would be the devil and he the angel. I wonder, Papi, whether it was this way with me and my brother, only he didn't live long enough to play the part of the angel, so all you got was the devil.*

*Today, Ehrlingen received a letter that will interest you. It seems that the Eichenhohl hunting party will be kept under wraps after all, because the police identified the blackmailer. He is an officer in the regiment and has shot himself. My husband thinks he probably had gambling debts. Apparently he also had a wife and children. I feel very sorry for them.*

*Papi, you and your cello are very much missed. There won't be any more piano trios at the beach villa, I fear. Ehrlingen has decided that we will play only four-hands in your absence, though I have suggested violin sonatas. But I suppose he thinks I will have my fill of violin sonatas if Fürst Wittenbach shows up in July, which I hope he will. We are planning to invite him, and I have a feeling he won't refuse.*

*And so, Ehrlingen and I are working through all the Schubert duets. Do you remember the last time Mami and I played the F minor Fantasy? We quarreled so, because she said she couldn't possibly play the "Allegro Vivace" at the tempo I wanted to take; but then she played it so nicely once she had practiced it. She just never wanted to practice; I suppose because she thought there were other, more worthwhile things she could do with her time! But there really weren't, because what could possibly be more worthwhile than music, which is the very soul of life?*

*Oh, and you will never guess, Papi! But you mustn't say anything to anyone. Ehrlingen confessed to Wilhelm that he plans to marry again. My husband says she is at least thirty—very poor, very plain, and a first cousin of Baron Flenheim (Botho). Apparently, she has a lovely soprano voice. Perfect for Ehrlingen, actually, since musically he is otherwise completely self-sufficient!*

*I shall come and visit soon with the babies, I promise—as soon as the weather cools off, perhaps in mid-September, for the Jewish holidays.*

*And something else, Papi: I read that the Phoenix will soon have a four-cylinder engine! I think you would love to have the newest model automobile, wouldn't you?*

*Your loving daughter,*

*L.*


*Heringsdorf, Usedom*
*June 25, 1898*
*Lieber Fürst Egon!*
*My husband has specifically requested I write to you to ask whether you would be willing to bring the children to us for a few days at Heringsdorf, where we have rented a lovely seaside villa and will be living until the end of July. As you know, we had planned to come to Kleinneubach this summer, but I don't see how it can be possible with two infants and the associated paraphernalia, even were we to bring two nurses! It would, I think, be a very unwelcome invasion, and the opposite of a sociable visit.*

*The good news is that I have procured a fairly decent piano here, and in between motherly duties, it would be such a pleasure to play chamber music! We could even set it up so that we manage all the Beethoven and Brahms violin sonatas. And we will divide them up according to the number of days you agree to stay. Perhaps my father-in-law will even agree to come for one or two days. Though he is very hard to budge, I cannot imagine he would refuse the chance to see his grandchildren.*

*Do let us know at your earliest convenience. We both very much miss your company.*

*As ever,*

*Lisi v. Boening*

*Berlin*

*June 29, 1898*

*Lisi, my dear!*

*You mustn't be angry with me that I didn't care to meet Fräulein* Doktor *Weingarten. Only that I cannot imagine what I would have in common with her. And yes, my dear, I am sure you are very grateful for everything she has done for you. And you will, by now, have repaid her with a thousand kindnesses, all of which she deserves, and all of which reflect your loving nature and your devotion to family.*

*And now, to the purpose of my letter, which, you will forgive me, is gossip. But not idle gossip, I hope, for it is told in a good cause. It turns out that Caroline von Schillingen will not get her divorce. From the beginning, she had no support from her family. And especially not after her husband pursued her to her parents' house with passionate and weepy declarations of contrition. And now that Schillingen's blackmailer has quietly ended his life, she has no hope of any publicity—not at least without being blamed for ruining a widow and three innocent children. But even aside from the issue of proper social discretion, Harden wishes to put the Eichenhohl affair to bed. Apparently, those involved were not close enough to the Kaiser to suit Harden's purposes. What he is after is the Kaiser and the fiasco that has become the Kaiser's personal rule. So that he is well-advised not to be distracted in his pursuit of the main prize.*

*At any rate, Caroline came to me last week with tears and laments (and also very affectionate things to say about you) and announced she was going back to Pomerania with Schillingen. That means she will need a friend now more than ever. And though her own situation is unenviable, it puts you in the fortunate position that you will not lose her as a neighbor and confidante. She is truly a model of goodness, and the image of beauty. And she is loved everywhere. You will be very well-placed as her favorite.*

*Wittenbach was here last night and said he had a letter from you inviting him to Heringsdorf with his children. I think he is truly tempted, as he knows you get to Berlin so seldom, and he loves your playing so. Whether he brings his children, of course, is another story.*

*Lisi, you should tell your husband that he must establish his family somewhere in Berlin—and if not in the Kadettenweg, then at least in an apartment in the center. Not that I have any experience in the matter, but I would imagine that wives who produce babies under harrowing circumstances might have a certain moral advantage over their husbands. At any rate, if you think it is so, you must not hesitate to use that advantage before Boening forgets all about nearly losing you.*

*Your father claims you will visit him in September. I hope you do, my dear. And that I will have the pleasure of your company often.*

*Your devoted cousin,*

*Babette*

*Herringsdorf, Usedom*
*July 2, 1898*
*Liebe Klara!*

*I miss you already. That is, I've missed you from the moment you left, and probably more than I otherwise would have if we had not had words. Though it's not as if I have had a lot of time to miss you, because the babies really do take up a lot of time. You were right that Wilhelm is becoming impatient with the breast feeding. And now that I'm feeling stronger again, he wants to undertake more activities, especially in the evenings. Particularly with Ehrlingen here, Willi feels we should attend social gatherings.*

*At least that is what he says—in those ever rarer moments when he isn't in the nursery visiting the babies or on his way there. Or sitting by me while I feed one or the other, and saying how nice it is to watch me, like a* tableau vivant *of the Holy Mother, but with little gulping sounds to go with it. He has started to sketch me while nursing, because he claims that it is an ideal way to get a study of my face in waking repose, which it isn't very often, apparently. He says I am very hard to sketch when animated, and that it's like trying to capture a kinetoscope frame. Klara, I am afraid to ask my husband, but isn't a kinetoscope one of those machines that are used to display dirty pictures?*

*But I'm sorry we had those words, Klara. I am sorry I was cranky. Of course, I am spoiled—I know I am spoiled. But I cannot play an unplayable piano, and I cannot eat inedible food. And while I have both a father and a husband to spoil me, they are in a competition to the death. So they spoil the spoiling and just make me feel guilty that I don't love either of them as much as I should.*

*If the truth be known, I am jealous of you that you have a career, while I am now chained to two tiny creatures who are physically dependent on me for their nourishment. Which means, first, that I cannot stop eating, which I would so dearly love to do; and second, that everything I worked for all my life—or at least I thought I did—is in a choke hold. When I think that at one time I was convinced I could "emancipate" myself! That seems a lifetime ago! Well, no emancipation for me! I fear my fate is sealed—that I am destined to be no more than a mere wife and mother, and that I will never again have any real control over my life.*

*But you, I think, will always be sovereign!*

*I wonder which impulses drive women to realize their goals no matter what the struggle, and which impulses stop them short, as I have been stopped. I cannot think that love and marriage are totally to blame! I think, rather, that the issue is one of confidence. You have so much confidence, and that will serve you whether you marry or not. But perhaps it is a different thing to be a doctor than to be a musician. Because I have the burden of such great expectations. Klara, I may have nearly died bearing my two children, but only once. One must be willing to die a thousand times to birth a late Beethoven sonata on the concert stage, and perhaps still not achieve the thing one is after, which is high art.*

*Yesterday, at sunrise, Willi and I took a walk into the lovely beech forest at Bansin, at the edge of which one has a view of the sea from a height of about 50 or 60 meters. We brought the babies, each in a basket, along with Willi's sketchbook and pencils, and we ensconced ourselves comfortably on the edge of the hill, feeling very private. I would say that were were* en famille *in a way that was quite profound. It was lovely to listen to the sea from there, and even little Ricki must have liked the ocean sounds, because she stopped howling for a change, and slept quite peacefully next to her brother.*

*Wilhelm took to sketching the view, but starting with shadows rather than lines. So I asked him about it, and he said it was something that my cousin Babette had suggested to him as an exercise—to draw the lines out of the shadows, rather than starting with the lines. (I regret so that Babette Meyer didn't make herself available to meet you, because she is such a force of nature!)*

*I mentioned to Willi how strange I thought it was that Babette did not hang her own work, which had been highly praised, but was nowhere to be seen. And he answered in a very matter-of-fact way that this was because she had burned all of her paintings. Klara, I was so shocked that I practically tore his shirt sleeve, grabbing at it! I asked if this could possibly be true, and if it was, how he could know this? And he said that she had told him. And that he wasn't aware it was a secret, but perhaps it was, and it should go no further.*

*At any rate, when he asked her why she had destroyed her work, she said that it was an act of spiritual discipline; a way, in fact, to prove to herself that she had taken her conversion to Christianity seriously. And then she had laughed and said that perhaps, in the end, the Devil made her do it because, as Goethe's Mephistopheles so famously put it, "All things called forth from the Void deserve to perish."*

*I told him that the whole thing struck me as an act of self-immolation, and that I couldn't imagine engaging in such violence against my life's work, no matter what my religious principles. And could he? And he said that his own work could not be compared to Babette's, since it was just a series of exercises—efforts to train himself to really look at things that bore looking at. So it could never disappoint. Whereas, he guessed that Babette was a perfectionist and painted to produce art, not just to enjoy some familiarity with the artistic process.*

*And then he said that perhaps Cousin Babette wanted to be released from her own nagging aspirations. Perhaps, he said, she wanted to be delivered from her ambitious Jewish milieu. Because the Jews are always bragging and showing off in some way or other. Always reaching for some performance or feat, always working so zealously to be remarkable. Always searching for the next thing, and never accepting the thing that is. And that is why people hated the Jews, he said, and were even beginning to talk of destroying them. Because everywhere the Jews wanted to be noticed. And the desire to be noticed is, after all, an obnoxious thing.*

*"When it comes down to it, Lisi," he said, "perhaps you married me for the same reasons Babette stopped painting. Because though you insist*

*you live for your music, you would never have married had you really wanted to be on the concert stage. And so you have chosen the path most becoming to you. You have married and put away your Jewishness."*

*Klara, all that talk made me want to run away and play some concerts, just to prove my husband wrong! And perhaps I will run away someday, if I ever can gather up the courage!*

*But right now, I have the children.*

*I sometimes wonder what would have happened had you not come to Pulow, and I had died in childbirth. Of course, nobody would have an easier time finding a second wife than my very handsome husband.*

*But I am conceited enough to think that he wouldn't have wanted a second wife too soon, and that he would always have missed me, even were his new wife more useful in the way good German wives are useful.*

*Klara, I will always need you. So don't be a stranger to your,*

*Lisi*

# END

# AFTERWORD

THE IDEA OF WRITING A STORY ABOUT A GERMAN-
Jewish woman in an aristocratic mixed marriage came to me in
the early 1980s, when I was a graduate student in East Central
European History. At the time, I had just encountered two historical works: The first was Fritz Stern's *Gold and Iron,* a brilliant,
painstakingly researched biography of Gerson Bleichroeder, personal banker to Otto von Bismarck, the political leader who uni-
fied Germany. The second work was a short but very provocative
study in social history by Lamar Cecil. Published in the Leo Baeck
Yearbook of 1975, it was entitled "Jews and *Junkers* in Imperial
Berlin," and summarized the uneasy social relations between rich
Jews and the Prussian nobility. Both works suggested that not-
withstanding the important contributions of Germany's Jews to
their nation's economic, scientific, and cultural achievements in
the nineteenth and twentieth centuries, even the most assimilated
Jews—baptized and intermarried—were subject to invidious anti-semitism long before Hitler's seizure of power.

Looking backward through the lens of the Holocaust, Jewish historians have regretted the lack of dialogue between Germany's Christian and Jewish communities on the subject of anti-semitism. Indeed, several prominent German emigrés have traced the Holocaust, in some part, to a failure on the part of educated, tolerant Germans to seriously engage with resurgences of Jew-hatred in the late nineteenth century and between the World Wars. The great scholar of Jewish mysticism, Gershom Scholem, for example, had this to say in 1962:

> "I deny that there has ever been such a German-Jewish dialogue in any genuine sense whatsoever, i.e. as a historical phenomenon. It takes two to have such a dialogue, who listen to each other, who are prepared to perceive the other as what he is and represents, and to respond to him....
>
> To be sure, the Jews attempted a dialogue with the Germans, starting from all possible points of view and situations, ... imploringly, and entreatingly, servile and defiant, with a dignity employing all manner of tones and a godforsaken lack of dignity; and today, when the symphony is over, the time may be ripe for studying their motifs and attempting a critique of their tones. No one, not even one who always grasped the hopelessness of this cry into the void, will belittle the latter's passionate intensity and the tones of hope and grief that were in resonance with it...."

How is it that there was no dialogue, when it was obvious that German-Jewish overtures to their host nation were far from empty? Not only did Germany's Jews zealously adopt the German language, culture, and customs, but a significant number stood prepared to give up their ancient religion and even their biological separateness. One of the most striking characteristics of German-Jewish assimilation in the late nineteenth and early twentieth centuries is the amount of intermarriage that took place—an amount that increased steadily and substantially during the very years anti-semitism took flight as a powerful political movement. By the 1930s, rates of intermarriage among Jews in many communities approached fifty percent. And this was intermarriage not just between men and women of the lower and middle classes, but in the highest reaches of society. Many of these mixed marriages were between highly educated men and women representing two powerful civilizations in the process of at once melding and colliding.

As a Jewish woman in a mixed marriage, I can attest that married couples ignore ethnic and cultural differences at their peril. Every day offers not simply an opportunity for dialogue, but the necessity for dialogue. So the question is: Were there dialogues in these marriages?

While it is true that German-Jewish women who entered into marriages with Christian men tended to put away Jewish life entirely (the story is a bit different for German-Jewish men who married Christian women), it cannot possibly have been the case that they did this without reflection and in absolute silence. One only need peruse the writings of the early nineteenth-century salon Jewess Rachel Levin Varnhagen to come to the conclusion that to live as a baptized Jew with a Prussian nobleman in the early nineteenth century was to live between two very separate worlds, which, at various points in time, had to be explicitly negotiated. Of course, a Jewish woman of the late nineteenth century might have felt less internal contradictions in settling into intermarriage (the Jews of Germany, in general, having by this time far more assimilated to the values and lifestyles of the host culture). But that doesn't mean the road to marital bliss had been made a smooth one. In fact, the statistics on intermarriage in Germany during both the Wilhelmine and Weimar periods tell us that mixed marriages were significantly more prone to failure than endogamous unions. And probably one of the factors in the frequency of marital failure was the reality that regardless of what was going on inside the marriage itself, the outside world could not let a Jew or "Jewess" forget his or her origins. It took a strong union to sustain itself against the social pressure of such widely ingrained racism. Such, for example, was the case with the Stresemans. Kaete Kleefeld Stresemann, wife of the German Chancellor and Foreign Minister, Gustav Streseman, came from a Jewish family. Lucky her marriage was a secure one. Even the Weimar-friendly American press made sure, during the 1920s, to mention Frau Streseman's origins, though these certainly had no bearing on any aspect of German foreign or domestic policy.

And now a few words about the historical people and places in *All Things That Deserve to Perish*. First, I want to say that Pulow is an actual place in Mecklenburg-Vorpommern, Germany. I have borrowed the name (which somehow appealed to me as both simple to pronounce and typical of the area) along with many of the natural features of the general area for my novel. I have also borrowed some parts of the legend of Pulow's conquering by the

Germans, and its first German lord, in the twelfth century. But I want it to be understood that any resemblance between the manor house in my novel and the actual manor house of Pulow, or between the characters of my novel and the lords of the manor or inhabitants of Pulow in the nineteenth and twentieth centuries is purely coincidental. In fact, it seems that between the 13$^{th}$ and 20$^{th}$ centuries, the estate of Pulow belonged to a succession of families, not to one single family. And I have purposely avoided learning anything about either the manor house of the estate or its current inhabitants and their family history, for fear that impressions of these things might find their way unwittingly into my manuscript. The name Boening, while an authentic Saxon name, was to my knowledge never associated with this place.

There are several historical personages in my novel who may or may not be known to the reader, and who play significant roles. Perhaps the most well-developed character is that of Babette Meyer von Kalckreuth (1835-1916). In bringing her into my novel, I have cleaved to the rough outlines of her life as gleaned from historical works. She seems to have been a fascinating woman—a baptized Jew, gifted artist, and patron of the arts (although also vitally interested in the sciences), and an influential socialite who had the ability to attract aristocratic and bourgeois politicians and intellectuals to her home, where they engaged in discussions of liberal reform. It may interest the reader to know that having married (alas, briefly and disastrously) the painter Stanislaus von Kalckreuth made Babette the step great-grandmother of the prominent Lutheran theologian Dietrich Bonhoeffer, who had very fond childhood memories of visiting her Berlin home. I hope that in creating a relationship between her and the fictional

Schwabacher family, I have remained true to an enticing figure of turn-of-the-century Berlin.

Here are some of the historical personages revolving around Wilhelm von Boening who also appear in *All Things:* the Iron Chancellor, Prince Otto von Bismarck; Kaiser Wilhelm II; and two of the Kaiser's more infamous cronies—Prince Philipp zu Eulenburg (whose life story, were it written up as fiction, would be rejected as ludicrous invention) and Count Kuno von Moltke. Poking around that *Junker* milieu, there is also the journalist Maximilian Harden, whose investigations of the effete political circle surrounding Kaiser Wilhelm II uncovered, in 1907, one of the most famous gay sex scandals of the twentieth century.

Then there are the Bleichroeders, the Israels, the Fürstenburgs, and Therese Simon-Sonneman—all wealthy and accomplished Jews who belong, in the novel, to the Schwabacher family's social circle. Not to be forgotten are the Musik-Wolffs, Luise and Hermann, who dominated Berlin's musical life for nearly half a century. The widowed Luise Wolff died in 1936, just after her concert agency was forcibly Aryanized.

Finally, there are the many artistic personages who are mentioned in my work. Theodore Leschetizky, Teresa Carreño, and Artur Schnabel, three great musicians I have made influences in Elisabeth von Schwabacher's music pursuits, were major figures of the concert world. Maestro Leschetizky was perhaps the most celebrated piano teacher of the *fin de siècle* period. Among his many students who went on to artistic fame were Schnabel, Ignaz Friedman, Rudolf Serkin, Anna Yesipova, Benno Moiseiwitsch, Paul Wittgenstein, and Mieczyslaw Horszowsky. Madame Carreño was one of the most brilliant pianists of the late nineteenth century. Her often convulsive personal life was reflective of her passionate nature and her near obsessive devotion to her art. I have endeavored not only to remain true to the characters of all these historical musicians, but to allow them, in some cases, to speak in their own words.

It is necessary here to say something about the *Junker* (pronounced "Yoonker") class, the demise of which ran pretty much parallel to the destruction of Germany's Jews in World War II. This largely poor and pious class of landed aristocrats brokered much power in Imperial Germany, virtually dominating the civil service and the military. At the end of World War I, the *Junkers'* legal and economic privileges were formally abolished, as was noble rank, altogether. Although as a class, the *Junkers* had been on the economic downswing for over three-quarters of a century, they continued to hang on to their estates in the east during the interwar period, retaining much of their social, political, and military prestige.

When the Nazis came to power, the *Junkers* tended to look down socially upon Hitler and his political coterie. But they nevertheless provided the regime critical political support, and not only out of fears of socialist or communist revolution. Filled with pride of blood, these aristocrats harbored very strong anti-semitic prejudices and found Nazi racial theory quite appealing. In fact, convictions of racial superiority were so widespread among the *Junker* class that when Berthold von Stauffenberg, an architect of the July 20th assassination attempt on Hitler, was interrogated by the Gestapo after his arrest in the summer of 1944, he made sure to declare himself a proponent of ethnic cleansing. When asked about his attitude toward the Final Solution, the Count answered that in principle, he approved of Nazi racial theory, only that it had "been grossly betrayed in this war in that the best German blood is being irrevocably sacrificed." This, from a man whose twin brother had a Jewish wife!

Historians agree that without *Junker* support, the Nazis could neither have established nor retained legitimacy. But in the end, *Junker* collaboration came at a very high price. These noblemen were expropriated *en masse* by the Soviet occupation of eastern Germany in 1945. Those *Junkers* who did not flee to the West during the Soviet invasion were either executed on sight or died in Soviet prison camps.

Finally, I want to say something on the subject of abortion in Germany of the late nineteenth and early twentieth centuries—the reason being that several readers of my novel in manuscript form found the idea that my heroine should have an abortion a huge stretch of credibility. The fact is, in the late nineteenth century, when all forms of birth control were illegal in German-speaking lands, abortion turned out to be the single practicable form of birth control available to women. And as the nascent socialist and feminist movements caught on, women of all social classes increasingly availed themselves of it. Between 1870 and 1930, live birth rates declined precipitously in Germany. This was to a large extent due to the fact that German and Austrian doctors—unlike their counterparts in the United States—appear not to have shrunk from performing terminations of pregnancy, even though they were illegal. By the eve of World War I, statisticians were alleging that fully half of German women had aborted at least one pregnancy, and politicians were talking openly about a national "birth strike." It may interest the reader to know that by 1930, the number of terminations of pregnancy in Germany exceeded the number of births.

I wish to note here that in the more than thirty years since I first conceived of *All Things That Deserve to Perish,* a lot of historical literature has appeared on the subject of politics, culture, and family life in Imperial Germany, as well as on the subject of the German Jews. From Barbara Hahn's provocative study of the Berlin "salon Jewesses" (*The Jewess Pallas Athena*) to Bryan Mark Rigg's study of the half and quarter Jews (many of whom considered themselves *Junkers*) who served in the Wehrmacht in World War II (*Hitler's Jewish Soldiers),* dozens of monographs and memoirs have helped me to flesh out my story. I hope that I have interested the reader in learning more about this fascinating period of history.

D.M.

# ACKNOWLEDGMENTS

I AM VERY GRATEFUL TO SEVERAL TALENTED writers who were kind enough to comment extensively on this novel in manuscript. I am most especially indebted to my wonderful daughter, Nadia Prinz, and to my good friend, Anne McKay-Smith Vance, both of whom slogged through revision after revision uncomplainingly. Similarly, I would like to thank Cheryl Mendelson for two patient and insightful readings, as well as Leslie Wells, whose critical appraisal and thorough line-editing was a great help to me just when I needed it.

Adrienne McDonnell, Brenda Kahn, Carol Kaelin, and Judy Wilkins provided much encouragement as readers and as listening ears. A writer spends a lot of time alone, which makes her friendships all the more precious to her.

These acknowledgments would not be complete without thanking my competent copy editor, Mariann Bigelow.

Self-publishing is a huge undertaking, and I could not have done it without her.

Lastly, I wish to thank my very dear husband, Herbert Prinz, who insists he has no intention of ever reading this novel, but who entertained me with an incalculable number of ideas for its characters.

D.M.

# BOOK DISCUSSION QUESTIONS

1. To what extent can you relate to the lives of the main characters? In what way were their lifestyles modern, and in what way old-world?

2. Was Lisi von Schwabacher a feminist? How did her take on the choices society offered women influence her personal choices and her fate?

3. Which characters in the novel do you think exhibited mere social snobbery where Jews were concerned, and which a more pernicious racial bigotry?

4. What do you think of the relationships Lisi had with her mother and father?

5. Several characters in the novel demonstrate polarizing hostility toward other political, religious, racial, and sexual identity groups. Do you think the current political and racial climate is similar in any way to that of *fin de siècle* Germany?

6. Was Wilhelm von Boening's courtship of Lisi romantic?

7. Do you think Wilhelm was a good husband to Lisi? Was she a good wife to him?

8. Why do you think Lisi's relationship with her cousin Klara was both close and contentious?

9. To what extent do you think Lisi's choices reflected her confidence or lack of confidence in her musical talent?

10. To what extent do you think the characters in this novel reflect or challenge literary and religious stereotypes and archetypes?

Made in the USA
Middletown, DE
18 April 2021